JUST ONE MORE

JUST
ONE
MORE

A Novel of Suspense

ANNETTE LYON

SCARLET
NEW YORK

JUST ONE MORE

Scarlet
An Imprint of Penzler Publishers
58 Warren Street
New York, N.Y. 10007

Copyright © 2023 by Annette Lyon

First Scarlet Press edition

Interior design by Maria Fernandez

Library of Congress Control Number: 2022917395

Cloth ISBN: 978-1-61316-375-7
eBook ISBN: 978-1-61316-376-4

10 9 8 7 6 5 4 3 2 1

Printed in the United States of America
Distributed by W. W. Norton & Company

Dedicated to the two librarians
who have had the greatest impact on my life:
Clare Peterson and the late Lu Ann Brobst Staheli.

CHAPTER ONE

BECCA

March 19

With five-month-old Ivy on my hip, I stare at my cell. *Buzz,* I order it. *Come on.* It remains silent and blank. Might as well be a glass brick. Should I text again? Call?

Jenn was supposed to be back at eleven to pick up the baby. It's eleven-thirty. And while she tends to run a little late most days, it's usually by five or ten minutes, not thirty.

I'd chalk it up to her being busy and focused on getting ready for their trip to Cherry Reservoir, if not for the fact that she looked . . . off . . . when she brought Ivy over. Her eyes looked glassy. She seemed almost sick. I thought maybe she'd told Rick that she didn't want to go on the trip, and they'd had a fight.

But my "Hey, are you feeling all right?" was met with "I'm fine! Be back soon."

"You're heading out at noon, right?" I asked. "So see you around eleven?"

"Yep," she said, not elaborating. She waved to Ivy, who waved back. "Bye!" Then Jenn got in her car. Backing out of my driveway took her a little longer than usual. Enough that I almost ran over to see if she *was* sick, if I could drive her to urgent care or something. But she reached the street, waved one last time, and drove away.

Maybe all I saw was her anxiety about the trip ramping up. Rick has been looking forward to his new boat's maiden voyage with their little family. Jenn has been worried about it ever since he got the boat a couple of weeks ago; I know that much. She doesn't want her baby on the water—let alone in the middle of March—when it's still so cold out.

Last week, when I suggested she refuse to go, she shrugged and shook her head. "I can't change his mind on this one," she said. "I've tried. Believe me."

That was more than she usually does. She typically goes along with whatever crazy idea Rick gets into his head, which frustrates me to no end.

"I feel bad saying no," she says. I've heard it a dozen times if once.

Just as often, she adds some version of "He's never been able to do anything like this before."

His first wife, Chloe, died tragically before they had kids. Forever the optimist, Jenn is determined to heal Rick's grief with her love. She tries to give him everything he's missed out on due to Chloe's death, even when it's stuff Jenn doesn't like—or in this case, something she feels uneasy about. She usually blows me off when I stick my finger in their business. I try to stay out of it, especially when I can hear the unspoken *you don't understand; you're divorced.* And she's right. What do I know about keeping a marriage together? I tried and failed, so maybe my advice sucks.

Regardless, the facts of the day remain: Jenn is half an hour late, and Rick will be home soon. In his view, if you're on time, you're late. Sometimes Jenn can be disorganized and flaky, but she goes out of her way to be on time (read: early) for him. My watching Ivy this morning was supposed to help her get everything done.

She's scooting all over the place, Jenn texted yesterday when asking if I'd babysit. *I can't get packed with her underfoot.*

I said yes. It meant rescheduling a meeting with a client to another day and working from home, but I had the sense Jenn needed me today, more than usual. Typically, if I watch Ivy during the week, it's on a Monday, when I work from home. That's the kids' early-out day, and I like to be here when they get back from school.

The twins have been with their dad overnight. They'll be home around four, so it's been just me and Ivy, and I've loved it. My little ones have turned into gangly tweens with braces and hints of acne. I miss the baby era with the snuggly softness and skin that smells like a fresh promise. Plus, I never had one baby at a time. In theory, I'd love to play with Ivy all day.

Instead, I worry that Jenn fell asleep because she's sick, or she's stressed out and could use an extra set of hands.

Ivy's mouth moves instinctively in a sucking motion as if she's drinking from a bottle or her mother's breast. So peaceful. After a moment, she fusses, so I adjust her in my arms and pat her. She takes a deep breath, which comes out unevenly as she relaxes against me. Making sure I keep the same left-right, left-right rocking motion I did with my babies, I check my phone again. My message is still unread.

I open my front door and peer down the street, hoping to see a flash of red: Jenn's Prius turning around the corner. No red, only a white van that looks like it belongs to a utility company. I can't get her glassy eyes out of my head. *Was* she sick? I think back to when she got in the car, and I *think* I remember her wiping her cheek—though, at the time, I thought she was brushing away a piece of hair or something, but maybe it was a tear. I could be imagining that memory. I don't know.

Regardless, something feels off. I don't know what.

I glance at the car seat. What if I head over to check on things? I'll find Jenn frazzled, and I'll help her with any final packing. Worst-case scenario, if she is sick, she could have passed out or thrown up, in which case, a friend coming over to help would be a comfort. I carefully shift Ivy into it, then ease her arms through the straps. As I secure the buckles, her face screws up with the threat of a cry.

"Sh . . ." I rock the carrier and slip her pacifier into her mouth. I seem to slip into the autopilot motions I did when the twins were this age. I suppose a mother never forgets. My body remembers. I watch my hands instinctively secure the car seat into the back of my car. I open the garage and start up the car, eager to get to Jenn's. I'll probably find her organizing stuff in the boat while her phone is in the house, which is why she hasn't replied. I'll help her out for a few minutes.

When I turn onto Jenn's street, the boat is clearly visible, parked on the cement pad. The top is off, which means Jenn's been getting it ready. She could appear at any moment. All is well. I overreacted.

I park in the driveway and hurry to get Ivy's carrier out. With my hip, I push the doors shut, and then I lock the car and head for the front door. The carrier jostles as it bumps against my leg. Fortunately, Ivy is falling asleep.

When I reach the door, I glance back toward to boat. Shoot. Should have checked it first. I set the carrier down and hurry over.

"Jenn?" No response. I climb up the ladder to check inside. The boat is new and gorgeous. I go down a short flight of stairs and find a full-size bed and kitchenette. Several grocery sacks of food are on the counter and bed. She must be inside the house.

Feeling more assured, I climb down from the boat and head back to Ivy. I'll find Jenn inside, distracted by something—maybe by a headline on Twitter. We'll laugh about my worry and her forgetfulness.

Don't worry, I picture myself telling her. *We'll get the packing done.*

I ring the doorbell. As I wait, an awful possibility plays out in my mind: Jenn is eating lunch, maybe a bowl of reheated stew, and she chokes on a piece of meat. She's unable to perform the Heimlich on herself. As a single mother, I've envisioned plenty of similar things like that about myself when I'm alone. It's one more reason it's nice my kids are a little older now. They know to call Maura, the nurse down the street, or 911.

When I hear no footsteps, I press the doorbell again, but I wait all of two seconds before deciding to use the keyless entry pad. Jenn and Rick gave me the code for when they go out of town so I can water their plants and bring in their mail.

"Jenn?" I call, stepping inside. "It's me. Just came over to be sure you're okay."

I step deeper into the house and look around. Jenn isn't in the kitchen. She's not behind the island on the floor either. A choking incident is unlikely. The thought doesn't reassure me as I expected it to.

Jenn's lime-green purse sits on the edge of the island. Her phone is beside it. I peer inside the purse; her keys and wallet are inside. A dirty glass is on the counter with what looks like remnants of a green smoothie. She's got to be here somewhere. After setting the baby carrier onto the kitchen floor, I walk to the laundry room and half bath. Both are off the kitchen. Both are empty. I open the door to the garage. There's Jenn's car. She's got to be home.

I close the garage door and turn around. The sliding glass door to the backyard greets me. Jenn's probably not out there. I check anyway. I walk over and peer through the glass. No sign of her, but I can't see the entire yard from this vantage, so I unlock the door and slide it open. Stepping onto the deck, I call, "Jenn?"

No response. I nearly close the door, but then imagine her collapsed behind a bush. I race across the deck and run around the yard. Within a minute, I've searched the entire backyard but found nothing. When I close the sliding door behind me, Ivy starts to fuss. I find her pacifier and pop it into her mouth, then pick up the carrier again. I slip my phone into my back pocket and head upstairs. I'll look there next.

With each stair, the carrier feels heavier. My anxiety multiplies, making my stomach twist. What I wouldn't give to hear my phone go off with Jenn's ring tone, Steven Tyler's high-pitched scream from "Dream On."

At the doorway to the master bedroom, I stop, as if stepping inside would be encroaching on a space I have no right to be in. That's odd, seeing as I've been there lots of times. Jenn and I have watched movies on the king-size bed. We've spent hours talking in there, especially when Rick's out of town when the kids are with their dad.

This feels different. Maybe it's the drawn curtains dimming the room. Or the double doors leading into the master bathroom. They're closed. I've never seen them closed. "Jenn?"

Nothing.

Hesitantly, I cross the threshold into the bedroom. Jenn isn't on the bed. I check the floor on both sides. Reluctantly, I turn to the closed bathroom doors. My middle tightens. Swallowing is impossible. I set the baby carrier down. She's starting to protest, but I can't hold her right now.

I reach for the door handles with shaking hands and send a prayer to anyone listening, asking for the guts to open them. Because in some horrible way, I'm afraid to. I'm afraid I'll see something I'll never be able to erase from my mind. I want to run away, go back home, forget I ever came over.

But I can't. Jenn is my best friend. If she's in the bathroom and something is wrong, I need to be brave enough to help her. I push the doors open.

And there, Jenn lies in the large corner tub, eyes staring up sightlessly through the water.

CHAPTER TWO

JENN

October 14
Seventeen Months before Drowning

After my lunch hour, I returned to work, having done something I never thought I would. I'd gotten a tattoo on the back of my shoulder for my husband's birthday. The drive from the tattoo parlor back to the library was only about five minutes. In that time, I somehow managed to bump the bandage—and wince—at least twenty times.

After parking and taking a couple of ibuprofen, I headed into the library, where I'd return to updating the audiobook catalog and making notes of new titles we should order.

Right as I entered the quiet of the library, my phone dinged loudly. Very un-librarian-like. Giving a sheepish smile to the patrons whose heads turned toward me—and ignoring the silent laugh that my coworker Tim wasn't even trying to hide—I quickly silenced my phone.

The notification was a text from Becca. *Did you do it? Pics or it didn't happen!*

I'd taken several pictures of my new ink before the bandage went on top, so I sent a couple, then replied, *Pretty sure I yelled some things that have never crossed my lips before. Worth it! Can't wait to see his face.*

Pics and text sent, I passed Tim, sending him a silent raspberry in response to his laugher, and returned to my desk. Only a few more hours and I'd head home to celebrate Rick's first birthday as my husband—his first birthday with me at all, thanks to a whirlwind courtship. In less than a year, I'd met him and become his wife. I couldn't have guessed the things that would happen as a result of one moment in the produce section of Trader Joe's. He'd knocked several oranges to the floor, and I bent to pick them up. As cliché as it sounds, that's how we met.

Rick filled the weeks that followed with one adrenaline rush after another. His passion for life—and for me—drew me in. Filled me up. Every hour without him was gray and dim.

Falling in love hard is probably inevitable when you're an orphan with no siblings. The entire concept of an extended family had never been a thing for me. As an adult, I'd found a sister in Becca, and then I found my person in Rick. They were my family.

So here I was, married with a tattoo as a gift to Rick—something deeply personal. He had several of his own tats but had never mentioned how much getting them hurt. I had to hold back tears from the moment the needle touched my skin until the tattoo artist finished.

"How's that look?" he'd asked as he handed me a mirror. I peered into it, at the reflection in a larger mirror on the wall behind me. There it was, my new ink on the back of my shoulder, a script font following the curves of an ocean wave: *Just one more.*

Rick had grown up in Orange County, where he barely graduated from high school because he'd been so focused on surfing. He was really good and even won contests. He credited surfing and SoCal swimming culture in general. I credited it with his V-silhouette that had belonged to every heartthrob on the posters that graced my middle-school-era bedroom walls.

On our third date, we went water-skiing, and he told me all about how it was different from surfing. How surfing had become almost a religion for him, a way of life.

"Surfing teaches you to enjoy every moment, seize every opportunity. The same wave will never come again, so you better ride the one you have right now," he'd said.

"Is the surfer motto *Seize the Wave*?" I asked teasingly, then wondered what that would be in Latin—*carpe* something-or-other. I decided to look it up at work.

"Might as well be," he'd said with a wink. "I couldn't get enough of the water." His face lit up, and his eyes looked dreamy as if seeing it all again. The joy there brought me joy too. "When you're riding the perfect wave . . . man, there's *nothing* like it. I never wanted to go home from the beach. Each wave was different. I always wanted *just . . . one . . . more*." His emphasis on the last few words had me repeating them.

"Just one more," I'd said, and heard the sentiment in my ears. "That sounds like a pretty good motto."

"Yeah. That's totally it," he'd said with a nod. "I always wanted just one more." He looked away from me then, staring over my shoulder as if watching a vision of the past. His eyes narrowed slightly. What memories were playing in his head? A particularly good day at the beach? Injuries? Mourning friends lost to the sea? Feeling the old tug of the water, calling him to it like a siren song?

About the time I opened my mouth to break the silence, he whispered, "Just one more," as if making a wish he desperately hoped would come true.

The buzzing of my phone brought me back to my computer at the library. Becca had replied. *It's perfect!*

I thought so too, scrolling up to admire the pictures I sent. I never forget the look he wore after telling me about the waves, the wistful way he'd said the words *just one more*.

At the time, I suggested going to a nearby mock surfing place, where they created waves indoors, so he could teach me. He nixed that, I assume because it wouldn't be anywhere near close enough to the real thing. I still wanted to learn to surf, but I put it on my mental marriage bucket list. The Rockies were pretty far from any ocean, but we had plenty of time for trips like that in the future.

Rick tended to be close-lipped about his past, not wanting to dwell on it. I got it; my foster-system childhood wasn't something I liked to dredge up either. That glimpse into his surfing era was the most detail he'd shared with me about his younger years, and I cherished every morsel.

I decided to do something with that memory, with those words. Something private, not a flawlessly wrapped gift to flaunt in front of others at a party. A gift so intimate that it would tell him that I heard him, understood him. Remembered everything he told me—and *cared* about all of it, everything that made Rick who he was. That I'd really seen him. He'd know I internalized his motto and would make it my own.

When I got off work and headed for the exit, Tim headed my way, having been replaced at the circulation desk by Stacie. "Nice volume earlier. I don't think the large-print section heard, though."

"Ha-ha," I said but with a smile—I liked the fact that a coworker knew he could tease me. That kind of thing didn't happen much during my younger years when I was the weird foster girl with no friends.

"See ya tomorrow," Tim added as he passed me, patting my back on his way.

"Aaaah!" The sound of pain came involuntarily.

Tim whirled around. "Did I hurt you? I'm sorry. Are you sunburned or something?"

"Or something." The pain was easing up, so my voice loosened. "Think the large-print section heard that?"

"Very likely," Tim said. "Seriously, you okay?"

"I got this today." I pulled up one of the pictures on my phone and showed it to him. "It's still tender."

"Wow, color me impressed," Tim said. "I didn't know Marion had it in her." A reference to the buttoned-up, bun-wearing librarian from *The Music Man*.

"It's for my husband's birthday."

Tim nodded approvingly, looking at the picture again. "It's *hot*." His eyes went wide, and he shook his head. "That came out wrong. Not trying to be inappropriate or get in trouble with HR—"

"No worries, Tiny," I assured him, referring to Cratchit's son in *A Christmas Carol*. "I hope he thinks so."

I assumed we'd go to a restaurant of his choosing and then maybe go to a movie, but when he returned from work at the law firm, he didn't seem to even remember that it was his birthday.

He turned on the news, and I curled up beside him on the couch, leaning my right side against him because the tattoo side was tender. "What did you want to do tonight?"

"For . . ." His eye moved to me quickly, then back to the television.

"Your birthday dinner," I said, kissing his cheek. "You deserve something better than I can cook up."

"Oh, right." He kissed my forehead and kept watching the news.

"Well, let me know when you decide where you want to eat, and I'll call in a reservation." I shifted my position a bit to relieve the pressure on my sore shoulder.

After a romantic dinner at Rocky's, his favorite steakhouse, we came home and started to fool around. Rick unbuttoned my blouse and slipped it over my head. I twisted so the back of my left shoulder faced him, showing off the bandage covering my gift, my one and only, brand-new tattoo. My heart started beating erratically, and I dug my toes into the carpet, waiting for his reaction—for understanding, appreciation, *love*   to wash over his face, followed by a big smile, and then an amazing night together.

"What happened there?" he asked, pointing to the bandage.

"Look under it," I told him.

"Why? Did you hurt yourself?"

I nudged my shoulder closer to him and smiled. "Take it off and see."

He did, carefully pulling off the tape. When he peeled off the gauze, he said nothing for a few seconds, then, "What's. That." He said the words as two statements, almost an accusation.

That was a tone I knew, but not the one I'd expected. It was the one that accompanied a certain tension in the muscles of his jaw and possibly a slammed door or two.

A zip of fear shot through me, along with the thought, *Shit. What did I do wrong?*

"*Just one more*," I said stupidly as if he hadn't just read it. "Your motto, remember?"

He looked back blankly.

"From your surfing days," I said.

If he didn't like women with tattoos, he could have said so. That's what he was annoyed about, right? He probably didn't even register what the tattoo was, let alone what it meant. He still didn't say anything else.

"Remember?" I said again. It came out as a squeak.

Please don't be mad, I thought, begged. What were all the ways I could have screwed this up? Maybe he didn't mind tats on women, but he thought mine was ugly. Did I remember the phrase incorrectly? Had the tattoo artist misspelled it? With that look and tone, *something* was wrong.

Rick breathed out heavily through his nostrils, his arms folded. "It's a tattoo," he said flatly.

"Yeah," I said tightly; I couldn't get enough air. "*Just one more*," I said, again, as if repeating it would change something. "I—thought you'd like it."

"I hate tattoos. They're ugly. They make you look like a tramp."

"You have three." I bit my tongue as soon as I said the words, then focused on slipping my blouse back on to cover myself.

"Ink's different on men. Dudes can't be tramps."

We'd never discussed tattoos, and while he probably wouldn't want me to have full sleeves, I assumed that because he sported a few—one on his bicep, two on his back—I figured he'd be okay with my having one, especially one meant for him, in a spot no one would ever see unless I was in a swimsuit. A tiny part of my heart had even pictured Rick getting a matching one.

Just one more could be our motto: one more day together, one more kiss, one more year, one more day to love each other.

"Why the wave?" The muscles around his eyes tightened further, making the pit in my stomach deeper.

I looked over my shoulder, not that I could see the tattoo with my blouse back in place. "Because it's from when you used to surf." Worry and confusion mixed with fear.

"I have no idea what you're talking about."

"Yes, you do," I insisted.

"You probably heard it in a movie or something and then misremembered it as being me." Rick grunted in annoyance and pushed past me on his way to our bathroom. The heavy tread he used when he was close to blowing a gasket.

The sound twisted something inside my middle the same way as when he came home from work unexpectedly and burst through the door, already upset about something.

"I didn't imagine it or make it up," I said quietly.

He stopped walking but didn't turn around. Those words were a very big mistake. After a moment, he clenched his fists and then disappeared through the double-door entry of the bathroom. A couple of seconds later, he reappeared and pointed his toothbrush at me. "You *are* getting that tramp stamp removed. It's disgusting." He went back in to spit, kicking the doors closed. The sound made me jump.

A little voice in my head wanted to keep arguing, to insist that he'd told me stories of championships he'd won, difficulties learning to surf, and more. To point out that a tramp stamp isn't on the shoulder.

After he came out, any magic that might have been in the air was gone. Nothing romantic would be happening tonight, and he'd blame me for it. He went to bed, and I quietly went to the bathroom to wash my face and brush my teeth. By the time I slipped into bed, he was already breathing heavily.

Lying beside him, I stared into the darkness, trying to comprehend what had just happened. Rick had denied ever surfing, but I *knew* he'd told me stories about it. I couldn't have made up *Just one more*. Could I?

His annoyance and insistence were compelling enough to make me wonder if I was remembering wrong. Maybe, as Rick said, I'd seen a movie or TV show with something similar and projected it onto him, like the Mandela Effect—a phenomenon I learned about when helping a patron with some research a year ago, where we have memories of things that didn't happen—but I didn't think so.

My husband had basically called me crazy. He insisted that I'd made up an entire past for him, including a motto. But I hadn't made anything up.

Unless . . .

Could *he* have early-onset dementia?

In the dark, I came up with three possible explanations for what had happened: I was losing my memory. He was losing his memory. Or he was lying to me.

Unable to sleep, I got out of bed and went downstairs to do what I did best: research. I grabbed my phone and went through several notes I'd made, diary-style, while we dated. I'd read them before, but tonight I had to read them again to know for sure.

These were words I'd written right after the events they described. I'd even typed out a couple of his surfing stories, like the one about the old surfer dude who claimed he coined the term *gnarly*.

I'd looked up the etymology and learned that no, the old man hadn't coined the word. I read about how Rick got annoyed that I bothered to look it up. "Why try to prove me wrong? You have to always feel superior, don't you?"

I shook my head to clear the memory and scrolled some more. There it was, the story about *Just one more.*

I *did* remember correctly. This wasn't some Hollywood-created mirage or personal Mandela Effect.

Okay, so I'd just proven to myself that *my* memory was fine. There was no way for me to research Rick's memory, at least none I could come up with in the middle of the night. But something in my gut said that Rick's brain was as healthy as ever.

Which left the third explanation: Rick was lying to me. If true, that brought with it all kinds of disturbing questions. They plagued me all night, even after I went back to bed, where I stared at the ceiling until morning.

Because all of the questions swirled round and round one central point: my husband was lying to me, and I had no idea what the hell was going on.

CHAPTER THREE

BECCA

For a moment, I'm frozen, unable to think or move. Unable to process what I see. A scream sticks in my throat and turns into a cry. The high-pitched sound thaws me enough for some level of instinct to kick in.

Jenn's eyes are open, her body floating just under the surface. Panic and fear are overshadowed by the pressing need to help Jenn, to get her out of the water, to get her breathing.

As I approach the tub, I take out my phone but nearly drop it into the water. I hold it with both hands to be sure it's secure and dial 911. Hands trembling, I somehow manage to put it on speaker and lay it on the floor. The phone can't fall from there. Hopefully, dispatch will be able to hear me. I whip around to the tub and plunge my arms into the warm water up to my shoulders. I'm hugging Jenn as hard as I can with my arms wrapped under her arms.

"911," a female voice says through the phone. "What is your emergency?"

I'm pulling, grunting, trying to heave Jenn from the tub, splashing water onto the floor but, I hope, not onto my phone. I need this call to stay live. Her frame—we're about the same size—feels twice as heavy as it actually is. The term *deadweight* flashes into my mind, but I refuse to let it stay. Jenn's clothes have soaked up a lot of water, which makes getting her out of the tub harder. The bathwater also seems to have its own gravitational force. More than once, I loosen my grip, adjust, and try to heave and lift again.

"Hello?" the dispatch operator says insistently. "Can you hear me? This is 911. What's your emergency?"

"I hear you," I say, more grunt than words. I hope my voice carries to the phone. "Please send an ambulance. I found my friend unconscious in her tub."

"Did you say that someone is unconscious?"

"Yes. In the bathtub."

"Who is in the tub?" The operator remains calm—annoyingly so.

"My friend. Jenn." I breathe heavily and try to think. "Jennifer Banks."

Clacking on a keyboard comes through the line. "Did you say Banks?"

"Yes." I'm still trying to drag Jenn out of the water. This is a corner tub with the faucet along the open side, and the hardware is getting in the way. It's dead center, digging into my stomach. I have Jenn's head and shoulders out, but I'm starting to feel lightheaded. "Her name is Jenn . . . Jennifer . . . Banks. Please. Hurry." I'm panting heavily now.

"Is she breathing?"

"No!" I say, frustrated. "Send help!" I want to yell at the dispatch operator and demand that she send an ambulance already. The operator asks the same things over and over, and I give the same answers between huffs, trying not to break down into tears. Her constant requests for repetition are more than I can take. I don't know how many times I can say the same awful things.

The operator confirms the address, and then I realize that the front door is locked; it locks automatically when closed. I yell the code to the operator so the EMTs can let themselves in.

Finally, with my shoe wedged against the tub and the floor, I have the leverage I need. I can do this. Get her up and over the side. Her jeans pocket catches on one of the faucet handles, stalling my momentum, but I manage to yank free after shoving the handle with my shoe. With both feet braced, I give one final pull, and Jenn's body thumps and sloshes onto the floor. Water rolls off her and down my arms, darkening the thin beige rug. I'm glad she didn't hit the tile directly.

"Please," I say to the operator, now panting with exertion. "She's not breathing. Hurry!" Again, I rattle off her address in case the operator didn't hear or believe me the last four times.

I roll Jenn to her side like I've seen in movies, hoping to get water out of her lungs. Only a little drips out. I start rescue breathing and chest compressions, cursing myself for not taking that refresher course at work when it was offered last year. The million-dollar Prescott account seemed more important at the time. I do remember that afterward, another manager, Jodee, said that the techniques had changed. But how?

After what feels like an eternity, the operator assures me that help is on the way. "Stay on the line with me until they arrive, all right?"

I mutter something in agreement. I'm far enough from my phone that hanging up would take both time and effort, neither of which I'm willing or able to expend.

The operator stays calm as a robot, but at least now she's talking me through doing whatever I can to save Jenn. She tells me to focus on chest compressions only, ignoring rescue breathing altogether. For now, keeping the blood moving is what matters most.

After a couple of minutes of chest compressions, my body tires out and my arms feel like rubber. Am I doing this right? Am I doing any good? I remember the old CPR course from a few years ago where they said to do compressions to the beat of the Bee Gees' "Stayin' Alive," which sounds horrifically macabre now. I try to do compressions to the song's tempo anyway, in case it helps.

Does Jenn's blood still have any oxygen to circulate to her organs? To her brain? I shoo the thoughts away by playing the Bee Gees in my head. I glance at the clock beside the sink. The fire station is maybe a three-minute drive from here. I've always been glad we live so close to help but never imagined needing it at a time like this. It's been *five* minutes since dispatch said help was coming. Where are they? Finally, I hear sirens and relief floods me. I pray the EMTs will get up here fast; I can't keep up the compressions much longer.

Beeps sound below, then the front door opening. At last, someone rushes inside, calling out.

"Upstairs!" I yell to them. "In the master bathroom!"

One set of heavy footsteps thunders up the stairs, and a moment later, a man bursts into the bedroom, barely missing Ivy's carrier; good thing I set it to the side. He's not an EMT. He's a cop.

I want to yell and ask what took him so long and where the ambulance is. Instead, I back away in a crab crawl, then stand and watch from the double doors, vaguely aware that Ivy is screaming. I can't comfort her right now. I watch, expecting the cop to get right to work, doing compressions better than I could as we wait for the EMTs.

But he doesn't. Instead, after looking at Jenn, he pushes a button on the radio at his shoulder and speaks into it, using numbers and codes that mean nothing to me. Then he steps out of the bathroom and addresses me.

"I need to secure the scene—"

"What's going on?" I demand, not letting him finish. I point to the doors behind him. "She's dying! You have to help her!"

"I'm sorry, miss, but she's obviously . . ." He shakes his head. "This is a clear fatality under unusual circumstances, so I have to treat this as a crime scene."

Eyes wide, I back up, but the bed stops me from gaining any distance. "Are you saying she was—and that you think I—"

"I'm not saying anything other than that I need to do my job," he says. "We'll need to talk with you, get a statement, of course, but for the moment, my priority is securing the scene. I need you to take the baby outside."

I nod robotically and kneel by Ivy. He may still be speaking, but I can't make out anything through the roar of my panic and confusion and whatever else is rushing through me.

"Hello? Hello? Can you still hear me?" a voice says, and I realize my phone is still on the bathroom floor.

The cop opens the door and retrieves it. He speaks to the dispatch operator, hangs up, and hands it to me.

I slip my phone into my back pocket again and unbuckle the carrier's straps. I take Ivy out and then go to the hall, down the stairs, and out the front door. No five-month-old should see her mother like that. She's fussing, clearly terrified by the commotion, and my freak-out isn't helping.

"We'll wait out here," I tell her, putting the pacifier into her mouth and rocking side to side, patting her back. I wish I'd been thinking clearly enough to grab a towel and attempt to dry off a bit, but there's no going back in now.

Just when I think the baby is calming down, her face screws up into an expression of misery. The pacifier falls from her mouth, and she wails at the top of her lungs. I hold her in the shade of a tree out front, bouncing and rocking her. She refuses the pacifier now. Tears stream down her face, which makes me cry too. And I can't stop. Her cries get louder, maybe because I'm crying. Maybe because my clothes are drenched in water, making her uncomfortable. Maybe because she's home, but something is terribly wrong and she can sense it.

At long last, an ambulance shows up—no lights or sirens. Several other patrol cars do too, and soon the place feels not like my best friend's home but like a crime scene out of a movie. I turn my back to the house, but blocking it out won't end a nightmare I can't wake from.

CHAPTER FOUR

JENN

January 21
Fourteen Months before Drowning

Life changed completely on Rick's birthday. From then on, I thought of life as before and after the tattoo: BT and AT. Everything began to unravel that day. Slowly at first.

I'd done my best to patch things up since I wanted this marriage to work more than anything. And I had something else in the back of my mind that could add another wrench into things, so I had to tread lightly.

It was a cold snowy morning, far from spring in this valley of the Rockies. I made Rick's favorite breakfast of bacon, eggs over medium—a tough order for someone like me, who didn't know much about cooking—and bran muffins. I sat across the table from him and offered to pour some orange juice.

He made a face and moved his glass out of range. "That stuff is liquid sugar. Might as well mainline heroin." And he returned to reading the news on his phone.

Strike one. I hoped the orange juice hadn't dented his mood by much, that my efforts at breakfast would provide plenty of positive energy, and he'd be back to the adoring man I'd said *I do* to. Debating whether to wait to mention the topic on my mind, I got up and put the orange juice back in the fridge. When I closed it and turned back, I opted to be open and honest, lay all my chips on the table.

My heart picked up its pace as I took my seat again. "Hey, hon?"

"Mm?" Rick glanced up from his phone and back again.

"I'm curious—when do you picture us having kids?"

This time, his head came up and stayed there. "What?"

"No rush, I swear," I said quickly. "I'm in no hurry, and I want time together as a couple." I reached for his hand across the table and held it between both of mine. "How about, you know, maybe in a few years, after you make partner?"

I wanted a baby. At least one. Preferably two or three, but I'd take it one step at a time. Our courtship had been fast, and while I didn't doubt for a second that we were meant to be together, we had a lot to learn about each other, things most couples know way before they reach the altar.

"Babe, I don't *want* kids." His voice sounded flat, but his expression was one of confusion as if us never having kids was a long-established fact.

It wasn't. I'd always wanted to be a mom. I would have remembered a conversation where my boyfriend or fiancé had nixed that dream. That guy wouldn't have become my husband. My face must have registered alarm because he sighed heavily and pulled his hand away. I wanted to grab it again; seeing him withdraw across the table felt like my hopes of having a baby were moving out of my reach.

"I *do* want kids." I wrapped my arms around my waist. "You never said you didn't."

"And you never said you did." Rick stood quickly, making the kitchen chair bump and scratch against the tile floor. He stepped to the side and shoved the chair back under the table as if that ended the discussion. His attention returned to his phone, still in one hand.

"But—" My voice cut off, along with my brain. Sure, there were a lot of things we hadn't talked about, but I knew for a fact that we'd talked about *this*. We'd talked about how fun it would be with a little Rick or Jenn running around, whether a child would have his eyes or my freckles. "We talked about having kids."

"If you say so, but I've never wanted any."

"We talked about it last summer," I said.

"No, we didn't."

"Yes, we did," I insisted. "We went on a moonlight ride on the ski lift. For the solstice?"

"The only times I've been on a ski lift are to go skiing." He returned to reading news on his phone, a clear message that the conversation was over.

I sat there, confused and frustrated. We *did* ride the ski lift last June. I'd worn my pink hoodie, and he'd worn an expensive pair of sunglasses that made him look even more handsome than usual. I'd never forget it. "But—"

"Stop it," Rick said, looking up from his phone and nailing me with a glare. "You're making it up."

"No, I'm not." What else could I say? I could hear a hint of surrender in my voice. I hated that.

Rick leaned against the back of his chair. "*If* we took that ride, then that's where I told you I didn't want kids." Almost a concession.

"You said you didn't want them *right away*," I countered. The accusation in his voice made me tense up inside.

"Not ever." His tone had shifted to one of hurt as if I were intentionally injuring him.

I sat there, listening to him lie. That was a blatant, outright, no-question-about-it lie. He'd said it with such serious intent—not angry, but wounded that I'd accuse him of not being honest with me.

Maybe I'd misheard him that night, but I knew we'd talked about having kids on the ski lift. *Knew* it. Maybe I misunderstood. Or maybe *I* wasn't clear in what I meant and he misunderstood me. Somehow, our wires had crossed.

The truth remained: I wanted kids. Plural. I'd told him as much. Whether he remembered the ski lift conversation or not, he couldn't deny *this* conversation. Now he knew that I wanted kids. More than anything, I *needed* to be a mom.

His phone vibrated with an incoming call. He answered it and talked for a few seconds, then looked over to me as if nothing were amiss. "Thanks for the breakfast, babe." He leaned across the table and gave me a quick kiss. "This won't be a quick call."

He trotted down the hall and up the stairs to our bedroom as he resumed the conversation—a client or colleague at the law firm, probably—and a few minutes later, he reappeared, still on the call but now with his shoes on and a blazer draped over one arm. He grabbed his leather messenger bag and mouthed "Have a good day."

"You too," I said quietly to not interrupt.

He left through the door to the garage. When the door closed, I stood and began gathering dishes. Rick started up his Lexus, and I paused, holding a stack of plates. The car pulled out of the garage, but I didn't quite manage a full breath until I heard the garage door lowering and then stopping. Then I carried the plates to the sink.

I had so much to learn about Rick and about being a wife, but throughout our brief marriage, I had learned that surprises upset Rick. He needed a gradual build-up of expectations. No springing things on him. Give plenty of lead time.

That's what this morning's breakfast conversation was supposed to be: a gradual build-up. He'd viewed it as the upsetting main event, a surprise I'd thrown at him.

What would he think when he learned what I'd planned to build toward? I suspected that I was already pregnant. My period was four days late, and I hadn't been late in years. My body felt strange. My chest was tender, and my stomach was queasy.

And as of that morning, I'd learned that the smell of bacon wasn't one I could stand. I wrapped the bacon-grease-soaked paper towels into a plastic bag, tied off the top, and put it in the garbage that way, hoping to trap the smell inside. Mechanically, I began loading the dishwasher, feeling even more nauseated. From the bacon, or from worry?

I'd hoped that over breakfast, we'd talk about the future, our hopes for our children, and get a little excited over the idea. That way, if I turned out to be pregnant, it would be an unplanned shock, sure, but a happy one.

Rick had a great job at a law firm, so we could easily afford a child. While I loved my job at the library, we didn't need the income. I'd already daydreamed about quitting to be a full-time mom, of meeting the librarian who replaced me when I brought my own toddler to reading time.

I'd wanted a family—a real family—for as long as I could remember. Foster homes never counted, and aging out of the system had a way of making you feel that you lacked whatever it was that made a person lovable. The closest thing I'd ever had to family was Becca.

With a sigh, I started the dishwasher and dampened a dishcloth to wipe the table down. Everything would work out. I was married to a great guy, and there had been many times I'd been sure I'd never get married at all. If no one could love the child me, and the teenage me was vile and intolerable—or so my foster siblings and foster fathers had said—why would anyone love the grown me? Then Rick swept me off my feet, and I became a wife.

Married life hadn't been a fairy tale, of course; real life goes on after the bride and groom ride off into the sunset on their gallant steeds. Those stories never show Cinderella or Snow White working on their relationships with their princes. We never learn that those steeds need oil changes and transmission repairs, and that even Prince Charming wakes up with morning breath.

Ours was a journey in progress, but I'd reached the trailhead for the path that led to the family and life I'd always yearned for. I headed along that path the day we exchanged vows. At least I thought I had.

Prince Charming seemed to have other plans. Now what?

CHAPTER FIVE

BECCA

"**E**xcuse me, are you the one who found the victim?"

I turn to see the person speaking—a police officer. My eyebrows draw together, something I'm aware of doing, though I didn't mean to. It's as if I'm observing myself from somewhere else. None of this feels real. None of it *can* be. "Um, yeah. I mean, yes, I am."

"Is she your sister?"

"N-no."

"Are you related?"

"No," I say again, hating that biology keeps us from being considered family when that's what she is to me. *Was* to me? "She's a friend." That word almost sounds traitorous. Jenn is so much more. That word can describe someone from high school geometry that you haven't seen since but happen to be connected to on Facebook. My head pounds. I reach up with one hand and feel my forehead. The muscles are all scrunched up. I rub them and add, "Jenn is a close friend. My best friend."

Standing by the garage, I rock side to side with Ivy, vaguely aware of more vehicles and people moving around than before. I think one of them is a reporter. The idea of Jenn becoming the subject of the evening news makes me cringe. Ivy's not screaming anymore. She looks more unsure than anything at the activity around us. I stroke her hair and kiss the top of her head.

"I'm hoping you can help us with a few things. May I ask you some questions?"

"Um . . ." I look at my phone as if looking for a message from Mark about a work meeting. "I think I need to . . ." My voice trails off, and I have no idea how to finish the thought.

"We need to ask you some questions, now. It could help us catch who did this."

That brings my focus around. "Okay." I'll do anything to catch the monster who did this.

"I understand from dispatch that her name was Jennifer Banks. Is that correct?"

Was. The word is jarring.

"She goes by Jenn," I say. "But yes. It's Jennifer Banks."

"Is she married?" The officer's tag reads *J. Michaels.* "She wasn't wearing a ring."

This time I nod.

"What's her husband's name?"

"Rick." How have I not thought of him at all? Where is he? He was supposed to be back by now, right? He needs to know.

"Rick," the officer says. "Is that short for *Richard?*"

"I . . . don't know."

"Do you know how we can contact Mr. Banks?"

"Yeah. I have his number." I grab my phone from my pocket and nearly drop it, clearly as clumsy now as I was earlier. Holding Ivy as I try to unlock it makes the phone unable to see me well enough for face ID, so I have to type in my password with my fat thumb on the tiny keyboard. Eventually, I unlock it and pull up Rick's contact page, then hold my phone face out so Officer Michaels can see it. "He's a lawyer at Hancock, Donaldson, and Cleese."

Officer Michaels takes a picture of my phone screen to capture Rick's information. "And you found her body, correct?"

Her *body.* I hate that word. I glance at the house and remember how sure the responding cop was that she was already dead. Of course she was. I knew

26

she was gone the moment I saw her. I arrived way too late. "Yeah. I found her." The air coming out scratches my throat.

Saying those words makes reality crash down. My life force drains out of me, down my legs, disappearing into the ground like water on parched soil. I'm simultaneously empty and filled with pain all at once, and I *know* she's gone. I don't want to know. I don't want to accept it. No one is inside, in the master bathroom, resuscitating her. Jenn's just gone, period.

"Was anyone else in the house at the time? Any children? I noticed a room with toys and a crib. I assume Mr. and Mrs. Banks have children."

"Just one." A tear falls down my cheek as I look at little Ivy and stroke her downy hair. She's getting squirmy. I hold on so I don't drop her. "This is their daughter. I was babysitting." My vision begins to narrow, darkness pressing on the edges.

"You look a bit pale," the cop says. "Let's walk over to the lawn. I'll hold the baby."

I follow his lead. Two steps onto the grass, he takes Ivy just as my arms give out. My knees lose all strength. I feel myself lowering and manage to catch myself with one hand and then the other before I collapse entirely. My arms threaten to give way, so I push myself sideways and lie on my back.

Each breath is a stab, and my vision narrows further. Nothing feels real, as if I'm watching myself from a distance, like one of those stories of people who claim to have died and returned to their bodies later. Am I dying? Will I see a bright light and find Jenn soon? No. And I don't want to; I can't leave my kids.

The cold, prickly grass pokes me, almost sharp against the back of my neck and elbows. I'm not dying. I'm simply incapable of understanding this pain, of processing what this day means. For me. For Rick. For the twins. For poor little Ivy.

Once more, Officer Michaels clears his throat. "Your color is looking a little better. Just breathe."

"Thanks," I whisper.

"So she's their only child?"

"Yeah," I say, but unsure whether I made any sound, I nod too.

"Do you know her name and birthdate?"

A blip of clarity breaks through the fog. "Wait, why do you need that information right now?" I find the strength to sit up. I reach for Ivy, and when she reaches for me, he surrenders her. She curls up against me, glad to be in familiar arms. "She isn't going to be taken into state custody, is she?" I think of the many horror stories Jenn has told me about growing up in the foster care system.

"That's not up to me. A judge will make that determination. But chances are good that if her father can care for her, she'll remain in his custody."

"Oh, g-good." I can hardly speak without stuttering with uneven breaths.

Someone calls the officer away, and he excuses himself.

Rick's not the most hands-on father, but as far as I know, he's done a decent job to this point. I'd much rather Ivy stay with him than lose both parents in a single day. Feeling slightly stronger now that I'm not worried about Ivy on top of everything else, I gingerly get to my feet and head toward the front door of the house.

Another officer by the door steps into my path. He looks younger than Officer Michaels, and his tag says *D. Berger.*

"You can't go in there," he says.

I gesture at my clothes, which are still damp. "I need a towel." Then I notice another officer blocking the door entirely. How many are swarming the place? "The diaper bag and car seat are in there, and my purse . . ."

"No one can go inside right now," Officer Michaels says, returning from whatever had interrupted him. He stands next to the guy blocking my way.

"Wh-why not?" My teeth are chattering. I am a little cold, but not that cold. Is this what shock feels like?

"Let's get you a blanket from the ambulance. Come with me." He takes my arm firmly but not painfully, as if to tell me that I have to obey. As weak as I feel, he doesn't need to use that much pressure. A piece of yarn tied to my wrist would be enough to lead me anywhere.

He takes me to the back of one of two ambulances. I don't know when they arrived. One is parked a few houses down, and I assume it'll carry Jenn's body when they remove it from the house. From the back of the other one, Officer Michaels gets what looks like a giant piece of tinfoil. He unfolds it and wraps it around me and Ivy, who is suddenly fascinated by the shiny material and the noises she can make with it.

"That'll help warm you up," Officer Michaels says.

"Can someone get my purse?" I ask. "I think it's by the front door."

"I'll see what I can do. A couple more questions first, though. Can you think of anyone who would want Mrs. Banks dead?"

"No," I say. "Everyone loves her." I don't mention that her marriage wasn't perfect. Whose is? It's not as if being a crappy husband means Rick did this.

The officer asks a few more questions, but I can't think clearly. "We've had reports of a suspicious white van in the area. Did you see anything like that today?"

"No." The cobwebs in my mind clear a bit. "Wait. I did see a white van earlier. It was on my street—a few blocks over." I wave in that general direction. "It looked a little weird. Maybe suspicious."

"Did you get a look at the driver?"

I think back but shake my head. "I didn't. Sorry. Only that it looked like a utility vehicle but didn't have any logos or anything, and it was moving slowly from house to house. Do you think the van could be connected?"

"We have to follow all leads," he says vaguely. "Do you know the make or model?"

Of a van? I can barely point out a Prius, and that's only because Jenn drives one. "No, sorry. Just white and boxy."

"No problem," he says. "Stay here, okay?"

I nod, and after he leaves, I sit on the curb with Ivy. No matter how much I try to wrap the blanket around her, she'll have none of it. She crinkles it between her fists and tries to eat it. I don't force the issue; she doesn't seem cold.

Time plays tricks on me. So does my memory of what's happened. It's as if my brain refuses to believe I'm living the reality that is this hell, so it periodically freezes like an overwhelmed computer. I have no idea how long Ivy and I are sitting there—long enough for her to fall asleep on my shoulder and for Rick to arrive home. His silver Lexus—I guess I can identify two models besides my Corolla—passes the first ambulance and then pulls next to the patrol car that's parked at the curb.

Rick jumps out of the car and races over to a couple of officers talking intently nearby. "What happened? What's going on? Where's my wife?" He's red-faced and sweating as if he just ran a marathon in his business suit.

His familiar face is the only adult connection to Jenn that I have left. I stand from the curb, careful to cradle Ivy so she won't wake, and walk to him. When I reach Rick, I throw my free arm around him and cry into his dress shirt and tie.

"What happened?" Rick leans back, trying to pry himself far enough away to look me in the eye. "Becca, look at me. Is she okay?"

"She's—she's gone." My teeth are chattering, making speech hard. Maybe I should give Ivy to him to hold, in case I get weak again. But his wide eyes and pale face say otherwise—*he's* about to go into shock now.

He releases me and turns as if to run inside the house. He's stopped from entering too. Yellow police tape is stretched across the door frame now. "This is my house!" Rick yells. "What happened to my wife? Someone tell me what's going on!"

"Your wife was found unconscious in the tub," Officer Berger says.

"Is she at the hospital? I need to see her." Rick is starting to look as frantic as I felt when I opened the bathroom door.

"She's still inside," Berger says. "I'm sorry, she didn't make it."

Rick takes a step back, and presses his fisted hand to his mouth. "No. No, no, no. Let me in. I have to see her."

Officer Michaels steps in. "That's not possible right now, Mr. Banks. Let's go to the station. I'll fill you in on everything we know so far, and you can help us figure out some more."

Rick nods like a man on a mission. "I'll meet you there." He strides purposefully to his sleek car and gets inside.

I look to Officer Michaels. "Should I keep Ivy with me for now? I can go back home and wait for Rick."

"Actually, we need you to come to the station too. I'll make sure we get you some coffee to warm you up."

"Oh. Okay." I look around. "I'll need my purse, though."

"It's right there." Officer Michaels points to the spot on the curb where I'd been sitting. He'd brought my purse to me as I'd asked, and I didn't notice. He looks at me with a gentle expression, as if he knows what kind of chaos my brain is in right now.

"Thanks," I manage. "The car seat is—"

"We can't go back inside," Michaels says. "If your purse hadn't been right by the door, we couldn't have gotten it for you either. We can't contaminate the scene."

"Oh. Right. Of course," I say, but the reality of everything is hammering home, too much too fast. The yellow tape reading *CRIME SCENE* seems to flash in my peripheral vision. I clear my throat so I can speak. "I have an old car seat in my garage," I say. "It's probably expired, but I guess it's better than nothing." Thanks to having twins, technically I have two car seats. I'm suddenly glad I didn't get rid of all the baby stuff.

"Are you up to driving? You can ride over in my patrol car." Officer Michaels looks at me, concerned.

"I'm fine. I'd rather drive so I have my car," I say, and somehow, he believes me. I don't want to be stuck at the station waiting for a ride after . . . whatever this is. "It's only a couple of miles, right?"

"Right." He seems to debate for a second but finishes with "Hold on." He calls the station and arranges for someone to bring over a newer car seat. Soon it's installed in my car and Ivy's buckled inside. "Follow me, okay?" He probably wants to make sure I get there in one piece. Or that I actually drive to the station instead of home.

Wait, could I be a suspect? The person who finds the body often is, right?

"I'll follow," I promise and pull my keys out of my purse as Officers Berger and Michaels head to their patrol cars. Berger disappears into the small crowd now gathered around the house, including several neighbors and a few reporters—I can tell from the logos emblazoned on the sides of the satellite trucks. Jenn and her family are going to be news fodder. There's no avoiding it. The details of our private tragedy will become public and turned into clickbait.

After getting in my car and starting it, I look around and wonder how I'll get out of the cul de sac with so many emergency vehicles everywhere. Officer Michaels gets into the patrol car parked right by the driveway, which is no longer boxed in now that Rick's driven off. Michaels pulls out, and I follow, which makes my getting out easy; the path opens for him, and I slip through right after. As I drive, my foggy brain begins to grasp why I'm heading to the police station. To be questioned.

Jenn's death is suspicious. I finally ask the question that should have registered right away: What *did* happen? Jenn wasn't taking a regular bath; she was fully clothed. Maybe she was planning to take one, and then a home invasion went bad, and the man—or more than one—knocked her out and held her under the water. I didn't see any signs of a break-in or of anything that would hint of theft: no rifling through drawers and other belongings, no stolen television or computer, nothing damaged that I noticed.

Was it murder by someone who knew her, then? Who would want to kill Jenn? No one.

The hum of the pavement, even for the few minutes it takes to get to the police station, is soothing enough to let me think more clearly than I have since I opened that door. By the time I find a spot to park, I've concluded one thing and decided another.

First, Jenn's death was not an accident.

Second, I'll do whatever is in my power to find the monster who killed my best friend and make sure they pay.

CHAPTER SIX

JENN

March 12
One Year before Drowning

I got a lot of flak in college over wanting to be "just" a stay-at-home mom, as if I were some backward girl who'd grown up in the Warren Jeffs compound. Granted, my dreams held a distinct commonality with June Cleaver, sans pearls. I had no ambition to become a high-powered career woman. I got my bachelor's degree in journalism. My master's degree was in library science, but despite the term *science*, it wasn't exactly a STEM field.

Rick was working late on a case, so I invited Becca over for a movie night. At one point, I mentioned my guilt about wanting to be a SAHM—not during a serious conversation but in passing as we watched a comedy from the eighties. She pulled the popcorn bowl onto her lap and hugged it as if she might crush it.

"Hey, give me some," I said, trying to take the bowl.

She sat up from the pile of pillows she'd been leaning against, grabbed the remote, and paused the show. "All of those women who came before us worked hard and faced obstacles of all kinds. They did that so you and I could have a *choice* about what we do. You *do* have a choice. You have an education, you have a job so you can support yourself if needed, and you have a husband who makes what I assume is a good salary. You have the option of being a stay-at-home mom when you have kids. If that's what will make you happy, then that's the right choice for you."

"You won't think less of me?" I asked.

Becca herself had a pretty great career in advertising, and she'd had it through marriage, twin babies, the accompanying maternity leave, and later, a divorce. Honestly, I didn't know if she had a choice about her career even before the divorce—had her ex made enough for her to stay home if she'd wanted to? That detail shouldn't have mattered, but I did wonder. Then again, Becca, a career woman, seemed intent on making me believe that being "just" a stay-at-home-mom was a good thing.

Her usual lighthearted let's-have-fun expression wasn't there. She was serious. Any nervous laughter that might have threatened to show on my face sublimated.

"I will *always* think the world of you," Becca said. "And I can't wait for you to have a baby. Any kid would be lucky to have you as a mom."

"You're the best, you know that?" I said. "Fine. No more guilt. I'm going to be a mom, and if Gloria Steinem has a problem with that, she can go suck it."

"That's what I'm talking about," Becca said, grabbing a handful of popcorn before passing me the bowl. She reached for the remote, and we were back to watching Dolly Parton and her coworkers plan ways to get back at their jerk of a boss.

What I didn't tell Becca then—or anyone, not even Rick—was that I was already pregnant, at least ten weeks along, which didn't seem like "barely." It wasn't far from the end of the first trimester. My husband thought I should have big career aspirations like Becca but then sacrifice them for his career. The firm had an unspoken understanding that men with career wives didn't make partner. But having a wife who *could* have been in a C-suite but chose not to for the sake of her husband? The only thing better was if said wife was a former beauty queen.

Becca probably suspected my unease with Rick on the topic, but we didn't talk about it. We rarely talked about Rick—or my marriage. It was the one thorn in our friendship, the only taboo topic. She had warned me against rushing to the altar, and I hadn't listened. Every so often, she'd suggest I push back against Rick, but she knew I hated getting her advice. She probably thought I didn't want input from a divorced woman. That wasn't true. I didn't want it from someone who couldn't understand my need to have a family and make it work no matter what.

That, and Rick would feel betrayed if he knew what little about our marriage I had shared with Becca. Our business was our business, not anyone else's, he always said.

She wouldn't ever say she told me so about rushing to the altar, and I avoided giving her reason to. I think we both knew I wasn't exactly living a happily-ever-after tale, but we never addressed the elephant wearing the Cinderella ball gown in the room. For me, walking away wasn't an option, at least not until I'd exhausted everything else, and this marriage was too young for that. Adults who aged out of the foster system have much higher divorce rates than the typical population. I was determined to not be another statistic.

Becca rewound the movie a few minutes so we could catch the part we'd missed while talking. My hands settled over my tummy. The living thing growing inside me was more than a blob multiplying cells. According to the app I'd quietly downloaded when Rick wasn't home, the baby was about the size of a chicken egg. It looked to be mostly head, but the little torso had tiny arms and legs. A few weeks ago, they'd been little stumps that made the fetus look like a gummy bear.

I wanted to tell Becca about it so badly, but Rick had the right to know before anyone else. Even if Becca would swear to keep it a secret, Rick had an uncanny way of figuring things out. Somehow, he'd know I'd told her and be justifiably hurt that he didn't know first.

As things stood, I already dreaded telling him. He didn't want a family. In my head, he didn't want one *anymore*. According to him, he never had.

On that ski lift, though, I know what he'd said. Why had he said he wanted kids, because that's what I wanted to hear? I couldn't believe that he'd really wanted kids and had forgotten.

Truthfully, I wouldn't have married him if I'd known he didn't want kids. Which he knew, so he lied. I clutched a throw pillow to my lap as if that could protect my tiny baby.

The movie went on, but I paid less and less attention to it, instead trying to come up with ways to tell Rick about the baby without him blowing up—and without him thinking that I'd gotten pregnant on purpose.

My phone vibrated with Rick's tone, so I glanced at it and read his message: *It's going to be a later night than I thought. Don't wait up.*

I sent back a heart emoji as a reply, then clicked my phone off and breathed a bit easier. No dealing with Rick and the baby conversation tonight. Becca believed I was going to be a great mom someday. Only I knew just how soon that day would be. The app said I was due September 17.

CHAPTER SEVEN

BECCA

The next few hours are a blur. A man introduces himself as Detective Andrus, then leads me to a small interview room. Interrogation room? Same thing, probably. The walls look like they used to be white but have an aged tinge like yellowed newspaper. A small table stands against the wall opposite the door, and two chairs are pushed under it.

"Have a seat," Andrus says. "I'll be right back."

I've got Ivy in the carrier. She's asleep, so I gently set her on the floor before taking a seat in one of the chairs as instructed. Looking around the room, I rock the carrier with my foot in hopes of extending the nap. A camera is mounted above the door, trained right at the table, and it makes me weirdly self-conscious. I've seen enough episodes of *Dateline* to know that these rooms record everything. Actually seeing the room, the camera is something else altogether.

I'm alone for what feels like a long time but is probably only ten minutes or so, long enough to sit back in the chair and slump from fatigue rather than sitting ramrod straight. My phone buzzes, and when I pull it out of my pocket, I half expect it to be a text from Jenn.

Remembering again is another emotional crash landing.

The text is from my ex, Jason. *Where are you?*

The old irritation flares in me, and I let it eclipse my anguish. What business is it of his where I am? He probably tried dropping off the kids early. I'm about to reply with a vague boundary-setting message, but I stop to check the time to be sure.

How in the world is it nearly five? I look in the diaper bag and mentally count—yes, I've changed her diaper and fed Ivy several times. The math works, but I still can't grasp the day or the passage of time.

This whole thing has taken up the entire day? Jason *isn't* early. He's late. He was supposed to bring the kids home at four, and if he had, I would've heard from him then. That doesn't matter because *I'm* even later. I'm not home and don't know when I will be. He'll throw this in my face for months, if not years, to come. I pinch the bridge of my nose and call him. Under the circumstances, it'll be better to talk to him instead of trying to explain via text. So I call.

"Where are you?" he says without preamble. "I'm not leaving them in an empty house."

One of these days, I'll get past the point where the sound of Jason's voice puts my teeth on edge, but today is not that day. I think quickly—what can I tell him that will explain enough without telling too much? Having Jason, of all people, learn about Jenn in this way would feel like a betrayal. Besides, I don't want to field any prying questions he's bound to have. Not to mention he'd probably let it slip to the kids, and they are *not* going to learn about this from him. "There's been an emergency," I say vaguely.

"Are you at the hospital?" He *almost* sounds worried. I'll take it.

"At the police station," I say.

"The *police* station?" Jason repeats the phrase as if I've said I'm a radicalized terrorist.

"I'm a witness to something. I didn't *do* anything." The call is waking up Ivy; she squirms in her seat, and I resume rocking it with one foot. "I don't know when I'll be able to get home, but I'll be there as soon as I can."

"Look," Jason says, annoyed, "the decree says—"

"I know what it says," I interrupt. "This isn't something I have control over. Something happened at Jenn's house, and they need to interview me."

"Wait, what? What happened?"

That got his attention, for better or worse.

"I can't talk about it," I tell him. I might be allowed to, but I physically can't get myself to do it, and I don't want to. "I'll call Nancy right now. The kids can hang out at her place until I get home. I bet she'll even feed them dinner. I'm sure she's home."

Nancy lives a few doors down and has kids close to the same age as mine. Maggie and Davis hang out there often, especially after school when I'm still at work.

After a few seconds of silence, during which I wonder if I need to remind Jason who Nancy is, he finally grunts. It's a minor win. "I guess that's okay. This time."

This time. I roll my eyes but keep my voice even. "Drop them off at Nancy's. I'll let her know they're coming." I'm close to reminding him which house is hers but stop myself. If he's forgotten, the kids can tell him, and he hates being talked down to.

As soon as I hang up with Jason, I call Nancy, and though I don't explain the details of the situation, she must hear the fatigue and stress in my voice because she says, "Don't you worry at all. I'm making macaroni and cheese, and the twins are more than welcome to stay and have dinner. Take all the time you need."

"Thanks, Nancy, you're the best," I say. "Hopefully it won't take long." Call ended, I drop my head to my arm on the table in front of me. I'm so tired I can hardly think straight. I've missed lunch, and it's basically dinnertime. I'm going to need to eat something to get through whatever awaits me here.

The door opens, and I look up. Detective Andrus appears but pauses in the doorway as if someone got his attention. He leans back into the hall, talking to someone. Then he comes into the room, carrying a plastic-wrapped sub sandwich and a bottle of water. The door thunks shut behind him as he offers me the food.

"Figured you'd be hungry," he says.

"I am. Thanks." The sub looks soggy and probably tastes gross, but for the moment, I don't care; it's food.

Andrus nods at Ivy. "Does she need anything?"

Good question. I pick up the diaper bag and look through it. "There's enough formula for a couple more bottles. I might need some water to mix with it later if we're here much longer."

He nods and sets a legal-size notebook on the table. "So. Big day, huh?"

I glance at the camera above the door. While it makes me nervous, it's good that I'm here. Better that the police talk to me now. I'll do anything to speed up the process to help catch the person who . . . did this to Jenn. Even in my head, I can't use the words for what that person did to her.

As I set the diaper bag back onto the floor, I look at Ivy and my heart twists. "What will happen to her?" I ask the detective. "Will she have to go into foster care?" Yes, I already asked one of the officers at the scene, but maybe this detective knows more.

"We're figuring some of that out now, at least a temporary arrangement. Detective Moffett's talking with Mr. Banks now," Andrus says, jotting the date and time at the top of the notepad. "For now, we're assuming she'll be able to stay with her father."

Oh good.

"I've watched Ivy lots of times. I'm happy to take care of her if I can, for however long."

"I'll make a note of that. How do you spell your name? First and last."

I tell him, and as he writes, I look down at my clothes. My top has dried after being drenched down the front with bathwater, making it wrinkled. I'd care if I were on my way to work, but not here, not now. Nothing much matters besides the fact that my best friend is . . .

Gone. Expired. Passed. I wonder when I'll be able to use the real word.

My jeans are still slightly damp. If I were to stand, I'd probably see a wet mark on the vinyl chair, which is uncomfortable to sit on and probably is no matter what you're wearing. I bet they make sure of that for interrogating actual criminals. I'd give a lot for a cushioned office chair.

As soon as the thought crosses my mind, I feel guilty. Here I am annoyed by an achy backside when Jenn is gone forever. My stomach gurgles, and my head throbs. I finish unwrapping the sub and take a bite. It's even soggier than expected. The bread feels like paste in my mouth, but I chew and swallow anyway.

I wish I had something to distract me—a show to watch during the spells the cops leave me alone. Like *Friends* or even something older like *M*A*S*H,* both of which Jenn and I often quoted from.

Everything circles back to Jenn.

Everything but the twins. Maggie and Davis don't circle back. So as Andrus makes a few notes and replies to a text, I think of them. They'll be thrilled to eat Nancy's macaroni and cheese. After that, they'll probably play video games in the basement with her kids, also a boy and a girl, only one of them is two years older. They'll get more screen time than I allow, which they'll love.

I didn't tell Nancy where I am for the same reason I didn't tell Jason. The kids need to hear it from me. Crap. I should have told her not to turn on the news so they don't hear about their Aunt Jenn that way.

She was their only aunt besides Jason's sister Miranda, who lives back east and hasn't seen them since before they could speak.

I was an only child, so I was thrilled to have a friend so involved in my kids' lives. I'd hoped that one day, Jenn's children would be my kids' surrogate cousins.

So much for the twins not circling back to Jenn.

The door opens, and Andrus waves in a woman with a camera and a folder of papers. She hands the latter to Detective Andrus and addresses me.

"Need to take some pictures for evidence," she says cheerfully. She's smiling as she tells me to stand against the wall and she clicks away. She has me raise my arms, and she takes pictures, front and back. For what? Evidence of defensive wounds?

Wait, am I a suspect?

My throat tightens, so as I obey the photographer's instructions, holding up my arms, turning to face the wall, and on and on, I focus on thoughts of the twins.

Maggie and Davis sitting around Nancy's kitchen table, eating dinner. Hopefully, they won't need to spend the night there, but if so, Nancy is more than up to the task. I'll bring her something as a thank you. In the past, I've given her a note with some of my decadent homemade brownies or flowers. What do you give for babysitting in a pinch when your best friend is . . .

Gone. Expired. Passed.

Dead.

Killed. Murdered.

Between pictures, the photographer makes notes. Just when I think she's got to be done, she asks me to lift my shirt.

"Excuse me?" I say.

"Not all the way. Just need to see if you've got any marks on your abdomen." She glances at the detective. "Would you like him to leave?"

My eyes flick up to the camera and back. What would the point be of having Andrus leave when everyone in the department will be able to see this later? I shake my head and lift my blouse.

That's when Andrus says, "Hm."

At first, I figure he's reacting to something on his phone. Then the photographer gets closer and snaps more pictures of my stomach, just to the right of my naval. Where, of course, the faucet dug into me as I heaved Jenn's body out of the tub. I have a developing bruise. Great. Click, click, click.

Ivy's awake now and looking around with big eyes that portend a crying jag if I don't get to her soon. Fortunately, the photo session seems to be over. The photographer makes a few last notes, smiles at me, then leaves.

I'm about to pick up Ivy when another woman enters the room, this time holding a small stack of what looks like scrubs and a t-shirt. "We'll need your clothes to process for evidence," she says, then gestures the ones she's holding, but she doesn't give them to me. "Here's something you can change into. I'll come with you to the restroom."

As I'm about to say that I can change clothes on my own, thanks, I realize that she needs to be there because my clothes, weirdly, are evidence. They're wet with the bathwater Jenn died in. That's about all they'll find. I gesture toward Ivy. "Can I—"

Andrus interrupts me. "I'll watch the baby till you get back."

"Oh. Okay."

She and I go to the restroom, and I put on the clothes she hands me. She puts my clothes in a paper bag, which she then seals, labels, and signs across the seal. This day is getting more surreal by the minute.

Back in the small room, I take a crying Ivy from Andrus's arms. I can tell he tried to keep her calm, something that softens my heart toward him a bit, but she's understandably scared and relieved to see me. I calm her cries, which can probably be heard on the other side of the station.

"I'll go get that water so you can feed her," Andrus says, and he slips out before I can thank him.

The sudden kindness makes me grateful, and that lift gives me a little hope. Maybe I'll be out of here soon and on my way home.

When he returns, he hands me a room-temperature bottle of water and waits until Ivy's quietly eating. Then he settles in with his notepad and looks at me expectantly as if I have something to say. A warning bell goes off in my head, one that says to keep my mouth shut unless they ask specific questions.

I want him to say that there's been some terrible mistake, that Jenn is fine, that they managed to revive her, and there's no brain damage from being without oxygen for so long. A pipedream.

Instead, we go through every detail of what I experienced and saw. Everything I can remember, from checking inside the boat to searching the backyard, then going to the master bathroom and finding Jenn in the tub. Pulling her out—the source of my new bruise—the 911 phone call. Everything.

As gross as the sandwich was, I've finished it, and the calories help me think a bit more clearly.

After combing through details again and again, Detective Andrus finally gives me a half smile. "Thank you for staying so long and for being so thorough."

"Of course."

He stands. "You're free to go," he says. "We may have more questions for you later."

"I'm happy to help however I can," I say, then begin strapping Ivy back into the car seat. She protests, but this time a binkie helps. I pick up my purse, the diaper bag, and the carrier. I want to be home and wearing my own clothes.

"Is there anything else you need?" I ask. As much as I want to leave, I'll stay if it means not having to come back to answer more questions, ever. "I'm happy to take a polygraph or—"

"Not now," he says, lifting one hand and giving a slight shake of his head. "I'll be in touch."

"Will you keep me updated on the investigation?" I sound like I'm begging for a promise. I guess that's exactly what I'm doing. I need to know that if there's anything—*anything*—I can do to help, that they'll reach out and tell me.

"Sure," he says with a nod in a tone that makes me believe him not at all. He's still half smiling, but his eyes look tired. I'm sure mine look worse, and that I look a mess in every other way too—hair, makeup smeared from the water, and that's on top of the weird, baggy clothes they gave me.

"I'll wait to hear from you, then," I say, slowly moving from the table as if it's a dog that might bite if I move too fast. "If I think of something I haven't told you, I'll call."

"Sounds good." He holds the door open for me to exit. "You did good today, Ms. Kalos."

His words make my step come up short as I stand on the threshold. I'm in the doorway, not in the interrogation room, but not in the corridor either. I look up at him. "I did?"

"Absolutely. You did everything you could for her. And you've been extremely helpful to us."

"Thanks," I say, then duck my head and step into the hallway, once again walking with Ivy's carrier bumping against my leg every other step.

Halfway to the outside doors, I nearly run into someone. "Excuse me," I say, but then the smell of a cologne whisks me right back to finding Jenn. Not until that moment do I realize that I associate that cologne with Rick. My head snaps up, and sure enough, Jenn's husband is standing there.

"Hey," he says, eyes looking as bloodshot as mine feel. "They're letting me take a bathroom break." He nods toward the door beside him, which looks identical to the one I just exited. He's not done being interviewed, and he wasn't even there. Poor guy.

"Rick," I say, breathing his name with the relief of finding someone else experiencing the same grief. I set Ivy's carrier on the floor and give him a hug. He wraps his arms around me, and for the first time since I entered their house today, I feel safe. I'm not alone in this.

"It's going to be okay," he says quietly and rubs my back with a gentle touch. This is the closest we've ever been, the most we've ever touched. It should feel odd but doesn't.

Stepping back, I wipe my cheeks with both hands, the tears falling anew. I heft the carrier and feel a twinge. Ivy belongs to him, not me. "Do you want to take her or . . . ?"

"Oh. Um . . ." He looks behind him at his interrogation room, then back at me.

"She can stay with me for now."

He lets out a huge sigh. "That would be a huge relief. Thanks."

"Of course. Talk to you later, then, when you're done here?"

"Definitely."

I give a small wave then head toward the exit. A cop, badge hanging from a belt loop, stands by the restrooms a little farther down the hall, past some vending machines. Rick follows me until he reaches the restrooms, and then we exchange waves.

My feet take me outside. I don't stop moving until I reach my car. I get Ivy buckled in. She protests, of course, reaching out for me to hold her. "It's a short ride," I assure her, but she's not having it.

Getting inside the car myself, I click my seatbelt into place, grab the steering wheel, then stare out the windshield. I'm anxious and fidgety and just want to be home. I start the car and think through the interview with Detective Andrus, living it a second time as if watching a video on high speed.

I *think* I did enough to remove myself as a person of interest. Detective Andrus warned me that as the person who found the . . . who found Jenn . . . I am automatically a person of interest.

He also mentioned, though, that the profile of the kind of person who commits . . . this kind of crime . . . is generally male, so I didn't have any reason to worry unless I was guilty and hiding something. Which, of course, I'm not.

As I drive away, I glance into my rearview mirror at the brown-brick police station and wonder how much longer Rick will be in there. If Jenn's best friend, the person who discovered her body, was automatically a person of interest, then surely her husband is too.

The sooner they clear him, the better. Then he and I can plan a memorial.

Raindrops splat against the windshield, big and full, all of a sudden. I turn on my wipers and get rid of them, but more follow. More and more until I have to adjust the speed to high. I realize that my vision is mostly blurred by tears.

CHAPTER EIGHT

JENN

March 19
One Year before Drowning

I'd been living with constant worry for over a month. How to tell Rick about the baby. Convince him that it didn't happen intentionally. That, surprise or not, I was going to carry this child.

When I got sick at night—because of course my "morning" sickness struck at any time of day—I faked a migraine or anything else I could think of. The time I spent two hours throwing up, I blamed it on food poisoning from a work lunch.

The longer he didn't know, the worse things would be when he found out. I'd learned to avoid certain topics as if they were land mines, though I always found new ones, "buttons" I'd better not push. An unexpected pregnancy? That would be a land mine of a button if ever there was one. And the longer I waited before telling him, the worse the explosion would be.

At around eleven weeks, I attended a library conference in Junction City, more than an hour away. Typically, as head librarian, Kathy went to things like that, but she was recovering from a fender bender, and sitting for long periods was hard. I was happy to go in her place.

I got a full day of library science, new books and authors, innovations in library tech. It should have been my personal Disneyland.

Instead, a cloud hovered over me. I couldn't shake the worry over how to tell Rick about the baby. Since I couldn't focus on the speakers, my notes turned into doodles, some of which looked like baby things: a rattle, a bottle, a smiley face with a spiral of hair on top. A heart.

The heaviness didn't lift even when I won a door prize, but it did provide a distraction. I won a smartpen, and my tablemates handed the box around, talking amongst themselves about how cool the pen was and how it could be a game-changer for students with learning disabilities. Maybe it could help Emily, a young patron of mine. Her parents thought she was lazy and stupid, so they sent her to the library to study after school, where I often tutored her. I suspected she had undiagnosed inattentive ADHD. Armchair psychologist of me, sure, but between a few college classes and loads of research as a librarian trying to help patrons, I had more than a passing knowledge of some conditions. Listening to recorded lectures helped a lot of kids. The pen could sync audio to the time stamp when a note was written. Definitely worth trying with her.

Once I was driving home without the buzz and chatter of conference attendees around me, my thoughts returned to Rick and the baby. Halfway down the wide canyon road back from Junction City, my phone rang—Becca.

I happily answered with the button on the steering wheel. "Hey," I said.

"Hey you." Becca's voice was a cool drink of water after a long day.

"I'm driving in the canyon. Hopefully the speaker phone will be clear. Can you hear me okay?"

"Sure can," she said. "I stopped by the library hoping to steal you away from the bookshelves long enough for lunch but didn't see you."

"Bummer," I said, meaning it. Becca and I hadn't managed to get together face to face in over a week, and while we texted all the time, it wasn't the same as commiserating and laughing together over comfort food. "I took Kathy's place at a conference today. I'm heading home now from Junction."

"How was it?" Becca asked. "I can't picture what a librarian conference looks like."

"Much louder than you'd expect, for starters," I said with a laugh. My non-morning sickness nausea decided to come in like a tide. I pressed my lips together and gripped the steering wheel tighter. After managing a breath or two without losing what was left of my lunch, I launched into the topic at the forefront of my mind. I was going to break my own rule by telling Becca first, but that would force me to tell Rick today too.

"Glad you called, because I have some news."

"Oh?" Becca said, then added, "Wait. Hold on." I heard her order a pork burrito from our favorite place, and after a fuzzy speaker voice told her to pull forward, she got back to me. "Okay. Sorry about that. Grabbing myself some dinner. The twins are getting pizza at a birthday party, so it's just me. Okay, so what's your news?"

The baby nausea flipped into excitement—not entirely dissimilar feelings. "Well, it's a bit of a surprise, but . . ."

"You're pregnant?"

Coming from anyone else, that would have felt like taking the wind out of my sails, but not with Becca, who would be as excited as I was. "How did you know?" I asked with a laugh.

"Then you *are*? Aaaah!" She squealed a couple more times, quieted briefly—sounded like she was handing over a card to pay for her meal—and then returned to the call. "When are you due?"

"Middle of September. Haven't been to a doctor yet or anything."

"What did Rick say?" She still sounded excited, with a note of justified wariness. She knew my husband didn't exactly relish surprises.

"He . . . doesn't know yet." I breathed out heavily. The nerves didn't go out with it. "I'm telling him tonight."

"It'll be great," Becca said, and though it wasn't clear whether she meant telling Rick or actually having the baby, I appreciated it.

"Thanks, Bex. First thing is to figure out what to make for dinner, since I won't have time to bake the lasagna I'd planned on. I need him in a good mood."

"He loves Mr. Pizza, right?" Becca said. "Especially their garlic knots?"

"Yeah. I'm impressed you remember that."

"I'm pulling over, and I'm going to place an order for delivery to your house. You won't need to worry about anything, not even tipping the driver. That's on me."

I sighed again, and this time, some of the stress did leave me; my shoulders felt a bit looser. "You're the best, you know that?"

"For ordering pizza?" Becca laughed. "Sure. I'll take it. But Jenn, seriously, you've got this. You're going to be a *mom*. That's the best news *ever*."

"Can't wait," I admitted, my eyes misting. "Love ya, Bex. Talk to you soon."

By the time I pulled into the garage, the knots in my stomach had relaxed a bit, no longer resembling something a Boy Scout would be proud of.

The pizza hadn't arrived, and neither had Rick. I knew my nerves would jack themselves up if I didn't distract myself. I glanced at my work bag and remembered the pen. Maybe trying it out would fill the time. The box had both a bulky black pen and a special notebook. Tiny dots covered the paper, which gave it a slight gray tone.

I frowned at that, doubting Emily's parents would be willing to spring for the special paper. They had money; that wasn't the problem. Her mom's parade of Kate Spade bags, perfect manicures, and lash extensions was evidence of that. But if they wouldn't pay for a professional tutor, they probably wouldn't pay for special paper.

I experimented with the pen—tapping on the paper to set a position, recording my voice, and syncing it to what I'd written.

The rumble of the garage door startled me back to the present. The doorbell rang right after. I left the pen and notebook on the table and answered the door. I entered the kitchen with the pizza as Rick came in from the garage.

"Pizza!" I called cheerfully.

"Ooh—nice," Rick said. He set his leather satchel on a barstool and his keys beside it. As I set the boxes on the table, he came over and kissed me. "Thanks."

"You're welcome," I said, keeping my voice ultra cheerful and *not* mentioning that it was Becca's treat. That could open the can of worms I was preparing to open but wasn't quite ready to. "I'll get some dishes."

At the table, I handed Rick a plate and sat down across from him, nudging the pen and notebook to the side. He loaded his plate with two pieces of combination pizza and two garlic twists. "This smells so good."

Stay in a good mood, I thought.

After a bite of pizza, I ventured, "How's the Lambert case going? Do you think it'll go to trial?"

Rick lifted one shoulder in a shrug. "After all the work we've put into it, I hope so, but I doubt it. The investors in the golf course seem eager to settle."

"Miss the courtroom?" I asked knowingly.

"It's been too long." He smiled and shook his head. "Such a rush."

He talked about the case a bit, and as I nodded and made all the right sympathetic responses, my stomach buzzed.

I knew that feeling. I got it whenever I had to speak up about something hard. I'd felt it when a foster sister was being molested by our foster dad, and I had to tell the caseworker. I felt it during my job interview at the library when asked about my stance on banned books, and I was sure that my rather liberal view wouldn't be welcome in the super-conservative community we lived in. Both of those situations turned out how they needed to, so maybe this one would too.

"So . . ." I ran a finger along the edge of my plate. "I think I figured out why I've been feeling so gross lately."

"Oh yeah?" he said, glancing up from his phone.

"I'm going to see a doctor about it."

"Sounds like a good idea." He wasn't asking any questions. Getting to the point would be entirely up to me.

The buzzing increased. It wouldn't go away until I'd said what needed saying.

"I'll need to see my OB-GYN."

"Lady troubles," he said knowingly.

"Not exactly." The buzzing made me unable to eat another bite. I pushed my plate away.

Rick glanced up, curious but not cluing in.

"It's unexpected, and a total accident, but now that it's happened, I'm kind of excited." I felt lightheaded and had to stop to take a breath.

His eyes narrowed, but not in an angry way. "About . . ."

I swallowed against a thick knot. "We're going to have a baby." As I waited for his reaction, I took in every movement of his face. One emotion after another registered, almost like the pictures on a slot machine rolling and rolling. Which would Rick land on?

He stared at his plate without saying a word. Each second he didn't speak was pure torture. I opened my mouth to repeat that this was an accident and to argue that a baby would be good for us, but that's when he spoke.

"You *know* I don't want kids." His focus remained on pizza crumbs.

"*Now* I do—"

"Are you trying to trap me?" Now he looked up, and his narrowed eyes made the hair on my neck stand on end. The buzzing dropped like a hammer.

"Of course not," I said hurriedly. "I didn't plan for it to happen. It just . . . did."

He pushed away from the table. Chair and table both thud-screeched. My pulse spiked, and I trembled. He stood and rested his hands against the tabletop. Not leaning away took everything I had. "Is this about your weird obsession with surfing? About that disgusting tattoo you got?"

"Wait, what?"

He pushed off the table, kicked one of its legs, and headed for the fridge. "You can't let things lie, can you?" He opened the freezer, took out a bottle of vodka, and poured himself a shot. He downed it and poured another, then put the vodka bottle back into the freezer. He closed the door with more force than necessary, then began counting off on his fingers.

"You knew I hate tattoos but got one anyway. You keep making up shit and claiming that *I'm* the liar. Now you go and get pregnant, even though I've *always* said I never wanted kids. How can I trust you?"

The buzzing returned to my middle, giving me a little strength. I sat up straight. "None of that is true, and you know it." I was sick of being told I was imagining things, that *I* was the liar. I ticked things off on *my* fingers. "We talked about having kids on the ski lift when we were dating. You said that you hoped for a girl with my eyes. I wanted a boy with your hair."

"Bitch," he said under his breath.

"You told me stories about surfing. I thought you'd *like* the tattoo. I'd *never* have gotten one if I thought you'd hate it."

The hard set of his jaw told me I'd crossed a line, said too much. I nearly choked on my tongue. My pulse throbbed in my neck as I waited to find out what his rage would do this time. He said nothing, just stared. The sword of Damocles remained above me. He withdrew the vodka bottle and drank straight from it.

So that's how his rage would go today—he'd get blackout drunk so he couldn't be blamed for anything he did later.

I stayed in my chair. What should I do? Say? Contradicting him when he was already mad only poked the bear.

I should have taken a different tack—but what? Was there any way to tell him without pissing him off? I'd had to tell him. This was our baby, potentially the only biological family I'd ever have. But I'd poked the bear.

"I'm so sorry," I said, hugging myself. Tears built up and spilled over. Not a single tear was from guilt—I'd done nothing wrong. They were from worry and fear, from upsetting him but not knowing how I could've avoided it. "You have to believe me—I didn't mean for it to happen. Sometimes birth control fails. I hoped this could be something good for us." My voice grew weaker until it was nearly a whisper.

He downed another gulp of vodka and put the bottle on the counter, hard. "Well, it's *not* a 'good thing.'" He even used his fingers for air quotes to make his point. He walked right up to me, so close his breath smelled of alcohol. I forced myself not to recoil. "You'll regret this."

He grabbed his keys and headed out to his car. I stayed stock-still until he'd driven away. Then my face fell into my hands, and I cried.

What should I do now, leave? Becca would want me to. But I knew the soft, kind Rick that was inside the monstrous shell.

If I left tonight, I'd be back, and leaving at all would only piss him off more. Would staying be as bad? Was I going to become one of those women people shook their heads over, wondering why she stayed?

I wanted to see Becca, or at least to call her and tell her everything, but I couldn't. If I told her the truth, she'd think me weak. If Rick found out that I'd talked to her tonight, he'd know I'd "aired our dirty laundry."

There was no winning. I shuddered. My husband terrified me. My growing baby depended on me for literally everything.

Did I want a child more than my husband? Yes. I loved my baby already. The man who'd driven off was not the man I fell in love with. That man, I hoped, still existed somewhere.

What if this was the new, permanent Rick? The thought flashed through my head like an over-bright neon sign. If I left Rick, would he try to take the baby from me? Use his legal expertise to get full custody?

My head pounded. I went to the cupboard for some Excedrin, only to remember you shouldn't take medications during pregnancy without doctor approval. I cleaned up the kitchen instead. My work bag and the stuff from the conference were still on the table, so I began putting it all into the bag. When I picked up the pen, the little screen showed a flashing low-battery icon.

I must not have turned it off earlier. I turned it off, planning to charge it up at work. I put the work bag in my car and went to bed.

Sometime after one, Rick came home, so drunk he barely made it upstairs into our room. I was still awake but pretended to sleep when he collapsed on the bed. Within seconds, he was snoring, fully clothed, in a smashed stupor.

My hand slipped to my stomach, just under my navel. *What are we going to do, little one?*

CHAPTER NINE

BECCA

I drive home, tears blurring my vision as much as the rain. Not until I'm in my garage and turn off the car do I remember that the twins are at Nancy's. Nothing about this day feels real, so I check my phone to be sure that yes, I did call both Jason and Nancy. I didn't imagine those conversations. Before that, the call log reads *911*. That call lasted only eleven minutes. It felt like at least an hour.

I move to get out of the car, and I realize the scrubs pants are a bit damp. My soaked jeans must have gotten the seat wet. Another reminder that everything else about this day really happened. I wish I could wake up, but this nightmare is reality. I call Nancy.

"I'm home," I tell her. "You can send them on up. I'll wait for them outside."

"Will do," Nancy says. "Hey, everything all right?"

Has my tone has tipped her off to my worry and exhaustion, or did she guess that something is wrong based on the last-minute babysitting favor on a school night? Maybe Jason was his usual jerk self when he dropped them off at her place. Or she's seen something on the news.

"It's . . . been a day," I say vaguely. "I'll tell you about it later."

"I'm glad you called, then. You can send the kids over anytime," Nancy says. "You know that, right? And if you need anything else, just say the word."

"Thanks," I tell her. "I do know, and I will. You're the best."

I hang up and stare at my phone. Nancy is one of the best people around, the best neighbor I could ever ask for. But she'll never be Jenn. *She's* gone.

After getting Ivy out of the car, I wait inside the garage, out of the rain, for the twins. I have no desire to get wet again. Nancy's front door opens, and Maggie's and Davis's figures hop out, down the stairs, and they head up the street. They turn back to wave to her. They even call, "Thanks, Nancy!" It's nice to see them having manners when I'm not right there.

When they spot me from the sidewalk, Maggie starts running. "Is that Ivy?" she calls. With each stride, the overnight backpack she brought to her dad's shifts side to side.

Davis jogs behind her. He picks up speed but falls behind Maggie because he's pulling his overnight bag, which is an actual carry-on. The wheels bump on the sidewalk seams and make the bag lurch. The twins are so different, something that is visible in everything, down to the way they approach something as mundane as packing for a night away. Maggie wants to have her hands free, and she loves pink, so her choice was that jumbo pink backpack with a glittery unicorn. Davis picked that gray hard-surface carry-on with wheels, which he informed me is tough enough to survive a Blast Burn charge attack by a Charizard, his favorite Pokémon. He's always been my careful, attentive child, while Maggie is the impulsive, loud one.

I love them so much it hurts.

My grip on the baby carrier tightens with emotion, which reminds me that Ivy no longer has a mother. I picture leaving my babies motherless, and I fight tears. The twins don't need to see me falling apart right now. They'll learn about Jenn soon enough, along with things about the world that no little kids should ever have to face. None of the parenting books have prepared me to explain murder.

Maggie reaches me with outstretched arms. She nearly bowls me over as she throws herself in my direction and I try to keep hold of the baby carrier. She pulls back nearly as quickly, then swoops over to Ivy, who's awake and kicking happily in her seat.

"Hey, Ivy. Hey! Can you smile? Do you need your binkie?" She tickles Ivy's cheek and is rewarded with a giggle. Maggie whirls about to face me. "Is she staying the night? Can she? Please? Ask Jenn."

Ask Jenn. Never have two words from my child punched me so hard in the gut.

Davis arrives. "What's up?" He wears a familiar look—curious, observing, trying to piece together clues, but not worried. His simple question is not a query about how I'm feeling. He's asking why I wasn't home when their dad tried to drop them off—something that's never happened before. And he's asking about why Ivy is with me after dinner, so close to their bedtime. Fortunately, he's quickly distracted by Ivy, but even as he plays peekaboo with her, I can see the wheels turning in his head.

I can't keep the truth from the twins for long. How do you explain something to a couple of third graders that's filled with more questions than answers even for the adults? How can I explain something to kids that I don't yet understand?

"Come inside," I call. "Ivy's getting cold."

Since they've already eaten at Nancy's, I begin our regular bedtime routine. The big difference tonight is that I have a baby in tow who proves to be an adorable but constant distraction. The process takes more than an hour instead of the usual thirty minutes. Thank heaven for Ivy, though; without her, I'd be having a much harder time holding myself together. I put on leggings, a sweatshirt, and fuzzy socks: comfort clothes.

The twins have separate rooms now, something I realized was necessary a few months ago when Davis insisted on dressing inside their cramped closet, away from his sister's eyes. I've kept up the tradition of singing to them before bedtime, though now from the hall outside their rooms, where I'm visible from both beds. I find myself rocking side to side with Ivy as I did when they were babies. She leans her head on my shoulder. When the song is over, I blow kisses, and the kids return them. They send extra kisses to Ivy. When I reach to close their doors, Davis breaks his silence.

"Mom?"

So close.

"Yeah? Do you need a drink of water?" I know he doesn't.

"What happened?"

A simple question that contains multitudes. Spoken with complete trust that I'll give him the truth. I *cannot* open that can of worms right now.

"Nothing you need to worry about tonight. Let's talk about it tomorrow after school, buddy, okay? It's way past your bedtime."

Davis gazes at me through the dimness of his room as if studying my face like a lie detector. "Okay." He lies down, unsatisfied but not pressing the issue.

The doorbell rings. I hurry to answer, grateful for anything to pull me away from my son's question, even if it turns out to be a college kid trying to sell me pest control. I look out a window to see who might be at the door. A silver Lexus is parked in the driveway. Rick's car. He's here for Ivy. At last, someone I can talk to.

On the other side of the door, Rick looks ashen, with bloodshot eyes and mussed hair. His tie hangs loose, and the top two buttons of his dress shirt are undone. This is the first time I've seen him looking even close to disheveled.

"Come in," I say, ushering him inside. With the door closed behind him, I lock it, as if that might keep out further tragedies. "I left the base for the car seat in my car. Diaper bag too. I'll be right back."

Rick raises a hand to stop me. "Can we talk for a second?" He walks to the couch and drops there like a sack of sand.

"Of course." I sit on the other side of the couch and wait for him to speak—and to take Ivy from me. He does the first but not the second. She's happily snuggled in my arms, so we sit like that for a minute.

"They won't say so," Rick begins, "but I'm pretty sure they think I did it."

"They always look at the spouse first. But of course you didn't do it."

"You believe that?" He turns to look at me, pleading in his drawn eyes.

"Yes," I say firmly. "I don't believe that you . . ." I glance over my shoulder, keenly aware that the twins might be able to hear, so I lower my voice. "I know you didn't . . ." A deep breath. "You didn't kill Jenn."

He lets out a sigh that's half groan, half sob. "I can't tell you how relieved that makes me. But *they* do. I—I don't know what to do."

"Give them anything they want," I say. "I'm pretty sure they suspect me too because I found her. The sooner they can clear both of us, the sooner they can find the real guy."

He leans forward, elbows on his knees and hands raking through his hair. "They kept me at the station for a lot longer than you, and they want me to go back in the morning." With a shake of his head, he adds, "Maybe I should get a lawyer. I probably shouldn't go back until I have one."

"Spoken like a lawyer," I say. "Go back in the morning, *without* one. You have nothing to hide, so you won't need representation. It'll look bad if you lawyer up now."

"I didn't do this," Rick says, resting his face in his palms, his fingers reaching his hair, which stands up, mussed. After a moment, he lifts his face and his hands as if in surrender. "I didn't."

"*I* know that, but *they* don't. They have to be thorough. Help them clear you."

"The kinds of things they're asking . . . I really think I should get a lawyer. I don't care what it looks like if it keeps me out of prison for something I didn't do."

"No, don't," I say, putting a hand on his arm to show my solidarity. "I know that might seem like a good idea because you *are* a lawyer, but to the rest of the world, that will make you look guilty. Remember Jon Benet Ramsey's parents?"

"Fair," he says, then drags a hand down his face wearily. "But what if they don't move on to find the real murderer?"

"They will," I insist. "That's literally their job. Without evidence, no charges would stick, and there can't possibly be evidence if you didn't do anything."

"What about my DNA? They'll find it all over the house."

"*Not* finding your DNA in your own house would be suspicious."

"True." He pushes against his knees to stand and then begins pacing. "They were so nasty, so accusatory. They acted as if they already have evidence against me."

"That's what detectives do," I assure him. "Is there any evidence for them to find?"

"Of course not."

"Then you have nothing to worry about."

He stops pacing, but his eyes are wild, and he seems to be thinking hard. "Yeah. Yeah, you're right. There's no evidence because I didn't do anything. Of course." He lets out a huge breath as if expelling hours of worry.

"Your daughter won't grow up without her father." No need to say anything about her mother.

Mentioning Ivy seems to flip a switch in Rick's head. He looks at her in my arms and again scrubs a hand down his face. "What am I supposed to do with her? I don't know her schedule or anything. Jenn did all that stuff." He resumes pacing. I debate whether to speak again, but he decides for me. He returns to the couch and leans in. "Would you take care of Ivy?" He rushes on to clarify. "Not forever. Just for a few days, until things with the cops blow over and I can see straight?"

"I work full time . . ." Has he forgotten that little detail?

"Oh yeah. Right. I mean evenings and overnight and stuff. We have daycare for when Jenn worked."

I'm a bit uneasy about the idea. I don't know if Ivy sleeps through the night yet, but if she does, a change in routine and environment will likely upset that. I should make sure Detective Andrus is aware of any arrangement we make so I don't screw up some procedure that will land Ivy in foster care after all.

"We could probably find a way to give you temporary custody," Rick suggests, his lawyer hat on.

"I don't want to cause any problems for Ivy . . . or you." Can a custody order—even a temporary one—mess things up for a biological parent? I have no idea. Jenn would know; she had plenty of experience in the system. I'd do anything for her, and that extends to her family. She'd want me to take care of Ivy; I do not doubt that. "Sure. Let's look into it."

"You're a lifesaver." Rick almost smiles. "You have no idea."

"Oh, I have some idea," I say. "Could you give me info on the daycare Jenn used? Keeping things as normal as possible for Ivy would be good."

"Oh, um . . . I should be able to find that stuff. Sure. I'll look for it as soon as they let me back in the house." He gets up and heads for the door.

I follow. "Where are you staying now?"

"At the motel on Main." He lifts one shoulder and drops it. "Not exactly the Ritz, but it'll do until I can get back into the house and the media circus outside dies down." As he steps outside, I hold Ivy out to him so he can say goodnight. He doesn't seem to notice, just keeps moving toward his car, no doubt in the same kind of otherworldly haze I've been in for much of the day. As he starts his car, I lift Ivy's hand and give her daddy a wave. He lowers the window, ostensibly to wave back, but instead, he says, "I'll let you know how tomorrow morning's interview goes."

Then he pulls out of the driveway, and his taillights slowly disappear into the night.

CHAPTER TEN

JENN

April 2
11½ Months before Drowning

I cleaned up the mess left over from story time—scissors, paste, and paper scraps left over from the craft—then collapsed in my chair at the admin station. Stacie had taken the day off to care for a son who got his wisdom teeth out, so I filled in for her. Pregnancy kept me constantly exhausted. I picked up my phone and texted Becca.

Someone gave the story time toddlers coffee this morning, I'm sure of it.

Becca texted back, along with a hilarious GIF of a woman with burned hair sticking up in all directions. *I thought you loved kids . . .*

I laughed and replied. *Turns out that when you're exhausted and not sleeping anyway, little kids sense you're vulnerable. Like a lion smelling a wounded gazelle.*

I didn't elaborate on why I wasn't sleeping well. Either I lay awake, or I slept fitfully and woke from nightmares. When the reason you can't sleep is that you're afraid your husband's lying to you, and you're exhausted from a pregnancy he doesn't want, even a pretty great job can be miserable.

Hang in there! Becca wrote. *I'll bring you a treat tonight. You've earned it.*

You're the best. I'll go back to appreciating my awesome job now.

Most days, I thought that being a librarian was the best job in the world. It didn't have long, stressful hours or tense meetings. No project managers breathing down my neck. Always something new to do. One of the bigger stresses, if you could call it that, was getting behind on cataloging new shipments of much-anticipated books. Readers got impatient to get their hands on new releases.

Even with toddlers that seemed jacked up on caffeine, I loved my job. I was surrounded by books all day. I got to recommend titles to people, and sometimes those authors became new favorites. I helped people with research, watching them find nuggets of information they were searching for. I helped patrons register to vote, find literacy classes, write resumes, and more.

After the story-time crowd left, the library grew strangely quiet. The place usually had a bit of a buzz from soft noises: whispers, footsteps on carpet, page turns, clicking keyboards. Occasional louder sounds punctuated the quiet: a book dropping to the floor, a kid trying to show a parent something, followed by the parent shushing said child, an older gentleman with hearing loss asking the same question four times of the ever-patient Kathy.

At that moment, the library felt downright tomb-like, empty yet filled with something intangible. Throughout the morning, my attention left the rows of books and compulsively returned, again and again, to the two rows of computers on one side of the central desk.

I had to do some research, and not the kind I found on any of our shelves. I needed to go online. Not from home. I couldn't risk leaving a digital footprint or Rick would fly off the handle. Having my journal on my laptop was enough to freak me out, even though it had a fingerprint reader and I changed the password regularly. I'd started keeping my laptop under a floor mat in my car so he wouldn't come across it. Glance in the car window, and you couldn't even tell it was there. If we ever went somewhere together, it was in his Lexus. He'd never step foot into my oh-so-practical Prius.

The library's public computers were safe for my purposes; any digital trace couldn't be linked to me directly. I eyed that bank of computers for hours, debating whether to use one, if I could discreetly do my digging on one of the main library computers in the public area instead of at an admin one at the central desk where we did most of our work. Kathy and Tim, who worked the same shift I did that day, would notice if I suddenly started Googling stuff on the public computers. They'd also notice if I wasn't doing actual *work* in the admin area, and I couldn't risk having any connection between myself and my searches.

I wanted to tell Becca, but I couldn't get myself to until I knew more. And hopefully, I could get myself to eat crow sooner than later, admitting to her that she'd been right about Rick and our super-fast courtship. I was loath to admit that; she might pity me, see me differently, when she knew the truth.

I opted to use my lunch hour to slip over to the public computers. Kathy and Tim thought I was going out to eat, and I didn't correct the assumption. I sat at the station farthest from the central desk, and I put on the black cardigan I had in my bag. I tended to get cold from the air conditioning, so I often brought layers with me, but I hadn't put the sweater on yet today. I waited until I was at the computer station in the hopes that if Kathy or Tim glanced my way, the black sweater would keep their eyes moving past me and they wouldn't realize it was me, not seeing my pale-blue top.

The first thing I did was a search for Wagner High in Del Marita, California, a tiny suburb of L.A. where Rick said he grew up. I'd never heard of it, but California was huge, with hundreds of tiny neighborhoods, each with a Spanish-sounding name, so my not recognizing it didn't mean much. As I pressed enter, I wondered if the high school or the town even existed. Turned out, both did. I let out a sigh of relief, but my hands were trembling after that one search, and I had a long way to go.

I searched for Wagner High School alumni and got several hits—Facebook reunion groups, several individuals' business profiles, bios on various websites. Nothing that stood out at first glance, but I combed through dozens of hits, hoping to find something about Rick.

Any time I found a list of alumni from the year he said he'd graduated—three years ahead of me—I searched for a Rick Banks. Thinking of a boy I'd known in foster care who went by his middle name, I checked for other variations using Rick's middle name, Christopher. I tried every version I could think of, including Christopher Banks, R. Christopher Banks, and on and on.

Nothing.

I broadened the date range. No dice.

Maybe he didn't graduate and wasn't considered alumni. I searched deeper, and by some miracle, found an archive of Wagner High yearbooks going back twenty years. I looked for him in every grade of every year he would have been in high school and five years on either side.

Never found him. Not in a student picture, not in any activities or clubs, not even in the index of not-pictured students. I was quite sure that even with dated hair, braces, and acne, I'd recognize Rick. He wasn't there.

My phone's alarm went off, telling me that lunch hour was over. While I didn't want to get back to work, I also didn't know what to look for next or how to feel about what I'd learned—that my husband had lied to me about something else.

What was I going to do about it?

Did I dare confront Rick over his lies about high school? After he denied knowing anything about surfing or *Just one more*, I didn't know what was safe to bring up. He was wrong about this too, whether he was intentionally lying or not. Maybe he hadn't been a surfer at all and made up that story. Or maybe he was concocting a new lie to deny his past. In a weird way, I hoped he'd forgotten—that maybe he'd had a concussion that wiped out a few years of his memory. *Something* besides outright lies to explain everything.

For a brief moment, I wondered if I'd gotten the name of the high school wrong, but no. I distinctly remembered because when he first mentioned it and I found out the school was near the coast in southern California, I shuddered, wondering if it had been named after Robert Wagner, celebrity actor and possible murderer. A school near Hollywood might very well pick a celebrity as a namesake.

"How did the school get its name?" I'd asked Rick. "Tell me it's *not* for the TV star."

Rick had said nothing, just laughed, which gave me pause.

I insisted on an answer. "Are you telling me that your high school honors the guy who probably killed Natalie Wood?"

I knew her best from *West Side Story* and had been disturbed as a kid when I learned how she'd died mysteriously. Back then, I was morbidly fascinated and horrified by the story. Then, a few years ago, the case had been reopened after decades as a possible murder investigation. Whether a conviction could be secured so many years later without new evidence was anyone's guess. Regardless, I'd never been able to stomach the sight of the eighties heartthrob Robert Wagner.

"Tell me the school's Wagner was a war hero, a scientist, or, heck, a different non-homicidal star."

Once again, Rick laughed, as if my reaction was a severe overreaction. He waved his hand as if brushing off a nonexistent fly. "The school was built before all that. I think it was named after some guy who donated the land—the farmer who owned the orange grove that used to be there."

Sitting in the library, staring at the monitor and the spread of the Wagner High yearbook that should have contained Rick's senior picture, I couldn't stop thinking about that months-old conversation. As I heard Rick's laugh in my head now, it sounded amused, with a dangerous edge to it. But maybe I was remembering it wrong and reading too much into it. Even so, the basic substance of the conversation was seared into my brain. No *way* did I make up the name of his high school.

"Hey," a voice whispered over my shoulder.

I yelped—quietly in any other setting, like a foghorn in a library—and whirled around, my heart nearly jumping out of my chest. Tim looked back as if he thought I'd lost a few marbles. So help me, if one more man suggested I was losing my mind . . .

I tilted the monitor so Tim wouldn't have a good view of it. Then I realized that might make me look guilty as if I were watching porn or something on the library computer.

"Hey," I said back, trying to sound airy. Good thing I had to whisper; I couldn't have used my vocal cords if I'd wanted to. In a series of quick motions, I swiveled frontward, exited the browser, and stood, slipping the chair back into place. Only then did I look up at Tim. He was a little taller than I was but slight; he probably weighed less than I did. The guy would have had a hard time killing a spider. I had no reason to be afraid of him. "What's up?"

The questioning look left his face, and he didn't so much as glance at the computer. "Do you know where the new James Patterson books are? I can't find them in the back room."

"I'm still cataloging them," I said, glad he was after something utterly mundane. A glance at my watch made me feel guilty for having spent time past my lunch hour on the computer instead of getting the Patterson books ready to be checked out. "They're under the desk." I led the way to the admin area.

Generally, when cataloging new books, I kept them on a cart next to me. But Patterson titles tended to walk out of the library if they weren't attended, so I'd slipped them under the desk for my lunch break, where they'd be less visible. They were all Tim had wanted. When we got to the desk, an eager fan awaited us, and I informed him that the books would be ready to be checked out tomorrow, but that they already had a pretty long waiting list. He informed me that he was number one on the list, then left, half happy and half disappointed.

I spent the rest of my workday in a fuzz, trying to process what I'd learned—rather, hadn't learned—and comparing that information to what I did know about Rick.

Turns out, I didn't know as much about him as I had believed. He had no yearbooks at home. No memorabilia from childhood. No friends from childhood or teenage years that he kept in touch with. Only friends from college onward. Not many of those, and he was rarely in contact with them.

Did I know for sure that he had no family? Or did I just swallow that information, hook, line and sinker, so happy to find a fellow orphan looking for a family that I ignored the red flags waving all around me?

After my shift ended at five, I slipped over to another public computer and did one more search; I wanted to request a copy of my husband's birth certificate. The website asked questions that only someone close, like a spouse, was likely to know—past addresses and the like. The instructions looked pretty straightforward. I figured I'd fill out the form on my laptop later, maybe at Becca's house. I'd for sure have the new birth certificate mailed to her house. Most days, I got home before Rick, but I wasn't about to chance him getting to the mailbox first and finding that envelope inside.

I decided that the birth certificate was how I'd tell Becca about all of this madness. Our texting conversations this week had been light and funny, filled with silly *Friends* GIFs and other things. I hadn't told her about Rick's reaction to the tattoo or the baby. Now I was too scared *not* to bring up Rick's past and the blanks I was starting to find in it.

Becca had been right all along. Despite her warnings when I rushed into marriage, she still loved me and swore she'd be in my corner no matter what. She had noticed little things here and there that bothered her, things that didn't seem to ring true or line up. Things I didn't want but agreed to because how could I say no to a trip to Manhattan when the one he planned with Chloe never happened?

Yes, marriage to Rick turned out to be far harder than I'd expected, and his temper, among other things, was exactly what Becca had feared.

I'd justified my silence about the topic of Rick not only because he'd get upset if I talked about us—plus, all of the advice books and Dr. Phil said the same thing—but also because complaining about my problems might hurt her: rub salt in the wounds of Becca's own failed marriage and bitter divorce.

Oh gee, I have a husband and no financial problems. I didn't want to be that friend.

But now . . .

Good husbands don't lie to their wives about who they are.

While the thought of telling Becca everything was awful, the idea of going through all of this alone—especially when I didn't have any clear idea what "all of this" was yet—was unthinkable.

An urgent need to know more came over me. Before I left the library, I pulled out my laptop and connected it to my phone's hot spot for a secure connection. I went back to the Orange County website to request Rick's birth certificate right away.

They had no record of his birth. As I had with the yearbooks, I tried variations of his name, expanded the search to the entire state of California. I couldn't find anyone that matched.

Nausea twisted through my middle. I put my hand against my stomach, wondering briefly if it was morning sickness, but this was something more. It was a deep cold fear that I didn't know my husband at all. That maybe I was about to bring a child into a very bad situation.

Oh, I was going to be sick.

So much for telling Becca when the birth certificate arrived. I packed up my laptop and headed to my car. When I had facts—indisputable facts—I'd tell her. I needed something to give me a direction, a next step, something Becca and I could do together to figure this mess out.

After getting into my car, I locked the doors, then promptly burst into tears as the meaning of what I'd *not* found washed over me. I felt orphaned again, alone. I didn't even have the tiny family with Rick that I'd believed I had. I thought of the little faces of the children at story time, and my arms ached from the pain of wanting to hold a child of my own.

I pressed a palm to my belly, which was growing, but not much yet. I needed something else in my life, now. The husband I trusted had been yanked away from me.

As I drove toward home, I tried to come up with a way to fill the strange, painful void in my chest that would bridge me to the day when I had my baby to hold.

On the freeway, I passed a billboard for a new pet store. That was the answer. I could have a pet to care for. Something small to care for. No animal would satisfy my maternal yearnings—only a baby would do that—but caring for a living creature might take the edge off the pain. A living presence that relied on me, that I could love, might help me get through the rest of this pregnancy.

Rick had refused to have any kind of pet, saying he was allergic to all animal dander. Was he, though? If I brought home a little furball, would he break out into hives and go into anaphylaxis? I'd never doubted it before, but now, nothing was a given.

I got off the freeway and headed for Walmart to grab a few groceries. As I parked, I realized that the store carried other things too. I could go home with a pet fish.

Fish didn't have dander. I could take care of one entirely by myself, and inexpensively. No shots or getting a fish fixed or trained. No daily walks needed. No time or money needed from Rick. No messes on the carpet. No reason to object.

I pushed my cart through the store, on a mission. I'd get the smallest aquarium and put it on my dresser so it wasn't in Rick's space. I'd clean it out more often than recommended to be absolutely sure there weren't any smells he could complain about.

The whole thing felt like a sneaky plan, but about something so minor as to be laughable.

So why did I feel triumphant about it?

CHAPTER ELEVEN

BECCA

My first night with Ivy proves far more challenging than anticipated. She's fussy, crying much of the night, refusing to eat or be comforted. I walk the floor in a way I haven't since the twins were this age. Halfway through the night, I'm sure I've never been this tired, but I must have been. The twins didn't sleep through the night until they were a good six or so months old.

Maybe I get tired more easily now that I'm a bit older.

Or maybe I'm less able to manage stress thanks to, oh, my best friend getting murdered.

And maybe Ivy's fussier than she would be if she weren't away from home overnight at such a young age. Ivy knows me and isn't scared to be babysat, but she also knows full well that I'm not her mother. I cry over Jenn, and Ivy surely senses my grief—and feels her own despite being unable to grasp what's happened.

Some parts of the night, we cry together.

I still have my old glider rocker, only now it's in the family room by the TV. I cradle Ivy late into the night, gliding back and forth. She eventually calms enough to curl against me, her head tucked under my chin. Even then, she trembles with sadness and exhaustion.

"I know, baby girl," I whisper, rubbing her back with one hand as tears stream down my face. I kissed the top of her head. "I know."

My phone's morning alarm wakes me with a start—Ivy too. When she looks around and realizes she still isn't home, that her mom isn't here, the screams begin again. I turn off the alarm and head upstairs to wake the twins.

"Time to get up for school, kiddos!" I call cheerfully, then realize that Ivy's diaper is in dire need of changing.

While I keep tabs on the kids' progress, I change Ivy and make a mental note to buy diapers and wipes to have on hand. Who knows how long Rick will need me to care for Ivy? Hopefully, this whole thing will blow over fast, and she'll be able to go home to be with her dad. For all I know, I'll be on pinch-hitting babysitting duty for the foreseeable future.

Did Rick say what time his interview is today? When will he call or text to update me? I glance at the clock on the living room wall and try to guess when he'll be done while snapping Ivy's pajamas closed. They're technically a pair of Maggie's footies that I kept to hand down to her when she becomes a mom. I may need to go buy Ivy some clothes or ask Rick if I can raid her dresser at their house.

Maggie and Davis bound down the stairs, both spotting Ivy and demanding to hold her first. "Nope," I say, holding her out of reach. "Go eat breakfast, and make sure your backpacks are ready."

"Fine," Maggie says with what is surely an embryonic teenage eye roll.

Normally, I make hot breakfasts—French toast, pancakes, or at the very least, scrambled eggs or oatmeal. Good meals are one of many ways I try to make up for the guilt I still feel about being a full-time working mom. This morning, though, I'm happy to let them forage for cold cereal. A flicker of guilt threatens to invade my mind, but at the same moment, my phone buzzes with a text from Rick.

Going in now. Wish me luck.

He wasn't kidding about a meeting first thing in the morning.

You'll do great, I tell him. *Update me as soon as you can.*

While the twins finish their breakfasts, which for Maggie consists mostly of picking marshmallow pieces out of the Lucky Charms, I feed Ivy a bottle. Right now, I don't care that Maggie's starting her day off with sugar. It won't put me in the running for Mother of the Year, but the kids aren't complaining, and they'll have something in their stomachs for school. Today, that's a win. If my mothering devolves into feeding them cold cereal three meals a day, then I'll reassess. For the time being, I need to focus on getting through this moment, and then the one after that, and the one after that.

That's the only way I can keep myself from obsessing over stuff like Jenn having an autopsy or where the police investigation will lead. Nope. I focus on feeding Ivy the last half of the bottle and keeping an eye on the clock. If I let my mind wander, breathing gets hard, my chest clamps tight, and I feel like I'm having a heart attack.

"Eat. Hurry or you'll miss the bus," I tell Davis for the fourth time as he makes faces at the baby. She giggles and pumps her fat little legs, formula dripping down her chin. I indicate his bowl with my head and shift a quarter-turn away from the table to block the kids' view of Ivy.

A few minutes later, they put their dishes into the dishwasher, and I usher them off to brush their teeth. When they return, I sit Ivy on the floor so I can help with their jackets and backpacks. I kiss Davis and Maggie goodbye in turn, then wave at the door as they trot out together. About two seconds after they reach the corner, the bus appears. We cut it close. After they and several other children board, the bus coughs black exhaust and drives away.

Ivy's whine, combined with her arms reaching, reminds me that she didn't finish her bottle, and it's rolled out of her reach. I pick her up and head for the counter. When she realizes I'm retrieving it, she starts waving her arms up and down. She grabs the bottle and immediately goes to town on it. I smooth her hair back with one hand, then slowly walk around the house with her in my arms. When she's suckling peacefully, I let myself sway side to side, deliberately slowing down. My typical morning pace is one of go, go, go—get the kids out the door, go for a run, take a shower, get to work.

But I won't be going to work today. I've already told my team that I'm taking the day off, and when Theo, my manager, heard about the situation, he arranged for most of my meetings to be pushed to next week. The few that can't be rescheduled will be virtual. I hope they happen when Ivy is napping, though I can't count on that. If she had a routine before, Rick didn't know it, and now it's flown out the window with every other sure thing in her world.

I'm grateful for the flexibility at work. Theo said he's giving me an unorthodox maternity leave of sorts, but that it won't last. He hinted that he expected it to be a week. We'll see.

Soon the formula is gone, and Ivy is asleep with a dribble of milk coming out of the corner of her mouth. I adjust her position so I can burp her, hoping not to wake her. The peaceful quiet lets my mind roam and wander.

Ivy is so sweet and adorable. I should snap a picture to send to Jenn.

I unlock my phone, open the messenger app, and there are the last few texts I sent to Jenn yesterday, asking if she was okay. I scroll up to a meme she sent over the weekend about chocolate making everything better.

Only then do I realize the impossibility of what I was about to do, and it sucks my breath away.

Never again will I get a meme from Jenn. I'll never send her a picture of Ivy while babysitting her. I'll never send her another text or anything else. We'll never take another selfie together. We've had our last late-night walk. We've seen our last rom-com. We've been to our last concert.

No more crying on each other's shoulders or talking late into the night about our hopes and dreams. No more sitting in glorious silence watching a stunning sunset.

I wish I'd known that when she did her impression of Buddy the Elf that she'd never again make me laugh so hard that Diet Coke came out my nose. What I wouldn't give for one more carbonation headache from her.

Stop it, I order myself, still patting Ivy's back to coax a burp.

My brain obeys, sort of. It abandons thoughts of the happy past. Instead, it flashes to Jenn's face underwater. So much water.

Water everywhere—as I try to pull her from the tub, grasping her lifeless body, which drew me downward toward the wet surface. Water sloshing out of the tub as I got her out and she thudded to the floor. Water spreading from her body to the floor. Water drenching the front of my clothes as I futilely attempted to revive her.

I close my eyes, trying to block out the images. The darkness of my eyelids won't shut out the nightmare.

Will this be my life now? A constant effort to mourn Jenn while not getting so sucked into the grief that I can't function?

The day will come when Ivy will want to hear about her mother. I need to keep the memories fresh because I am the only one who can tell some of her stories. I'm the only one Jenn told about how at fifteen, she almost set a field on fire trying to impress a boy with an illegal bottle rocket. Only I know about her first kiss, her first school dance.

I got to witness the pregnancy with Ivy, to see Jenn stroke her belly, and talk about things she'd do with her baby girl—go to the zoo, read books, paint, explore the mountains, collect rocks. All kinds of things. I'm the only one who knows those priceless details.

I decide to write down everything I can think of so Ivy can read it later. Not yet. When things are less chaotic. For now, my focus needs to stay on being a rock for Ivy, the best mom I can be for her and the twins. I need to do my work at the firm so well that no one will balk at my time off—or at my taking even more time off if I need it.

That means no more seeking quiet and calm for myself, but staying as busy as possible and filling my brain to capacity. That'll keep my thoughts from wandering toward the hot stove that will blister my heart every time I get near it.

I kiss Ivy's soft head. When I lift my face, I find a wet spot on her hair. Only then do I realize I'm crying.

CHAPTER TWELVE

JENN

April 5
11½ Months before Drowning

I named my goldfish Edward. He'd been in the house for three days. Any time he got attention from me, Rick grew annoyed. He turned up the volume on the TV, scowled at his show, and refused to look at me. He wouldn't even touch me. I think that's the real reason he never wanted a pet—any snuggle a dog or cat got from me was attention he didn't. Fish couldn't be cuddled, but I did watch Edward and talk to him.

After three days of Rick's silent treatment, I couldn't stand it. I sat on the bed and waited for his police procedural to end. I'd come armed with a pack of Red Vines, one of his few sugary vices. Maybe that would win me a point or two.

Pretending to watch the show, I wordlessly held out the open package. He didn't move his head, but his eyes darted to the candy and then to me. He took the whole package and tucked into it. Didn't offer me any.

When the credits rolled, I summoned my courage. "Did I do something to upset you?"

"You know what you did." Rick snapped a bite off the licorice without looking at me. He navigated to the next episode. If it started before we cleared the air, the topic would be closed for the night.

"Do you mean . . . that?" I pointed to the aquarium. I'd almost said *Edward.*

"I can't believe you'd make such a big decision without consulting me." He finally looked at to me, his eyes narrowing.

A fish is not a big decision, I wanted to say. *A dog, maybe. Not a little fish.*

"I honestly didn't think a fish would be a problem," I said quietly, hoping I didn't sound argumentative. "I'm sorry."

Another glance my way, but no words, only folded arms and a tight jaw.

"It cost hardly anything, and since I'm the one cleaning the tank and everything, I figured it wouldn't be a big deal."

"You figured wrong." His tone gave me chills. "You never bothered to wonder if the smell would gross me out, or if the lights in the tank would annoy me, or how much the supplies would cost—a lot of them ongoing expenses. It's more than a few bucks for a fish."

"You're right. I'm sorry." I hated how cowed my voice sounded.

"You *knew* I didn't want pets. We talked about it, lots of times. Tell me you remember *that.*"

I nodded and ignored the dig.

"I would *never* be so disrespectful to you, but I suppose we have different values and priorities. I guess I'll have to get used to that."

I pulled back as if slapped. How could he say that I hadn't been respectful to him? Didn't he know that he was on my mind virtually every waking moment? Not because of being in love. Because I was always afraid that I'd screw up.

And I could never avoid ticking him off, and then I had to live through my personal Chernobyl for however long he decided. *Stop pushing my buttons,* he often said. But the man had more buttons than an accordion, and most of them weren't labeled.

I wanted to call Becca and have a girls' night streaming a movie. Not happening. Rick would assume I'd gone over to trash talk him. As if I dared.

We used to be happy, back in our honeymoon period. No one warns you to prepare for when marriage settles into something painful. It's called a honeymoon *period* because it ends.

Rick started the next episode. The tension between us was palpable. All over a fish.

I brushed my teeth and returned to bed, hoping he'd think I was asleep so we wouldn't fight.

I slept fitfully and woke early, leaving for work before Rick even got up. I didn't want to talk to him or feel obligated to kiss him goodbye.

The workday was a good distraction, but when it ended, I had to face home again.

I went to our room to change into sweats and feed Edward. Three steps in, I saw Edward belly up at the top of the water. I hurried over and stared at him, wondering what to do. As if CPR could save him. Any triumph from bringing him home was squelched.

Goldfish have short lifespans and small brains. They can't feel pain—I don't think.

Maybe Edward had been unhealthy or older than the store knew. He might've died no matter who bought him or what care he got.

I grabbed the paperwork and the tank's manual and reread it all. I found nothing new, only confirmation: his habitat was perfect. He'd gotten fed the right amount. Even as a first-timer, I knew not to overfeed a fish. The filter was clean. The bubbler was doing its job. I'd done everything right.

Then why was he dead?

Rick killed my fish. The thought flashed through my mind. *Ridiculous idea.* Or was it?

Had Rick overfed Edward? I grabbed the food container and took off the lid. It was still nearly full. Maybe Rick had nothing to do with this.

I sat on the bed, thinking. Edward had been perfectly fine that morning when I left for work. Rick had been asleep, something highly unusual for Mr. Lawyer-who-never-wastes-a-billable-minute. He had the opportunity to do something to Edward before going to work. He had a motive too.

I'm starting to sound like a true-crime podcast.

A surprising wave of grief overtook me. I fought it. I'd lost a goldfish, not a geriatric cat who'd seen me through college. This was a fish. Just a fish. I didn't even know if he'd been a *he*. Maybe Edward should've been Edwina.

What had happened? Rick could've taken him out of the water and let him suffocate. A warning from one article popped into my mind: abrupt temperature changes could kill a small fish. I looked at the tank more closely. Several drops of water were on the dresser next to it, on two sides, as if something had splashed out. A few of the drops were the size of coins. Unless Rick came home to do the deed during his lunch break, these drops had been bigger in the morning. Could pieces of ice have landed and melted there?

My phone buzzed, startling me. A quick check showed a Waze notification saying that Rick was on his way home. I left the little orange corpse and headed to the kitchen.

I'd originally planned to make enchiladas for dinner, but I needed something faster. I'd cook the salmon now and do the enchiladas tomorrow. With the salmon in the oven, I made a green salad. The whole time, I kept glancing at the clock on the microwave and guessing how much time remained until Rick got home.

I started setting the table. When I grabbed our usual water pitcher from the cupboard, it was wet inside. And I knew.

The pitcher wasn't wet from yesterday's dinner. It had been filled with water or ice today, then dumped into the tank, which had shocked Edward's nervous system and killed him.

My hands shook as I filled the pitcher from the fridge's dispenser. Rick had deliberately killed Edward. Such a petty thing to do. *Edward was only a fish.*

I knew why Rick did it—jealousy. He couldn't stand the thought of anyone or anything but him having my love or attention.

Rick arrived as I walked the pitcher to the table, my hands shaking. "Hey, babe," he said, coming in from the garage. "How was your day?"

"My fish is dead." I *wanted* to say *You killed Edward.*

"Too bad." He set his satchel on a barstool by the kitchen island and took off his suit coat, which he laid on top of the satchel. "Dinner smells great." He loosened his tie and opened his top button on his way to the table. When he sat across from me, I didn't look at him. "Earth to Jenn," he said with an amused half smile. "Are you seriously upset over a fish? Their lifespans aren't much bigger than a fruit fly's." He unbuttoned his sleeves and rolled them up.

"Their *natural* lifespans," I said under my breath, then immediately regretted it.

His hand paused mid-sleeve roll. "What?"

"Nothing."

He dished himself up the bigger of the salmon pieces. "You flushed it, didn't you? We don't have a fish rotting in our room, right?"

"I'll take care of it."

He grimaced, then forked a big piece of salmon into his mouth. "That's gross. Do it now."

Honestly, I would have preferred to have a private moment to dispose of Edward's remains. Silly, yes. He was only a goldfish, and I wasn't six.

But I obeyed. I set my napkin on the table and headed to the bedroom to fetch and flush Edward. If I didn't do it soon, Rick would.

With the little net, I scooped the body out of the tank, then held my hand under it to contain any drips. A better scenario would've been standing on a bridge in the canyon, then tossing the tiny remains into the rushing river below.

Earth to earth for people. Water to water for a fish.

That would've been better than sending him off through a sewage pipe. I knelt by the toilet and whispered a tiny goodbye, then tipped the net right above the bowl so he fell and made only a slight noise—*bloop*. I stood and flushed. Edward's lifeless form swirled around a few times and then disappeared.

"Did you do it?" Rick's voice startled me.

I looked over to see him standing outside the toilet room door.

"Yep." I headed back to the kitchen. Rick followed. Instead of sitting down to eat, I grabbed my purse and headed for the garage.

"Where are you going?"

"For a drive. I need to clear my head. Finish dinner without me. I'll clean it up when I get back."

I left, not breathing easy until I was out of our subdivision and I was certain that Rick hadn't followed. At the turn out of our subdivision, I glanced to the right, toward the canyon. Maybe I could've taken Edward there. Oh well.

I turned left and headed for a little mom-and-pop drive-in, where I ordered a fresh raspberry shake and fries. I ate in silence, my phone powered off so Rick couldn't track me or try to call or text. Tears welled up.

It was just a fish.

My fish.

A fish named Edward.

His death was not an accident, but a message: no more rebellions from me, no matter how small.

I found myself smiling sardonically at that. If there was one thing my husband didn't know about me, it was that I didn't take ultimatums well. My childhood stubbornness gave my foster mothers fits. The same stubbornness drove my high school teachers crazy.

The tiny act of rebellion of buying a pet had awoken that stubborn child. The eight-year-old who spent five hours falling off a bicycle, well after the sun went down, because she refused to go inside until she could ride. The seventeen-year-old who gave her teachers crap about due dates and missed classes and aced tests anyway.

Rick wanted me to stay within the lines he drew, did he? That might have been what he meant to say, but that was *not* what he'd get. I'd wait a few days, let him simmer down a bit. And then I'd tell him what I knew: he'd never attended Wagner High. He wasn't born in California. He'd been lying to me for our entire relationship.

And *I* was the disrespectful, disloyal one?

If I could get myself to say all that, he'd lose his mind.

More than that, I'd keep looking into who Rick really was. Not even Mr. Lawyer could convince me to do otherwise, I thought, then bit into a shake-covered fry with satisfaction.

CHAPTER THIRTEEN

BECCA

In some ways, it feels more like a year since I found Jenn. Each hour of the day drags. Sometimes I wake up, grab my phone, and start scrolling through the morning news. If I ever come across something that makes me laugh—a clip of a monologue from one of the late-night comics or a funny Twitter thread—it's like a gulp of cool water down a parched throat.

But that feeling is followed immediately by the memory of *why* laughing feels good, and that's when a waterfall of guilt knocks me flat. How could I, even in the haze of morning-grog brain, forget that Jenn is gone? How can I laugh when her daughter will grow up not knowing her? How can I find even a split second of happiness when her life was snuffed out? The pain comes on as fast as a car crash, then sits on my chest, heavy as a dump truck.

I go through the motions of my daily routine with the twins and Ivy, who I'm still taking care of. Jenn's body hasn't been released by authorities; they're still waiting on autopsy results and who knows what else. I manage to hide the worst of the pain from Davis and Maggie. At least I think I do. Despite being up half of every night with Ivy, I wake them up with the same lighthearted voice I've always used. If they notice anything different, it's that I'm feeding them toaster waffles instead of making whole wheat ones from scratch. A step up from cold cereal, at least.

The sink already has more to wash, thanks to the addition of baby bottles and nipples. The amount of household laundry has spiked; you'd think several new people live here instead of a single baby who spits up and has diaper blowouts. I've forgotten how much laundry a baby can make—and I had twins.

With Ivy in the highchair that I took from Rick and Jenn's kitchen, I go about getting breakfast for everyone. I'm in a total haze, staring into the pantry, unable to find the syrup bottle to save my life. At least part of that has to because my sleep is pure crap right now. When I do manage to sleep for a few hours, nightmares are inevitable.

"Right there, next to the chocolate chips," Maggie says helpfully.

Sure enough, the syrup bottle is right where it belongs, beside the basket that holds nuts, raisins, and chocolate chips. "Good eye," I say, doing my all to maintain a cheery tone.

Last night's nightmare was particularly gruesome: Jenn under the water, her face a skull, her hair intact, floating under the surface. The skinless face spoke with bitter accusation. *Why didn't you save me?*

"Mom?" Maggie's voice breaks through the image, and I snap back to the present. She's holding out her hand for the syrup bottle.

"Oops. Sorry about that. Here, sweetie." I laugh and hand it over, but even that draws attention.

Davis cocks his head. "You're going to let her pour it?" he asks as his sister is gleefully taking advantage of the situation, covering her waffle with syrup. She's filled every square, and now she's squeezing out more to encircle the waffle so it's sitting in a puddle of syrup barely contained by her plate. This is why I pour the syrup. Usually, anyway.

"Just this once," I say with a shrug as if I intended it all along. To Maggie, I add, "Enjoy it, missy."

Judging by the look on her face, she totally is. When she puts the bottle down, syrup drips down the side, but it doesn't reach the table because Davis picks it up and nearly empties the bottle onto his plate. He looks at me with delight in his eyes, as well as a little suspicion, as if he wonders if he'll get in trouble for using up so much syrup—or as if his mom has lost her mind.

I can't show the kids that I'm teetering mentally, so I head to the dishwasher to empty it from last night's dishes. "Don't feed Ivy," I tell the kids as I pass them. "She's got her own food."

As I unload the utensil basket, last night's nightmare creeps back into my mind, and I shove it away so I won't cry in front of the kids.

Dreams mean I'm getting REM sleep, I tell myself. *Even bad dreams are a good sign.* Though calling that image a *bad dream* is like calling a passing kidney stone a discomfort. At what point will getting more REM mean I don't feel exhausted and burned out all the time?

As I reach into the utensil holder, a fork stabs my palm, and I suck in my breath. Do I dare drive to work if I'm so sleep-deprived that I can't empty the dishwasher without hurting myself?

I send the kids off to the bus stop, get myself and Ivy ready for the day, and drop her off at the daycare center on my way to work. When I walk into the ad agency building, I inhale deeply. They say that smells are one of the best triggers for memory, and for the next eight hours, I hope the smells will help me stay mentally at work—to think solely about work and *not* think about what the outside world holds for me when I leave.

When I walk past the break room on the way to my office, I smell coffee and pastries, and I realize that while I might have fed three children enough sugar to outdo the Energizer bunny, I forgot to get myself anything eat. I grab a coffee, add vanilla creamer, and snag a maple bar. Might as well complete the sugar-filled breakfast pattern for the day.

After a quick stop in my office to check email, then grab some files and my tablet, I head to a conference room for a meeting where I'll lead my team in coming up with slogans for an athletic clothing campaign. I get to the meeting room a few minutes before it's supposed to start and get set up, review my notes, and finish the pastry. No one has shown up yet—odd for everyone except Todd, who's notoriously late. But not even Leslie is here, who usually shows up before I do. I pull up my phone calendar to be sure I didn't miss the meeting; I wouldn't put that past my cobwebby brain.

The meeting is on the calendar, all right, but it's at two. I could have sworn it was at nine. Was I told about the new time? I don't know. My memory feels like a sieve. I set an alarm on my phone so I won't forget to return to the room this afternoon, then go to my desk, fully intending to work. In theory, I should be able to do my job without thinking about Jenn at all. At least, that was my intent yesterday when I tucked the three pictures I had displayed of us into a desk drawer. Their old places feel empty, so I rearrange the remaining picture frames to fill in the gaps.

Not having her pictures out feels wrong, but I can't focus on my work with them there. They'll go back to their rightful spots eventually, maybe one by one, when I can look at them without a sudden breath piercing in my solar plexus.

Still unable to concentrate, I pull out noise-canceling headphones and stream classical music at a high volume, something in my arsenal that I use only in dire situations. It worked in college when I had to spend hours on projects, and it doesn't fail me now. I get sucked into work, and the next thing I know, an alarm goes off. The noise pulls me away from drafting a campaign proposal for a medical cannabis company and back to my desk.

The alarm keeps going, and I remember that the noise is coming from my phone. For a few seconds, I stare at it, confused. I look at the clock in the bottom corner of my computer, convinced that I couldn't have just lost five hours, but sure enough, it's time for the two o'clock meeting.

I turn off the alarm and look around my office. So bland. It needs life. Maybe a Ficus. Some color. And something on the walls besides framed posters from old campaigns and a few awards.

I successfully open the meeting. Soon, the room has plenty of energy and ideas bouncing around. I tell Joni to take notes, mostly so I don't have to. When the meeting adjourns two hours later, I head to my office without any idea about what we decided or whether I agree with any of it. Instead of going back to my desk, I decide that caffeine would be a wise move before attempting to drive home. Caffeine and donuts are all I've consumed today, but something needs to wake my brain up.

As I walk down the hall, a new receptionist approaches from the other direction. We smile our hellos, but as soon as she passes, I step into the wake of something that screams Jenn. I stop in the hall and look around. I feel as if Jenn is nearby, so close I should be able to reach out and touch her.

Where is she? Then I realize that I'm *smelling* her, or rather, her perfume, one rare enough that I've encountered it on only a few other people. The new receptionist must wear it.

Frozen, I'm unable to take another step as I stand there in the cloud of her scent. Images of Jenn fill my mind faster than I would have believed possible. I press one hand against the wall to steady my lightheaded dizziness. I can't escape. Memories and reminders of Jenn are everywhere. Not even a hallway is safe. Couldn't Jenn have worn a common perfume, like Chanel No. 5?

I stumble toward the break room, then think better of it and hurry to my office. I shut the door and collapse at my desk. I rest my head against my folded arms and try to breathe, but soon, I'm sobbing.

A text from Davis breaks me out of the crying jag. *Can I bring my video games to Dad's?*

It's Wednesday, which means a night at Jason's. I usually dread the weekday visits because the kids come home after having stayed up late and not having any consistent rules or schedule. Jason gets them to school late, picks them up late, forgets to send their backpacks, often doesn't bother feeding them, and on and on. He often takes them out for big adventures I can't afford. Getting them back on schedule and doing things like chores is exhausting, a battle I hate and resent. Maggie recently came home with some new salty words in her vocabulary that she'd picked up from her dad. I hope it doesn't slip out at school.

Before answering Davis's text, I straighten in the chair and wipe my cheeks. I can be a strong mom. There's a lot I can't do right now, but I've got this. Strong Mom is a role I've taken on for my kids since their births, and more so since the divorce three years ago.

Is your homework done? I send the question back, not answering his query. I probably won't let him take any games to his dad's; they're likely to stay there, end up lost, or get broken.

No, but I'll bring it with me and do it there. Pleeeeease?

As if Jason will even check to see if they have homework or insist it gets done if he did. He makes sure to be the fun parent, and unfortunately, that means I can't ever stop being the responsible one.

Sorry, buddy, I type. *Not this time.*

Time to head home. If I miss something in the last hour of the workday, someone will fill me in later. That's what email and texts are for, right? Besides, Theo keeps telling me that I'm free to take as much time off as I need. I know that doesn't mean a blank check to stay on the payroll and not work for a year. I'll take off a day here and there, but I work as often as I can manage it.

My phone vibrates with Davis's reply. A sad emoji and one word: *Fine...*

I pocket my phone, glad that the battle is over. He's pouting, no doubt, but I made the right call.

For the first time since the divorce decree was finalized, I look forward to having the twins at their dad's. I need the time alone. I've been go-go-going to avoid thinking about Jenn, but I know that eventually, if I hold the grief down for too long, it will burst out uncontrolled, like an exploding can of pop in the freezer. Tonight, I'll do some deliberate mourning when the twins aren't home. I'll watch a ten-tissue movie and eat a couple of pints of ice cream. I'll cry all of the tears that have been building up, releasing some pressure so I don't break into a million pieces with the kids.

I have a sense that they feel a bit ignored. My best right now isn't enough for them. Ivy needs so much attention, and while they love her, they're acting up. They may resent me—or her. We all need a break.

Time to head to the daycare center, pick up Ivy, and check in with Rick. He's been bad about replying to texts the last few days, so I have no idea what's going on with him or when he plans to take Ivy home. If he doesn't return any of my calls or texts soon, I'll talk with Detective Andrus to get an idea of what to expect. I don't want to stress Rick out even more, but I need to have *some* idea of what to expect day to day.

Just when I think my emotions are enough under control to head home, another wave of sobs comes over me.

Later, I command myself. *After the twins go with their dad, you can cry all you want.*

It doesn't work.

CHAPTER FOURTEEN
JENN

April 17
Eleven months before Drowning

Rick sat beside me in the women's clinic waiting room as I filled out pages and pages of forms. The room was decorated with giant framed photographs of mothers and babies and furnished with chairs and tables designed with simple lines and colors like an IKEA showroom. Rick was on his phone doing I don't know what when I reached the personal and family medical history section. I glanced at him from the corner of my eye, grateful that he agreed to come to my first prenatal visit.

With reluctance, I returned to the form. My personal medical history was straightforward enough, but I knew nothing of my biological medical history. I didn't know if I had a family history of female cancers or whether any woman in my line had lost children during pregnancy, or anything else. My child would know the history of at least one generation before her, something I'd never have.

Eventually, we were brought back to an area decorated, as the waiting room had been, with poster-size photos of babies and pregnant women. A young nurse took my weight and blood pressure, then led us to an office-type room, complete with bookshelves, a desk, and a couch. There we waited—me nervous, Rick looking bored—until a quiet knock sounded on the door. The knob turned, and the door opened, revealing a dark-haired woman who I guessed to be in her late fifties.

"Hi," she said, entering with her hand extended to me. "I'm Tiffany." This was the nurse practitioner I'd made the appointment with a month ago. The clinic was highly recommended online, but they also had a long waiting list, so I was in the middle of my second trimester—much later than recommended for a first prenatal exam.

"Jenn," I said, shaking her hand and smiling. "And this is my husband, Rick."

"Hey," he said, putting his phone down and shaking her hand as he flashed a smile of his own. It was the first real energy or emotion I'd seen from him since we left the house. I took it as a hopeful sign.

"Nice to meet you." Tiffany took a seat at the desk and went over my paperwork. She asked a few questions here and there, including why I had such a scant family medical history, though she made me comfortable even with that sensitive subject. She was kind and warm, and I felt instantly at ease. She consulted a small chart. "Looks like you're about fifteen, sixteen weeks. Does that sound right?"

"Yes." I reached over and took Rick's hand in mine. For the moment, I felt as if we were on the same team.

She spent a lot of time talking with us, asking me about my nausea and other symptoms, wondering if I'd given any thought to a birth plan, what my hopes and desires would be in the delivery room. Many of the questions were things I hadn't known to think about, and my mind began swimming.

"I don't know," I said more than once, and Tiffany assured me that I had plenty of time to make those decisions.

She shifted away from the computer and faced us directly. "If you don't have any other questions—"

"I have one," Rick interjected.

"Sure," Tiffany said.

"Is it too late for an abortion?"

All air seemed to have been sucked out of the room; I couldn't breathe. A flicker of shock passed across Tiffany's eyes, but she recovered quickly, so fast that Rick might not have picked up on it.

"Here? Yes. A few states allow them later, but even then, we're getting close to that line," Tiffany said.

"So how much time do we have? I mean, hypothetically, if we went to another state where it's legal longer?"

Rick's question took Tiffany off guard. She glanced at me, then spoke with measured words. "Two weeks at most," she said. "According to the date of Jenn's last menstrual period, she's between weeks, which gives you closer to ten days." When she stopped speaking, an uncomfortable quiet fell over the room as if the gravity had been turned up.

"Gotcha," Rick said, leaning back, seemingly satisfied.

Tiffany glanced between me and Rick a couple of times before putting her hands together and standing. "Okay, well, we'll do the standard first-visit exam in another room. Rick, you can go wait in the lobby for the first part. I'll call you back in a few minutes. It shouldn't take long." She smiled warmly and went to the door, which she opened and held for us. Rick passed through and kept going, back toward the waiting room.

"Excited to hear the heartbeat?" Tiffany asked as she led me to an exam room.

"The heartbeat?" I said breathlessly. Of course I'd hear it. I hadn't thought about what hearing that would be like, or really considered that it would be today. My eyes watered.

In the exam room, I expected Tiffany to give me instructions for undressing and putting on the gown or whatever came next, but instead, she gestured to a chair. "Have a seat."

The look on her face had me worried. Did she know already that something was wrong with my baby? I sat on the chair, and she sat on the rolling stool.

"I have a question." The concerned tone didn't help my nerves.

"Yes?"

"I usually have the fathers come in for the whole exam instead of having them wait in the lobby during the first part, but . . . I wanted to be sure that *you* want him here. I don't need to call him back at all. Your medical information is private, and we can keep it from him if you want us to."

My brow furrowed. "Why would I want to hide anything from him?"

"Maybe you don't. But part of my job is to keep a patient's medical information private and to make sure my patients feel safe."

"Oh," I said, still unsure where she was going. "He's on my forms as someone who can have access to my information, so . . ."

"Permission you can revoke at any time."

Alarm raced through me like ice water through my veins. "Why would I want to?"

Tiffany licked her lips in thought and then scooted a bit closer so we could look at each other eye to eye. "Do you want this baby?"

"I do." The words made my eyes burn. "More than anything."

"Then I can safely infer that you won't want to sign a consent form for an abortion?"

"That's the *last* thing I want to do," I said, my voice a whisper. I knew that with Rick, my opinion—my voice—meant little. If I was presented with a consent form with him at my side, I might find myself shakily signing it against my will.

"That's what I thought," Tiffany said. "The truth is that you could have one, no questions asked, for several more weeks. Longer in some states if you wanted to travel there."

She lied to Rick for me?

"But I'm happy to tell him that your situation is one in which it wouldn't be legal."

"But—"

"And it would be the truth," she said over my near protest. "Patient consent is required, and you don't want to consent. That makes the procedure illegal. I'll make sure you're not put into a position to be pressured into it."

The burning behind my eyes increased, and tears finally spilled over. I dropped my face into my hands. "Thank you," I murmured, not knowing if she could hear or understand me.

Tiffany pulled two tissues from a box on the counter and handed them to me.

My breath hitched. "Thank you," I said again.

She put a hand on my arm and looked me in the eyes. "We'll get your baby here safely. I'll do everything in my power to make sure of that."

CHAPTER FIFTEEN

BECCA

I pick up Ivy from daycare and drive home. In a couple of days, we'll reach the two-week mark since Jenn's death. We're settling into the routine of having her live with us. I make sure to update Rick on how she's doing every day. In my last few texts and phone messages, I've left hints asking about his plans for Ivy moving forward. What should I expect? Whether she's going to be with me long term or going back to live with him soon, I need to know.

The idea of giving her back to her dad makes my eyes water. I want her with me. I blink the tears away and sing to Ivy. When she laughs, I glance at her through the rearview mirror. She's grinning and flapping her arms.

We get home and enter the house, where the smell of freshly removed sneakers hits me. Davis and Maggie are back from school.

"All right," I say, clapping my hands to get their attention from the TV. "Time to pack for Dad's!" I'm wearing my happy face in hopes that it'll make getting them ready and out the door with Jason a bit easier. Predictably, they rush to Ivy, who's in her carrier by my feet. They make faces at her, tickling her toes, and otherwise being cute but unhelpful. I hold my foot out between them and the carrier. "If you pack quickly, you might have time to play with her before Dad gets here."

The twins pause long enough to process my words. They look at each other, communicating silently as only twins can, then race up to their rooms. I spend the next half hour feeding and changing Ivy and making sure the kids pack everything they need.

"*Not* your video games," I tell Davis when I check his carry-on. "Nice try, but it's not happening."

He groans and whines that it's not fair, then marches back to his room.

Soon, I have the house to myself. I take off my ad-executive business clothes and put on something easier to move in. An hour-long walk with Ivy in a stroller—another thing borrowed from Jenn's house—gives me the exercise and endorphins needed to relax. Better yet, by the time I get back, Ivy is drowsy. A warm bath, a new diaper, sleeper jammies, and a bottle are all she needs; she quickly nods off and stays deeply asleep when I set her in the portable crib in my home office. She's gotten used to me and the house, and we even have some semblance of a routine here now. She usually sleeps through the night.

I take a quick shower, then slip into comfy pajama pants and a big Lakers tee.

I wash my face and go through my regular skin-care routine for the first time in several days. Would a therapist think that's a good sign? I don't recall routines and skin care being anywhere in the stages of grief. As I squeeze a tiny chocolate-chip-shaped bit of eye cream onto my finger, I pause. Does any of this mean I'm getting over Jenn's death already? That I didn't love her as much as I thought I did? No, that's stupid. I lean into the mirror and dab the cream around my eyes with my ring finger. From my nightstand, my phone rings.

Usually, I put it on Do Not Disturb mode after work so no one can bug me during off-hours when my focus is my kids. Most days, the twins need me, and on nights like tonight, when they're with their dad, I need time alone, untethered from the office, to regroup. If I'm being honest with myself, since Jenn's death, any time I've spent alone has been more wallowing than restorative.

The phone keeps ringing, and I continue to be unwilling to answer it. The volume is low enough that the sound is unlikely to wake Ivy in the other room, especially with the office door closed. I'm reluctant but curious, so I walk to my bedside and check the screen to be sure it's not one of the twins or Jason. Maybe I did remember to turn on Do Not Disturb mode, but their numbers get to bypass that.

It's Rick. Good. Maybe he's calling with answers to my questions. I steel myself for whatever he's going to tell me, even if it means not having Ivy with me anymore.

I sit on the edge of my bed and stack a couple of pillows behind me as if I'm about to talk to Jenn. I can't count how many times I've sat on this bed, with these pillows behind me, chatting and laughing and crying with her. Rick and I have never had a nighttime chat or anything remotely resembling one. He's also the only living person who was as close to her as I was. The only other person mourning her as I am.

"Hey," I say.

Rick doesn't answer for several seconds.

Unsure if the call dropped, I say, "Rick? Are you there?"

"Yeah." His voice doesn't sound normal, but I'm not sure how to read it. He clears his throat and adds, "Um, sorry." A long sniff comes through the line, and my worry antennae goes up.

I sit up straight. "What's wrong?"

Aside from the fact that he's lost his wife? I'm such an idiot.

"I mean, is there something new that's gone wrong?" I clarify. Maybe he needs me to take care of Ivy for longer. *Please, please, please.* I don't dare ask, so I probe from a different direction. "Is everything hitting you harder tonight? Because I know what that's like—the grief comes in waves, often when you least expect it. My dad died fifteen years ago, but sometimes I break down if I see an older man who walks like him or wears the same glasses. It can come right back, knocking you off your feet like a tsunami. It just . . . sucks."

"Yeah," he says. "It does."

"Sometimes you need to cry it out."

Great. Now instead of sounding like a callous idiot, I'm sounding like Ann Landers. Normally, I'm not so, well, weird, but this is Jenn's husband, a man I hardly know. This is new territory for both of us. How am I supposed to speak or act? I absolutely can't face the idea of pushing away the one person who also knew and loved Jenn. We are her only family. The stakes to say the right thing feel awfully high, and I seem to be screwing it up.

"Thanks, Becca." Rick sniffs again, more loudly. He sounds sincere, not distant or annoyed. A good sign, I hope. "There *is* something wrong. Something new, I mean."

My stomach sinks. "Oh no. What is it?" Both of my hands hold the phone to my ear as if the extra fingers somehow add support through the airwaves to him.

"I've been . . . oh, Becca." Sobs come through now, whimpers and sniffs. Actual sobs. He's crying.

I've never heard Rick cry. If this were Jenn, I'd know exactly what she needed. I could read her tone so well that she hardly needed to say more than a word before I'd know which kind of comfort she needed.

Not with Rick. Sitting on my bed, I realize how little I know Jenn's husband.

"What is it?" I ask.

A deep breath and then he goes on. "I'm officially a person of interest."

My brain takes a few seconds to catch up. "Not a suspect?" I say, thinking back to the news magazine shows I've seen.

"No, not officially. Not yet." He sounds as if his life is over. In some respects, it probably feels over. So does mine sometimes. Our lives will go on. How, I don't know.

"They always investigate the spouse first," I remind him. "If they *weren't* looking at you to rule you out, I'd worry they weren't doing their job."

"I know," he says. "They have to investigate me so they can rule me out, but I don't know if I can handle much more of it. They keep asking me to come in, again and again."

That seems odd. He hasn't mentioned Ivy, though, so he's probably not calling about her at all. I force my shoulders to relax. "What are they looking for?"

"No clue. The interviews are feeling more like interrogations. I'm this close to getting an attorney."

This doesn't sound like the strong guy I know Rick to be. Then again, do I *know* him to be anything?

Rick groans on the other end. "I wouldn't be surprised if they ask me to take a polygraph."

"Jump at the chance," I tell him. "Hell, suggest it. Clear your name."

"They're going to try to pin this on me," he says, his voice weak. "I could see it in the detective's eyes. He told me I couldn't leave town. Did he tell you the same thing?"

"No," I say quietly. A weight has fallen over the conversation, and a new worry goes through me. What if Ivy loses her father too?

"Becca, you have to believe me," Rick says through a hiccup between tears. "I didn't do it."

"I know you didn't," I say quickly. "Just remember, the sooner they eliminate you as a suspect, the sooner they can find the person who *is* responsible."

"I guess." He sounds as if fatigue is messing with his head as much as it is with mine. He needs someone to talk him out of this slump.

"Rick, listen. Cooperate with anything they ask for. Anything and everything. Again and again, even if they ask the same questions over and over. Whatever it takes. They can't pin this on you without evidence, right? And there can't be any if you didn't do it."

"You're right," he says. "It's just—" Another deep breath as if he's trying to calm down. "I thought they'd be past that point by now."

"The investigation is just starting," I remind him. "Hang in there. When the toxicology, DNA, and other reports are all in, and they've cleared you, we can start getting some closure. What other suspects are they looking at?"

"None that I know of."

"Well, let's correct that. There's got to be something pointing to who did this."

"I haven't even been able to bury her," Rick says. The pain in his voice is palpable. "She deserves a proper burial."

"She does," I agree. I try not to choke up.

"Will we be able to have an open casket after an autopsy?"

"I think so."

"Maybe I'll have her cremated."

I don't answer. I have a feeling that Jenn wouldn't want to be cremated. Her body has already been through so much. Autopsies seem so violent, with saws and knives and who knows what else. And fire is utterly destructive. Which, I suppose, is the point. My vision blurs, and I hear him sniffing again, which makes my own tears fall.

"This sucks," I say. "There's no other good word. It plain old sucks."

"Yeah."

I wait for him to go on. The silence on the line stretches and stretches.

"Anything I can help with?"

"Uh, yeah," he says quickly. "I thought I should come over to see Ivy. Don't want her to forget who I am, right?"

"Right," I say. She's been asleep for half an hour, but maybe I should wake her up if he misses his daughter and wants to bond with her. "She's down already, but if you want to play with her for a bit, we can wake her up. You could put her back down for the night."

"I wouldn't know how to do that."

He doesn't know how to put his own child to bed? I feel like a question mark is hanging over my head now. Jenn did most of the heavy lifting when it came to caring for their baby. I know that. But even if he never put his daughter down for the night, he had to have noticed how Jenn did it, or he'd want to learn now, you'd think.

On the other hand, he also isn't showing interest in learning anything about Ivy's schedule and patterns, so maybe he doesn't have plans to.

"Do you want me to wake her up?" I ask again.

"That would throw off her schedule or something, wouldn't it?"

"Well, yeah . . ."

"Then no," he says. "But can I come over tonight anyway? To talk with someone who gets it?"

"Sure," I say. "I can make you some of my famous Mexican hot chocolate. Maybe we can try to figure out where the cops should be looking."

"Deal," he says. "I'll be there in a few."

CHAPTER SIXTEEN

JENN

April 25-26
One Month before Drowning

Time began to feel both fast and slow. Every day dragged, but every week that passed surprised me with its swiftness. Each Monday when I went to work, I stared down another week stretching out ahead of me like a long road that disappeared into the horizon. Then, seven eternal days later, Monday arrived again and it started all over.

I felt safe and comfortable being myself at the library, but work was still work, stressful at times. It was also tiring during pregnancy. But going home wasn't exactly a place I could unwind.

It's Thursday, I realized as I checked out books at the circulation desk, covering for a college student who had to take the morning off for a final. I handed a stack of five books and the patron's card back to her, an older woman with silver hair.

"Oh, are you expecting?" she cooed, noting my slightly rounder middle.

For both of us, I was glad that yes, I was pregnant, because I didn't necessarily look it. I could have just put on a few pounds. I'd been told by plenty of people that all the significant growth happens in the second half. I was sure I'd be a whale in no time. Happily, mind you—I wanted this baby so much—but a whale nonetheless.

"Due in September," I told the woman.

"How wonderful," she said, and I could tell she was getting ready to launch into a speech about the blissful life of grandmotherhood—I'd heard several versions from other patrons already—and I wanted to avoid the awkward part where I had to say that my baby wouldn't have a grandma.

"Have a great day," I told her, a clear goodbye, and I greeted the next patron, though my mind was stuck on thoughts of the baby, of Rick, of life outside the library. So much had happened in recent weeks.

The ebb and flow of library patrons were like a clock for me; I could tell when the university classes were about to start because students rushed out to get there on time. A rush of teenagers in the afternoon always hit twenty minutes after the nearest high school let out. The students seemed so happy and free, with nothing to tie them down, not even worry about their futures. What would that be like?

I'd never known. Kids in the foster system grow up awfully fast and worry about the future every waking hour. Part of me wanted to warn them about the joys and heartbreaks the future might bring, tell them to cherish the now because it would be fleeting. Of course, if I said anything, they would either look at me as if I had horns, or they'd take me seriously and lose some of their innocent joy.

I kept eying the bank of public computers, waiting for when I had time to do more Google searching about Rick. I rarely found a chance to do research during work hours, and the few times I could have snuck away, I was held back by something else: I was scared to learn more. Things had been relatively fine for a while now. Not great, but okay. The things I found out before—not even a month ago—seemed like another lifetime.

Last night, something flicked a switch inside me. Rick commented on my tattoo again, calling it trampy. I didn't sleep well, and when I got to work today, I couldn't get Rick's nasty tone out of my head. It echoed on repeat like the worst kind of earworm. When my shift was over, I went back to the staff room to get my purse, where I noticed a goldfish magnet I'd stuck onto a file cabinet in the back corner.

It was handmade, carved of wood, and bright orange. I'd bought it at Walmart the same time I bought Edward. I walked over and took the magnet in hand, turning it around and around, running my thumb across the smooth edges. The day after Edward died, I'd taken everything fish-related out of the house and donated it to Goodwill. Everything but this magnet, which I'd taken from the fridge and put on the file cabinet here, where Rick wouldn't see it. This last little reminder of my fish, I kept. One more tiny way to rebel, I supposed.

As silly as it sounded, my fish was killed by my husband. Standing there in the staff room, a goldfish magnet in one hand, made me think of who else he might have hurt. Killing animals was a sign of being a psychopath, right? But did ice-shocking a goldfish indicate a red flag in the same way mutilating cats did? Edward's death wasn't long and tortuous, but the emotion behind it felt similar in a way I couldn't quite explain.

Then I felt a sudden . . . *something* . . . inside my body. Something not me. I caught my breath.

The baby. One hand cradled my swelling tummy, and my eyes filled with tears. That was a kick; I was sure of it. "I love you, baby girl," I whispered, having learned the sex at my last appointment.

When families returned from summer break and school started up again, my little girl would be here. That wasn't far away. I looked from the magnet in one hand to my other hand resting on my belly. I needed to protect my baby. I needed to find out more about Rick and then . . . *do* something. I didn't know what yet. But I had a limited amount of time before she'd be here, and I needed to decide what to do about the family she would have. About her father and his place in her life.

I picked up my purse, but before leaving for my car, I stopped at Kathy's desk. "I need to take tomorrow off," I told her.

"Well, good," she said. "You never take vacation time."

I gave a half smile and shrugged. "Can't go on a lot of vacations when your spouse is always preparing the next court case. It'll just be me resting up a bit."

"Well, get yourself a pedicure, at least."

"Deal," I said, though I wasn't sure I'd make good on the promise.

At home, I didn't tell Rick that I'd be taking a day off. As far as he was concerned, I would have a typical workday.

The next morning, I drove to the Harvest Valley city library, as always. Once there, I checked the app Rick insisted I use, supposedly so we could make sure to find each other in case of an accident or other emergency. Today, I needed it to record me as being at work. I didn't go inside the building, but that didn't matter. For the app, the parking lot was close enough.

Once I was sure it registered my location as the library, I turned off my phone's location services. If Rick checked up on me with the app, which he did a few times a month, my last known location would be the library, as expected. He'd have no reason to suspect anything else.

With my ties to GPS severed, I drove to the library in neighboring Red Grove. Along the way, I planned what I'd look up. I also reminded myself why I was doing this, because looking into your husband's past seemed creepy and stalkerish. I had to know who Rick was and who he had been. I needed to understand the wounds and scars he still bore. He was the kind of man who didn't express his feelings, who thought that sharing emotions and being vulnerable meant you were weak and a sissy. If he wouldn't tell me what was behind the Rick Banks I knew, the only way to find out was to find out for myself.

I'd never been to the Red Grove Library. It was much smaller than Harvest Valley's. I didn't think I knew any of the librarians. Even so, I tried to stay inconspicuous while finding a computer to work at. One in the far corner was shielded from view and available. I took it. My heartbeat picked up speed as I pulled a notebook and pen out of my work bag to begin the research I'd intended to do ever since Rick killed Edward.

I'm really doing this. Am I nuts?

I went through the reasons this was important. Rick had lied to me repeatedly about his past—either when he first spoke of it or later, I didn't know. He'd killed the only living thing I'd ever called my own. Most of all, I was still pregnant. We weren't quite at the point that I was legally unable to have an abortion, and until I was, I wouldn't relax on that count. With a simple internet search, Rick could learn the truth and pile the pressure back on. I couldn't wait until we were past the stage where it was legal in any state, so no amount of Rick harping on how I was trying to trap him would help.

A tiny voice told me that I was reading things into the past, that I'd misread what I'd found, and that I should just go home. One thing was for sure: if I stayed, and I learned more—if there was more to learn—I couldn't ever *unknow* it. I was standing at a metaphorical doorway, and though I knew I needed to step across the threshold, taking that first step was proving to be nerve-racking.

The baby kicked again. It reminded me that I had to prepare in every way for her arrival, and that included figuring all of this stuff out. How could I figure out how to be a mother, how to guide a child, when I didn't know my husband at all, or how we got here? That knowledge would come from figuring out my husband and whether our marriage was doomed.

And *that* meant digging to learn who he was.

I put on my librarian science hat and dove into the research as objectively as I could. Determining where to start proved to be harder than expected. No search of Rick's name, in any combination, brought up any useful leads. The only hits were things like his LinkedIn profile and his bio on the law firm's website, with the picture of him that matched all of the other lawyers, all with the same bluish background, taken on the same day, at the same studio.

In a notebook, I wrote out everything I thought I knew about Rick and researched each piece of information. First up was Wagner High School in Del Marita, California to look for any record of him as student there in case I'd missed something before.

Then I searched public records of all kinds, unable to find any indication that Rick had ever lived in California; I already knew he hadn't been born there. I found no driver's license, no property records, no speeding or parking tickets, and nothing on social media. I sat back against the wood chair and stared at the screen, unsure what to do next.

Hire a private investigator?

That would be ideal, but how would I pay for one without Rick finding out? I considered setting up a bank account he wouldn't know about, using Becca's street address so no statements or promotional mailers got sent home that would tip Rick off. I'd have to do that if I wanted to have any kind of money to spend on a private investigator. I could take on one of those MLM side hustles that were mostly excuses to throw parties and get free products. Plenty of wives in the area did this. If I pitched it as a way to make friends rather than money, Rick might not balk at it. After all, I could tell him, so many nights when he worked late were lonely. Hosting little parties might be the perfect thing to cheer up his wife, which would make *his* life happier.

Instead of getting free or discounted stuff, I'd—hopefully—earn money here and there that I could deposit into a new account that Rick wouldn't know about. He controlled the finances and knew to the penny what I earned. I could make up a reason for wanting extra money: I was saving up for a surprise for him, maybe a big trip together.

But eventually, I'd have to come up with the grand gesture of the surprise I'd supposedly been saving up for. I'd also have to tell Becca something about it all, but I could come up with an excuse that she wouldn't press me on.

Shaking my head, I decided to search the other schools that Rick claimed as alma maters. His biography on the law firm's site said that he received his bachelor's degree in political science from UCLA and his law degree from Stanford. Again, California ties.

A quick search turned up phone numbers for both institutions. I looked around the Red Grove Library and found a small hallway where I placed calls to both universities, pretending to be a recruiter looking into references on Rick's resume. I soon had my answers: neither school had any record of him as a student. I'd expected as much, but finding out for certain made my steps heavy as I walked back to the carrel I'd been using.

I felt queasy, and even if it was due to my research, it also had to be related to hunger and pregnancy. I opted to grab a bite to eat, paying with cash so there would be no digital record, then go to another nearby city and use their library. I ate a shake and fries in the car—I could keep those down on an upset stomach *and* drive while eating them—and headed toward Maple Fork, our city library. Being close to home would be smart if I found a research rabbit hole that sucked the rest of the day away.

With my notebook open, I read over everything I'd written. I'd had an idea a couple of hours ago, one I'd put a star by, and now it seemed brilliant: doing a reverse-image search on the one picture I had of Rick as a boy.

I no longer had it on my phone's camera roll, but I'd posted it on Instagram last year for his birthday. I scrolled through my feed to find it. There he was, a young boy wearing a bright-yellow tee, with crooked teeth too big for his mouth and an untamed cowlick. I took a screenshot, emailed the picture to myself, then used a public computer to log on to my inbox and download it.

I set up the image search, but my finger hovered over the mouse button for several seconds; I suddenly didn't have the nerve to click it.

The tattoo seemed to be suddenly burning on the back of my shoulder. I scratched it, took a deep breath, let it out, and then, eyes closed, clicked the button. At first, I thought the results were fruitless, but as I scrolled, I found a newspaper article with a grainy black-and-white picture that looked like the one of Rick as a boy. It wasn't the same picture, but it was strikingly similar, down to the same cowlick and teeth crooked in the same way—canines up high, the front two teeth overlapping.

The article was a scanned newspaper image, so I magnified it enough to read the text. I learned of a tragic boating accident in the middle of the night that claimed the lives of a father and mother. They reportedly had an argument on deck after heavy drinking and had likely fallen overboard, unbeknownst to the two other people on the boat: their ten-year-old son Ryan, and the captain of the yacht. The boy in the picture was identified as Ryan.

Could Ryan be Rick?

The family's name was Brockbank. Ours was Banks. Had he created a new identity, keeping his initials and shortening his last name? Was I reading too much into the similarities?

Based on the article's date, the boy was ten, the same age as Rick was in my picture. The newspaper photo looked just like him.

Was this Ryan Brockbank my husband as a child? Is that how his parents died? Weirdly, the idea wasn't disturbing; on our second date, he'd said that he, too, was an orphan. Maybe *something* he'd told me about himself was true. Changing his name could have been a way to start fresh, leave a tragic past behind.

Biting my lip, I felt an uneasy energy building in my chest, a strange mix of both relief and disappointment at not finding more.

Something deep inside me said that Rick's birth name was Ryan Brockbank.

Did that mean I was really Jennifer Brockbank? That had a nice ring to it. It also sounded like someone else. He married me as Rick Banks. Was our marriage valid? I was being silly. If he changed his name legally, of course it was.

Shaking, I printed off the article, then went on to the next item on my list. I had to keep focused. Who knew when I'd have the time—and courage—to do more research? This might be my last shot for a while. I kept digging, reading everything I could about the boating accident that had killed his parents. Interestingly enough, it happened in southern California. Maybe he *had* grown up there.

Unfortunately, the story hadn't stayed in the papers for long, and a few months afterward, the only mention I found was a tiny update when the toxicology report came back, confirming blood-alcohol levels right in line with the medical examiner's theory of a terrible "drunken row," as he put it, a tragic accident in the middle of the night.

I found nothing about what happened to the boy, Ryan—not that he'd been put into relatives' custody or the state's or anything else. The trail went cold.

The alarm I'd set on my phone went off, yanking me back to the present. Time to head home and get dinner ready—and turn on my phone's location services again.

As I packed up my stuff, I felt a small measure of peace. Rick had been raised in California. He was an orphan. Changing his name would explain why his schools had no record of him. I'd have to check them for Ryan Brockbank, but I suddenly wasn't afraid of what the search would turn up.

Rick had been through a lot. He might have blocked out parts of his past from his memory as a coping device.

If anyone had empathy for trauma, I did. And if anyone could help her husband heal from that kind of trauma, it would be me. I'd spend the rest of my life trying.

CHAPTER SEVENTEEN

BECCA

I order Thai for delivery; I remember Jenn saying how much Rick likes Pad Thai, and I can never get enough of Massaman curry. He said he'll be here in five minutes. He probably will, since they live so close.

No, I correct myself. *Rick* lives nearby. Jenn doesn't live *anywhere* anymore. The reminder twists a knife in my chest. I know she's gone. I saw her body—hell, I *found* it. I'm taking care of her daughter because she can't.

Yet whenever my phone buzzes, I still expect it to be a text from Jenn. The doorbell rings, and for a split second, I wonder if it's Jenn. Even when I'm thinking about her death, I keep thinking she's alive. Of course, it's Rick—I check my phone—arriving fifteen seconds short of the promised five minutes.

I open the door. "Hey there."

"Hey." His eyes are bloodshot, and for the first time in memory, his hair sticks out in several directions, as if he slept on it funny. This is far more disheveled than last time, after his first police interviews. That evening, you could tell he'd done his hair with gel or pomade or whatever and had later mussed it up by raking his fingers through it. Normally, he doesn't have so much as a cowlick untamed. His hair looks . . . *greasy.* Did he even shower today?

Equally unlike him is his clothing: dark blue sweats with a small hole in the left knee, a Dodgers t-shirt, and a pair of beat-up sneakers. He removes the latter at the door when I invite him in and he steps inside. He glances toward the stairs. "Do you think she'll stay asleep?"

"I think so," I say, closing and locking the door behind him. "She sleeps like a baby." I try to muster a smile at my humor attempt.

His clothes mirror my navy pajama bottoms and Lakers shirt. I'm wearing my favorite fuzzy socks—a gift from Jenn. I normally wear socks or slippers around the house, regardless of the season, because my feet get cold on air-conditioned floors. I've been wearing these ones a lot lately because they're one of my last gifts from Jenn. They're pink with purple and white hearts and bright red heels. A bit louder than I'd pick out for myself, but so Jenn. She got them for me on Valentine's Day, which we celebrated as friends every year. Not as "Galentine's Day," but because, according to her, February fourteenth is "friendship day" in some other countries. I've never looked it up, but I'm sure she's right, and we had fun celebrating our friendship each year.

I wash them as little as I can get away with; I don't want to lose whatever "Jenn" essence remains on them. As often as I wear them, they'll have holes soon. I may need to learn how to darn socks.

"The food should be here soon," I say, heading toward the stairs and the family room, gesturing for him to follow. "I ordered Thai." I plop onto one side of the cozy chocolate-brown couch and pick up two remotes. "Live TV or streaming?" I ask, holding up one remote for each. "Netflix? Hulu? Amazon?" I rock the remotes back and forth, waiting for him to decide.

He looks overwhelmed at making even that small of a decision. He shrugs and sits on the center cushion of the couch, right next to me. As in *right* next to me. At his sudden closeness, my hands freeze midair. I've never been one for needing a large personal bubble, but I've also never spent time on a couch with Rick, ever. Aside from two hugs the day Jenn died, I'm not sure I've ever had physical contact with him until now.

He means exactly nothing by it, I tell myself. *He's here as a friend because you asked him to come, knowing he's going through a rough time. Be his friend. It'll help me too. We're both grieving.*

Rick sighs. "I don't know what I want to watch." His tone sounds strangely flat, something I totally understand—the world has less color to me too.

I vaguely remember her mentioning that he's preparing to take a case to trial, but that happened a lot. Is he still working on the same case Jenn talked about a couple of months ago? A different one? A few times a year, he works extra-long hours, and Jenn had many evenings alone while he stayed to work late at the office, so she came over a lot. Judging by Maggie's and Davis's reactions to seeing her several nights a week, you would have thought Jenn was Santa.

Jenn hated the lead-up to trial and all the work that entailed. Cases tend to settle out of court, but, like a corporate game of chicken, never until the last minute. Both sides have to be ready for court, just in case. Jenn was a law widow those weeks—part of being the wife of a lawyer. She also knew how much the firm didn't get how hard those realities were on families, but by golly, they wanted their lawyers to be family men.

Everyone knew—and Donaldson himself hinted vaguely at it—that only the men with families, defined as a wife *and* kids, would ever make partner. Bonus points for a wife who stayed at home before having babies. A wife who worked a minor job—like Jenn's at the library—might be okay, but a wife with an important career? Deal-breaker.

On more than one occasion, I wondered aloud to Jenn whether Rick's firm was in a wormhole that led to the 1960s.

Jenn understood all too well that long hours and heavy work were the only way for Rick to make partner, but knowing didn't make long stretches of late nights easier. I got the sense that Rick found her loneliness annoying. I'd always figured he was clueless, a bit egotistical, but not mean.

Whatever the truth was then, he and I are absolutely on the same page now, mourning Jenn's death.

I need to ask about whether he'll be getting time off soon—the firm has to have a good bereavement policy—and what his plans are for Ivy. Is he here tonight because he's taken that time off? Because the case settled? Doesn't matter. I'll simply have to watch for an opening to bring up Ivy's care and everything else that's up in the air.

As we sit side by side on the couch in nearly matching outfits, the awkward silence gets to be too much. Have the two of us ever been alone for longer than it took Jenn to use the bathroom? If so, I can't remember it. I decide to break the silence. If Rick wants to talk, I'll do my best to listen. But if I don't find a way to lighten the mood, I'll lose my mind.

"Hmm." I tap the remote on my chin in thought. "Pretty sure I have at least five episodes of *Dr. Phil* saved up."

Rick's eyes widen in what can only be dismay mixed with worry over offending me.

"Kidding!" I add, then laugh to assure him that I *am* kidding.

I lean back into the corner of the couch, very aware of the heat and slight pressure of Rick's leg against the entire length of my thigh. Our arms rest against each other. He's never acted this . . . *friendly* around me. Maybe because sitting this close to any woman would have been inappropriate when Jenn was still around.

Wait, does that mean this is different? I can't deny that his physical closeness, the scent of his cologne, and, yes, his total vulnerability, feel nice, comfortable. And *that* feels equal parts strange and alarming.

He rests an arm on the back of the couch. It's sort of touching my shoulders. Is he sitting like that to be comfortable, or is he signaling something more? I want to scoot away, but there's nowhere to go unless I make an obvious move and leave the couch altogether.

This is Rick, I remind myself. *He may be a small personal bubble person. He's probably unsure how to handle Jenn's death. Don't jump to conclusions.*

"I know just the show," I say hurriedly, eager to get my brain to shut up. "Okay."

I bring up YouTube and search for a channel that Davis and Maggie are currently obsessed with. The videos are made by a twenty-something kid who illustrates and talks about funny stuff, usually stories from his childhood. I've found myself laughing more than once right along with the twins as they watch new videos and rewatch their favorites. Sometimes at night, I secretly watch the channel by myself, especially when I'm stressed out and can't sleep. Once, I laughed so hard that it turned into racking sobs. An amazingly effective catharsis.

"What's this?" Rick asks, nodding toward the TV and the young man addressing the audience.

"Watch and see," I say, glancing at him.

Something weird occurs to me: he's been crying, and his eyes are blood-shot, which means he probably isn't wearing contacts because those hurt in already irritated eyes. But he's not wearing glasses either. Jenn mentioned his plans for Lasik when he had the time because he has really bad eyesight without lenses. Did he drive over without glasses *or* contacts? Or did he recently have laser surgery that Jenn didn't mention?

He slouches into the couch, which lowers his arm more onto my shoulders and makes him lean against me slightly. Within a few minutes, I find my head easing into the hollow between his shoulder and his chest as if we've watched shows together a thousand times.

Having a human—an adult—this close makes me realize how much I've missed physical contact that isn't kids pulling me in a hundred directions. I've missed touch. Nothing sexual, just *contact*. I relax more, but as I lean toward him, I smell a subtle hint of alcohol on his breath. He doesn't seem buzzed. Did he drink a little before coming over? Or was it hours ago and the smell's still lingering?

Quite possibly, he drove here after drinking, without lenses. I can't help hearing Dr. Phil chastising Rick in my head, the same outrage he's expressed to dozens of guests on his stage: *Who gave you the right to drive a two-thousand-pound missile on the streets where others' loved ones walk and live?*

I take a deep breath in an attempt to get rid of the thoughts, but that only makes it worse, because I inhale more of the alcohol smell—something stronger than beer. A second video begins on the channel, the first having failed to elicit much of a reaction from Rick. During this one, he chuckles. I take it as a win.

When the food arrives, I pause the video and hurry to the door, returning a moment later to the couch. We divvy up the food and dive in while talking, not needing the distraction of the television for the moment. Very quickly, the conversation moves to Jenn, but in a good way. We share memories and laugh and cry. I retrieve a tissue box from the kitchen counter and offer it to him. He waves it off. He looks miserable, but he must be cried out. When he talks, he still sounds like he's crying, but there aren't tears anymore. Meanwhile, I blow my nose and sound like the trumpet section of a marching band.

"Did you know that Jenn could wiggle her ears?" Rick asks.

I put the tissue box on the side table by the couch. "No way," I say. "I don't suppose you have that on video."

"Unfortunately, no."

"I bet you loved watching her paint. She used to sketch ideas for me to take to work and pitch to companies to show my advertising ideas, but that was the tip of the iceberg. I told her she should illustrate children's books or something—she had some serious talent."

"She didn't like being watched when she drew, so I didn't see much," Rick says with a shrug. "I don't know if she was afraid of her work being judged before it was ready or what. Of course, I didn't expect perfection with every stroke, but she still refused to draw if I was even in the room. She never let me see what she was working on until it was finished."

I nod, picking at the carrots in my Massaman, but I don't relate. I saw Jenn's art unfold on paper and canvas lots of times. Sometimes I sat directly next to her, and she knew I was looking over her shoulder. She often asked my opinion should she add more shading here? Did the proportions look off there? She never believed in her talent, no matter how much I praised her. Now that I thought about it, she'd done a lot less art since marrying Rick. When was the last time I saw her so much as doodling? I can't remember.

People change when they get married. Jason sure did. Honestly, I changed too. Neither of us divorced the spouse we married. The possibility that Jenn had let her art die after the wedding makes me sad, and more so that I didn't notice.

When we're done eating, I start gathering empty takeout containers. Rick pipes up. "Thanks for dinner. I haven't been eating well lately. That was my first real meal in a few days."

Holding containers in each hand, I pause and smile at him. "Glad I opted for more than hot cocoa, then."

"Can I still take you up on the cocoa?" He smiles back, looking almost like himself again, a little less miserable. A little spark of something appears in my chest—not happiness, precisely, but a lightness. A warmth. I helped him tonight. I lifted his burden for a moment.

"Mexican hot chocolate coming right up."

"Here," he says, standing and reaching out to take the containers from me. "I'll clean this up while you make the cocoa. I'd offer to make it, but I have a feeling I'd screw it up."

"Oh, it's incredibly difficult," I say with a grin. "Heating milk in a saucepan and melting chocolate into it. Brutal stuff."

We head to the kitchen together. As the chocolate and a bit of water melt in a saucepan, I stir it, and we talk more about Jenn. I tell him about the P!nk concert we went to a couple of years ago and how amazing it was. He tells me about how they met and how he asked her out. I've heard the story from her, but his version has details Jenn's didn't.

I pour the hot cocoa into two big mugs, spike them with drops of almond extract, and top each with a squirt of whipped cream, followed by shavings of chocolate. I push Rick's mug across the counter to him. It's black and reads *Literally the Best*, a reference to *Parks and Recreation*.

He rotates the mug, admiring the contents. "I *really* would have screwed it up. This is almost too pretty to drink."

"You'd better," I say, walking past him with my mug. "That's the whole point. And hurry; the whipped cream will melt, ruining the whole effect."

"Your wish is my command." He hops off his stool and follows me to the kitchen table.

That's when I pull out my phone and pull up some notes about the case. "So," I begin, "did they ask you if you'd seen a white van?"

My question takes him off guard. He considers it and then, eyes widening, he nods. "They did. Driving around suspiciously in the neighborhood? They did, and yeah, I saw it."

"I did too," I say, excited. "Not on your street, but mine. And look." I pull up the city's Facebook page and scroll a bit. "Two houses on this end of the city were broken into the day before she died. One of them was right around the corner from you."

Rick's sitting straighter and looking more alive than I've seen him since this all began. "Do you think this could be a botched home invasion? I wonder if anyone has security camera footage." He shakes his head. "Getting cameras was always on my to-do list. Never got around to it."

I show him the posts on the city page. One is from a father sure that his kid was nearly abducted by a man in the white van. Another post, this one on the Maple Fork PD page, mentions sightings of the white van and includes a description of the driver, which sounds like about seventy percent of men in town: white, around six feet, twenty to forty-five years old. Wearing a baseball cap, so no info on hair color. The post ends with a reminder to keep your doors locked, especially after dark. A lot of good that advice would have done to prevent Jenn's death.

I get a notebook from the cupboard and imagine turning on Jenn's library science mindset. "Let's come up with ideas for where the authorities could look and ways to clear your name."

There have been too many sightings of the white van to all be connected to the same vehicle and driver, and the variety of crimes don't fit one perpetrator. Chances are good that people have jumped to conclusions with some of the sightings, so I'm hopeful that the van could turn up to be useful in solving this, somehow.

"Okay, so the van isn't giving us much yet. What about your alibi? Can anyone at the firm vouch for your meeting that morning?"

"Unfortunately, no," Rick says. He sighs. "I'd officially taken the day off, so I slipped in the back door to have the meeting over Zoom. No one saw me."

"But the client can vouch for what your office looked like," I say.

"They could if I didn't have a green-screen image of it that I've used at home in a pinch so it looks like I'm there. Before the baby, of course. It's impossible to do now. I used my laptop, which has a VPN, so I can't even use an IP address to prove I wasn't home."

I make a few notes and rack my brain. "What about the timing? Let's set aside proving that you were in the building that day for a minute. What time was the meeting? If it overlapped the time the ME says she died, then you couldn't have done it, right?"

"I doubt that'll make much difference. The initial estimated window for the time of death was a couple of hours."

"Humor me," I say.

"Fine. I left the house at eight-thirty. Meeting was nine to about ten. Then I left the building and went to the store for some last-minute trip supplies. Got home late because a semitruck jackknifed and had a spill on the freeway."

I'm making notes of everything he says. He pauses, so I look up. There's a glimmer of something in his eyes. "Did you figure something out?" I ask.

"If I'd come home on time, I would've found Jenn." He shook his head, staring over my shoulder into the distance. "Damn. So glad I didn't."

Great. Thanks, dude. I *did* find her body, and it was traumatic. Does he hear himself—or remember who he's talking to?

"Yeah," I say. "I guess you would have."

"Maybe pointing that out could help take the focus off me," he says, looking at me again. The energy I saw before is building in his face.

"How do you mean?" I'm not sure I want to know.

"Isn't the person who found the body the most likely to be the guilty party?"

I gape at him, saying nothing, only blinking in shock.

"Oh wait," he says, waving his hands as if brushing away his last words. "I didn't mean *you* did it or that they should suspect you or anything." He laughs and shakes his head. "I meant that since I obviously wasn't there—you and a bunch of cops and EMTs can testify to that—then it's pretty unlikely I did it, right?"

"I don't know. . . ." My voice trails off as I return to scribbling in my notebook as fast as I can. My writing is illegible, and I'm not making sense on the page anyway. I keep writing as a way to not look at Rick right now. The last few minutes have given me the creeps. If I look focused on my notes, maybe he won't sense my unease. Suddenly, his not-quite-inappropriate-and-not-really-touching touchiness from earlier unsettles me.

"Okay, we have the white van with a Caucasian male at the wheel," I say. "Not much there, but we can keep looking." I point to another part of my notes. "We should look into aspects of your alibi—did you have your smart watch on you? That would tell us where you were."

"Couldn't find it that morning. It was at home. And before you ask, my car's GPS is busted. I haven't gotten around to getting it fixed at the dealership. And no, I didn't use an app on my phone for traffic. I had my phone on airplane mode so anyone trying to reach me at work would go straight to voicemail—and I wouldn't see any notifications, which means I wouldn't be tempted to look at messages and reply to them."

"Oh. That's pretty smart, though it makes an alibi trickier," I say. "There were news reports of the spill on the freeway, I assume, so we can prove that timing, right?"

"I guess so." Rick shrugs both shoulders. "I haven't exactly been watching the news lately."

Touché.

"We need to dig into Jenn's phone and email," Rick says. He reaches across the table and taps a finger on my notebook. "Write that down."

I nod and start writing.

"See if she was in contact with anyone suspicious," he continues.

My pen slows, and my head comes up. "Like who?"

He raises a hand palm up. "Oh, I don't know. Maybe someone was blackmailing her."

"Over what?" I say with a laugh.

"Maybe she was having an affair and wanted to run away with some guy."

I almost laugh again, but he's serious. I set the pen down and level a stare at him. "No way can you think she was cheating on you. You know Jenn."

Rick looks at the table for several seconds before meeting my gaze. "I thought I did. But who knows? Maybe I didn't know her like I thought I did."

I reach across the table and touch his hand. "*I* know that she wasn't cheating on you. I know that as clearly as I know you're sitting in my kitchen. She would *never* have done that to you."

He gives a single-shoulder shrug. "Write it down anyway. We're brainstorming all ideas, no matter how outlandish, right?"

I didn't bother telling him that the old theory of brainstorming had been proven to be full of shit. Instead, I sigh and reluctantly write down his crazy suggestions so we can move on. "Done. Now let's think deeper—what about social media accounts and messaging? Maybe she had a stalker."

That brings him around and opens his mind enough to think of other options, and the unease fades as we join forces to come up with possible leads. Our animated discussion gradually slows as we fade with fatigue.

We settle into silence, and that's when the emotion hits again. My eyes burn. A tear drops onto the tablecloth and spreads through the fibers. I press a finger against that spot. "I'd give anything to be able to hug her one last time."

This time, Rick reaches across the table and rests a hand over mine. In a tender tone, he says, "Me too, Becca. Me too."

His touch is heavy, and I want to pull away, but I don't dare. His gaze has a weight that holds me in place. "Tell me," he says, "what did you and Becca talk about? I mean, about us. Her and me. Our marriage and stuff." He's trying to sound light and casual, but a dark undercurrent of accusation comes through anyway.

"Honestly, she rarely talked about it. She always said it wasn't appropriate to discuss a marriage outside of it." It's my turn to shrug. "So I only heard about restaurants, movies, parties at the firm, and stuff like that."

"Huh," Rick says. "That surprises me."

"Well, it's the truth," I say, and now I do slip my hand out from under his, free at last. Suddenly, I understand Jenn a bit better than I ever have. She had very good reasons to not confide in me about her husband. I never thought I'd be grateful for that, but right now, as he's staring at me in a way that I swear he can read my soul, I'm glad that my words are the truth: she didn't tell me much of anything about their marriage.

And my guesses? They weren't accurate.

If that darkness in Rick's affect was any indication, her life was far worse than I ever suspected.

CHAPTER EIGHTEEN

JENN

May 2
10½ Months before Drowning

Rick and I went on with our lives, one day at a time as if nothing had changed, though for me, after learning what little I had about his parents' deaths, everything had. My efforts at being extra supportive and loving seemed to be paying off in some respects; Rick wasn't as irritable of late, and he even brought me a half pound of my favorite chocolates the other day, just because.

As pregnancy brain fog grew, I tried to throw myself into every bit of my job, but focusing for long stretches became hard. I kept forgetting things, like giving Emily the smartpen. I kept it in my purse, and it stayed there for weeks. I wondered if it would be particularly useful now, with the end of the school year so close, and decided to hold on to it. I'd give it to her at the end of the summer before the new school year. That might be even better because it would give me time to learn its features so I could teach her all about it.

Between the pen and a blizzard of sticky notes I'd posted all over the library workstation, inside my car, on the fridge, and everywhere else, I began to get a handle on things again. The chocolate helped too, as did the night after he gave them to me—I had my husband back for a bit, and I hoped he'd stick around.

The biggest thing that helped my anxiety, though, was passing the legal abortion cutoff date that morning—in any state. I hadn't realized just how tense I'd been, how much I'd been watching the calendar. Not until I woke up, remembered the date, and sobbed silently into my pillow with relief. I no longer had to be strong. No longer had to worry that Rick would find out that the nurse practitioner had lied to him. No longer had to worry about pushing back against Rick's pressure to end the pregnancy. Now the law wouldn't *let* me give in, and no doctor would either. My baby was safe.

I got out of bed feeling lighter, as if a weight had been lifted from my shoulders. I got ready for work with a brighter step and happier tone, something Rick picked up on. He was *not* a morning person, but my cheerful mood that day caught his attention. He grabbed me as I walked to the bedroom door and pulled me in for a long kiss.

"What was that for?" I asked.

"Just because. You're extra sexy today, I guess."

I wasn't dressed or wearing makeup or anything, so the only thing I could chalk it up to was my mood. "Good thing I brushed my teeth already, then." I giggled and then kissed him again. He held me close, and for a minute, I remembered all of the reasons I fell for this man. His humor. His spontaneity. The warmth and utter safety I felt wrapped in his arms.

"I don't want to go to work," he murmured into my hair.

"I could stay like this forever," I said, relishing the embrace.

"I love you, Jenn Banks," Rick said. He leaned in, kissed me soundly, and we found our way back to the bed.

Afterward, he rested his hand over my growing belly. "You know, this little guy might be good for us."

"Oh?" I said, hoping my surprise and delight weren't too much. He was in a good mood, so I didn't point out that it was a girl.

"Donaldson always wants partners who are family men. Right now, it's a race between me and Gordon Hayward as to who will make partner first. He's married, but he's not a father." Rick grinned. "*I* will be."

We were both late to work, but neither of us cared. Kathy didn't mind too much when I showed up half an hour late, but I made it up to her. She was *very* happy with how productive I was that day. I was able to get a ton of books cataloged that had been waiting for over a week.

Some of my work was repetitive enough that my mind wandered back to Rick—the man who'd brought me chocolate and had consumed me that morning with his love. Twice.

I thought of the little boy he'd been—Ryan Brockbank—and how scared he must have been to wake up on that yacht without his parents anywhere to be seen. Unresolved trauma can linger throughout an entire life. I knew that well.

Maybe I could help him heal from some of the dark spots of his past so that the Rick of that morning would be the husband I always knew he could be, the man I always saw and believed in.

I was entering a new set of young adult books into the computer when muffled voices sounded behind me—a recording, maybe. I turned around to find Tim with earbuds in, listening, no doubt, to one of his dozens of podcasts. I waved him over, knowing that if he was going to hear me, I'd have to practically yell—not ideal for a library.

He pulled one of the wireless earbuds out. "Yeah?"

"Turn that down," I said. "I can hear it from way over here."

"You're five feet from me."

"This is a library," I countered. "But I shouldn't ever be able to hear anything from earbuds this far away. You're going to lose your hearing."

"Fine, *Mom*," he said with an exaggerated roll of his eyes that made me laugh. He turned the volume down. "Don't blame me when I miss out on becoming the next top FBI profiler because you wouldn't let me listen to my true-crime podcasts."

I laughed. "I'll keep that in mind."

We lapsed into silence, and I finished the backlog of cataloging books. I kept thinking of ten-year-old Rick and wanting to find out more.

"Do you think Kathy would mind if I left early?" I asked Tim.

He pulled out an earbud. "On the day you showed up late?"

I stared him down as if he were my little brother.

"I'm sure she'd be fine with it."

I looked around the library, making sure I could justify leaving. The place was pretty dead and would probably stay that way; this wasn't a time of the school year when kids were still doing research papers. It was standardized testing season. I'd already done story time for the little kids. We weren't swamped by new releases, and I'd just finished the backlog.

After finding Kathy in the back room with her lunch, I gave her the report, and she told me to clock out. "Go get that pedicure you didn't get last time you took the day off."

"No promises," I said, grabbing my purse from the hook by a file cabinet and waving as I left.

I drove to the Red Grove Library again, and after a quick detour to the restroom—pregnancy bladder was as real as pregnancy brain—I settled into a workstation in a quiet corner in the basement of the library. The spot had little foot traffic, which made me feel safer, somehow.

I withdrew the notebook from my bag that I jokingly always called my "brain," which contained everything from calendar items and to-do lists to phone numbers. I wrote down some of the questions that had been tickling my brain all day about Rick.

Where to begin my search today? The one successful thing from my last time here was the image search of Rick's childhood photo. I decided to do a similar search using his headshot from the firm's website. I didn't have much hope that it would turn up anything, but it would be one more thing to check off the list. I ran the search as if I were doing it for a patron.

The search engine spat out several hits of men that looked like Rick in general terms, but they were all too grainy or blurry for me to know for sure if any were Rick. I clicked to various sources, feeling like an archaeologist uncovering a tiny hint of a bone under a rock, as if I were slowly excavating to find Rick's past. I didn't know what chain of links I clicked on to get there, but suddenly, I was staring at a face that *was* most definitely Rick—but *not* the Rick I knew.

This was a mugshot from Washington state of a man named Ryan Brockbank. He looked slightly younger than the man I knew, but that was definitely the same face, including the light scar cutting through one eyebrow—what he'd told me was the remnant of a childhood fall from a bike. He had the same scar, which confirmed that the boy who'd lost his parents had grown up, changed his name, and become my husband.

The mugshot showed two tiny moles on his nose, which Rick hated, and his uneven eyebrows—a unique feature that had drawn me to him. They made him look quirky in a handsome way.

I blinked, reminding myself to read and learn. I wasn't here to stare at a mugshot. I read on, doing additional searches to fill out the picture that was slowly forming of Rick's not-so-distant past.

Ryan Brockbank had been arrested on charges of second-degree murder in the drowning death of his wife, Chloe, in the bathtub.

For a moment, I couldn't breathe. I knew he was widowed. I knew his late wife's name. He'd always said Chloe had died in tragic circumstances, an accident he didn't want to talk about.

But this . . .

When I could breathe again, I kept digging.

I found several state-level papers reporting on the death. With each account, I kept coming back to two details circled in my mind like ships caught in a whirlpool: first, Chloe had died by drowning, just as Rick's parents had. And second, when he was married to her, he was still Ryan Brockbank. My first assumption was wrong: he hadn't changed his name to leave his childhood behind.

In the mugshot after he'd been arrested for Chloe's murder, he had some scruff, as if he hadn't shaved for a few days. His eyes were bloodshot, and his hair was greasy and stuck out in several directions. His shirt was obviously a Tom Ford, the expensive brand he'd worn as long as I'd known him. For once, the shirt wasn't starched and perfectly flat but dirty and rumpled.

For the next two hours, I read everything about the case that I could get my hands on. A husband arrested for his wife's murder piqued public interest more than the accidental death of a set of parents did.

News clips, TV interviews, newspaper articles, court proceedings—videos in some cases, transcripts in others—took up my day. I found several blogs devoted to the case, two insisting he was guilty, another that he was innocent. I found podcasts analyzing the case, playing armchair detective and armchair psychiatrist—and a couple of former FBI profilers putting in their two cents. Everyone had an opinion, and each time I thought I'd decided on mine, something made me reconsider.

The Pacific Northwest seemed to have been in a bit of a local frenzy for a year and a half after Chloe Brockbanks's death, as the media followed the arrest and trial.

The case ended in a mistrial. Ryan Brockbank was allowed to go home, pending new charges being filed. But he vanished. At least, I couldn't find anything else about him after the mistrial.

I had eighteen months of material to go through. I drafted myself an email where I could drop all of the many links I was collecting. Before I sent the message, I changed my password, but I hesitated even then. Rick could still find a way to see my inbox. If he was already checking it periodically, he'd see all of my research, and I wouldn't have a chance to explain that I'd dug up the past to try to help him heal.

Instead of emailing myself the links right then, I created a new email address on a different platform, then used it to send myself about a hundred links. After a quick check of the clock, I printed out a bunch of articles so I could mark up the hard copies. I'd just need to hide them somewhere. Good thing I had a couple of twenties in my purse. As I paid for them, I made a mental note to get some extra cash the next time I went to the grocery store.

Another phone check said I was cutting it close on time; I'd need to head back soon.

On a blank sheet in my notebook, I quickly made a list of the open tabs so I could return to them when I had the opportunity.

I was about to log off when one last article, published about six months after the mistrial, caught my eye. Rick had been released on bail while awaiting a new trial. I read on.

Detective Keith Jensen called giving Brockbank bail a mistake, saying, "He was a clear flight risk. Brockbank appears to have gone into hiding. We may not get another chance to give Chloe Brockbank justice."

Rod Andreason, county DA, agreed, saying, "Brockbank fled because he was guilty of his wife's murder, and if we can't find him, we can't try him again. He knows that in a second trial, he'd be found guilty."

Harrison Martin, Brockbank's defense attorney, insists his client is innocent and simply needs to recover emotionally after the harrowing ordeal of going on trial for a murder he did not commit. Martin added, "Who can blame him for retreating from the public eye for a bit?"

Both sides had valid points. I was more confused than ever.

My phone buzzed with a text from Becca. I opened it to find a meme she'd found somewhere about pregnancy bladders being microscopic. Normally, I would have laughed, but right then, I couldn't. All I could think of was that Rick had been on trial for Chloe's murder.

He didn't lie when he said her death was traumatic for him, but if he didn't tell me that he'd been on *trial* for her death, had run while on bail, and then changed his name, what else hadn't he told me?

A bell sounded over the library PA, noting the hour: five o'clock.

Shit.

Getting home on time was paramount, but I couldn't risk bringing any of this material under the same roof as Rick. Ryan. Whoever.

After closing my searches on the computer, I packed up my notebook and the photocopies and headed for my car, trying to find a solution about where to hide the notebook and papers. To be sure Becca wouldn't think anything was wrong, I quickly replied to her meme with a pair of emojis to show that I thought the meme was as hilarious as she did.

While driving, I considered stopping by Becca's on my way to drop off the papers. No. She'd ask questions that I couldn't answer yet, and I didn't want to put her in Rick's crosshairs either.

Approaching a traffic light, I spotted the gym. I had a membership, which I used a few times a week. And inside, I had a locker with a combination lock. Rick wouldn't stumble across my papers there. If he thought I was hiding something, he wouldn't know to go there, and he wouldn't be able to get in if he tried.

I swung into the gym parking lot. I checked in at the desk where a teen girl was working. She gave me an odd look, likely because I wasn't dressed for a workout. I threw her a smile and headed to the women's locker room.

My hands shook so much that opening the lock took three tries. I had to get home, and soon. As the lock opened, I realized I hadn't turned off my phone's location services before driving to Red Grove. My heart stopped. What if Rick had checked on me during the day and I wasn't at work?

If he confronted me, I'd make up some excuse about why I, a librarian, needed to visit a neighboring library. I could find a reason that would make sense. Tonight wasn't the time to tell him that I knew about how Chloe had died.

I yanked the locker door open and shoved the photocopies and note-book inside. I slipped the lock on and clicked it back into place. Job done, I wanted to drop to the bench and catch my breath, but I didn't have that luxury. Rick would be home in about ten minutes. I was at least seven minutes from home, and I'd need to come up with a dinner I could throw together fast so it would look like I'd been home longer than that.

I practically ran to my car. By the time I had my seat belt buckled—something that took three tries as well—I knew I'd never be able to come up with a fast dinner Rick wouldn't think was beneath him. Instead, I drove across the large parking lot to the chain grocery store. I bought a rotisserie chicken, salad fixings, and something from the bakery for dessert.

By some miracle, Rick was fifteen minutes late, which meant I got home before he did—barely—and he didn't ask questions. Over dinner, I did my best to thrust everything about my day out of my head.

He didn't ask any questions, and the morning's good mood seemed to have lasted. Not until I lay awake in the dark did I confront what I'd learned.

What did it mean to be married to a man living under an assumed name?

Did Chloe die in a terrible accident? The articles made a point of saying that cocaine and meth were in her system. Had she accidentally overdosed?

Or was Rick guilty of killing her as the prosecutors claimed?

I thought of a blog post that declared Rick's innocence. The writer's impassioned words insisted that the broken man they'd seen in the courtroom could not be a murderer. Besides, the only evidence had been circumstantial. Rick, the author declared, did not commit this crime. He was entirely innocent.

Innocent. The word repeated in my head. Could it be true? If so, Rick was still guilty of hiding so much from me, of *living* a lie with me. The betrayal cut deep.

In the darkness, I broke down and cried. My body shook with a bizarre kaleidoscope of emotions. I couldn't point to one thing I was crying about. In a way, I was relieved that Rick wasn't convicted of killing his first wife, but he wasn't exonerated either. I was devastated that Chloe's death wasn't a car accident or some other easily explained, if tragic, event. I felt deceived and abandoned. I didn't even know my husband's real name or that he'd changed it.

Worst of all, I was afraid that he got off after actually killing Chloe.

I put my hands over my face to muffle any sound as I slipped out of bed and hurried downstairs so my crying wouldn't wake him. Slumped on the couch, I sobbed. My shoulders heaved, but I kept my mouth over my forearm to keep the sound from carrying to our bedroom.

I was so . . . scared. About many things, including the future. I was afraid about what all of this meant for our marriage. For our baby. I was scared to tell him what I knew. Yet how could I keep all of this to myself?

Was it only that morning that we'd been happy again? That'd he'd desired me and said he loved me? Was it only a few hours ago that I learned how Chloe had died?

I couldn't keep going along as if things were normal. I couldn't pretend that I didn't know the things sending a web of cracks through the foundation under my feet.

That would be living a lie too, and I refused to do that.

CHAPTER NINETEEN

BECCA

It's been a week since I gave Detective Andrus the list of leads that Rick and I came up with. It's also been a week of waiting to hear back from him beyond his initial acknowledgment that he'd gotten it.

Rick hasn't been able to figure out Jenn's social media or email passwords, but her phone and laptop are with the police, ostensibly so they can try to get into them. My hopes are on the mysterious white van, but my voicemails to Andrus haven't been returned.

I have to wait, which meant attempting to return life to relative normalcy—at least as normal as it can be when you're giving full-time care to the baby of your best friend who was murdered, and you jump every time your phone buzzes because you hope it's a detective with an update.

The twins are off traveling to various amusement parks in California with their dad. They'll be gone for the next two weeks, and only one of those weeks is spring break. They'll have to make up a lot of schoolwork when they get back, but it's not as if Jason will have to deal with that. That'll be my job after he has fun with the kids.

I hate having them gone, but under the circumstances, it's also a relief. Talk about a paradox of emotion. Ivy is in daycare while I'm at work, though I'm working from home as often as possible—right now, two days a week—and doing Zoom calls for meetings when I can. She's adjusting well—another bittersweet thing. On one hand, I'm so glad she's not showing signs of anxiety and fear. She's sleeping through the night, eating well, and seems as happy as a typical almost seven-month-old.

Even so, I can't help but wonder if her adjustment means she's forgetting Jenn already. How long does a baby remember anything or anyone, including a mother who vanished from her life one day?

Ever since our Thai food and hot cocoa night, Rick and I have been in close contact. We text multiple times a day, call at least once with updates, and sometimes he comes over for dinner—as much to see a friend as to see Ivy, I'm sure. A few days ago, I finally got an answer out of him about her, not one with a clear timeline or period at the end, but something. I can plan on having Ivy with me indefinitely, until Rick's no longer a person of interest and this whole thing is resolved.

As of last night, when we had takeout at my place, the detectives had told Rick that they were waiting on the toxicology report.

"Should be back any day now," he told me. When I expressed surprise, he clarified. Our little valley and its surrounding areas didn't have too many suspicious deaths, so the labs were able to get the results faster than most.

As I sit in a meeting at work, I can't focus on the advertising campaign my team is working on. My thoughts keep drifting back to when we'll be able to have a memorial. Life feels chaotic, as if I'm floundering in the wind like a tarp flapping, about to fly away. I need something to tie me back to Earth, back to normalcy. A memorial won't provide closure, but maybe it'll tie down one corner of that tarp.

Toxicology is the last thing we're waiting on before they'll release her body. Apparently, holding funerals before test results were returned used to be common, but after another case in a neighboring state that ended up requiring the family to exhume the body, Detective Andrus insisted on waiting to be on the safe side.

"Rebecca?"

I snap back to the moment. "Sorry. I was waiting for a message." I put my phone on the table face down so I won't be tempted to look at it. "You were saying?"

My team is brainstorming campaign ideas for Alcestis Dresses, our newest client. The company was named after a character from Greek mythology who offered to die so her husband could return from the underworld. Then Hercules rescued her from death after all, allowing her to remain with her husband.

Too bad we didn't all have a Hercules to show up and keep loved ones from dying.

I sit up straighter and nudge my chair closer to the table to get my attention back to the meeting. This time, I'm determined to focus, and somehow, I manage to. Maybe it's the graphics my team has come up with. Maybe it's the jolt of caffeine in the cup Tim slid over to me. Whatever the reason, for the first time since Jenn's death, I find myself in the zone. I'm energized as we sit around the table, thinking of new angles for the campaign. Winning the Alcestis account was a huge coup; we wooed them away from our biggest competitor. Their account alone will guarantee a nice bonus at the end of the quarter for me, and bonuses for my whole team as well. If we can nail this upcoming campaign, this will be a very good year for us.

Pete, our social media expert, is pumped, and he's talking so fast that soon I give up on trying to take notes and just listen, taking pictures on my phone of the whiteboard instead. He has better handwriting than I do anyway; I'll be able to read his scribbles easier than my notes.

"Okay, so that's the idea for Instagram," Pete says, drawing double lines under one section of the board. "And we can apply a lot of the same ideas to Facebook, seeing as they're integrated and have the same algorithms. I have some ideas for Twitter, though based on the sales data, more of the company's base is on Instagram and Facebook. So for Twitter . . ."

He swaps his red marker for a blue one and writes *Twitter,* then circles the word. Before he can dive into his ideas, the door opens and Mark pops his head in, looking around. I assume he's searching for me, so I wave.

"Over here," I say, then nod toward the whiteboard. "Check it out. Pete's telling us how we'll sell ten million in product for Alcestis Dresses."

"Get this," Melinda says, piping with excitement. "All of their dresses have pockets." She sits back and nods as if waiting for expressions of awe. Mark doesn't get it, but the women in the room murmur their approval.

"You have no idea what a huge selling point that is," I say. Then to Mark, I add, "If I didn't already know that Alcestis was founded by a woman, that fact alone would tell me."

He doesn't laugh or even smile. The room quiets as if a pall has landed over it. We're all staring at Mark, waiting for whatever it is he came to say. It had better be important if he interrupted this meeting to say it. Mark looks pale and serious.

"What is it?" I ask. All thoughts of social media and dresses with pockets have fled my mind, and in their place, I feel a nervous dread. Is the company going under? Are we all getting laid off?

"Turn on the TV." Mark gestures toward the flat-screen that's mounted in the corner.

Pete grabs the remote. "What channel?" he asks as he turns on the TV and navigates to live programming. We soon realize that the channel doesn't matter; all of the networks are covering breaking local news.

A female reporter is speaking to the camera in front of a polished stone building. "I'll step aside so the camera can zoom in on the door and we can see what's happening," she says. "They should be exiting at any moment."

The camera moves to the side and zooms in to show the door leading into the building, all glass and chrome. Beside the door, gold-filled text is engraved into the side of the building: *Hancock, Donaldson, and Cleese, Attorneys at Law.*

That's Rick's firm, I'm almost positive. A hundred questions push from inside me, trying to get out. I fight the urge to vocalize them, but I watch and wait.

The camera is still focused on the door, but nothing is happening. The journalist's voice returns.

"For those just joining us, we're watching a live shot of what should shortly be the arrest of Rick Banks for the murder of his wife, Jennifer Banks, whose body was found in the couple's bathtub last month."

My jaw drops. Hardly able to breathe, I walk around the table to get closer to the television, not wanting to miss a frame. Rick didn't kill Jenn. He couldn't have. He has an alibi—that big meeting at the firm.

What about the driver in the white van? They haven't gotten into Jenn's social media or email or followed any of the other possible leads we came up with.

Why would they make an arrest before looking at everything?

What's changed for them to move Rick from being *a person of interest* to *suspect?*

What does this mean for Ivy?

After what feels like an eternity but was probably no more than a few minutes with the voices of a couple of anchors recapping the case so far, the screen finally shows movement at the door. It opens, and sure enough, two cops push a handcuffed Rick through. He's wearing one of his high-end suits and Italian leather shoes. His hair is slicked back in place as usual, but his tie hangs askew. Camera flashes go off all over, and as they navigate through the small crowd that's gathered, I expect Rick to lower his head and angle it away to avoid the cameras.

Instead, he walks with his chin raised, defiant, and when reporters call out questions, his face screws up with rage and what might be fear. "This is bullshit! You hear me? Bullshit! You can't lock me up for something I didn't do."

I wince. Yelling it to cameras in front of cops probably isn't the smartest move when you're trying to prove your innocence.

You're a lawyer, Rick. Act like one.

The officers at his sides jerk him along to keep him moving but otherwise don't react. When they reach the patrol car at the curb, Rick raises his head and speaks over the roof at the cameras in the distance. "I'll be out on bail in an hour or two. And then I'm going to sue these clowns for defamation."

Now he's acting like a lawyer, but not in a good way.

One of the officers pushes Rick down by the head. At first, he fights it, screaming "I didn't kill my wife! You can't *do* this!" Soon, he's sitting in the back of the police car, subdued. The camera tries to focus on him through the side window. The image isn't clear, but his profile says plenty. He's not ducking to avoid being seen. He's still screaming, but the mic can't pick up the words now that the door is closed.

As the cop pulls away, I see one thing very clearly. Rick leans toward the window behind the driver's seat, and he's holding up his cuffed hands—one of them flipping off the public and everyone watching the news. This is an angry side to Rick that I've never seen.

After the patrol car is gone, the camera pans back to the reporter covering the story. "We're told that Chief Harris of the Maple Fork police department will be holding a press conference at the top of the hour. We'll stream it live here as well as on our social media feeds. Stay with us for the most up-to-date information on this story."

The feed returns to a pair of anchors at a news desk talking to a retired detective from a nearby county chiming in with his opinions on the case. The longer I watch, the more I want to hurl a remote at the TV to break it, shut it off entirely, while at the same time, I'm glued to the screen.

For the first time since Jenn's death, I let myself wonder, even briefly: *could* Rick be responsible for her death? I've been so sure that he wasn't involved, but what if he was? He doesn't seem capable of that kind of thing. But isn't that what neighbors and friends of murderers always say? Monsters are never the ones with saliva dripping from pointy teeth. They live among us.

"Hey, Becca, you okay?"

Mark's voice brings me back to the meeting room. I scan the room to find my team looking on with concerned expressions. My arms are tightly folded. I don't remember folding them. I sense my hands balled up in fists, my shoulder muscles tensed, my jaw clenched.

Deliberately, I release my arms, take a slow breath through my nose, and force myself to unlock my jaw. I attempt a smile, but even though I can't see it, I know it's a sad imitation. "I'm fine." Arguably the biggest lie I've ever uttered.

Everyone in the room seems on edge, and no one speaks. I'm an eggshell they're all afraid of cracking. I turn away from the screen and look at the table, which now seems twice as long, with my notebook, pens, and phone on the far side. "I, uh—"

"Why don't you take an early lunch?" Mark says gently. "I'll finish up with your team."

"Yeah," I say. "Okay. Thanks." Nodding but not entirely sure what he said besides excusing me from the room, I pick up my belongings and leave in a daze.

Halfway to my office, I'm spitting mad. Andrus is going to hear an earful from me.

CHAPTER TWENTY

JENN

May 10
10 Months before Drowning

I tried to see through the chaos I found myself in. I felt as if I were in a snow globe and someone had shaken it up so hard that I was blinded by white flakes. Instead of calming and settling, the white flecks were stirred up again and again. There was no making sense of this upside-down world I'd landed in, where the man in a mugshot, accused of killing Chloe, was now my husband.

Pregnancy hormones didn't make me nauseated anymore. The stress that Rick would find out that the OB/GYN had lied to him was gone. But I still felt sick to my stomach. Being the most loving, supporting wife possible wouldn't heal whatever wounds my husband was carrying, not by itself. I had to know what those wounds were.

Part of me was a little worried to find out everything. I didn't really know the man I'd married, but how *much* didn't I know? I needed to learn more about Chloe, their life together, her death.

I went to the gym before work. I'd come a few times over the last few weeks, mostly to walk the track, because doing any high-impact exercise was getting harder. Each time, I avoided the things inside my locker. But that morning, one glance at the notebook made the nausea rush back. I closed the locker and headed to the track.

What do I do? I thought as I walked around and around. *I have to keep digging.* I'd trust in what I always had, where my career had led me: learn more because knowledge is power.

In this case, the more I learned about Rick, the more unnerved I became, but if I stopped trying to learn the full picture, those worries would only grow.

After returning to the locker room and wiping my sweaty face with a towel, I sat on a bench, and, for the first time since frantically locking up the papers in April, I reached into the locker and pulled them out. The corner of the notebook snagged as it released. I refreshed my memory on the basics of Chloe's death in the bathtub, including the toxicology results saying she had significant amounts of meth and high doses of Xanax in her system. I read about how Rick was on trial, how it ended in a mistrial, and then he disappeared on bail before another trial could be held.

I desperately wanted to find out that I was wrong, that his first wife had died, as he'd told me on our second date, in a tragic accident. I knew some of the details of that accident now, that was all. He hadn't mentioned any substance abuse or even that she drowned. But again, this was a guy whose parents had died in the water when he was a boy. He'd been through a lot. He had learned to survive on his own, to get by without needing anyone else.

Considering all of that, of course he kept the details to himself.

On that second date, when he told me about Chloe, if he *had* spilled his entire past and expressed the pain and sadness it had caused him . . . wouldn't *that* have been odd?

All true.

There were simply a lot of unsettling facts, no matter how I wanted to interpret them. I married my husband without even knowing his real birth name. I hadn't even known how his parents died.

Did I know how they died now? I mean, sure, they drowned; I knew that much. But his parents accidentally drowned, and then his wife mysteriously drowned too? What were the odds? Were both of them tragedies made all the more heartbreaking because he'd lost family to drowning—twice?

Or . . . I didn't want to think it, but the question popped into my head anyway. Could Rick have somehow been responsible for Chloe's death . . . and his parents' deaths too?

Research. I had to dig to find out more. I didn't know enough yet to come to any clear conclusions.

I need to talk to Rick.

Another thought appeared, and one I fought. I didn't want to talk to him about any of this, but silence is what got us here, right? I slipped the notebook back into the locker. I promised myself I wouldn't pull it out again until after I talked to Rick.

When I arrived home after work, the garage door opened to show Rick's car already there. Did I know he was coming home early? Was something wrong?

I'd scarcely turned off my car before the inside kitchen door swung open to reveal a grinning Rick. "Hey, beautiful! Good news!"

My heart resumed beating and my chest warmed. "What's up?" I asked, closing the car door and heading toward him.

"My case settled—and in our client's favor. Big time." His eyes danced.

"That's fantastic!" I said, hugging him. "You worked so hard on it." I pulled back and gave him a kiss.

"It means a huge bonus at the end of the quarter—this, plus this little one"—he placed a hand over my belly—"means I'm closer to making partner." He kissed me hard and swung me around. "Let's go out to eat to celebrate. How does Rocky's sound? A medium-rare ribeye sounds perfect right now."

I pulled up my phone to search for the number. "I wonder how long the wait is."

"I already made a reservation. Come on. Let's go."

"Can I freshen up real quick?"

He checked his watch. "Sure. If we're on the road in six minutes, we'll be five minutes early, even with traffic."

"Great." I kissed him again. "Congratulations again. I'll be right back."

I jogged upstairs to our room, where I unloaded my work bag and purse. After a quick restroom stop, I slipped on a black dress he liked, touched up my makeup, added a spritz of perfume, then grabbed my purse from the bed. As I headed downstairs, I checked my watch and grinned. "One minute to spare."

Traffic was light, so we arrived nearly ten minutes early, but they had a table ready for us. We ordered, and our drinks were brought to us.

He took a sip of his. "Just think what this case means. I'll make partner even sooner, and we'll be able to build our dream home, travel the world, do anything we want."

"Partners still work long hours," I said with a chuckle. "And you're a workaholic."

"Well, sure, but I'll be able to pull back a bit and enjoy life."

"If you don't keep working sixty-hour weeks."

He reached across the table and took my hands in his. "Think about how great life will be for the two of us."

Three of us, I thought, and baby kicked as if hearing me. I didn't think my face had registered a reaction, but it must have because Rick tilted his head and narrowed his eyes.

"Something on your mind?"

Why, hello, Pandora's box.

I dropped my gaze to the table but kept my hands wrapped in his, grateful I'd left the research in my gym locker instead of bringing it home—and had done all my research on a computer that *wasn't* my laptop.

"We don't have to build a new house if you don't want to move," he said.

"It's not that." I looked up and smiled. "But there is something on my mind."

Rocky's Steakhouse was always full of diners, and tonight was no exception. Not a single booth was empty in our half of the restaurant. Servers and customers regularly passed us going opposite directions. I felt safer than I had in some time. Rick wouldn't dare yell or make a scene here. This would be the best opportunity I might get to ask about his past.

Better take the chance.

"I learned a few things," I began.

"Hold that thought," he said, lifting a finger as he released both of my hands. "I should have gone to the little boy's room before we left. I'll be right back."

My heart started to beat faster, and my stomach tightened. I reached for my purse and fished inside for the bottle of Tums I kept inside—something I *could* take while pregnant that sometimes calmed my stomach and heartburn. My hand hit something else, and at first, I didn't realize what it was—long, thick, smooth, plastic. The smartpen. I'd forgotten about it. I could record the conversation for . . . proof of something? I didn't know, but I felt crazy half the time, and maybe being able to hear this conversation back would help me untangle some of this.

The pen could make an audio recording. No need to write or use the fancy paper. Just push a button. I glanced at my phone—its audio capability was probably better than the pen's—but no. Rick could hack into my phone or pressure me into giving up my password and find anything I'd put onto the phone. He didn't know about the pen.

I glanced toward the back corner, where he'd gone to the restroom. My fingers shook so much that turning the pen on took a couple of tries, but I finally did it—and started an audio recording. Then I popped a couple of Tums and drank some water just as he returned.

He sat down, reached across the table again, and squeezed the tips of my fingers. "Where were we? Oh, right. You were going to say something?"

Where do I begin?

Once I spoke up, there would be no undoing this moment. The same old trembling returned, first in my chest, then spreading to my legs. I did my best to keep it from reaching my arms and hands. He'd detect that. But even my teeth were on the verge of chattering.

While I didn't want to open this door, the pain of staying on this side of it was worse. I had to walk through. Staring at his hands, I took a deep breath and finally spoke. "Why didn't you ever tell me who you really are?"

His expression darkened, his eyes suddenly looking hooded as he dropped my hands. "Excuse me?"

Two words, but I heard two different ones: *Back. Off.*

CHAPTER TWENTY-ONE

BECCA

The evening following the arrest, I go on autopilot for Ivy until I get her down for the night. The twins are still with their dad. I reheat some leftovers for myself, but instead of eating, I pick at the food as I remember Rick's arrest. How could Andrus go after Rick so soon after we handed him a list of leads on a silver platter? What about the guy in the white van?

I call Detective Andrus and leave a message. "Hey, detective. Becca Kalos here. I saw the news today, and um, well, I couldn't help but wonder if you'd taken a look at the leads I sent over the other day. Could you call me? Thanks."

Somehow, I sound polite, even though I'm raging inside. The cops have let themselves be blinded.

I try to call Andrus again—maybe he'll pick up?—but my phone rings with an incoming call. It's Mark from work.

"Hey," I say.

"Becca, hi. I've been thinking about you ever since . . ." His voice trails off.

"Yeah," I say, saving him the need to expound on how everyone in the conference room watched Rick's arrest on live TV.

"Why don't you stay home tomorrow? Take a bit of a break. Take the rest of the week off. You've been under a lot of pressure."

Pressure feels like an understatement, but I don't know what else to call this sense of unreality, of swirling in emotional chaos. I'm unable to concentrate on anything. It's a good thing the twins are with their dad; I don't want them to see me like this. Davis would worry, and Maggie would be her hyped-up, cheerful self, bouncing—often literally—on the couch or even foot to foot as she excitedly tells stories.

"You're right," I say. "My team will do fine working on the Alcestis campaign for a day without me."

After a slight pause and a chuckle, Mark says, "Who are you and what did you do with control-freak Becca?"

I manage a light chuckle too, rather surprised myself that for once, I'm not worried about what my team will do with a campaign without my constant supervision. They're competent. They're the best in the business. They know the standard I expect.

And I desperately need a break.

"Thanks, Mark. You're the best. I really appreciate it. See you Monday."

"Or Tuesday, if you need another day."

I'm not about to commit to that, but I won't reject it either. "We'll see. Thanks for the offer."

"Absolutely," he says. "And seriously, let me know how else I can help."

My eyes sting as they tear up. Refusing to cry, I shake my head and blink a bunch to get rid of the tears. "Will do," I say. "Thanks."

The next morning, I take Ivy on a long walk in her stroller. I take her to a park, though she's too little to do anything but sit in the baby swing and giggle as I push her. When I've exhausted ideas for entertaining her outside the house, we go back home with Mexican takeout for me and plans to binge nineties romantic comedies.

Around six o'clock, my phone rings with a call from a local number I don't recognize. I usually let calls like that go straight to voicemail, figuring that if it's not spam, the person will leave a message. This time, I hesitate. It could be Andrus returning my call from an office number. Whenever the kids are gone, I'm more likely to pick up in case it's an emergency call.

"Hello, I'm looking for Rebecca Kalos." The voice I hear is unfamiliar—a man's, deep and smooth.

"Speaking."

"This is Jeffrey Arrington. I'm the defense attorney of Rick Banks."

"Oh. Hi." I'm frozen, unsure what to expect next.

"As he can't have regular contact with others at this trying time, I am reaching out to you with a message from him."

"Oh. Okay. Hold on." I have no idea how to prepare myself because I have no idea what's coming. The one thing I can think of is to be sure I write the message down. I scramble to the kitchen to find something to write on, settling on a scratch pad in the kitchen junk drawer and a pencil in dire need of sharpening. "All right. I'm ready."

"I understand that you are—or, I suppose I should say *were*—the best friend of my client's late wife."

Why doesn't he say her name? My heart rate and breath both speed up—the anger toward Andrus shifting toward this Arrington guy. "Jenn was my best friend, yes," I say, and manage it without clenched teeth.

"I see that Mrs. Banks had a membership at the, uh, let me see . . . yes, at the Venus Fitness gym in Maple Fork. I've canceled the membership. They have indicated that she had a locker there that held some personal effects and have asked that someone come to retrieve those items. I'm rather swamped with work, as you can imagine, and Mr. Banks said you'd be willing to retrieve his late wife's belongings on his behalf."

"He . . . did?" It comes out as a question because, for a second, I'm trying to remember a conversation where Rick asked me to get Jenn's things from the gym, but of course, that conversation never happened. He told his lawyer I'd be willing to run the errand, and I guess he's right. A phone call takes a lot less time than an errand, which means Rick paying his lawyer less. I can run the errand for him.

"Sure. I'm happy to."

"That's wonderful to hear," Arrington says.

"Do they have the combination to the lock?"

"The gym has it in their records. It's Venus Fitness in Maple Fork. Do you know where that is?"

"I do, yes." I write the name down anyway, though I know full well that it's the only gym in our small town.

"Wonderful," he says again. "They'll be expecting you. They'll ask for your ID, of course. Mention me, and they'll handle it from there. Thank you in advance. If you have any questions, don't hesitate to call."

He rattles off his number, which I write down even though it's already on my caller ID. There wasn't anything else *to* write down.

When the call ends, I stare at the number, above which I add *Jeffrey Arrington*, as if that should mean something to me. Jeffrey Arrington. It means nothing personally, but I'm sure this man is the best criminal defense lawyer money can buy.

Suddenly, I have something I can do for Jenn. I can go get her things from the gym. It's small, but it's *something*.

I call Nancy down the street to see if her daughter Aimie can babysit—basically housesit while Ivy sleeps—while I run to the gym. Aimie shows up five minutes later, and I'm out the door like a shot.

As Arrington said, they're expecting me. I thought they'd have me go open the locker myself, but they've already done that, I guess because they have the locker's combination code. I'm annoyed when they hand over a plastic grocery sack with her belongings—did they go through her stuff? Did they take anything? Couldn't they at least have handled her things, I don't know, more solemnly, in some way that noted the loss behind my errand? Maybe they don't know why the locker needed to be cleaned out.

They check my ID, and then I take the bag. I peer briefly inside as if that will tell me if anything's missing. I didn't expect to see a notebook and a binder of papers. Trust Jenn to track her workouts on spreadsheets or whatever. I have no idea if anything is missing.

The scent of Jenn's perfume wafts out, enveloping me and overwhelming my emotions and thoughts.

"Ma'am? Are you all right?" the receptionist, likely no older than nineteen, asks.

I look over and force myself back to the present. "I'm fine," I say, though weakly. "Thank you."

I hold tight onto my emotions during the drive home, paying Aimie for her time and checking on Ivy. She's still sound asleep. Good.

Only then do I go to my bed and spill the contents of the bag. A sports bra, leggings, tank, socks, a small bottle of perfume, a makeup bag, running shoes, and other expected items lie before me. So do the things that drew my attention when I first looked inside: a notebook, a bunch of papers, and what looks like a bulky marker.

I reach for the notebook, yearning to see Jenn's even, beautifully angled handwriting, but my hand stops midair. Am I invading Jenn's privacy? Should I hand over the bag's contents to Arrington sight unseen?

What kind of privacy am I violating? I demand of myself. I'll find a record of her workouts, maybe a schedule showing arm and leg days. Arrington didn't ask me to bring him the bag. He asked me to pick it up.

Unsure, I reach for the marker and realize it's not what I thought. At first, I can't figure it out—the cap on the tip blends in so well I almost miss it. It's a *pen*. There's a tiny screen on the side showing the time and battery strength. I play with the buttons to see what they do.

I hear something—a recording coming from the pen. Is that Jenn's voice?

For a second, my heart nearly stops, but then it revs up and patters hard, like hail on a roof. I find the control for increasing the volume and listen. I hear Jenn's voice, a ghost from the past.

"Why didn't you ever tell me who you really are?"

My eyes widen. Who is she talking to? I learn the answer a second later when Rick's voice comes through.

"Excuse me?"

Wait, what? I stop the recording, back it up to the beginning, sure I missed something crucial or that I misheard.

I hear the same words again, followed by another question from Jenn, one that makes my skin crawl.

"Why didn't you ever tell me your real name?"

I press stop and then stare at the pen/recorder thing.

Rick *isn't* his real name? Who is he?

A local news notification pops up on my phone—*Husband Arrested in Maple Fork Woman's Death*—and suddenly I wonder . . .

Who is Rick Banks?

Is Andrus right to have arrested him?

Did Rick have anything to do with Jenn's death?

CHAPTER TWENTY-TWO

JENN

November 19
Four Months before Drowning

My little girl was born on the tenth of September, a birth that was, in the words of my nurse practitioner, Tiffany, "uneventful." I knew that was medical speak for no complications, but for me, giving birth was the opposite of uneventful. From the moment I heard her cry, and even more so when she was placed into my arms, I was transformed.

The next eight weeks of maternity leave were a sleep-deprived blur of feedings, diaperings, and taking naps when she did. Would I get to have another child? I doubted it, so I soaked in every feeding, every bath, every snuggle, every diaper blowout, and every bout of colic.

Those were some of the hardest days of my life, but some of the best too. I was so grateful that I got eight solid weeks off work. My heart and mind were split on going back. Of course, we didn't need the money. I'd always wanted to be a stay-at-home mom. But I also missed my colleagues, and I had a feeling that working a few hours here and there a few days a week would feed that part of me.

Rick didn't take paternity leave, and I didn't ask if the firm would give it to him. He seemed to have a real soft spot for her, but I could never shake the knowledge that if he'd had his way, she wouldn't exist.

Despite not being home much, Rick was definitely more affectionate, and even patient with Ivy at times. One evening, I found him sitting on the couch, holding her facing him and gazing into her eyes. He looked absolutely besotted.

I sat beside them. "She's perfect, isn't she?"

"I never got to have this with Chloe," Rick said. "Did I tell you that . . ."

I waited for him to finish the sentence. When he didn't, I prompted, "Did you tell me . . ."

He glanced at me and then looked back at Ivy. "We were trying for a baby when she died." With a shrug, he added, "I've wondered if she was pregnant that day. It would have been barely—probably not something an autopsy would catch—but still. I wonder . . ."

He might have lost a wife *and* a child that day.

"Oh, honey," I said, leaning against his arm and wrapping my arms around it. "You have it now. A perfect little girl, a wife who loves you. You have it all."

"Yeah," he said, nodding. He turned his head and pressed a kiss to my forehead.

Mid-November, when Ivy was just over two months old, I hired Ruth, a retired kindergarten teacher two blocks away, who was thrilled to tend Ivy while I worked. I didn't tell her or Rick that I wasn't working full days, only that I was working three days a week instead of five.

After work, I'd head to the Red Grove Library. What I'd found before had already given me perspective and insight into Rick that had helped our marriage. Now that Ivy was here, I felt driven to learn even more. Rick had come so far in a short time. How much more of his real self could he reveal, how many of his childhood wounds could he heal from, if I knew more? How much better of a father would he be to Ivy if those hurting parts of him were soothed?

On my first day back at work, a nip was in the air, the leaves had changed colors, and our lawn had tips of frost. I drove Ivy to Ruth's house, sure I'd be a complete wreck dropping her off. I did better than expected. I didn't cry, but I *did* worry. That was normal, or so all the Instagram mommy accounts said.

My coworkers greeted me with enthusiasm—and a bit more volume than a library technically warranted. The four hours flew by, but I was worried about Ivy, and frankly, I missed her so much that I skipped my research trip to Red Grove Library. I headed to the gym in Maple Fork. I'd do a quick workout, which would please Rick, and then I'd get Ivy.

In the locker room, I glanced at the notebook and papers, bound with a thick clip and rubber band. Not for the first time, I wished I'd known what was in there when we were dating. How much more compassionate and patient would I have been toward him in the last year if I'd known about how he was orphaned, how his first wife died, and that he'd been tried for her death?

Looking at his life through the lens of tragedy, I could draw a line from his childhood traumas to his adult behavior. Of course he was a hot mess, which affected our marriage. Would therapy help? How could I approach the topic in a way that he'd at least give it a try?

I closed my locker and went to the cardio room. Fifteen minutes into a light treadmill jog, some cable show began on one of the many mounted televisions. It looked interesting enough. I set my earbuds to the frequency of that screen and watched.

The introduction was typical of true-crime mysteries—tense music and the reporter doing voice-over, mentioning the key players, and ending with a question that seemed both melodramatic and obvious. Yes, their lives had been changed by whatever we were about to learn. I'd missed the title of the episode, but then, most shows like this had episode titles that were essentially vague but scary and could practically fit any true-crime story—*Death in the Night, Disappearance of Elizabeth, Twisted Night, What Happened to Sandra?* All you had to do was swap a name out of a title with another victim's, and presto—new title. I had watched enough true crime that sometimes I forgot which detail went with which story, but I enjoyed them anyway.

As soon as the main story began, along with some news footage and pictures, I vaguely remembered the story when it broke across national news some time ago. It was a case of a man on trial for the death of his wife—pretty common as true crime went. I didn't remember much beyond the fact that the husband had been in the medical field. Sure enough, he'd been a dentist with a practice in eastern Washington state.

What his wife and patients didn't know, the reporter said dramatically, *was that he wasn't a dentist at all, despite having a fifteen-year-old practice and being highly respected in the small town of Crown City. He hadn't been to dental school. Hadn't even applied. For a decade and a half, he'd lived a lie.*

Jogging, I wondered how someone could fake a profession like that—and how others around him hadn't figured it out. Hadn't anyone ever checked to see if he'd actually gone to dental school?

His wife had died under suspicious circumstances. The husband claimed it was all a tragic accident. She'd had major back surgery after a car accident and then took too many painkillers before taking a bath. Where she drowned.

Similarities to Rick's life unnerved me so much that I had to slow the treadmill to a walk.

Rick's parents had drowned too. Rather, *Ryan's* parents.

Chloe drowned too. Very different circumstances from his parents' deaths, but the same ultimate cause of drowning. She had died, like the wife in the show had, with drugs in her system. The one thing that didn't fit was a parallel between the dentist faking his education and profession.

Or did it? What if Rick never graduated from law school or passed the bar?

My shoes caught on the belt, and I almost tripped, catching myself on the handrails. Breathing heavily, I stared at the TV screen and turned up the volume in my earbuds, but adrenaline zinged through me so intensely that I couldn't pay attention.

Was Rick really a lawyer? He had to be. But did I know that for sure? Had I seen a diploma? What did I *know*? The law firm must have checked all of that, right? Not necessarily, if he had an impressive resume they already believed, with references and who knew what else.

My heartbeat pounded in my ears anyway, muffling the sound. I tore out my earbuds. Suddenly, I couldn't get enough air. I shut off the treadmill and then stood there, bracing myself on the handrails until I felt steady enough to walk.

Finally, I reached the locker room, where one woman tilted her head and asked, "You okay?"

She walked on when I smiled back and murmured, "I'm fine." But then I slipped into one of the changing booths and locked the door. I dropped to the bench and leaned my head against the cool metal, eyes closed, unsure if I'd pass out after all.

I'm overreacting, I thought. *Take deep breaths. Everything is fine.*

My mind countered, *How do I know anything is fine?*

A month ago, after hearing Rick's version of Chloe's death, I'd slid into the safe place of believing him and trying to use the history I'd learned to make our life better.

I already knew that Rick didn't go to UCLA or Stanford as he'd claimed. Was the full truth even worse? Was he like the dentist in the true-crime show—not even a real lawyer? Was he practicing without having gone to law school or passing the bar?

The bizarre coincidence of his parents drowning *and* his first wife drowning unsettled me so much that I worried I'd throw up. I sat on the bench, breathing shallowly and hoping the nausea would pass. My whole body was shaking like an aspen in the wind.

What if Rick had killed his parents and his wife? On one hand, the drownings were different. His parents had drowned in the open sea, his wife in a bathtub.

He'd been a boy when his parents died, the incident ruled a tragic accident. Yet he'd been tried for Chloe's death. Not convicted. Not exonerated either.

I felt as if I was on a merry-go-round, spinning around as I tried to get my feet under me after learning one fact, only to be spun faster with something new coming to light. Consider this, each thing seemed to say. Only for that idea to be countered by another. The whole thing was dizzying.

A constant parade of *and yet, and yet, and yet.*

He hadn't told me everything; I could feel the truth of that in my bones, right along with the worry and fear that I now had coursing through my veins.

How could I have believed his latest story after knowing that he'd told me lie after lie? Sure, he finally copped to certain aspects of the truth, but only *after* I'd confronted him with what I knew. He hadn't confessed everything.

What would it take to get the rest of it out of him? Would I ever?

The reality weighed heavily with a cloak of grief. After a lifetime of not belonging, I finally had a home and a family, only to have the rug yanked out from under me again.

But maybe, if I learned the rest, if I found that he *was* innocent in Chloe's death, then I'd be able to move forward, continue building the life of my dreams.

I grabbed my purse and left, heading for Ruth's house to pick up Ivy. I'd hold my baby girl close. I needed to feel her in my arms. I needed to protect her. And that meant learning everything I could about her father.

I should have gone to Red Grove today, but I'd go tomorrow for sure. I *had* to know: who was Rick?

CHAPTER TWENTY-THREE

BECCA

After several minutes of staring at the smartpen, I get the courage to play the full recording. I start again at the beginning.

"Why didn't you ever tell me who you really are?" Jenn asks.

As before, Rick replies with "Excuse me?"

"Why didn't you ever tell me your real name?"

I hold my breath, waiting for whatever is coming next.

"What do you mean?" Rick asks.

Voice recordings don't always sound exactly like the real thing. Is there a chance the male voice isn't Rick?

"I mean," Jenn says, "that Rick isn't your real first name."

The fragile bubble of hope I nurtured pops.

"Your birth name is Ryan, and your last name was originally Brockbank. Your middle name really is Christopher." Her voice cuts off with a whimper, and she says something else, but it's muffled as if she's covering her face with her hands.

I find my hand covering my mouth in shock.

No one speaks for several seconds. I wait, my heart racing, adrenaline pumping through my body as if I'm watching the most intense suspense movie ever. But this is real. *Was* a real conversation.

I hear something I think is a glass returning to the table. Rick taking a slow sip of wine? I'm imagining the whole scene.

"Babe," he finally says, "I should have told you. You deserved to know."

Not the answer I expected. I hold the pen's mini speaker closer to my ear as if that'll make the words clearer.

Rick sighs loudly. I picture him shaking his head. "What can I say but that I had to run from the pain? Not only did I lose my wife—in a horrible, shocking way, but I was then accused of killing her and put on trial."

Whoa. He *what* now? I thought losing my best friend was horrible. I thought that having her husband arrested for her murder was the worst it could get. But now I'm finding out that he's been accused of murder before?

"That must have been so hard," Jenn says quietly.

"Can you imagine what that kind of thing does to a man? Losing your wife, only to be accused of killing her? It messes with your head. I had to escape it all."

"But you weren't convicted." I sense a glimmer of insistence—maybe a smidgen of hope?—in Jenn's otherwise tight voice.

"No, but a mistrial isn't an acquittal," Rick says. "The DA was planning to try me again. I could *not* go through that a second time. I would've been demonized by the press. I'd already been arrested, called a monster, and put in jail once. I couldn't bear the thought of going through it all again."

"Maybe a jury would have believed you."

"Maybe," Rick repeats and lets out a heavy breath. "Juries are notoriously unpredictable. You never know how they'll interpret testimony. Innocent men are convicted all the time. Another trial could have meant life behind bars for something I didn't do. I couldn't risk another trial. It's so hard to explain—it's surreal when it happens to you. I'm sure it sounds nuts when you're hearing it."

"No, not really," Jenn says. "I get why you'd want to start fresh."

"Yes, that's it exactly," Rick says. Excitement now laced his voice. "I hadn't been given any time to grieve or anything."

He had a point there. But I couldn't think straight to know what to believe. Too many new things were being thrown at me. The world seemed to spin, giving me emotional vertigo.

"One of the biggest pieces of so-called evidence was DNA. Of *course* Chloe had my DNA on her. I was her husband! My DNA was all over the house too. I just . . ." He sighed wearily.

"Ran away."

"Yeah." His voice sounds almost vulnerable now, tender. "I knew you'd understand."

I hear what must be the sound of him kissing her, and then Jenn speaks again. "Why did you change your name?"

"If yours were splashed across headlines like that, what would you do? No one would hire me if they looked me up and found out I'd been charged with murder. A mistrial doesn't mean much to a prospective employer. The charge was enough to blackball me."

His reasoning makes sense, though as I sit there on my bed, clutching a pillow to myself, I remain too overwhelmed to process what I'm hearing.

"Why didn't you *tell* me?" Jenn asks, voicing the question I'm thinking. "Imagine what it was like to find out about this stuff on my own. I mean, you were upset that I got a *goldfish* without telling you, but you hid your entire past life and your real name. I just . . . I don't know what to think."

A squeak like vinyl tells me that Rick probably shifts in his seat. He sighs. "As you said, I was running away from it all. First from the pain of losing the woman I loved."

Ouch, I think. Poor Jenn probably wasn't ready to hear his profession of love for his dead wife. Of course, someone can be in love with more than one person in a lifetime. Any semi-mature adult knows that. Still, his words must have stung.

"I had to start a new life," he continues. "That meant a new identity. I refused to be identified by tragedy." He pauses, and some sounds make me think he's leaning forward, maybe taking her hands. "Jenn," he says, lowering his voice to the sultry tone that likely first won her over, "we've both been through a lot in our lives. I knew you'd understand because you don't want to be defined by your parents' deaths any more than I did by the death of my first wife."

"Or . . . by the deaths of your parents by drowning?"

I stare at the pen in shock. Did I hear that right? I rewind and listen again. Yep. I hear Jenn saying the same words again, calmly, as if she isn't lobbing a shock grenade into the conversation.

After a moment of what I can only imagine is stunned silence, Rick lets out a breath. "Didn't know you'd found out about that, but yeah. Their deaths were sudden and unexpected and . . ."

"Traumatic?" Jenn sounds like her empathetic self. I know her. His story is softening her good heart to the point that she'll forgive him for not telling her about his trial, his real name . . . she'll forgive him for all of it.

She forgave him, past tense, I correct myself.

"Is there anything else I don't know?" Jenn asks.

"That's it."

"And you're innocent of the charges," she says as if reciting something memorized for a class. "You ran from the pain and the possibility of being tried again?" It only sort of comes out as a question.

"Exactly. I knew you'd understand."

"Any other secrets I should know about?"

I wish I could yell through the recording into the past, whenever this conversation happened, and ask what he's hiding. It's impossible to think that these are the only things he's lied about; if he's lied about things as big as life and death, he's undoubtedly been lying about other things.

I want to shake Rick and ask why an intelligent man with a law degree thinks that the best way to deal with tragic loss is to run from the authorities. That makes Rick look guilty. I have no idea if he is.

People react differently to situations, I remind myself. *Running out of fear of being locked up isn't proof that he killed someone.*

"I still don't understand why . . ." Jenn's voice trails off. That sentence could end in a thousand different ways.

"Why . . ." Rick repeats, but his voice has a thread of tension in it now. Did Jenn notice it?

Probably, because when she speaks again, it's in a rush, as if she needs to get it out while she has the nerve. "Why did you lie to me about surfing and going to Wagner High?" She sucks in a breath after that, as if the question took every molecule of oxygen in her lungs.

"I was running from my entire past," he says. I can picture the charming shrug.

"Rick," she says, using his name as if that might bring him back around, make him focus, and tell the truth. "I've been through tragedy too, remember? Of all people, *I* would have understood. I'm your *wife*. I deserved to know."

"You're right," Rick says. "I should have told you. That was wrong of me. I never knew when the right time would be to bring up the past. It's just that . . . this kind of thing isn't what you lead with on a first date. Or second or third. After a while, it felt too late to say anything, and I didn't feel the urgency to tell you because, I don't know if this makes sense, and it's not an excuse, but I felt like I was a different person now. The old me was gone. You and I got serious really fast, and I got caught up in the whirlwind. We began a great life together, and by then, I thought, what would be the point of ripping open an old wound? Ryan—the old me—he was long gone, dead. He's not me. I'm living a new life, with the love of my life." I hear something that could be Rick kissing her. "Babe, I apologize. I shouldn't have kept my past a secret. You deserved to know, a hundred percent."

The apology, the contrition, the gentle voice—all of it made my defenses stand back a bit. Imagining myself in his shoes, I saw how hard it would be to not only live through multiple tragedies but to also go through one of them publicly. He wouldn't want to be labeled by them. He was still wrong to hide his past, but if the reason he did it was to avoid being held back by it—*and* if he was innocent in Chloe's death—then some of his actions made sense. If you squinted a little.

Then again, a guilty man would run and change his name too.

Questions kept popping into my head like whack-a-moles.

"There's one more thing I don't understand," Jenn said.

Only one? I think.

"What's that?" Rick is starting to sound tired.

"Were you ever a surfer?"

"Actually . . . no."

My jaw opens in surprise. Why *this* revelation is the one that breaks the camel's back, I don't know, but it does. Jenn had been so sure that he'd love her tattoo, so devastated when he basically called her a whore for getting it. Maybe this hurts me more because the wound was directed at Jenn herself—literally at a part of her body.

"Oh, man," Rick says. I can picture him running his fingers through his hair as he thinks through what he's about to say—and calculates how he'll say it. "I grew up watching surfer movies and documentaries. I watched a few of them over and over until the VHS tapes or DVDs broke. I always *felt* like a surfer. Sounds crazy, I know, but in a way, I almost convinced myself that I *had* been a surfer." His voice quiets, and I almost miss his next words. "I'm such a loser. You deserve so much more than a jerk who lives in a fantasy world."

The rest of the recording is Rick putting himself down, insisting he's garbage, and Jenn offering assurances that he's not a loser, that she loves him, and that they'll get through this. That their love is enough.

When the recording ends, I sit in stunned silence, staring at the pen that holds their voices from the past. My eyes slide to the notebook and papers. I have to find out what's in them. I *should* turn everything over to Mr. Arrington or Detective Andrus and wash my hands of the whole thing. But Jenn won't rest in peace until I find answers to her questions, and *I* won't be able to live in peace either.

Where will this road take me? I'm terrified of the question, but I must face it. For Jenn. For Ivy. For myself.

I grab the stack of papers and start reading.

CHAPTER TWENTY-FOUR

JENN

December 23
Three Months before Drowning

The library was officially closed for the holidays. I was off work, but Rick was not. He still had to work late, swearing that his holiday vacation would begin tomorrow. That evening, when it got dark, Becca and I bundled up our kids—Ivy in a new snowsuit I'd just bought her—and took them to a nearby park where you could walk around acres of magical Christmas lights. Maggie and Davis doted on Ivy, who looked like a pink starfish-shaped puff with a face.

Becca's twins kept running ahead and pointing to things, then running back, talking to Ivy to get her to grin or attempting to get her to look at something they'd found. She could sit up in her stroller if I kept it reclined a bit, but more than once, the twins got a bit overexcited in their attentions, bumping the stroller so much that Ivy tilted and fell to one side or the other.

After setting her upright for the third time, I tucked a blanket tight around her and returned to the back of the stroller. "I worried I'd be judged for taking such a small baby out when it's so cold," I said to Becca as we walked along.

"Ivy is nowhere near the only baby here," Becca said, knowing what I needed to hear as a new mom uncertain in my abilities. "Plenty of others are here with babies."

"They all have older kids too."

"She's plenty warm and happy," Becca countered.

We followed winding cement paths, enjoying music from Bing Crosby, Mariah Carey, and others piped through speakers. The trees were wrapped in lights, and under them were figures created of wire and lights—animals, people, snowflakes, even a dragon, some with automated movements.

We stopped at a kiosk and ordered four hot chocolates.

"Wait," Maggie said. "Ivy needs one too."

"Oh, she's too little for that yet," I said.

"Really?" Maggie said, her face lighting up slightly at the idea she was big enough to have crossed a threshold that a smaller child hadn't.

"Jenn's right," Becca said. "Hot chocolate would hurt Ivy's tummy."

Davis nodded soberly. "Then we don't give her a drop."

As we walked along, the crisp snow crunching under our feet, our breath turning into puffy clouds, I let out a happy sigh. "I'm finally feeling the Christmas spirit."

"Just now?" Becca asked.

"What do you mean?"

"Let's see . . . you've decorated to the point that your place looks like a gingerbread house out of a magazine, your tree has been up since mid-November, you burn pumpkin spice and evergreen candles whenever you're home . . ."

"I got a sugar cookie one yesterday," I interjected.

"You're proving my point," she said. "And you've been listening to Christmas music nonstop for weeks. You've been drenching yourself in Christmas, but you're only now feeling it?"

I shrugged. "Guess I've been busy."

I didn't mention that I'd done a bit more research and uncovered one more startling piece of Rick's past that I didn't know what to do with: he'd had a second wife who died, named Natalie. I was still chasing breadcrumbs to figure out more about her. So far, I'd learned that he was Christopher Banks when he married her—so he'd changed his name not once, but twice. They'd been married for about a year. Natalie had died "unexpectedly," according to her obituary, which could mean almost anything.

"This is a different Christmas season for you," Becca said.

"Oh?" Had she sensed something was off? I hoped not.

"Of course." Becca took a sip of her hot chocolate. "I mean, you have a new baby, you're back to work after maternity leave, and apparently, you've decided to make Christmas a month-long event for Ivy. Anyone would be overwhelmed."

Oh good. She had plenty of reason to assume I was under stress for easily explainable reasons. I couldn't tell her about my other huge worry: what I had uncovered about Rick last month.

If I ever figured out what steps to take next, and if she could help, I'd bring it up. In the back of my head, I wondered if I'd have to take on a fake name and hide with Ivy to get safely away from Rick. If so, I might need Becca's help to pull that off.

Or maybe I'd have to keep her in the dark about it forever to keep *her* safe and to prevent Rick from finding us through some clue left behind that Becca had and didn't know he could find.

Man, the idea of dropping off the grid without her—without her knowing why—was heartbreaking. Hopefully, I'd find another way. Until I knew what I needed to do, and how I'd do it, I couldn't talk about any of it to anyone.

"I suppose it's silly of me to decorate and go all out when Ivy's so little," I said. "It's not as if she'll remember this Christmas."

"Keep it up," Becca said, looking straight ahead as we walked. "It's worth it even for a baby."

"What do you mean?"

Davis ran back then, yelling, "Mom, check out that polar bear!"

In the distance, sure enough, was a family of fiberglass polar bears, including one giant one in the back.

"Cool!" Becca said, and her enthusiasm must have been enough because he ran back to Maggie. She looked at me again. "Starting traditions is a big deal. She'll come to anticipate certain things much younger than you'd expect."

160

"She won't want to go see the lights next year because we did this year."

"No," Becca said thoughtfully. "But you never know what she'll remember. Even the scent of those candles will be imprinted somewhere in her head, and when she's older, when she smells pumpkin spice and whatever else, she'll remember you and happy times."

"I never thought of it like that." I was suddenly glad I'd gone overboard, even though much of the reason was that I finally had a family to celebrate with, in a house I called home.

"When they were little," Becca said, nodding toward the twins ahead, "I was stunned when they asked about watching a video I'd shown them the year before, or when they asked about my grandma's sugar cookies, which I make only at Christmas. They remembered all kinds of things from when they were very young."

"I hope she remembers," I said. I liked the idea that something of the sleepless nights would remain as an imprint on her little heart. "Sometimes, when I'm exhausted, I think about how she'll have no memory of how much I do for her. None. It could be a stranger changing her diaper and nursing her."

"No, it couldn't." Becca's voice had a seriousness that took me off guard. I stopped pushing the stroller and looked at her. She faced me and explained. "After the divorce, I went through a time when I was so pissed off at Jason. As far as the kids were concerned, Dad was this fun, awesome guy, and I was the mean parent who made them do chores and homework and had rules. They didn't remember the years when I was the only one taking care of them, how Jason traveled so much that when they were two, they thought that "Daddy" was a face on a phone who talked to them sometimes. I did all the heavy lifting, and I resented the hell out of it."

I hadn't known this part of Becca's past, a tender, vulnerable spot. Just as I rarely brought up Rick, she rarely brought up Jason.

"The twins are old enough now that they need less hands-on care," Becca went on. "What they need from me now—and, I imagine, will need even more of as they get into their teens—is a safe place, a soft place to fall. I'm already seeing it, though. When they have problems with friends, they come to me. When they fall and get hurt, they come to me. They never, ever seek out their dad for comfort or advice." She blinked back tears and swallowed hard. "I doubt they even realize that their dad doesn't cross their minds when they need help, but the reality is, when it matters, they always call for me."

"I hope Ivy will know I'm a safe space," I said quietly.

Becca turned to me with glassy, serious eyes. "She will. Maggie and Davis don't remember all of the things I did when they were little that created the bonds we have, and Ivy won't remember either. But those bonds will still be real, and they'll last. Jason will never have that with our kids—and, provided I don't completely torpedo their teenage years, I'll never lose it." She gestured toward Ivy. "Your little girl will *feel* the bond you're creating with her, hour by hour, day by day. When she's older, anytime she smells cinnamon at a bakery, she'll think of you and feel loved. When her first boyfriend breaks her heart, she'll know she can come to you, *not* because she remembers that you soothed her tears as a baby, but *because* you soothed them."

By that point, Becca and I were both crying rivers of tears. I took off a glove and wiped my cheeks. "Thanks, Bex."

⁂

December 24
About Three Months before Drowning

Rick had to work on Christmas Eve after all, but when he got home, he announced that he wanted a date night, just the two of us. Six o'clock on Christmas Eve is a bit late to make reservations, but I tried to come up with something special.

The first item of business was a babysitter. Every attempt landed in a dead-end. The daycare facility wasn't open, Becca was out of town with the twins visiting her grandma for Christmas, and I refused to hire the teenager around the corner to babysit a three-month-old.

"Teenagers babysit all the time."

"Toddlers, sure. It's flu season, and she's only three months—"

"Three and a *half* months," he countered. "You're being unreasonable."

As if two weeks made any difference in how well a teen who smelled of pot could care for such a young baby.

A nearly hour-long debate followed. Finally, I told him to go ahead and try to get a reservation, and if he managed to, *then* I'd get a babysitter. I won that debate only because he couldn't get in at any of his favorite restaurants. After twenty minutes of attempts, he went down to the couch and dropped to it with an exaggerated sigh. I couldn't celebrate or even look relieved or he'd get even more upset, so I held my features in a neutral expression as I followed him downstairs.

"Way to shackle me," he said. His words a not-so-subtle reminder that he hadn't wanted kids in the first place.

I quickly sat on the couch beside him. "Rick," I began, reaching for his hand.

He pulled away. "Look, I just don't appreciate someone coming between us." He jutted his chin toward Ivy, who was gumming teething toys on the floor. "She's your number one priority. I've been knocked quite aways down."

"No, you haven't," I insisted. "You're as important to me as ever."

My heart twisted slightly at the half truth. It wasn't *exactly* a lie, or so I reasoned with myself. My feelings for Rick hadn't changed, but until Ivy was born, I hadn't known what love was. She *did* come before Rick. As a tiny, fragile, completely dependent person, she had to. I still loved Rick. At least, I thought I did.

Rick looked away from me, so I put a hand on his thigh, hoping the touch would bring him back. "She's so little. She can't do anything on her own. It's my job to protect her. You can get dressed and feed yourself, but she can't do those things yet. But you—you are my husband, and I *love* you."

At that, he turned to look at me, looking hopeful and less angry. "Yeah?"

"Yeah. And our child deserves parents who love each other and have a strong bond. I *want* to have date nights at fancy restaurants and attend concerts and plays and—"

"And go skiing?" he added hopefully.

"That too," I said and chuckled. I tried not to think of how it was already ski season, and how soon, he might expect me to leave Ivy with someone for an entire day. I had a hard time leaving her for four or five hours when I went to work. "When I know she'll be safe with a babysitter." I shrugged. "I can't yet."

Rick sighed—only slightly mopey—and lifted his arm. I scooted close on the couch, and he rested his arm around me as I lay my head on his shoulder. "I get it," he said, then kissed my hair.

We ordered food and streamed movies to celebrate Christmas Eve, with only a few moments of annoyance directed at me. He seemed almost surprised that I'd shown signs of having developed a backbone. He'd just have to get used to it.

I put Ivy down for the night and then we watched a Marvel movie. After enough action fight scenes, my mind drifted off and replayed the conversation from earlier. And I realized some things.

Rick was so used to my going along with any suggestion he made that having me put my foot down had unnerved him. I'd always seen my agreeableness as a way to keep the peace and be selfless. Ivy gave me a reason to say no.

For our entire relationship, I'd been the one who compromised (read: did things his way). I'd cared for him, showed my love for him. I'd been selfless; heck, I usually even had dinner ready when he got home from work, like Donna Reed. In short, I'd tried to do all of the things the experts said to.

The experts said that if you put your spouse's needs in front of your own, you'd have a happy marriage. What they didn't say: selflessness has to go both ways. If only one partner is doing that, they turn into a doormat for the other.

How had I become someone who let herself get walked on? I certainly hadn't grown up spineless. I had to be tough to survive multiple foster homes, to survive the angry drunken binges of my first foster dad and the rage of a foster brother who gave me a black eye for going in his room without asking, and to get through six different high schools and graduate with some semblance of sanity.

None of that had prepared me for marriage. Early on, Rick *did* give me love and the family I had always dreamed of. I'd locked up my backbone, but it was always still there, ready to come out if needed.

The moment Ivy was born, my backbone reemerged, stronger than ever. No one could make me back down when it came to protecting her. Not even Rick's petty silent treatment, gaslighting, or throwing fits would sway me. He could be as pissed off at me all he wanted, call me every slur in the book. None of that mattered anymore. I had a new barrier—a shield like Captain America's—that he couldn't penetrate if the situation had the slightest thing to do with Ivy.

And because she was my world, *everything* had to do with Ivy.

CHAPTER TWENTY-FIVE

BECCA

After listening to the smartpen recording several times, I begin looking through the papers I found in Jenn's locker. First, I scan them to get an idea of what the papers contain. Jenn starred and highlighted some sections and wrote in the margins of others. Seeing her handwriting again makes me smile.

As I flip through the pages, a few photographs catch my attention. I stop and flip back a bit to find what caught my eye. There it is—a black-and-white photo of a young boy covers most of the page. It's pixelated, likely magnified. Nothing about the boy stands out to me; it looks like a regular school picture of a typical white kid. His hair and t-shirt don't tell me much; it could have been taken any time in the last couple of decades or so. Jenn wrote the boy's name under it: Ryan Brockbank.

That was the name Rick admitted was his original one, right? The longer I look at the photo, the more it looks like a young Rick. His hair is darker now, and the boyhood roundness is gone, but the eyes are his, and that's a young version of his adult nose.

The paper has a paperclip in the upper left corner, so I reach up and remove it, along with the small stack of other papers it's attached to, and flip through them. I find another photograph, one of a family—father, mother, son. The boy is the same kid as in the school photo; I'm sure of it. The headline above the photo and its accompanying article reads *Boy Orphaned As Parents Drown in Overnight Tragedy.*

My eyes dart to the caption: *Russell, Janet, and Ryan Brockbank, in happier times. Photo courtesy Wolf Photography.* Rick looks about a year younger in the family picture than in the school photo. The mother wears a plaid blazer and matching skirt that looks straight out of Alicia Silverstone's *Clueless* closet, and her hair is only slightly smaller than an 80s poof. The father wears a slightly baggy button-down shirt with large stripes. If all of that weren't enough to tell me that the photo was taken in the 90s, the parachute pants on Rick—known as Ryan back then—are a dead giveaway.

The article is about a boating accident, reported by a boy who called for help on the radio when he woke up and his parents weren't anywhere to be found. The bodies were found a day later, washed up on the shore. I knew Rick didn't have family, but I had no idea how he'd lost them. I feel sympathy for the boy who was, but I have too many questions to trust the man who is. I don't really know Rick and never did.

Neither did Jenn.

I go through the papers, not noticing or caring about the time. Jenn did so much research. She made lists of things to look up, each crossed off as she finished digging into them, and notes upon notes about what she'd found. She'd looked up all kinds of drowning stories, medical articles about drowning, and even common ways of murder that appear to be accidental. Drowning was high on the list, along with car crashes and skiing accidents. She looked into other legal cases where someone—usually the man, but not always—was charged with the death of their partners.

Sleepiness was starting to creep up on me, so I decided to make some coffee so I could get through everything. As I set the papers aside and moved to get off the bed, I noticed Jenn's writing in red at the top of the next page. Two sentences in red ink were starred and circled for good measure.

Many murders and suspected murders are disguised as drownings.
Proving drowning to be murder is very difficult.

167

A chill goes through me. I actually shudder. And now, without a drop of coffee, I'm wide awake.

I gather up the papers and head to the kitchen anyway, where I can eat and have that coffee without the siren call of my pillow. I haven't pulled a true all-nighter since college, but this night might turn into one.

I dig some ice cream out of the freezer and pull two mugs out of the cupboard. I fill one with hot coffee and the other with mint chocolate chip. Then I return to Jenn's research. How did she manage to get all of this information? I mean, I know that librarians are good at this stuff, but this is investigative journalism level.

First, I learn more about Chloe's death. I never knew how she died. I assumed cancer or something similar.

But no. Chloe Brockbank—*not* Banks—drowned in the bathtub. Goosebumps race up my arms.

The autopsy found hard drugs in her system—cocaine, meth, and a high dose of prescription anti-anxiety medication. She died late at night after an argument with her husband. He claimed to have gone out for a drive to cool off, only to return and find his wife dead in the tub.

When I turn the page, it only gets worse. Jenn learned of another woman who'd been married to Rick *after* Chloe.

Her name was Natalie Banks. The groom in the wedding photo is definitely Rick, but the wedding announcement from a small-town newspaper calls him Christopher Banks.

He must have changed his name more than once. I try to keep it all straight: he was born Ryan Christopher Brockbank. That's the person Chloe married.

By the time he married Natalie, he'd begun using his middle name, Christopher, and he'd also lopped off part of his last name, becoming Christopher Banks. But by the time he married Jenn, he'd become Rick Banks. Why did he change his name—twice?

My mind starts to spin as I try to keep it all straight. I decide that caffeine and sugar were good choices; they'll keep me going even if they make me jittery. I swallow some of each and turn the page.

I quickly pass over articles about other cases and printouts from medical sites, preferring to read Jenn's highlights and notes. I want to read it all but can't while I'm still processing the fact that Rick had a wife sandwiched between Chloe and Jenn.

How did his marriage to Natalie end? I flip through the pages quickly, scanning for a clue.

Jenn, tell me you found more about that.

And there it is. Not a divorce decree, medical file, an accident report, or anything else I expected to find. It's an obituary. Natalie Banks died shortly after their first anniversary. I hold my breath and look at the ceiling fan. I don't want to read on but know I can't avoid it. I force myself to lower my gaze and keep reading.

She drowned. I feel sick to my stomach, and it's not from the ice cream.

Behind the obituary is a 911 transcript of the call Rick made after finding Natalie's body. I drop the papers on the table as if they're hot coals. Reading the first few lines of the transcript is too much; it brings me right back to the call I made after finding Jenn.

This is all spooky and wrong.

Did Rick kill his parents too? Was that the only real accident, the thing that gave him the idea of drowning others? Or has he been a killer since the age of ten?

Either way, my best friend married a sociopathic serial killer.

I find a note Jenn wrote to herself: *Figure out how he forged his diplomas, licenses, etc. They're all fake. How did he get them?*

That's the last page in the stapled section, so I set it aside, face down. Several handwritten lines on the next page catch my eye. A couple of spots look like they've gotten wet and dried, smudging the ink a bit. Tears, maybe. I pick up the papers again and read her even, slanted writing:

> *I have to keep smiling. Have to pretend that everything is great and that I don't know the truth. I can't let him suspect anything. Who knows what he'll do to me? I can do this. I can smile and act normal*

*as if my life depends on it. Because it does. At least until I can figure
out what to do and how to get both myself and Ivy out of this.*

Tears build in my eyes and fall, grief over losing Jenn combined with the
horrors I had no idea she'd uncovered. Rick *is* responsible for her death.
Did she suffer? Did she see his eyes through the water as he held her under?

A strangled whimper escapes me as my tears increase. I wish she'd told
me, but I don't know if I could have helped her without tipping him off.
Could I have acted normally around Rick, knowing he's a killer? Could
I have protected her from a man who's gotten away with killing several
times before? Could the police have? I'll never know. I'll always wonder.
The what-ifs will keep me up at night.

Ivy is safe with me for now. There's that, at least. I'll do everything in
my power to keep her that way.

CHAPTER TWENTY-SIX

JENN

December 31
Two and a Half Months before Drowning

New Year's Eve was wonderful. We even found a way to get a baby-sitter that I felt comfortable with: a seventeen-year-old honors student trained in CPR who came over *after* Ivy was in bed for the night. Essentially, we'd be paying the girl to do homework or watch TV in a quiet house in case there was an emergency. Even though Rick thought I was going a bit overboard—and maybe I was—he was glad to get out of the house together for the firm's New Year's party.

I had to admit that getting myself glammed up, from hair to earrings to formal dress, was a breath of fresh air. I had bought a new dress because I had a good twenty pounds or so of baby weight yet to lose—and my shape might not ever be the same as before, no matter how much I lost. But when I looked in the mirror—black dress, red heels, red lipstick, an updo—I liked what I saw, and I smiled. Even my smile looked happy.

When the new year rang in, everyone toasted and kissed their significant others. The kiss Rick gave me was hot and intense, hungry in the way I hadn't felt from him in a long time. He pulled back, slightly out of breath. I was breathing heavily too. He grinned. I grinned back. At that moment, I felt as if we'd found our old selves again, that maybe we could work out after all. That I wouldn't have to run from him with our little girl.

For that brief spell, I was able to love him as I once had, to hope for our future, and forget the contention and stress of the past months. Maybe I'd made far too much of everything.

Maybe we really could be a forever family after all.

I wanted it so much. I wanted to believe it. I wanted to live it. That night, when he kissed me again and led me to our room, my knees melting as they hadn't since before Ivy was conceived, a little corner of my mind whispered questions.

Not tonight. I mentally slammed the door and let myself fall into Rick's embrace.

℗

22 February
About Seven Weeks before Drowning

After a Saturday morning of grocery shopping, I took Ivy from the car and got her settled into her highchair so I could unload the groceries more easily. When I returned on my last trip, she wasn't in the highchair but in Rick's arms at the top of the stairs.

Leaning over the banister edge, he held Ivy, suspended in the air with a thin blanket slipped over her head.

"What are you doing?" I gasped, grocery bags forgotten at my feet.

Rick laughed. "Aaah," he said in a sing-songy tone, once with every bounce of his arms. "Aaah, aaaah! Don't move, Ivy, or I might drop you!"

I raced toward the stairs, having nearly lost my mind. "What are you doing?" I repeated. "Pull her back up!" Before Rick said another word, I'd taken Ivy into my arms, yanked the blanket off her head, and held her close. "What were you *thinking*?"

"Sheesh. It was a joke," Rick said. "Remember how Michael Jackson did that with his baby?"

"How he *endangered* his baby?" I snapped. "Yeah, I remember. Not funny."

Ivy began to fuss, whether from her own fear or because she sensed mine, I didn't know. I made soothing noises and patted her back as I headed down to the kitchen.

"Lighten up," Rick said, following from behind. "It was just one floor indoors. He was outside a high-rise, dangling the kid a hundred feet above concrete. She's fine." He patted Ivy's head, then sat at the table. He scrolled on his phone, and I let the silence settle in as I put away groceries, never putting Ivy down.

With the groceries away, I felt uneasy and had to get out of the house. I decided to go to the gym, bringing Ivy along to be in the daycare there rather than at home with Rick. I didn't know when I'd feel safe leaving her with him again.

After getting Ivy fed and changed, I put some gym clothes on and gave Rick a quick kiss goodbye. "Off to work out."

"Good job," he said, eying my figure.

I forced a smile and headed out with Ivy. I worked out almost every weekday morning, though not every weekend. Today was an exception. I needed to work off the nervous energy from before and maybe read more of my research that I'd printed out and kept in my gym locker.

Sometimes that meant reading PDFs on my tablet. On other days, it meant listening to various true-crime podcasts at one-and-a-half speed. I found two devoted to Rick. Rather, one was about his parents' deaths, and the other was about Chloe's death and his trial.

As I started up a treadmill with my tablet propped on it, I thought through what I'd seen at home. *Would* Rick eventually hurt Ivy? He could easily have dropped her, and he could have pleaded an accident. No shaken-baby syndrome or anything like that. A horrible accident where she fell fifteen feet.

The more I learned about Rick's past—so much more than losing his first wife—the more I worried about me and Ivy. Things had been so much better between us since New Year's Eve. I'd let myself exercise without thinking about Rick's past, hoping that whoever he'd been, he was different and we would be different.

But seeing her held over the banister . . . that made my blood run cold. He wasn't different. He'd always been this person.

Why hadn't he walked away from me and Ivy already? He'd never had a wife as long as this, never had a child before. He'd always moved on.

I shook my head and increased the speed on the treadmill. I pulled up a blog post from the podcast I'd listened to about Natalie's death. It included all kinds of things they'd talked about on the show—episode transcripts, photos, and more.

The text was plenty big to read even while running. As I went through one page after another, I looked for any mention of either of his wives or his parents. There was nothing about them. In all of my research, I hadn't found anyone else who connected the other deaths to Rick in any way. Was I the only one?

After finishing one article, I went to another, one that discussed Chloe's autopsy. One claim nearly tripped me right there on the treadmill. I steadied myself on the side rails and zoomed in on the actual report to read the text myself.

Chloe had been six months pregnant when she died.

I knew everything else on the report: drugs in her system, accidental drowning declared the cause and manner of death. But she was pregnant. Estimated thirty weeks along.

Rick had told me that he wondered *if* she'd been pregnant. He had to have known she was. At thirty weeks, the baby would be moving like crazy, and Chloe would have been showing a lot. The baby had probably been viable if it had been given the chance to breathe.

Still standing on the rails of the treadmill, my breathing sped up as if I were still running. I slowed the belt to a walk and kept reading. The article pointed out that one of the most common ways for a pregnant woman to die was by murder at the hand of the baby's father. It went on to list Scott Peterson and other notorious murderers that fit the type.

A shiver went through me despite the heat of the room and the sweat on my forehead. I wiped my face with the hand towel I'd brought, hoping no one in the room wouldn realize that some of it was from tears.

Time to focus, not get emotional, I ordered myself. I took a long drink from my water bottle, then dove back in, but I went to a different post altogether, one under the site's *Victimology* tag, which would mean talking about who Chloe was, not about her death.

I learned that she'd been a special education teacher. Her students adored her, and she got a state award in Oregon for her work with special-needs students. The file had several stories in newspapers from towns so small that even minor events were written about. Like the one about her work with a nonverbal autistic boy, who, at the end of the school year, did what no one had believed possible—he gave her a hug. He didn't look her in the eye as he did it. His father was quoted:

> *It was a breakthrough moment. We've prayed so hard for such a small thing, and we'd almost given up hope. When I saw it on the last day of school, I cried like a little kid, and I'm not ashamed to admit it.*

The more I read about her life, the more it seemed eerily similar to mine. Before college, she'd gone through the foster system, bouncing from one house and school to another, thanks to her drugged-out birth parents. They eventually lost their parental rights, but she was never adopted. As I had, she'd simply aged out of the system.

I never met her, but I'd met dozens of girls like her. I *was* just like her. Her young-adult life mirrored so much of my own, with only minor details tweaked, like names and locations. The pain from my teen years and beyond roared back as I read about her.

Like me, after she'd graduated from high school, she had no family and she was on her own. With no one to support her emotionally or financially—not even a distant aunt or cousin—she had to pick her way through the jungle of new adulthood she suddenly found herself in.

The treadmill stayed at three miles per hour. I couldn't go back to running, not with my heart beating painfully from flashbacks of my own early adulthood. Couch-surfing when I could. Sleeping outside when I couldn't, sometimes on the less-visible side of a big tree in a city park, hoping no one would see or hurt me.

Eventually, as Chloe had, I graduated from college and ended up with a stable job doing what I loved—helping children find a love of books and learning, helping older patrons access the resources they needed to find employment and housing. Librarians had been a lifeline for me, and then I became one. *I* got to be that help and mentor to others. As my final triumph over the odds, I'd gotten married to a successful litigation attorney and had a child.

Would I become another sad statistic after all? Not an aged-out-of-the-system cautionary tale—I *had* overcome those odds—but a victim of the man I hadn't known I'd married.

Climbing out of the hole of my childhood wouldn't matter if, in the end, Rick took my life and the life of my baby girl.

I wiped my face again and kept walking on the treadmill, slowly, needing to keep reading. I took a short break, though, to gather my emotions.

Through college, Chloe had worked a variety of jobs, from retail to dog walking to custodial work at her community college. She applied for and received Pell Grants and scholarships.

Nothing I found explained how she met Rick, but I could've provided an approximation of what their courtship probably looked like: romantic, amazing, passionate, filled with gifts and attention, and, most of all, it had been fast. So had mine.

Clearly, Rick had a method that worked. Part of his pattern was to make a woman feel special, even though each of us was simply the next link in his chain. We were nearly identical as far as our lack of family. Regardless of what he said, how much adoration or gifts he showered us with, we weren't special at all. I found myself belonging to a terrible club of women who'd fallen for Rick Banks.

After my workout, I secured the research in my locker, as usual, then picked up Ivy from the daycare room. I held her so tight that she protested and tried to wriggle free. I kissed her head and laughed, thinking she'd start crawling as soon as she could figure it out.

I got her settled in the car and turned it on. And sat there for several minutes, thinking—processing.

If Rick had killed both Chloe—along with their unborn child—and Natalie, why had he let Ivy be born at all?

That's when the answer came to me, so clearly that I couldn't believe I hadn't seen it before. Ivy and I still served a purpose. More than anything, Rick wanted to make partner, but he couldn't unless he was married . . . *and* had a family.

He had both now. If my suspicions were correct, as soon as he made partner, our lives would be worth nothing to him. No one would take away a promotion after his poor wife and daughter died in a tragic "accident."

How much longer would it take him to make partner? Months? Years? Hopefully long enough for me to figure out how to extricate Ivy and myself safely.

The truth was glaring, now that I let myself look at it. Rick's hope of making partner was the only reason I was still alive. It was the only reason Ivy had been allowed to be born.

I felt sick. I sat in the car, gripping the steering wheel, holding back tears of shock and fear. Would I be able to make sure Ivy got to grow up?

She had lived long enough to learn how to roll over and sit on her own. Would she fully transition to solid foods? Learn to walk and run? Say *Mama*?

I had more research to do, not only about Rick but about how to escape, assume new identities, and most of all, hide from someone who already knew how to do all of that.

Someone who'd disappeared after committing murder. More than once. Someone who'd know how to find us.

Somehow, I had to get Ivy away from Rick in time.

CHAPTER TWENTY-SEVEN

BECCA

I never expected to visit anyone in jail, but here I am, standing in the doorway of a room where I'll be sitting across a wood table from Rick Banks, or whoever he is. I did expect to be separated by something more than a table. I'd pictured those booths with glass partitions and phones on either side—one for the arrested person and another for the visitor—like you see in movies. Maybe those are only in prisons or for inmates who are already convicted of serious crimes, not a county jail.

Maybe I've seen one too many movies.

Normally, I can camouflage nervousness by checking email on my phone, but I'm not allowed to have anything with me. I've been searched, and my purse is in a locker. I was told to not bring any metal, which means I'm wearing an uncomfortable sports bra—I wasn't going to take chances that an underwire would keep me out. I can't play with my keyring or run my fingers along the strap of my purse.

"Are you all right, ma'am?" The guard inside the visitation room has a gravelly voice—all practical, though not unkind, encouraging me to go into the room.

My mouth feels dry, my chest tight. "I'm fine. Thanks." I step across the threshold, and he gestures for me to sit in the chair on one side of the table.

"No touching. Stay on your side of the table for your safety."

I nod my understanding. "Thanks," I say, and though he probably thinks it's just a polite platitude, I'm grateful that the rules won't let Rick hug me. He'd try otherwise, and I wouldn't dare say no, but the idea of his arms around me, even for a quick hug, makes me shudder.

I sit on the chair but don't scoot it in. I don't want to be any closer to Rick than I have to be. If I could stand on the other side of the room and talk to him from there, I would. If I could have avoided coming altogether without raising alarms, I would have. But through his attorney, Rick specifically asked for me to visit—coating on the guilt by pointing out that he has no family, no other visitors.

I'm loath to see him again, though a piece of me is curious. Now that I know about his past—his parents, his past marriages, their tragic ends—will I be able to see the evil in him I missed before? Will I be able to weasel a bit of information out of him when he doesn't expect it?

The day after Mr. Arrington, his lawyer, contacted me about visiting Rick, I sent in the required application. It was approved in just over a week rather than the minimum three weeks the website said to expect. I can't help but wonder if Rick's deep pockets and a lawyer with clout managed to expedite my application.

However it happened, here I am. Will I regret coming?

The oak table is thick and heavy, with a honey-colored grain. The top looks worn, smoothed by time. As I wait, my heart rate speeding up alarmingly, I stare at a knot in the wood and try to breathe. In, out.

Another door heaves open, and I hear clinking metal. I picture the prisoners from news reports: hands and feet both bound and then a long chain connecting wrists and ankles. I hope Rick's hobbled like that so he can't try to touch me before the guards can stop him. I've never been afraid of Rick before. Now, I'm terrified. He killed my best friend and is guilty of many others. He's an unpredictable monster.

He enters my peripheral vision. Moments later, he sits across from me. I can't exactly pretend I don't see the bright-orange jumpsuit. He rests his hands—handcuffed, but not in chains, so maybe I was hearing ones connecting his ankles—atop the table and says nothing at first. I brace myself, then lift my gaze, unsure what I'll see.

Rick looks like nothing but a typical tired man. Clean, though he could use a shave. His hair is a lighter color than I've ever seen; whatever product he used to put in it must have made it look darker. His temples have hints of gray. He couldn't have grown gray hair in the time he's been here, so he must have colored it until the arrest.

He doesn't intimidate me as I thought he would. Looking at him here, no one would think he's a wealthy attorney. He looks sad, not arrogant. And he's not particularly attractive anymore.

Is it the jumpsuit? I don't think so, at least not entirely. I think it's partly because I know his secrets, or at least some of them. And he has no idea.

"Hey," he says.

"Hey," I echo. My mouth is still dry; I wish they'd have let me have a water bottle with me. "So, um . . . sorry I couldn't bring Ivy. I tried, but minors can't visit unless it's with a parent or legal guardian, and my guardianship isn't official yet, so they wouldn't approve it."

"It's okay." He doesn't sound mad, which sends a shaky sigh of relief from me.

"I'll keep trying," I say. "My visitor application got through a lot faster than most, so . . ." I hold up crossed fingers and attempt a smile.

"It's fine," he says, waving away my words, or sort of. It's a gesture I imagine would be a wave if his wrists weren't in handcuffs. "I wanted to see *you*."

"Oh." I try to keep surprise from registering on my face. Does he not care about seeing Ivy? I assumed she was the reason I would be visiting in the first place—to bring her along when I could. Does he want to see just *me*? If so, why? What if he thinks we had a connection that night he came over? Does he think I'll be his girlfriend on the outside?

Get me out of here.

Without meaning to, I glance back at the guard who's been my companion for the entire visit so far. "Fourteen minutes," he says as if I asked how much longer we have. "He can earn more time through good behavior."

I nod and look back at Rick. He has circles under his eyes, and his back is bowed slightly. Under other circumstances, I'd feel compassion for someone who looks frayed by stress. But I can't muster compassion for him.

When I don't speak, Rick does. "I was hoping you could help me."

Red flags pop up in my head. "With . . . what?" I ask, guarded.

"With proving I didn't do this."

But you did. You're a murderer. I can't say that, and I can't show it. I call on the lessons of Mr. Brower, my high school drama teacher, to keep my face straight.

"I don't know how *I* could help," I say, then immediately regret the phrasing; he'll tell me how. Then I'll have to tell him I don't *want* to help, that I know he's a killer who deserves to rot in prison.

Rick doesn't seem to think my behavior is anything but normal. Mr. Brower would be impressed. Rick leans forward on the table. I'm extra glad I kept my chair at a distance; I don't have to lean back to avoid his face. I *do* have to grip the sides of my wood chair to keep myself from standing.

This will be over soon.

"You were her best friend," Rick says.

I nod, and my eyes tear up despite my efforts.

"If she told anyone anything, it would have been you."

I nod again, but then shake my head no. "She probably would have, but she didn't say anything about someone trying to kill her."

"No text or emails or anything?"

"No."

"What about diaries? Did she keep one? They didn't find anything like that on her laptop, but maybe she wrote one by hand."

"As her husband, you'd know better than I would," I say. "A diary would be pretty easy to find, I'd think."

Rick drops back against the chair and sighs with frustration. "You'd think. They didn't find anything when they searched the house. After they were done with it, I had Jay poke around, but he couldn't find anything either."

"Jay?" I repeat.

"Sorry. Arrington, my lawyer. First name Jeffrey."

"And his friends call him Jay."

"Well, *I* do." He shrugs as if he's never wondered whether being referred to by his first initial bothers the man. "We haven't found anything at the house, and Jay searched the staff room at the library. Nothing. Have you cleared her locker at the gym yet?"

My stomach lurches, and I fear the unease registers on my face, if only in a flash. I suddenly know why Jenn kept her research and the smartpen there. "Yeah," I say. "I picked up her things."

His expression lightens. "Anything in there? A flash drive, jewelry, a will, anything you wouldn't expect in a gym locker?"

"Nothing like that," I say, counting off on my fingers as if remembering the list takes effort. "Workout clothes, a few toiletries, a towel . . . and um, oh yeah, a notebook and a pen. It wasn't a diary, though." I hold my breath, waiting to see if he'll ask to see them. While I'm not directly lying, I'm not telling him that there were pages and pages of printouts and that the pen wasn't your typical ballpoint. I'm careful with what I say here; they've got to have cameras on us. If he wants me to surrender everything I found to Arrington, I'll have to figure something out.

"Figures," he says. "She tracked every workout in a notebook, huh? Sounds like her."

"Yeah." I nod and attempt a chuckle. "It does sound like her." That's not what the pen or the notebook contained, but I won't be mentioning that.

"What did you . . ." How can I phrase this without ticking him off? I glance over my shoulder at the guard, who must be at least six-four. He gives me a reassuring nod, so I turn back to Rick. "Were you hoping to find anything specific besides a diary?"

"Just trying to find anything that she might have been hiding from me. They even searched her car. Nothing."

"Why would she have been hiding anything?" I dare ask only because he brought up the word—and because he seems defeated, even smaller and weaker.

"I don't know," he said, so casually that he might as well have been guessing about tomorrow's weather. "Maybe she was cheating on me and kept gifts from him—you know, necklaces or rings—somewhere. Maybe he wanted her to leave me, and she refused, so"—he makes a cutting gesture across his neck and a sound almost like a wrong-answer buzzer—"he finished her off."

How can a man speak of his murdered wife so casually—so *callously?*

"She would never have cheated on you."

My mouth must be hanging open, because his eyes flit downward and then he laughs, shaking his head side to side as if I just declared the Earth flat. "Man, are you really that naive?"

"I'm not naive," I say. "Maybe as a lawyer, you're used to being around unethical people so you assume everyone is one." The words tumble out, and the second I see his jaw muscle popping out as he clenches his teeth in anger, I regret them.

"Sorry," I say quickly. "I shouldn't have said that. But seriously, Rick, she wouldn't have done that. You knew her as well as anyone, right?" I question the statement as soon as I say it but soldier on. "You completed the family she always longed for. She would never have cheated on you."

Her vows were between her and God, she said, not between her and Rick, and she took them seriously. She'd never cheat. Period.

A light bulb turns on in my head. Not about cheating. I'm as sure about her being faithful as ever. But maybe she *was* miserable. Maybe she wanted a divorce, and Rick knew it, and because she was threatening divorce, *that* was why Rick, in his own words, "finished her off." Like every modern woman, I've heard over and over that the time right after you leave an abusive partner is the most dangerous. Jenn's death could easily be one more statistic proving it.

If I'd only known that things were rough, I would've offered help—I could've paid for Jenn to have a therapist so Rick would never know about it. She and Ivy could have moved in with me. The twins would have been over the moon. And Jenn might still be alive.

"Did she tell you anything that might help?" Rick asks.

The opposite, actually. "Like what?" I ask.

"Well, like some guy she found attractive, or things she got mad at me about, I don't know . . ." His voice trails off as if there's a lot he could add to the list.

"Nothing," I say.

Looking back, I can't see any clear signs that her death was imminent. Nothing the day of, the weekend before, the week before that . . . I keep thinking back in time, trying to remember, but the farther into the past I go, the murkier it gets. I'll have to check my calendar to remember specifics, but I'm relatively confident that Jenn never gave any inkling that things were as bad as they had to have been.

"In fact," I tell him, remembering one conversation that cemented the fact that she'd never cheat, "a few months ago, we watched *The Bridges of Madison County* together, and she *hated* it."

Rick raised an eyebrow skeptically. "Isn't that some big tragic romance? Chick-flick stuff?"

"A lot of women find it romantic." I'm half impressed he's even heard of it, both because it starred Meryl Streep instead of some plastic Barbie and because it's relatively old in film years. "But Jenn didn't like the movie because she couldn't get past the infidelity. She insisted that cheating wasn't an option—ever."

I remember a conversation with Jenn when we were watching the movie at my place, both of us on the couch, the twins asleep, Ivy nursing in Jenn's arms. "Cheating is *never* an option?" I pressed. "Even if you're miserable?"

"Never," she said. "Divorce, maybe, in a desperate situation. Not cheating."

At the time, I was both impressed and confused. Now as I sit across from Rick, I don't know what to think.

Rick shrugs. "I don't know what to think anymore," he says, hands spread as far out as the cuffs allow, which looks silly, makes him look powerless.

"Me neither," I say. What else is there to say?

We hold each other's eyes for a moment of silence, and in his, I see darkness, something that looks dead and angry at the same time. His gaze feels like a threat without a word.

What does he see in my eyes? I break the stare, not wanting him to attempt to control me or read me. Staring at the wood grain again, I ask, "How were things between you? Were you fighting?"

He slams the handcuffs against the table and jumps to his shackled feet. "*You* think I killed her too?" He leans over, arms against the table. Two security guards jump into action, one on each side, ready to step in.

"You need to calm down," one tells Rick.

As I try to calm my racing heart, I'm glad they're here, but I wish I hadn't come.

"I gave the police all of the leads we came up with," I say. "They followed up on all of them, including the white van. They came up with nothing."

"So they defaulted to the easy mark—the husband." Rick glares at me, teeth bared. "I shouldn't be in here!" He lurches forward, but the guards restrain him. "I should have gotten bail. This is bullshit," he yells, though within a second or two, he's held face-first on the table, one cheek pressed against the surface as a string of curses fly. Spit flies from his mouth. I lean away, back pressed against the chair. I can't breathe.

"I'll get out of here!" Rick screams. "And when I do, everyone who tried to get me in here is gonna pay."

The guards yank him into a position that makes him go silent. I'm not sure if he's taken the hint to shut up or if he's in too much pain to speak.

"You'd better go," the other guard says to me.

I stand and look for my purse out of habit before remembering I don't have it, then quickly move to the door. The guards watch me the whole way. So does Rick. I can feel his glare on my back. Only after the door slams shut behind me with a metallic thud, making me jump slightly, do I react to what I've just been through. My entire body begins to shake, and even as I leave the jail and walk to my car, I can hardly keep hold of my phone because my hands are trembling so badly.

I think of the monster Rick has shown himself to be.

I'll do everything in my power to make sure he never again walks free. Not only so Jenn gets justice, but so Ivy will never have to spend another moment with him.

Rick deserves to die for what he did, but, if necessary, I'll settle for a life sentence.

"I'll do whatever it takes, Jenn," I whisper from the driver seat in my car. "Anything to make sure Rick stays behind bars forever. And I'll keep Ivy safe. Promise."

CHAPTER TWENTY-EIGHT

JENN

March 3
16 Days before Drowning

Saturday. I lay in bed, scrolling on my phone during the quiet of an unusual morning of Ivy sleeping in. Rick was already up, and he was in a strangely good mood, seldom losing his temper or being irritable. He'd even helped out with dishes—something I'd long since stopped asking for.

It was enough to make me worry that he knew I was up to something, that he'd found the research hidden in my locker.

The Jenn from a year ago would have been thrilled that he was finally changing, being the man, the husband, I'd always wanted. Now, I didn't dare believe any of it. Not after everything I'd learned. Not after he'd put Ivy in danger by hanging her over the banister. Not when I had a pretty good idea of why he'd let Ivy be born and why we were still here.

I adjusted my position on my pillows and pulled up the calendar on my phone. I counted the days—ten since the stairs incident. Since then, he hadn't done anything worrisome with Ivy, though I hadn't left him alone with her even for a second. He had stayed positive and his old self with me. Every so often, I ached inside, wanting so much to believe that the old Rick was back. That after some bizarre anomaly that had made him seem so mean and cruel—maybe I could blame it on an aneurysm or temporary insanity—the guy I thought I'd married was back.

I knew better.

I just hated that I knew better.

In the week and a half since I decided I had to leave Rick, I hadn't managed to learn anything about taking on a new identity, living off the grid, or anything else that would be useful in hiding from him.

Scratch *useful*. Make that *necessary*.

The only things I'd uncovered were obvious things that had to be beginner level to someone who'd committed the same crime several times, as Rick had. Even I knew some of the basics going in: I was smart enough to know not to use social media or GPS when trying to get away and stay hidden.

For as much as my librarian research skills had helped me uncover Rick's past, they hadn't helped much in figuring out my future—a future that loomed ahead like a dark specter. Disappearing off the grid took intelligence, which I had. But it also took connections and money. I had neither.

Plus, no matter how smart you are, all it takes is one small obscure detail or slip-up to blow your cover. Rick would find any mistake I made, and he'd come after us. He'd hide our bodies and claim we were abducted. Or he'd stage an "accident." The end result would be me and Ivy dead.

I couldn't risk Ivy's life like that, so I tried to keep digging, wishing all the while I had an FBI contact who could get me and Ivy into the witness protection program, but even then, we might be out of luck. Everything I could find about the protection program said you had to be an important witness for a trial to get into it. No charges meant no trial, no witnesses, no testimony. No witness protection.

A successful escape would mean a lonely life. It meant changing my name—and Ivy's—and cutting off all ties. That included Becca. Losing her would be a kind of death all by itself, but letting Becca stay in my life could be a literal death. Mine, Ivy's, maybe Becca's. I had no way of knowing how far Rick's vendetta might go.

Until I knew we were safe, I'd have to avoid public cameras where possible, change my appearance somehow—dye my hair, at least.

I got out of bed to shower and get ready for the day. I'd be meeting Becca for lunch. How many more times would we get to hang out until I had to escape?

My hope was to be gone by Christmas, if not earlier. Getting us away safely would take months, but fortunately, Rick making partner could take years.

As I showered and then did my hair and makeup, I thought through what the next weeks should look like for me. More research was a priority. Maybe I should take a leave of absence from work but not tell Rick. I could maintain the same daily schedule, but I'd research at various city libraries instead of going to work. I'd have to account for why I wasn't bringing in a paycheck, though.

Ready for lunch, I looked myself over in the mirror and nodded. *You'll figure it out*, I thought. *Somehow.*

Half an hour later, after Ivy woke up and was fed and diapered, I drove with her to the restaurant to meet Becca.

I'm not supposed to be alive, I thought suddenly. *Neither is Ivy, if he'd followed his usual plans.*

Sitting at a red light, I heard Ivy giggling behind me, and that made me laugh. When she heard me, she laughed harder, and I couldn't help but laugh too. But that only released stress and worry, and tears flooded out. I covered my mouth to hold in a sob, not wanting to draw attention from other cars or have Ivy hear me and start crying too.

How was this my life? It felt like a reality TV show, that at some point, a host would pop out from around a corner and tell me where the hidden cameras were. None of it was real. None of it *should* be real.

When I pulled into the restaurant parking lot, there was no sign of Becca's car yet. I used the extra time to touch up my makeup in hopes of camouflaging my tears.

They were still falling, though. I need to get them under control.

Five minutes and a new layer of foundation later, I left the car and toted Ivy in her carrier into the restaurant. Becca arrived right behind me.

Lunch began as usual, with fun catch-up talk and food, but as it wound down, the conversation shifted to aspects of motherhood that didn't involve being spat up on or walking over Lego pieces and letting out a string of profanity—I laughed so hard at that one. I needed that laugh.

"You're such a good mom," I told Becca.

"Be sure to tell the twins that," she said with a chuckle. "In their minds, I'm not much better than a warden forcing them to do hard labor."

"Meaning toilets."

Becca nodded with mock soberness. "Yea. And—horrors—the *dishes*."

"Cruel," I said, with proper fake shock. "But seriously, I want to have the same connection with Ivy that you have with the twins. I'm thinking I might not keep going to work so I can have more time with her." That was one of the reasons, anyway.

What I didn't say was that I was desperate to build a bond so strong that nothing and no one could sever it. Not time, not Rick, not anything. I also didn't say that I knew the hourglass was emptying, that I didn't have ten years to create that bond. I probably didn't have ten months.

"Stay home if you want to," Becca said. "But don't stay home over guilt. You can't be the ideal mother all the time."

"I know," I said vaguely.

Becca pressed the issue. "We get enough pressure from, well, everywhere, to be the perfect everything. And motherhood is hard. The best moms screw up because they're human. Be kind to yourself."

"I will," I promised, but she didn't understand the stakes I was facing. I had to be perfect in keeping my daughter safe.

Ivy started blowing raspberries—her latest trick. I pulled out my phone to take a video of it.

"I just feel this need, this urgency, to be with her and cram in everything I can with her, pour my love into her little heart every moment." I click my phone off and took a sip of my drink. "I'm ridiculous. I know."

Becca's mouth quirked to one side in a smile. "Not ridiculous. It makes perfect sense." She spoke softly, in a tone I recognized as one where emotion hovered right under the surface. My throat tightened, and tears sprang to my eyes too. "You're giving your own daughter the love that *you* never had from your mother."

I nodded, my throat so tight with emotion I couldn't speak. She was right, but there was more to it, things I couldn't tell her yet, if ever. If I had to run with Ivy and assume a new identity, I might not ever be able to tell her. She'd be the first person he'd go to when trying to find me. I loved Becca and the twins too much to put them in potential danger.

If I tried to leave Rick and divorce him like a normal person, I'd have to win full custody of Ivy. I'd end up fighting Rick in court to get it, because even if he didn't want to be a father, even if he cared nothing for Ivy, he'd do everything in his power to ruin and control me. When it came to anything lawyerly, he was like a tiger with its jaws around prey—he'd never let go until forced to.

And I wouldn't have the money to fight him.

What I couldn't get over was that, no matter what happened, Rick's future looked about the same as his past. If I didn't succeed, and he managed to kill me and our baby, he'd pick a different name again, marry yet another unsuspecting woman, and kill her.

If I managed to divorce him *and* escape, he'd move on with his life just fine.

No matter what I did or didn't do, Rick would be a free man, a murderer ready to strike again. I couldn't bear the thought. My eyes began to burn, and I blinked, sending tears down my cheeks.

Becca reached across the table and covered my hand with hers. "You are the best mom I've ever seen," she said, not knowing that I wasn't crying about that.

We talked so long that I had to hurry home from lunch. Rick said he'd be out running errands for the afternoon, and I was sure he'd return home hungry, if not hangry.

I plopped Ivy in her highchair and let her play with Cheerios and a wooden spoon as I worked on dinner. The salmon was nearly done in the oven, so I grabbed the tongs to toss a salad. That's when I heard the garage door open. I glanced at the clock. He was about five minutes early; good thing dinner was almost ready.

A minute later, the inside door opened behind me, and I plastered on the same wide smile I'd been wearing around Rick since the day I got the tattoo that started all of this.

Half the time, I regretted getting it. The other half, I was grateful because it shined a light on secrets that needed to come to out. *Knowledge is good, right? Even when it's hard to accept?*

Yes. Yes, knowledge is good. I'd never go back to living in ignorance.

"Hey, babe," Rick said cheerfully from behind me. "How was lunch?"

Before I could answer, he took the tongs from me, set them in the bowl, then pulled me into his arms. I stiffened at first until he leaned in for a kiss. Not just a peck. A long, deep kiss.

He finally pulled back, wearing a smile bigger than my fake one. He looked like a little boy who'd been given a puppy. Something was up. I couldn't remember the last time he looked so . . . *gleeful.*

"What?" I asked tentatively, though still wearing my broad smile. A flash of happy energy zipped through me, but I didn't trust it. "Why do you look so excited?"

"I bought something." His eyes widened as if he'd said he just won the lottery. He tilted his head to one side. "Actually, two somethings."

"A new car?" I asked. He'd wanted a nicer car for a year now.

"Sort of," he said enigmatically. "Look at this." He revealed a glossy brochure in his hand of big trucks. "I bought this one. Only it's black."

"Seriously?" I said, looking at the picture. "It's gorgeous."

"And powerful," Rick said with an approving nod. He set the brochure on the counter. "I got the truck because I'll need it for the other thing."

"I don't understand," I said. "What's all of this about?"

His cheerful, mischievous look sent off alarm bells in my head, but I had no idea what they were alerting me to. We'd long since agreed that big purchases were something we decided on together, though he held me to that rule, not himself.

Something was different.

"The other thing is the part I'm really excited about."

"What is it?" I asked, feigning excitement. I looked around and pointed at his briefcase. "Is it in there?"

"Nope." He grinned even wider, then tilted his head toward the garage. "It's outside. Come see."

My eyes flitted to the door to the garage and back at him. "What is it?"

"Come *on*," he said, tugging me in that direction and squeezing my fingers almost to the point of pain.

"Okay," I said, following, though I didn't exactly have a choice.

Rick was utterly *stoked* about . . . something. I hadn't seen him in such a good mood since . . . I couldn't remember when. I'd never seen such excitement from him, even on our wedding day.

He turned the handle of the door leading to the garage, but before opening the door, he held up his free hand. "Close your eyes."

I raised an eyebrow, so he said it again and shielded my vision with his hand.

"They're closed," I said obediently.

I heard the door open and then he led me carefully through it, down the two concrete stairs, and into the garage itself. He turned me so we walked past the cool metal of my car, then kept going, toward the driveway.

"So what you should know," Rick said as he led me, blindfolded, "is that this morning I got some good news, so this is my way of celebrating. I think you'll agree it's worthy of something big."

My stomach twisted. "Oh?"

"We're almost there," he said, still leading me.

What he was up to? Had he bought a motorcycle? Another car? A jacuzzi? *Had* he won the lottery? Gotten money from embezzlement or something else illegal?

When I was standing in what I assumed was the middle of the driveway, facing the side yard, Rick stopped me and rotated me to face the side of the drive, but one hand remained over my eyes. "The good news is . . . I made partner!"

My heart stopped and I couldn't breathe.

"And here's what I bought to celebrate!" He removed his hand from my eyes with a flourish.

My jaw—and my stomach—dropped.

He interpreted my reaction as surprised or pleased. I *was* surprised. But my overarching emotion was pure terror, ice water in my veins.

"Isn't she gorgeous?" Rick clapped his hands and pumped the air with his fist. "I'm going to name her *The Jennifer.*"

And with that, Rick climbed aboard his new boat.

CHAPTER TWENTY-NINE

BECCA

've become the de facto landing place for anything that has to do with the Banks family. I suppose now that I'm Ivy's temporary legal guardian, things involving Jenn or Rick head my way too, as if the space-time continuum has bent, sending all kinds of stuff toward me to deal with.

Some days, it's Detective Andrus with questions or updates. Yes, he's followed up on the leads I gave him before. No, none of them panned out. Yes, he's sure. I gave him the papers and the pen from Jenn's locker—after making copies for myself—and though he thanked me, he won't say a word about whether he's doing anything with them.

Other days—far too often—Arrington calls with questions about Rick's defense.

The phone rings from a local number, but I don't recognize it.

I've become good at hanging up quickly on reporters—they call me more often now that Rick's not easily available for comment—but I still answer all calls to be sure I don't miss something important.

"Is this Rebecca Kalos?" a voice says. Middle-aged female, if I had to guess.

"Yes."

"This is Marianne Lobel, the M.E."

"The . . . excuse me?" I ask.

"Sorry. The M.E. The medical examiner? I'm calling about the remains of Jennifer Banks."

"Oh."

I've fielded calls about a lot of things relating to Jenn's death, but it's all been about the event itself, not about what's physically left of her. I'm suddenly lightheaded. I lower myself to a kitchen chair. Good thing Ivy's taking a nap; if I'd been holding her, I might have dropped her.

"What can I do for you?" And why was she calling me instead of Rick or Arrington?

"I'm calling to notify you that the remains can be released now, for whatever kind of memorial or burial you wish."

"Oh." Apparently, that's all I'm capable of saying. My mind spins in circles. I've had so many other things occupying my thoughts—among them, the latest Zoom meeting for work and several fires I have to put out on the Alcestis Dresses campaign. Now I need to refocus so I can finally give Jenn a proper burial and funeral.

"I tried to reach her husband, Mr. Banks, and I was directed to his attorney, who gave me your number. He said you'd be handling the remains. Is that correct?"

"That was never communicated to me, but I'm happy to do it."

The sound of riffling papers comes through the line. "Let's see, I understand that her husband is currently incarcerated and his phone privileges are restricted?"

"That's right."

"But I see here that you're on his approved call list. Are you family?"

Might as well have been. Jenn's, anyway. Not his.

"His wife and I were very close . . . friends." My voice sounds husky. If this call lasts much longer, I'll be sobbing by the end of it.

"I'm sorry for your loss," Ms. Lobel says. "If you could speak with her husband about his wishes and then call my office to let us know which funeral home will be retrieving the remains, that would be very helpful."

"Sure. Yeah, I can do that." I sound like someone with half a brain, but I've learned that shock surrounding your best friend's murder shows up at unexpected times, in giant waves. When a new one hits, it knocks you off your feet and does strange things to your ability to think and speak.

Ms. Lobel thanks me and hangs up. Before I forget her name and the entire point of her call, I write myself a note. Then I stare at it, still unable to fully grasp, in my core, that the "remains" are Jenn's body. All that's left of her. A shell of who she used to be, the flesh she once inhabited. And that it's been sitting around in a refrigerator for weeks. I can't stop images of finding Jenn from flashing through my mind.

Next to my notes about the call, I make a list of things to ask Rick regarding the memorial service. We can't put that conversation off forever. It will likely need to happen while he's awaiting trial because who knows how long that'll take, and if he'll ever get out.

Before I can call the county jail to request and schedule a phone call with Rick, my cell vibrates with several back-to-back texts coming in. I check the clock before looking at them, gauging how much time I have before Ivy will wake up from her nap. Fifteen minutes, probably. Thirty if I'm lucky.

The texts are from Mark at work, and they're long. Standing in my kitchen, wearing leggings, an old college sweatshirt, and a messy bun, I'm far from the advertising executive he knows me as.

I pace the kitchen, needing to walk and work off extra energy as I read Mark's words.

> *Hey, this is tough to write, but here goes. We've done everything we can to make this difficult time easier for you—time off that's usually for mourning family members, bending the rules on maternity leave so you could manage things with the baby, having you work remotely—but AS wants their main contact in the office, available for in-person meetings. They've asked to make Melinda their contact person.*

That's the first text. Melinda is a videographer and a baby in terms of seniority. I've relied on her a lot. I never guessed she'd try to take my place. Is that what Mark's saying? My stomach is uneasy as I scroll to read more.

Melinda has really stepped up lately getting the campaign ready, stuff that's way beyond her job description.

Read: she's caught some of the balls I've dropped. In my defense, no dropped balls have shattered. I've been working my ass off as much as I can—granted, not with the hours I used to, and I'm nowhere near as productive, but still. Hasn't my past work over years earned me some leeway, some benefit of the doubt? This is all temporary.

Melinda is a brilliant videographer, but *I'm* the team manager. Wary, I scroll to the third and final text.

We don't want to lose you, and Theo's not replacing you with Melinda.

Theo, company president, has gotten involved? Unbelievable.

I just thought you should know right away. I've got your back, but Theo's concerned. This isn't what I want. It's not what your team wants. It's not what Melinda wants.

Of course it's what she wants. She'd be stupid to not want the campaign, and if Melinda as team lead is what Alcestis wants, she'll probably get it.

This is a craptastic cherry on top of the nightmare that has been my life since the day Jenn died. I lean against the pantry door and slide to the floor and let myself cry. Not so much about the politics at work. I know I'll still have a job, but having Melinda pull an *All About Eve* sure sucks.

I'm crying, and the tears don't stop. I've been holding them back for too long.

I cry because I'm not being the mom Maggie and Davis need—or the one Ivy needs, now that she's lost both parents. Detective Andrus isn't making things easy there, nor is Rick's lawyer. And now I get to worry about someone getting promoted, trying to take my job?

I have to keep this part a secret; if Jason gets wind of any trouble at work, he'll gleefully take me back to court to revise our divorce decree so *he* gets primary custody. He's wanted it all along, not to be a dad but to avoid paying child support. And to make sure he wins and I get hurt.

I can't let him know anything about work or how Melinda may be taking my client. One more secret to keep tucked inside. I drop my face onto my knees, tight against my chest, and let out the pain I've been holding in.

Of course, that's when Ivy wakes up and screams.

I lift my head, stare at the ceiling as if to ask the fates *Are you kidding me?*, then wipe my face clear of tears and head upstairs. Ivy is innocent in all of this.

Once again, I put on the Super Mom armor I rely on—stronger than anything Captain America or Iron Man ever had—and I pick up Ivy, wearing a smile because Jenn's daughter deserves that much from me.

A bottle and a solid burp later, Ivy is happily sitting on the kitchen floor, banging a wooden spoon on some upside-down pots. That activity kept the twins busy at the same age better than actual toys did. It should give me a few minutes to make the most important call. Not to Mark—I haven't figured out what to say to him—but to Rick.

Instead of having to schedule the call, the jail puts me on hold and goes to get him. I'm glad I made that list of points.

When Rick picks up, he dives in without small talk. No surprise, it's all about him. "Find anything new that could help prove I didn't do it?"

It. I'll never stop being surprised at how callously he refers to Jenn's murder.

"The medical examiner is releasing her body," I say, ignoring his question. "They need to know which funeral home will be picking her up. We'll need to figure out what we're going to do for a memorial, a headstone, all of that—"

"Cremation," he interjects.

"What?" I didn't expect such a quick decision from him.

"No headstone. No burial plot. No embalming. Just cremate the body, and we'll find a place for the ashes. Less drama, much cheaper."

Why does Rick care about money, when he has plenty to ensure that his wife has a decent final resting place? He won't spring for the cost of a burial plot or headstone, but by all means, he'll hire the best criminal defense lawyer in the state.

"No memorial?" I ask.

"Who would we invite? It would be just you and me."

He forgot about Ivy.

Since when did *anyone* losing a spouse not care about a memorial?

I realize I'm grinding my teeth, so I force myself to stop before it makes my headache worse. I take a deep breath, hold it, then let it out. Hopefully, that'll make my voice sound normal instead of enraged. "Did Jenn *want* to be cremated?"

If so, then, of course that's what we'll do. But if this is just for convenience and saving a buck, no way.

"I assume so, but we never talked about that stuff," Rick says. "We didn't think something like this was going to happen."

I bet you didn't, I think, and I grind my teeth again.

"I think we should still hold a memorial. Something small, where friends can come to pay their respects. You know, coworkers, neighbors, library patrons who loved her—"

"No service if I can't be there," Rick says. "If you want to wait until the trial's over and I'm let out"—as if a not-guilty verdict is a given—"then you'd better cremate her; that could take months, and not even formaldehyde can keep a dead body fresh that long."

Revulsion comes over me. Not at the idea that Jenn's remains will disintegrate, but at how horribly clinical and distant—how cruel—he sounds when talking about her.

For the moment, I set aside the question of a memorial and take a different tack. Maybe I surprise him with a little about what I know. He might reveal something. Might as well try. I take a deep breath and innocently ask, "Did you cremate your other wives' bodies?"

"Did I—what?" He stammers inaudibly for a few seconds. "How do you know anything about that?"

"Just curious," I say, sidestepping the question. "Were they cremated too?" I'm highly tempted to use their names, but I don't want to press my luck.

After a long pause, he finally says one word. "Yes."

"So I guess that's what you're familiar with," I say, pretending as if everything is normal, as if I didn't just tip my hand and freak him out.

"Listen, *Rebecca*," he says slowly, his voice deeper now, threatening. He's never used my full name. The sounds make me grip my phone, and my breath halts for a moment. "I don't know what game you think you're playing, but if you know about my late wives, then you know I didn't kill Jenn. You'd better not be hiding evidence that shows I'm innocent, because if you are, I promise you, there will be hell to pay."

My heart starts racing, pounding against my ribcage as if I'm trying to outrun a bear. But he's in jail. He can't hurt me from in there. Could he contest Ivy's guardianship, take her away from me? He might, with Arrington's help. I wouldn't have the money to contest it for long.

Rick and Jenn have no family to lay claim on Ivy. I'm as close to a blood relative as she has. I don't think any judge would take her from me and put her into the foster system, but fighting the effort might be expensive and brutal.

With effort, I keep my voice even. "I'll call later to discuss arrangements, but for now, I'll have Gates Mortuary pick up her body. I'll ask them to wait for further instructions. Bye."

I end the call, drop my phone, and kick the pantry door shut so hard that Ivy startles and then starts laughing. I scoop her up and hold her tight, but she squirms, reaching for the floor and her "toys" of a wooden spoon and a pot. I set her back down, and she resumes smacking her makeshift drum.

My anger and fear toward Rick are encompassed by my growing love for Ivy and the sense that Jenn is watching us. If she is, she'll help me keep custody of Ivy.

Because I'll do whatever I can to keep her baby safe and happy—and away from Rick, so help me God.

CHAPTER THIRTY

JENN

"Isn't she a beauty?" Rick held his arms wide, almost as if he could embrace the boat. He breathed in deeply and let it out as if he were drinking in cool water after a long parched thirst. He climbed the ladder on the side, then turned around, only to find me still standing in the driveway. "Come on up and look around."

"You made partner!" I said with as much excitement as I could muster. "Hancock, Donaldson, Cleese, and *Banks*! I'm so proud of you!" If I said it loud enough, maybe I'd feel less vulnerable, less frightened. As it was, a paralysis threatened to grip my feet, keeping me planted on the driveway instead of running away. It's as if my body knew that the boat was how I'd die.

"Come on up and give me a proper celebratory kiss!" Rick called down, half coaxing, half mocking. "You look as if the boat's going to bite. You'll find no gators on board, if that's what you're thinking. Promise." He laughed a bit too hard at that.

"Later, 'kay?" I said, trying hard to keep my tone light.

"Come *on*." Those two words used to have so much power over me. They didn't anymore, and I wondered at my old self, why I so often caved to keep the peace.

I gestured toward the house and shrugged as if I were disappointed in not being able to join him. "I would, but Ivy's alone in her highchair, and the salmon's going to dry out if I don't take it out of the oven soon."

"Fine," Rick said with a sigh, then swung a leg over the side. "Later."

As he lowered himself, rung by rung, I worried he'd try to push me up the ladder after all. I turned to head back inside through the garage as he kept talking. "After dinner, you need to climb up and check it out. It'll be fun." His tone was what you'd expect from a parent coaxing a child to get into the bathtub because they're afraid they'll get sucked down the drain.

The big difference is that a child's fear about the drain could be shown to be irrational.

My fear over a boat showing up on my driveway wasn't irrational. I didn't have months to figure out how to run and disappear with Ivy. I had weeks or maybe just days.

Rick reached the last rung and then hopped down to the concrete beside me.

I nodded toward the boat. "She's beautiful," I said. I meant to turn and head back inside, but the look he gave pinned me to the ground.

I stood rooted in place. Did he know I'd found out more than what I'd told him over dinner at Rocky's Steakhouse? All of the names, the fake diplomas, the other wives, and their suspicious deaths? Most of all, I knew why he'd bought that boat—to get rid of me and Ivy now that he'd made partner. I had to get back in the house—*had* to. As if he'd know my thoughts just by looking at me if I stayed outside a second too long.

"Of course she's beautiful," Rick finally said after a silence that had pulled thin and tight. "She takes after her namesake."

"You're sweet," I said, pecked his cheek, then really did head back inside. Despite my hammering heartbeat, I made sure to keep my head up and my step light so he wouldn't ask questions or suspect anything. "She's really something," I said over my shoulder.

Something like a murder weapon.

Most wives would be upset over a sudden big-ticket purchase. A year ago, I might have been. Now, the issue of buying something as expensive as a boat *and* a truck—to pull it, I assumed—without telling me paled in comparison to what he planned to use them for.

Who cared about how much money he blew if it meant that the window of time Ivy and I had to get away from him was quickly closing?

The salad fixings still sat on the counter. I went to them, intending to put away the vegetables, but my hands started trembling. I pressed my hands against the counter to steady them.

Calm down fast, before Rick comes inside. As if calming down in a hurry weren't an oxymoron.

Breathe. Inhale for eight. Hold for four. Exhale for eight.

Rick's footsteps sounded in the doorway. I straightened and grabbed tongs and tossed the salad, pretending that I'd been finishing up the salad the whole time.

He closed the door to the garage, then stepped behind me. I could feel his warmth radiating along my back, a feeling that used to be one of comfort. Now it felt like danger. Setting down the tongs, I eyed the knife on the cutting board that I'd used to chop the vegetables. Could I defend myself with it? It looked more like a liability—he could grab it or wrench it from my grip.

Rick's arms wrapped around me, binding my arms to my sides. I inhaled sharply. I held my breath, not daring to move or struggle, though my eyes never left the knife blade.

"Mm, you smell good," he said. He nuzzled my neck as he used to. I felt like vampire prey, as if he were getting ready to bite my jugular.

I chuckled awkwardly, trying to keep my fear hidden. Tilting my head back to look at him, I said, "I can't finish your dinner without the use of my arms."

"Hmm, that *is* a problem," he said with fake thoughtfulness. "Maybe I'll have *dessert* first." He left kisses along one side of my neck.

Forcing myself to act casual, I managed to turn around in his arms and kiss him soundly on the lips. Then I pulled back and smiled flirtatiously. "Later. Dinner's ready. The salmon's going to be all dry if we wait . . ."

He gave a mock sigh of resignation, then kissed me again. "I guess I can wait for dessert. Hey, let's stream a movie while we eat."

I glanced at the table, which I'd already set. "Sure," I said. "I'll bring our plates down."

He walked off, letting his hand trail along, touching me as he passed and patting my butt at the last moment. I didn't breathe easily until he'd gone downstairs and sounds from the television drifted to the kitchen.

ANNETTE LYON

A few minutes later, I'd gotten Ivy and the highchair washed and plates dished up for me and Rick. I brought the baby down first, then fetched our dinners as Rick cued the movie.

"What are we watching?" I asked, handing him his plate.

"*The Prestige*," he said, lifting his brow in a show of interest.

"I haven't seen it."

"If the paralegals at work are to be believed, it stars two of the hottest men alive."

"Oh." What else could I say? Rick got weirdly jealous if I so much as hinted that a celebrity might be something other than ugly.

As the movie began, I learned that the stars were Hugh Jackman and Christian Bale. I made a point of not reacting to their names with anything other than a nod and "They're both very talented."

With Ivy chewing on a toy at my feet, I dug into my dinner.

Only a few minutes in, the magicians on stage put a female assistant in a tank of water. The bite of salad in my mouth suddenly tasted like cardboard. My eyes were riveted to the screen until the woman was safely out of the water.

I was able to eat some more until a few minutes later, when the same trick was performed, but this time, something went wrong. I swallowed, and a bite of salmon stuck in my tightened throat as I watched the woman fight and struggle and try to communicate that she was in trouble. By the time the men realized what was wrong, it was too late.

She'd drowned.

"What the hell?" Rick said suddenly.

I looked over and realized he said it at me, not the movie. My plate had fallen to the floor, scattering dressing, salad, and salmon pieces everywhere.

"Oh shoot." I got on my knees to clean up the mess. "I don't know what happened."

"You're going to have grease stains all over the carpet," Rick said with an annoyed shake of his head.

"I'll take care of it," I said, though I felt as if I had sticks and marbles in my mouth.

All I could think of was the woman who'd drowned on screen. My hands shook as I scooped the food onto my plate, and my legs felt weak as I took it back to the kitchen and returned with a spray bottle of stain remover and a rag. Rick halfheartedly offered to pause the movie. When I didn't answer, he kept watching.

With my back to the television, I worked the stains out of the carpet. I couldn't bear to watch more. When I returned the cleaning supplies to the kitchen, I stayed there for a few minutes and did more breathing exercises.

"Hurry!" Rick called. "You're going to miss some important parts."

How could I get out of watching the rest of the movie? "I should probably get Ivy to bed."

"Feed her down here. She can sleep here until later."

"I don't know . . ." Ivy did better when she got her full bedtime routine. And I didn't want to see another frame of that movie.

"Don't worry, the rest of it isn't scary."

Tentatively, I walked down the stairs. I picked up Ivy and looked at Rick. "It's not scary? Promise?"

"Scout's honor," he said, holding up a hand.

Boy Scouts held up three fingers close together, not a full hand. But then, he was no Boy Scout, literally or otherwise.

If I didn't watch the movie tonight, he'd make fun of me for being scared, and then he'd pester me until I finally watched it. Sometimes giving in was easier than fighting.

This is one of the last times I'll have to decide whether to fight a battle with him. The realization made the prospect of the movie less upsetting. Soon, I'd be far away from him, and I wouldn't have to pick my battles about dumb things like movies.

I'd have to fight battles with far greater stakes. I could handle a scary movie.

The film was interesting. A bit dark at times, confusing at others. Hidden identities became an important part of the story. A glance at Rick proved that he was enjoying himself immensely, probably loving the fact that he, too, had a hidden identity. Several. More than he realized I knew about.

Heaven only knew how much more existed that I *hadn't* found.

The movie had more drownings. Horrifying ones. Near the end, I couldn't take it anymore. Was this *pre*-traumatic stress? I dropped my head into my hands, covering my ears and pressing my eyes into my knees so I couldn't hear or see the screen. Too late, though—I had seen and heard enough to haunt my nightmares.

"Sheesh, what's the matter?" Rick said, laughing. He patted my back as if I were a first grader scared over a haunted house ride at an amusement park. "It's just a movie."

But it wasn't just a movie. It was my future.

CHAPTER THIRTY-ONE

BECCA

I t's been almost six weeks since Jenn died. Time feels oddly stagnant and fleeting at the same time.

It's also been four days since the call from the medical examiner. All I've done is decide to have Gates Mortuary collect the body—man, I hate that term—though the M.E. uses "remains," which also feels weird. Gates is the only mortuary I know off the top of my head, so *that* wasn't much of a decision. I haven't been able to think clearly enough to make any other choices about Jenn yet.

I can barely take care of my kids and Ivy. I'm barely pulling my weight at work. Sure, I'm lucky to be able to work from home, but getting much done, well, isn't happening, and my paranoia about losing my influence and position at work only makes me less productive, less competent.

Putting myself together each morning is harder than ever. I wake up, usually late, after a bad night's sleep, barely getting the twins to school. Then I decide to work from home—again—because I can't get myself to the office at a reasonable time—again. Besides, Ivy does better when she stays with me at home rather than going to daycare.

Maybe I'm kidding myself on that point, and I'm just a hot mess who can't handle basic adulting anymore.

As it is, my makeup and hair get done—half of the time, sans shower—and I throw on a professional-looking blouse or sweater for Zoom meetings. Sometimes I can't get myself to do even that, and on those days, I pretend my web cam's not working. So long as they have audio, it works. I basically live in leggings and sweatshirts.

I can't live like this forever. It's past time to make the final call on cremation or embalming and then figure out what kind of memorial to hold without Rick, and, ideally, without his input. I could probably figure out a way to live stream it to him in the county jail, but I'll happily use any hoops they require for that as an excuse to avoid it. Jenn's murderer shouldn't get to enjoy watching others say their goodbyes.

I officially take the day off, figuring I need a personal day, but I'm so used to having every minute of my day called for that without a schedule, I flounder. Ivy's naps are inconsistent right now; I think she's going through a growth spurt, the kind that makes a baby's schedule shift all over the place. The only semblance of a routine I have is the beginning and end of the twins' school day. When they're home, I put on my Super Mom hat, but only until they're in bed. Then the mask slips. I'm alone in the dark, rocking Ivy on the old glider, feeling adrift.

This morning, I went to the local craft store to get something to do on my day off. I bought a bunch of little acrylic paint bottles, brushes, and a variety of wood figures to decorate. I'm not a crafty person, but I need to do something, and tole painting seemed like an inexpensive way to funnel my energy today. At least the paint is cheap.

The kitchen table is covered with an old sheet and a few other projects I've begun since Jenn's death. At seven months, Ivy is happy in her high chair, though the banana pieces she's playing with are fully mushed now, and she'll need a good bath later. Cleaning the highchair tray will be a priority before the banana can dry. I've recently relearned that it can get almost as hard as the concrete that milk-soaked Cheerios turn into when they dry.

The doorbell rings, and my head comes up from the little dog I've been painting. A glance down confirms my worry—my old gray sweatshirt has splatters of paint. My hands are streaked with various colors. My hair's in a ponytail, and I'm wearing no makeup.

Please be a solicitor, I think, for the first time in my life. I don't want to see anyone I know right now.

I set the brush down, give Ivy a handful of Cheerios, then wipe my hands on an old cloth as I head to the door. I'd rather not answer it at all, but with everything going on, I'd better be sure it's not Detective Andrus or someone else who needs to reach me about Jenn.

Not Arrington, I think as I lean forward to look through the peephole. A visit from Rick's lawyer wouldn't be much better than one from Rick himself.

Two men stand on the other side, but I don't recognize them. The distortion of the peephole makes it hard to make out their features. One of them looks vaguely familiar. He's probably a regular driver for package deliveries. I've ordered a ton online of late to avoid having to leave the house as often. It's probably someone with a package. I open the door.

When I see them clearly, and the guy on the right holding a TV camera like a suitcase, I know immediately who they are, and I know one of them by name, though we've never met.

I curse silently. I shouldn't have answered. Reporters tried to me to talk here and there, but only for a few days after Jenn's death and then right after Rick's arrest. When I refused interviews on camera—and didn't provide even a decent quote or two—they moved on.

I should have expected more of the media would show up eventually.

Even without the local affiliate station's logo on the van parked in front of the house, on the camera, and the cameraman's shirt—I recognize Ben Winsley, the one reporter who's been covering the case as more than a tabloid story.

"I'm Ben Winsley with KTMP News," he says, pronouncing the station name as "K-Timp." He holds out a hand for me to shake.

"I recognize you," I say with a nod, and I grudgingly shake his hand. I can't help looking out to see if other reporters have camped outside my house again. "I've followed your coverage of Jenn Banks' murder."

He gives a shrug. "I hope that's a good thing."

"It is," I say, surprised at myself for complimenting a reporter. "You seem to care about the people and the truth, not about shocking viewers."

"Thank you," he says. "That's one of the nicest things a reporter can hope to hear." His cameraman gives an enthusiastic nod but says nothing.

"Is there something I can help you with?" I ask.

"Yes, actually," Ben says. He holds up a manila envelope. "I was wondering if you had any comment about the toxicology report released this morn—"

"It's been released?" I don't mean to interrupt, but this is big news. I point at the envelope. "And that's it?"

"Yeah," Ben says.

I stare at it. Why didn't the medical examiner tell me the results or offer to send a report? Probably because the autopsy was done for the authorities, not for me, and because I didn't think to ask for the results. Should I call Lobel's office and ask for a copy? Annoyance rises in my chest toward Detective Andrus. *He* should have called me, at the very least. I push it down and decide to call him later.

"I assumed you would have been notified," Ben says. "Would you like to see it? And maybe . . . comment on it?"

I can't tear my eyes from the envelope, which holds answers to how Jenn died. Did the M.E. find signs of a struggle, like bruising or a strike to the head? DNA under her fingernails from Jenn trying to break free? Not that Rick had any defensive wounds like scratches. At least, none I saw.

"Ms. Kalos?" Ben says, which pulls my ultra-distractable brain back.

"Can I read it first? I'm not sure if I can comment, but I definitely need to read it before I can know." I pause and then add, "I won't read it on camera, and I might not give a comment on the record. I don't know yet."

"Whatever you're comfortable with," Ben says. He nods toward his partner. "Tom can wait in the van if that makes you more comfortable."

"Thanks," I say. "I really appreciate it."

Cameraman Tom trots back to the station's vehicle, and I finally think clearly enough to invite Ben inside. "Have a seat." I gesture toward the couch. "I'll be right back."

Two minutes later, with a cleaned-up Ivy on my lap, I sit on the love seat, across from Ben on the couch, and wait to learn what happened to Jenn.

Ivy wriggles off my lap, so I set her on the floor and set a small basket of toys in front of her.

"So . . ." I say, voice trailing off in the hopes that he'll dive in without further prompting.

He opens the metal prongs that keep the envelope closed and slips out a stack of papers. "Do you want to read it first, or do you want me to tell you what it says?"

"Tell me the conclusions—the broad strokes," I say. "I'll want to read it too, though."

He shows me one page and points out various lines. "The manner of death is officially homicide."

"Oh, thank God," I say, breathing out heavily. I didn't realize how afraid I was that the autopsy would be inconclusive or say it was an accident, which would mean Rick could get off. "And the cause?"

"That's the interesting part," Ben says. "Or one of several interesting parts." He riffles through pages until he finds the one he's looking for and pulls it out of the stack. "Several substances were found in her system. Do you know if she had any prescription medications or used any drugs recreationally?"

I shake my head. "No prescriptions that I know of, and she was *not* one to share medications." I remembered that well—I once offered her a migraine pill, but because it was my prescription, she refused it even though it wasn't an opioid or anything like that. I gesture to the page. "I take it she had some drugs in her body?"

"Several, yes. All ones that suppress the nervous system, like slow breathing and heart rate."

"Sort of like how Heath Ledger died?" The question sounds silly to my ears, but it's a case I'm at least loosely familiar with. If I remember right, when the actor couldn't sleep, he combined legitimately prescribed medications that shouldn't have been put together, and at higher doses than prescribed. They eventually worked, but though they finally helped him fall asleep, they also stopped his heart.

Suddenly, I hope that Jenn was unconscious when she died. Nothing will bring her back, but I hope to find a tiny bit of comfort in the idea that if she was unconscious when she went under the bathwater, maybe she didn't feel herself gasping for air, taking in water, lungs feeling like they're about to explode. Maybe Rick didn't hold her under as she fought and she didn't lock eyes with him, begging for her life.

"She had multiple prescription drugs in her system, all depressants, plus Benadryl."

"That's a lot for her," I said, reading the lines Ben has highlighted. Jenn was very sensitive to medication. Half a dose of Benadryl would've knocked her out for hours all by itself.

"There's more."

"Oh?" I brace myself to hear about Jenn getting beaten, or that she died of asphyxiation, not from the drugs.

"She had crystals forming in her kidneys."

I have no idea what that means. My brow furrows. Ivy starts to fuss, so I pick her up to comfort her, only for her to squirm to get free and cry louder. I set her down again, now propping her between my legs against the coffee table—she likes standing with support now—and hand her a toy to play with. When she's calm, I ask, "Crystals?"

"Apparently, crystals in the kidneys can indicate that the individual ingested ethylene glycol—antifreeze."

"The drinking glass on the counter." I hear myself making the connection.

They found Rick's fingerprints on the glass by the sink, but none of Jenn's. And this wasn't an old plastic cup used to pour antifreeze into a car. It was a regular drinking glass that matched a dozen others in the cupboard.

"The glass had more than antifreeze in it," I say. "I'm pretty sure it had some of Rick's morning green smoothie."

"That's consistent with the report," Ben says with a nod.

Did she drink a green smoothie that Rick had laced with antifreeze? "Her DNA," I say under my breath. "Was it found on the glass?"

"On the rim," Ben says, nodding. "And a little inside. Her husband's too. They both drank from the glass."

"Then he drank his smoothie, made her another, and then laced hers with antifreeze."

"That's my guess," Ben says.

I take the toxicology report from him, needing to read and reread it myself. I go over it repeatedly, despite not understanding all of the scientific terms and abbreviations.

Ben shifts on the couch and coughs as if getting ready to say something uncomfortable. "It's not something anyone wants to consider, but there's also the possibility that Jenn took those medications and drank the ethylene glycol on purpose. Do you know if she was depressed or suic—"

"No." I shake my head. "Absolutely not. She never would have done this to herself. Being a mom was the most important thing in the world to her. Sure, she and Rick were having some problems, but she wasn't suicidal. You don't understand. *She* grew up without a mother or any family. Ivy was her everything. Leaving her own daughter without a mother on purpose?" I shook my head again. "Absolutely no way."

"That's what I figured," Ben says. "I just had to look at the possibility. I've spoken with some experts who say that antifreeze poisoning can be a pretty painful death, so while it's not awful to drink—apparently it tastes sweet—it's not a common way to die of suicide. And then there's the fact that she was in the bathtub, fully dressed."

"What does that mean?"

"For starters, that she didn't take a normal bath and accidentally fall asleep because of the medications."

We talk a bit more, with Ben showing me different parts of the report, but he's already given me the big stuff. When he finishes, I hold the report out to Ben. "Could I get a copy?"

"Sure. I'll email it to you. You can take pictures of it too."

I set the report on the coffee table. "Thanks." I take pictures of each page, then give the report back to him. My mind is churning, trying to figure out how what I've just learned fits into the rest of the picture.

I'm closer to knowing the full picture. Yet something isn't quite adding up.

Does knowing every single detail matter in the end? No matter why or how he did it, Rick is behind bars. I'm praying with everything in me that the report will be the final nail that ensures his conviction.

Whether I ever figure out the full picture doesn't matter so long as Rick pays for killing my best friend, my sister, my only family. And for killing Ivy's mother. The monster must pay.

CHAPTER THIRTY-TWO

JENN

March 11
Eight Days before Drowning

The boat was still parked on the concrete strip on the side of the house, and now the new truck was there. I continued to act as normally as I could around Rick, despite knowing that the countdown to how much time Ivy and I had left was officially ticking.

My research continued at a more frantic pace than before, which might have been why I wasn't finding what I needed; I couldn't think straight, nor could I be patient. About all I'd found: a few leads for where to get fake IDs. Needed, sure. Not nearly enough.

In the evening, I served Rick dinner with a smile. He ate his pot roast, clearly hungry, as I sliced homemade french bread, the satisfying crunch of the crust breaking under the pressure of the knife. After cutting two pieces, I began slathering them with butter and just said the words I'd been rehearsing all day.

"So when are you thinking of taking the boat on its maiden voyage? June?" I set one piece of buttered bread on his plate and held out the other. "Want two?"

"Sure. Thanks." He raised one eyebrow. "I'm not waiting to take that beauty out. I'm going as soon as I can arrange a trip. Definitely this month."

We were already a weekend and a half into March. "Really?" I said, trying to sound curious rather than freaked out. "Isn't everything still frozen?" Mountainous lakes and reservoirs could have some ice even into June, depending on elevation.

He lifted his head and studied my face. I smiled innocently wider. He slowly reached out and took the second slice I was offering, never taking his gaze from my face. "Why would you think I'd put off using the boat?" His words were even and measured. My past self wouldn't have worried whether I'd upset him, sparking a fight and, later, his silent treatment.

Current me knew that his tone and words meant something far more sinister. He was weighing me.

I took my seat, broke off a few small pieces of bread for Ivy in her high chair, and shrugged casually. "I mean, it *is* really cold still. We'll probably get a few more nights of frost. It's not even officially spring." I chuckled lightly and lifted one shoulder in a shrug—then worried I was overdoing the nonchalant thing. "Figured this would be the time of year boats would be on sale. You know, before the summer rush. Like how snowblowers are most expensive right after the first snowfall?" I was rambling and sounding like an idiot. I needed to shut up before Rick suspected anything. "Thought a trip when it's warm out would be more fun is all."

"Oh," he said, taking a bite of bread. He chewed for a second, then, with the bread in his cheek, said, "I didn't buy it now because it was on sale. I bought it to celebrate making partner."

"I know." I smiled.

"Money's not an issue."

"I know that too," I said sweetly, then laughed at myself. "Guess my penny-pinching years are showing again." I took a bite of my dinner, and for a moment, the only sounds were utensils clanging on plates, Ivy squealing and kicking, and bread being chewed.

"I'm actually thinking of going this week," Rick said suddenly.

I'd just swallowed a piece of meat, and it suddenly got stuck halfway down. I had to swallow again to free it.

216

"Sorry." He twirled his spoon to gesture as if rolling time along. "I meant *next* week."

I breathed out a shallow sigh of relief, hoping he wouldn't notice.

"A week from Thursday. It'll be an early weekend."

Now I sat there frozen. He was taking the boat out a week from tomorrow. I had *one* week to escape with Ivy unless I could push out the trip, delay it.

I couldn't feign a smile or say a cheerful word. I sat there like a stupid deer in the headlights. I wanted to yell at him, tell him that no way would I board that boat when it was on the water. That I knew he would only try to kill our daughter and me if I did.

"Th-Thursday," I managed, barely.

"Right." Rick's eyes flashed with excitement, a sight that sent my stomach acid churning. "Don't worry about work—I've got it covered. I have a meeting in the morning, but we can be on the road by noon and on the reservoir by, oh, four or so."

My mouth was so dry. I grabbed my glass of water and downed half of it. "Won't it be even colder in the evening?"

Rick grunted and took another bite of meat. "A bit. The sun won't be as high, and there could be some wind, but we'll be below deck until morning." With his foot, he nudged mine under the table. "It'll be cozy."

Not yanking my foot away took all the control I could muster. I tried to flirt. "Not so cozy when we've got a baby along to interrupt things." My tone probably didn't sound as airy as I intended, but hopefully, my point would make him reconsider.

If he didn't change the date, I might be screwed. If he was determined to drown us in the reservoir, he could easily force us into the truck and onto the boat—conscious or unconscious. Then he could certainly leave the valley—the state—and start over. By the time our bodies washed up, if they ever did, he'd be long gone.

But if I could prevent or at least postpone the boat trip . . .

I tried one more angle. "What can we even do on a boat this time of year? It's too cold to swim. We wouldn't be fishing—"

"We can totally fish."

"Oh." Now what? "Let's wait just a few weeks until things warm up a bit more so we can all enjoy the trip," I said. "The reservoir probably still has patches of ice. It would be a shame for your new boat to get scratched up."

"It'll have to get broken in eventually. A few scratches are inevitable," Rick said in an offhand tone I couldn't read—a fact that set my nerves on high alert. I'd become an expert at reading Rick's emotions, but my radar was suddenly off. Was he simply stating a fact, or was his statement a threat? Was he thinking about his past wives fighting for their lives, scratching not a boat but him?

I cut my meat into pieces, needing to do something with my hands while I avoided Rick's eye.

"It's all planned," he said. "The firm knows when I'll be gone, you don't have work, and I've checked the open dates for all the lakes and reservoirs in the area."

When I said nothing and just kept cutting my meat into smaller pieces, Rick laughed. "Oh, come on. Be a good sport. You're tough, right? Besides, the boat has a heater, and we can bring coats and blankets. We'll be fine." He reached across the table and rested his heavy hand on my forearm, pinning it against the table. "It'll be fun. You'll see."

"Sure," I said, the most blatant lie of my life. I had no intention of seeing how the trip would turn out. The very idea made my blood run cold.

✑

Tuesday, March 16
Two Days before Drowning

Five days of trying to get Rick to cancel or postpone the boat trip, five days of failure. Each felt like my personal sword of Damocles, swinging back and forth like a pendulum as it lowered ever closer.

My point about the cold weather was shot down with "The forecast is expecting a record high for the reservoir at this time of year."

"March isn't typical boating season," I said the next day, and he laughed.

"Right. We'll have the place to ourselves," he said.

The next day, I went more personal. "I don't *want* to go," I said while doing dinner dishes. "Ivy will be miserable. What if she falls down the stairs or gets into something that could hurt her? The boat isn't exactly baby-friendly."

"She'll be *fine*," he said, then grabbed the vodka bottle from the freezer.

I still wasn't used to the fact that he didn't have a chivalrous bone in his body. The guy I'd fallen in love with had pretended to. He'd had a sense of loyalty. He was kind and good.

He didn't exist.

For the real Rick, behavior that looked like loyalty and kindness were useful only as means to an end. That's how he got women to agree to marry him. I often felt like an idiot for not seeing the truth earlier, but the fact that I wasn't the first to fall for his ruse told me that he was an expert in pretending to be the perfect guy—and targeting vulnerable women.

I headed to a strip mall a couple of cities away to buy some things for St. Patrick's Day, which was the next day. For obvious reasons, I didn't grow up with family traditions, and I'd been determined to create ones for my new little family. That included "small" holidays like St. Patrick's Day.

As I searched for a store that carried lamb for classic Irish stew, I grew anxious over not finding the meat. I needed to make lamb stew. I *had* to, not only because that was a way to celebrate the holiday, and not only because I wanted to create traditions, but also because it was likely the last holiday of any kind that I'd celebrate with my family intact.

At the fourth store, I found some lamb and bought it, caring nothing for the jacked-up price tag. What did the grocery budget matter when Ivy and I wouldn't be around to spend any of the money in it much longer? I still had no idea how we'd escape.

No local women's shelters seemed safe enough—Rick could find us, I had no doubt, whether that was through lawyer connections or by chatting up a cop so they'd slip and reveal a location. I'd found a couple of possible leads, but they were out of state, and I needed to figure out how to get there, how to make contact, how to get money transferred somewhere so that Rick wouldn't notice it was missing too soon *and* wouldn't be able to track it, and so much more.

I needed time, and I was running out of it. There I was at the grocery store, desperately buying expensive lamb because it was something I could do for Ivy that day and distract myself from the fact that Thursday was the day after tomorrow.

From the grocery store, I went to a fabric and crafts one. Ivy sat in the cart, pretty steady now, and she loved the vantage. My original plan was to sew matching mom-and-me dresses covered in shamrocks. My sewing skills weren't good enough to make two full dresses in a day, so I went so a much simpler route: decorating existing aprons. Whether they'd end up with ruffles, puff paint, sequins, or sew-on patches, I wouldn't know until I looked around the store.

I pushed Ivy and the cart down one aisle and onto the next, really taking in the huge store and thinking of all the kinds of traditions and parties and fun times the products on the shelves could be used for. I passed a big cake-decorating section and imagined baking Ivy her first birthday cake—and wondered where we'd be then. Would I have a kitchen to myself? Be in a shelter? Or at the bottom of the reservoir after all?

Don't think like that. Maybe I'll make her wedding cake someday.

I passed an aisle with cross-stitch supplies, another with knitting and crochet tools, and beyond that, several aisles of yarn. The back corner was filled with painting stuff: oils, pastels, brushes, canvases.

I stopped along an aisle filled with picture frames, most with stock photos of fake families laughing and smiling. My throat closed up as I gazed at one little family—dad, mom, little girl.

Now that he'd made partner, Rick was planning to kill me and Ivy. That's why he bought the boat. He might do it on Thursday as soon as we got the boat onto the reservoir. Or maybe it would be that night. Or the day after. He'd be able to force me and Ivy into the truck and onto the boat.

That's exactly what he'd do if Ivy and I were still home. For now, it looked like we would be because I was no closer to finding a way to escape his reach than I had been when he admitted to having been widowed more than once.

I had nothing concrete for a plan of escape, and I wasn't about to bet my daughter's life on the *possibility* of leads panning out. I needed more time. I should have had more time—months, at least.

Reality crashed over me. Time was up for an escape. I'd failed to protect Ivy. If I didn't have an airtight getaway plan already, what chance did I have to escape Rick's reach? None. And neither did Ivy.

What could I do?

I pushed the cart onward and walked the perimeter of the store to think—and not cry.

If he got rid of me, that was one thing. Bad on its own. But worst of all, he'd kill Ivy. I wanted to think that he wasn't capable of killing his own flesh and blood, but if, as I suspected, he'd killed his parents, he was absolutely capable of anything. He'd already killed Chloe's baby, which probably would have been viable.

I could *not* allow that to happen.

Yet how could I prevent it, when I was dealing with someone smart enough and evil enough to get away with killing several times before?

I had two days. That wasn't enough time to *do* anything. It wasn't enough time for me to save us.

Rick would get away with murder. Again.

I blinked away tears and sniffed, hoping no one else in the store would see me crying, then kissed the top of Ivy's head. "What are we going to do, baby girl?" I murmured into her sweet downy hair.

We left the store without crafting supplies. I had the lamb for stew, and I'd be making soda bread for dinner, the ingredients for which I already had at home. That would have to be enough to celebrate the holiday tomorrow.

I drove home with the car audio off, unable to listen to talk shows or music. I had to think. But all I could process was fear and worry. How could I make any kind of plan when I had adrenaline shooting through me?

I pulled into our driveway and pushed the button to open the garage door. As I waited for it to go up, I stared at the boat, each slick curve and angle. The propeller looked like an angry corkscrew capable of drilling through anything. I imagined the boat churning water, cruising under the sun.

He'd do it after nightfall. He'd toss our bodies overboard. It would later be deemed a tragic accident. I shuddered.

If he was to get drowning as the cause of death, then we'd have to be alive when he dumped us in the water. Images from the movie the other night returned to mind, of the actress frantic underwater. My stomach clenched with fear. Maybe I could beg Rick to drug me, so I wasn't awake when my lungs felt ready to burst for want of oxygen. So that when the water finally filled them up, when I blacked out and finally died, I wouldn't feel pain or panic.

I pictured myself begging to be drugged and begging for him to spare Ivy.

No. Ivy and I would *not* get on that boat, ever. Whatever it took, we'd stay off it. Let Rick plan whatever trip he wanted to. We had to remain on dry land, breathing oxygen. Alive.

Rick had killed and gotten away with it. This was a game he'd always won. Somehow, this time had to be different.

I pulled into the garage and shut off the car. The drive had put Ivy to sleep, so I sat there for several minutes, thinking. Not panicking—I purposely shoved fear aside as best I could and just thought.

No matter what Rick did to me, was there a way I could make sure Ivy was safe?

If I failed and Rick killed us, could I somehow leave a trail so the police would know he did it—so he could never hurt anyone else ever again?

The kernel of a plan was starting to form in my mind. A completely crazy plan, something I never would have thought of without being thrust into an equally unthinkable position.

It might not work, but if it did . . .

I knew two things: first, I had to protect my daughter. And second, I'd do whatever it took to make that possible.

CHAPTER THIRTY-THREE

BECCA

I walk Ben Winsley to the door. After I open it, he hesitates, not stepping through.

"Thank you for talking to me," he says.

From where I stand, I can see Tom, his cameraman, still in the van. "Thank you for respecting my privacy."

"About that . . ." Ben says. "Is everything we talked about off the record?"

I hadn't considered that; I'm not used to thinking in journalistic terms. I think through our conversation, not remembering everything we talked about. I was—am—too emotional to remember it all, let alone be on my toes about statements on and off the record.

"I don't think so," I say and hope I don't regret it later.

"Thanks," Ben says.

I'm not too worried; Ben Winsley isn't known for tabloid or gotcha journalism. From what I've seen, he's about as unbiased as a reporter can be, and while he's a great storyteller, he sticks to the facts.

He reaches into his shirt pocket and pulls out a business card—likely the only thing in the pocket, placed there for this very purpose. He holds it out, and I take it. "If you think of anything else or want to reach me, please do. Call, email, or text anytime. I'm most likely to respond to texts quickly. Text me your email address so I can send you the report."

"Will do," I say, and he steps onto the porch.

With a wave, I close the door behind him, then go to the kitchen, where I grab my phone from the table and enter Ben's contact information. Aside from wanting a copy of the toxicology report, I don't know why I'd reach out to him. I can probably get it elsewhere if I need to, for that matter. But if the last month and a half has taught me anything, it's that there's no predicting the future.

Dropping into a chair at the kitchen table, I pull up the camera to snap a picture of the business card in case I've entered something wrong on Ben's contact page. My thumb taps the corner of the screen, bringing up my camera roll. I haven't had much of a reason to take pictures lately. Before all of this, whenever I babysat Ivy, I sent cute pictures to Jenn. I find myself scrolling through my camera roll. Most of the pictures are of Ivy and the twins.

I don't have to scroll far to find one of Jenn. I find three pictures taken on the same day, two with Jenn in them. The first is of Ivy, bundled up in her coat and hat, sitting in her stroller. She was facing backward, which meant Jenn and I could talk to her, pull faces, and make her laugh. That's exactly what Jenn's doing in the second picture: making a face at Ivy, who is giggling with pure joy. I took the picture from the side so it shows both of them.

The last picture is a selfie of me and Jenn. Neither of us is showered or wearing makeup. We're making the classic teenager duck lips and sultry eyes to be silly. She's even making gestures that she surely saw teens doing online. I swipe back and forth between her making Ivy laugh and the two of us acting like goofy high school kids, taking in how happy and *alive* she looks. My vision blurs. I swipe at my cheeks.

That walk was days before she died, when spring was promising to come, but winter hadn't quite released its hold. We often walked together on the mornings I worked from home—usually only on Mondays, but it was St. Patrick's Day and I promised to help with the twins' class party, so I'd opted to work from home that day.

I wish I'd had some inkling, some clue, that our time together would be cut short, that this was our last walk. Ever.

Sitting there, I try to remember her voice, her laugh, and I worry I'll forget both. What did we talk about on the hour-long loop through the neighborhood? Nothing of significance or I'd remember it. Maybe that's for the best; if I'd known that was the last hour-long conversation we'd ever have, it would have been sad, not fun and silly and happy.

A beep draws my attention, and for a moment, I don't know what it's from. Not my phone, not the doorbell or the TV. It's my new dishwasher, chiming with the finished cycle. Oh yeah. I got a new dishwasher. That's what we talked about on the walk.

The kid who arrived to install it must have been new; he was nervous and looked about sixteen, though he assured me he was an adult.

"Did you ask for ID?" Jenn asked.

"I considered it," I said. "But he already looked so nervous and pale that I worried he'd pass out, so I let it slide."

Only now do I remember that Jenn's laugh wasn't as chatty as usual. She'd been quiet much of that walk—not like her at all.

I remember more of our conversation. I told her about Kaden, the obnoxious intern at work who mansplained everything to every woman, no matter how senior in the company. "The guy thinks he'll be snapped up for a manager-level position as soon as he graduates from college. Not happening, kid." I laughed, and when she only chuckled shallowly, I looked over at her and found her brows pulled together, not laughing along with my story.

We reached the corner where we always did—where I always turned up to my house and she then walked the remaining blocks back to her place. "Are you . . . are you okay?" I asked—a detail I'd forgotten until now. A detail that seems so meaningful in hindsight that I can't believe I forgot about it. "You seem quiet today."

She smiled, not quite making eye contact, and shrugged. "Just tired." Jenn reached into the stroller and tickled Ivy's cheek, making her squeal and laugh. That was one of the pictures I had on my phone now. "But she's worth it."

"She certainly is," I remember telling Jenn. "She is so lucky to have you."

Jenn smiled at that but said nothing.

"I'm serious," I said. "Just so you know, I've put you as the twins' guardian if something were to happen to me. And honestly, you're such a good mom that they'd be lucky if they ended up being raised by you."

"Wow. Thank you." She tilted her head to one side. "What about Jason?"

"Well, yeah, he'd technically get custody if I'm out of the picture, but I wouldn't be surprised if he'd happily give up parental rights to not have to deal with the twins full time."

We were just standing there on the corner, but I could tell something was on her mind, so I stayed. I waited, knowing that when she thought through what she wanted to say, she'd say it. That's how Jenn was—thoughtful and deliberate.

"Speaking of estate planning . . ." Jenn's voice trailed off.

"Yeah?" I said, trying to sound supportive.

She swallowed hard and blew out a breath. "Estate planning and guardianship and all of that—it's all so easy to put off, you know? I'm married to a lawyer but don't have a will. How crazy is that?"

"No way," I said with a chuckle.

"A case of the shoemaker's family going barefoot." Jenn shrugged. "I really should set one up, especially now that I have Ivy."

"It's hard," I said. "As a mother, you know it's important, but *being* a mother, you don't want to think about things like your own mortality, let alone that anything could happen to you before they're grown, you know?"

"Exactly," Jenn said.

A bond of old wounds connected us; we both knew what it was like to lose family and be on our own much too young. Feeling an urgency to get her affairs in order even more strongly than the typical parent made sense. I'd felt the same thing, which is why I *had* made a will.

She went on, fiddling with the stroller brake with the toe of her sneaker. "I'd hate to have the courts decide that stuff."

I shook my head adamantly. "Oh gosh. That would be awful. That's it. I'm updating my will. I'm calling a lawyer today."

Jenn looked up then, right at me. "So you know, if anything ever happens to me, *you* are on deck to raise Ivy. No ifs, ands, or buts." I raised an eyebrow and looked at Becca. "I hope you're okay with that."

"Assuming Rick's out of the picture, but yes—of course," I told her. "I'd do anything for her—and for you."

Her gaze went to Ivy, and she looked lovingly at her baby, who was valiantly trying to shove her entire fist into her mouth. "You're practically a second mother to her, Becca. You love her as much as I do. You're an amazing mom to your kids. It just makes sense." She licked her lips in a way that now seemed nervous to me.

Was it nervousness? Maybe. Maybe not. I could be projecting meaning onto the memory after the fact.

Jenn hugged me then, and I hugged her just as hard. She pulled away with tearful eyes, which she apologized for. I didn't cry then, but I'm sobbing as I remember.

"Just so you know," I told her, "if something were to happen to you, but not to Rick, I'd steal her away from him anyway."

"Please do," she said quickly—more energetically this time. She laughed, sounding more like herself.

At the time, I assumed she'd simply been worried about asking me to be Ivy's guardian. As soon as that issue was settled, she was relieved and her old self. Right?

What if something else was on her mind that day?

"Rick has never been one for late-night feedings. Can you imagine what he'd be like during potty training? Or when she's a teenager?" She sounded entirely lighthearted now.

We both laughed like crazy, then hugged again. She held me tighter than usual, and as I remember it now, I wish I'd held on a little longer, relished the feeling of Jenn being close one last time.

I swipe to the most recent images on the camera roll—the ones I took of Ben's copy of the toxicology results. I'd dismissed the idea that Jenn had killed herself, but *could* she have? Did she know that morning on our walk that she wouldn't be around much longer? Is that why she asked me to be Ivy's guardian—and egged me on when I said I might "steal" Ivy from Rick?

That's not the Jenn I knew. Granted, over the last weeks since her death, I've learned a lot about her that I didn't know before. About Rick too. But I still can't accept the idea that she'd kill herself when it meant Ivy being without a mother and when it could mean Rick raising her.

Yet she made sure she wanted me to be there for Ivy.

Days before she died. I check the date on the picture to make sure I'm remembering the day right. Sure enough, that walk was on St. Patrick's Day—two days before she died. Did she know what was going to happen?

If so, what does that mean? I swipe one more time, to the picture of Ben's business card. Should I tell him about that conversation? Should I call Detective Andrus?

I tap the contacts icon on my phone but stare at the screen. If Jenn's death is ruled a suicide—no matter how incomprehensible that possibility is—then all charges will be dropped from Rick. He'll be free. Ivy will likely have to go back to live with him.

How long would he stay in town before slipping away, creating a new identity for himself, and continuing to kill innocent women?

From upstairs, a whimper marks the end of Ivy's nap. My head whips in her direction, and I think of what it would mean for her to return to her father's care. How long until Ivy went "missing" or had a fatal "accident"?

To think of what her life will be like if Rick gets her back makes my blood run cold. I race upstairs to Ivy's crib. She's crying, reaching for me. I scoop her into my arms and hold her tight.

I'll keep my promise to Jenn—I'll keep Ivy safe.

CHAPTER THIRTY-FOUR

JENN

March 18
One Day before Drowning

It was time. I had to act, to make every possible preparation that day because if Rick got his way, we'd go on the boat trip tomorrow. I had about twenty-four hours to get ready.

While Ivy was down for her late-morning nap, I slipped one of Rick's credit cards out of the box he kept in the top drawer of his nightstand. I'd just put it into my purse when Ivy woke up. After feeding and changing her, we headed out in the car.

First stop: the Maple Fork library for a few more research items. On the drive, my mind drifted to the day that started this entire mess: the day more than a year ago when I got the tattoo. Would my life have turned out like today if I hadn't gotten inked? That was arguably the thing that set off this unbelievable series of events.

I'd still have gotten pregnant. But if I hadn't started digging into who Rick was when I did, I probably wouldn't know enough now to stop his plans. I'd still be living with a murderer, but unwittingly. I certainly wouldn't be planning something as unthinkable as I was now.

If I could go back to change the last year, would I? No. Ivy was worth everything, and the steps I was taking now would, God willing, keep her alive and well. No matter what happened to me, a piece of me would live on in Ivy.

We arrived at the library, and I carried her inside, still buckled in her carrier. We wouldn't be here long. I smiled at the librarian at the reception desk but moved quickly enough to hint that I was in a hurry and couldn't talk.

I found an unclaimed computer along the back wall and sat at it, tilting the monitor so that others would have a harder time seeing it. I knew the librarians had set them up specifically so that no one could hide their screens—we had similar reasoning for the public computer setup at the Harvest Valley library. A slight tilt was all I could do without drawing attention to myself. It would have to do.

I took a few of the little slips of paper and a short pencil meant for taking notes. A couple of searches and about five minutes later, I knew what I'd be looking for at the grocery store. I closed out the browser and headed out of the library, Ivy babbling happily in her carrier, which sounded extra loud in a library—and when I was already on edge. I barely noted the librarian at the circulation desk as I left but hoped I gave her at least a polite smile.

Now I was on a mission: off to Mecham's Market—the biggest store in Maple Fork that wasn't a chain. I chose it because the security at the store wasn't the best. A neighbor, Valerie, used to work there and she once told me how she hoped cops would never need their security tapes because the recordings only went back a few days before getting recorded over. If my luck held, by the time anyone would ask for the tapes to verify who made purchases here today, they wouldn't exist.

I'd already made sure that Rick didn't have any official meetings on his calendar today, so he wouldn't be able to prove that he *didn't* make this trip. As I pulled into the grocery store parking lot, I got close to backing out of my plan. What if I went on the boat trip, knowing I'd die, but left Ivy with Becca to make sure she'd be safe?

No, that wouldn't work. For one thing, Rick would still be able to take care of—and hurt—Ivy. My body would probably never be found, and he'd disappear again. Kill again. I had to make sure that Rick would be stopped once and for all.

I stopped in the medication aisle to look for Benadryl. Rick could overpower me pretty easily: knock me out or drug me, then bind me with zip ties and drive me there. But if I was going to be drowned, hopefully I could make it less terrifying. Something better than being thrown into icy cold water, wide awake, like Rick was planning.

If my life was nearly over—and I was convinced it was—then it needed to end on my terms.

I grabbed a bottle of Benadryl and a few other cold medicines that I knew could make a person sleepy. Then I headed for the automotive aisle. When I reached the shelves of antifreeze, I found several colors.

I consulted my notes from the library and compared them with the labels on the jugs. I needed the kind with an ethylene glycol base, which, according to the colored chart I'd found, neither my Prius nor Rick's Lexus used. Having a jug of it lying around would be suspicious. Good.

After casually thunking a jug of the greenish stuff into my cart, I headed to the frozen food case. I'd get Phish Food, my favorite flavor of Ben and Jerry's, along with Rick's favorite, Red Velvet Cake, which I found to be a disgusting parody of a bakery classic.

I found a container of Red Velvet ice cream and got one—not to butter up Rick, but so that this trip would look that much more like one he'd made. I paid for it all with Rick's credit card. The total was small enough that I didn't have to sign for it. He tended to pay more attention to the transactions in the checking account in my name rather than his.

"Have a nice night," the checker said, handing me the bag of ice cream pints. I'd already hefted the jug into the cart.

"Thanks," I said, not wanting to say anything else that would make this transaction stand out in his memory.

As I left the store, I glanced up at a camera above the exit. Had the system been upgraded since Valerie told me about the backups? How long ago did she tell me about the cameras? A year ago, maybe?

I looked back down at Ivy and made faces so she'd laugh, shaking off the idea that the camera had caught anything that would ruin my plans.

Back home in the garage, I camouflaged the antifreeze in the back of my car with a blanket, making it look like it was just part of the same old pile of stuff usually back there: a blanket, a case of jumper cables, a first-aid kit, and a stack of reusable grocery bags. Rick rarely, if ever, looked in my car, but I wasn't taking chances.

As soon as I got Ivy settled in her high chair, I went upstairs to the master bedroom, where I replaced Rick's credit card exactly where I'd found it, making sure to wipe my prints from it first, then wipe the drawer handle after I pushed it closed.

A happy screech floated up from the kitchen—Ivy's babble that always made me smile. How many more times would I hear that adorable voice? Not enough.

Every time I hesitated about my plan, every time I wondered if I had what it would take to go through with it, all I had to do was think of Ivy.

I could do this. I *had* to do this.

CHAPTER THIRTY-FIVE

BECCA

After Ben leaves, I move through the hours in a fog. I keep thinking about his visit. About the toxicology report—how Rick poisoned Jenn on top of his usual MO of drowning his victims. I can't stop thinking about the last walk Jenn and I shared—of her worried, distracted expression. About how she'd planned for me to be guardian if she *and* Rick were both out of the picture as if she knew he was going to get rid of her soon.

None of it makes sense to me. But then, I'm not a detective or a sociopath.

I must be more in my head than I thought because, over dinner, Davis and Maggie keep calling, "Mom. Mom! Did you hear me?"

Each time, I haven't. Over and over, I have to pull myself back to the moment, determined to be present for my kids. Inevitably, morbid thoughts pull my attention away again. Finally, with dinner cleaned up and their homework done, I insist they get ready for bed earlier than usual.

"But whyyyyyy?" Maggie whines.

Instead of giving her a reason, I promise a treat tomorrow if they spend an extra half hour reading in their beds before turning out the lights.

"Ice cream?" Davis asks hopefully.

"At the Pink Pony," I promise—the mom-and-pop ice cream parlor in town.

Maggie pipes up with a request. "Can we get grown-up-size sundaes?"

"Yep. And a large order of fries . . . *each*," I say with a grin.

That's too much food for even an adult to finish, but that doesn't matter. The twins' eyes light right up, and they race to get the pajamas on. I get Ivy to bed without much trouble, and with the twins in their rooms, the house is very quiet. Too quiet. Maybe I should have kept the kids up. I wouldn't have been much company for them, but their chatter and energy would keep me from constantly circling back to Jenn and what I'm missing about her death.

I sleep a little, but not much, and that little bit isn't restful; I toss and turn. The only reason I know I slept at all is because of the brief but disturbing dream of walking through Jenn's house, trying to find her before it was too late.

Morning isn't much better. I get the kids off to school. After Ivy goes down for a nap, I head to the bathroom for a shower. Before I get there, my phone rings with a call from Gates Mortuary.

I dread answering, but I dread having to call them back even more, so I answer. "Hello?" My reflection in the bathroom vanity mirror reveals circles under my eyes and a messy bun that looks like a cartoon character that got hit by lightning.

"Ms. Kalos? This is Betty from Gates Mortuary calling to let you know that your loved one is ready to be retrieved."

"My—what?" I swear, my brain had better start working one of these days. *Oh, wait. She means Jenn. Her ashes.*

I forgot that I had the mortuary go ahead with cremation—not because I knew for sure that that's what Jenn wanted, and not because it's what Rick wanted, but because I'm paying for it, and I can't afford embalming, a casket, a vault, a gravesite, and all of the other expenses a widowed lawyer should be able to easily afford for his late wife. Granted, he's racking up legal fees, but still.

"Will you be coming to retrieve your loved one?" Betty asks.

"Yes."

"That would be great. We're open until five-thirty."

"I'll be in today," I say, ready to hang up, then another thought occurs to me. "Do I need to pick out and pay for an urn first?"

"We'll provide a temporary one. You can pick one out later if you wish."

"Oh. Great. Thank you." One less thing for my frazzled brain to deal with. After the usual pleasantries, I end the call and then imagine an urn on a shelf or fireplace mantel. That doesn't sound like Jenn. Would she want them scattered somewhere? Her ashes buried with a tree? I'll have to ponder that one.

I wish I had someone to bounce ideas off of, a sounding board. Still holding my phone, I find my thumb navigating to my texts. I catch myself, realizing that I was about to ask Jenn for her opinion on the situation, as I used to ask her about so many other things—the color I should paint my kitchen, which pair of heels were cuter, whether I should spring for a gorgeous dress that was on clearance even though I had no event to wear it to in the near future.

Urgency wells in me to get another person's opinion. I want to reach out to another human, another adult. The hole Jenn's death left in my life is ragged and keeps tearing bigger.

I need someone to talk about Jenn with. My colleagues at work aren't really an option, no matter that I consider Mark, Melinda, and the rest to be my friends. Before this all happened, I wouldn't have had the slightest clue what to say or do for a colleague in a similar position.

Looking at my phone, I tap the contacts icon. I hesitate for just a moment before typing in a B and then an E. Ben Winsley pops up. Am I crazy? I met the guy yesterday. He's a journalist, not a therapist. He wants to report breaking news, not give a hug to a vulnerable woman.

But he did say to reach out. At least if I thought of anything new about the case. This doesn't exactly qualify, but before I lose my nerve, I send him a text.

Becca Kalos here, I begin, doubting he added my info to his phone. I stare at the blinking cursor for a second, then type out a quick message. *I have to pick up Jenn's ashes today. Want to join me?*

Before I can overthink it, I click send, put my phone down, and turn on the shower. My phone isn't muted, something that's clear when my hair is covered with shampoo and my phone goes off with incoming messages, one after another. They've got to be from Ben, and I've got to know what he said.

I quickly rinse my hands, push open the shower door, and wipe them on a towel before grabbing my phone. As I guessed, all of the messages are from Ben, and they're all short.

Glad you reached out!

I'm happy to meet you anywhere.

Name the place and time. Just need 20 minutes' notice.

Shower water still falls behind me, and I can feel suds dripping down my body. I clear some from my vision with my forearm and type out a quick reply.

Gates Mortuary in an hour?

He replies almost immediately. *You got it. See you then.*

I'm strangely relieved that I texted him. Soon I'll have someone to talk to, reporter or not. I finish showering and get myself pulled together quickly so I won't be late.

Twenty-five minutes later, I'm ready to go. By some miracle, Ivy doesn't wake up when I put her in her carrier. On my way out, I grab my laptop. Maybe Ben can help me write the obituary. Maybe I'll show him some of Jenn's research, play the pen recording for him, which I uploaded before handing everything over to Detective Andrus.

I don't know what to expect at the mortuary—what I'll feel when I'm handed Jenn's ashes, what I'll tell Ben, how he'll react—but for the first time in weeks, I feel like I'm acting rather than being acted upon. I feel as if I have some power to do something, though what, I'm not sure.

Whatever is ahead of me, I feel as if a glimmer of light is ahead, and with that light, my old self might show up too.

"Let's do this," I whisper as I turn the key to start the car.

CHAPTER THIRTY-SIX

JENN

March 19
The Day of Drowning

Thursday—*the* day—arrived. As usual, Rick left for work at eight-thirty in his suit, suitcase in tow. He had an important consultation with a potential client via Zoom. Naturally, he'd never do something like that from home because of the potential for Ivy disrupting it. His wood-paneled office looked more lawyerly too, I guessed.

The call was confidential—a client that, if Rick could lure to the firm would be huge—but he didn't want anyone there knowing about the possibility until he had the company under contract with a retainer paid.

"Be sure you go in and out the back entrance," I reminded him. "Don't want Donaldson or Cleese wondering what you're doing when you're supposed to be on vacation."

"Right. Thanks for the reminder," Rick said, but he looked a bit annoyed and seemed to be searching for something. "Can't find my smartwatch. I swear it was charging right there last night." He pointed to the charging station on the counter.

"I'm sure it'll turn up," I said. "I'll keep an eye out for it."

"Thanks. Remember, I'll be back in time for us to head out by noon." He touched his bare wrist, still scanning the kitchen as if his watch would magically appear.

"Leaving at noon means you'll be back around eleven-thirty? Or quarter to?" I asked, smiling. "To be sure Ivy and I are ready." He detested being late, and that included anything on his personally manufactured schedule.

"I'll stop for some road-trip snacks on my way home, so let's say a quarter to."

"Sounds good," I said cheerfully, terrified that he'd be able to detect the lie, figure out my plans, and put a stop to them.

Put a stop to bringing him to justice and saving my daughter.

Ivy sat on my hip, gumming a cracker and drooling down her chin. I kissed her head and breathed her in. She made me smile sincerely. Rick wouldn't guess anything was amiss if I was smiling for real, and my joy over Ivy was as real as it got.

She reached up with drool-and-cracker hands and pressed her messy face to my cheek, her version of a kiss. My chest tightened with emotion that I could not let out—for her sake and mine, I could *not* cry right now. Her life literally might depend on Rick not detecting any unexpected emotion.

"Okay, now that's gross," Rick said with a laugh. He took a step toward the kitchen island and grabbed a burp cloth. He handed it to me. I used it to wipe my cheek off and clean Ivy's hands and face.

That gave me enough time to rein in my emotions. "There. All clean," I said, setting the dishcloth on the counter. "Good luck with your meeting, though I'm sure you don't need it. You'll bag that client for sure."

"Thanks." He leaned in for a goodbye kiss. My stomach went sour as I kissed him, but having Ivy clinging to my side provided enough motivation to keep up the act. Anything for her.

Rick, however, wasn't satisfied with his regular morning peck. He lingered, and I pretended to enjoy it, though it felt like I was kissing a snake. His lips tasted bitter and dry—cold. For months, everything about Rick had felt foreign, but something about the act of affection, today of all days, felt like entering an upside-down reality that sent the hackles rising on the back of my neck.

At last, he finished the kiss, but before he went into the garage, he slapped my butt. That was the second time he'd ever done that, the last time being the day he brought the boat home. I forced out a giggle; he clearly thought he'd done something clever and fun. This was a man who thought himself so smart that he couldn't be caught, who must have found pleasure in hurting others, having the ultimate power over them. Let him think I was just one more victim.

He grinned, then chuckled, trotting down the concrete steps in the garage to his car. He was the least spontaneous person I knew, yet he'd changed up our morning goodbye, first with a long kiss, then with the butt slap. Why?

Because today was different. It was the beginning of the end. My blood ran cold as he walked to his Lexus. I pasted a smile on my face. "Ivy, wave bye-bye to Daddy." That was one of her newer tricks. She and I both waved.

Rick didn't turn around, he just kept walking to his car and checking his phone.

I waited until he pulled out and the garage door closed. Then I closed the inside door and sighed heavily with relief; he hadn't noticed anything off. If anything, he seemed more cheerful than usual when he helped out with the dishcloth. Normally, he would have grunted and told me to wash off Ivy's drool before he kissed me.

Maybe he did notice that I was a bit off but attributed it to nerves over going on our maiden boat trip. Either way, he seemed confident that his plans were in motion. He seemed excited. Was he anticipating the thrill of killing again?

When did he think it would happen? This afternoon? Tonight?

I was sure that a lot of the thrill was getting away with it. This time, he wouldn't . . . *if* my plan worked.

With Ivy still on my hip, now chewing on a stuffed frog she loved, I went to the front room and watched the street from the window, making sure to stand far enough back that no one could see me through the sheers. I stood there, rocking side to side without realizing it—the mom rock, I'd heard others call it—and waited.

Rick's car turned the corner and went out of view, but I stayed there, needing to be sure that he wouldn't return for some reason, like forgetting a file for his meeting, or if he'd thought through the morning goodbye and realized that I hadn't been my normal self.

I stood there for a solid twenty minutes, still rocking Ivy, who was plenty happy playing with my hair and her frog until the clock on my phone assured me that Rick had to be at the firm by now. He'd never be late to a meeting, and his first one was supposed to begin six minutes ago. If he were going to come back, he would have already.

Rick had long since stopped sharing his location with me on our tracking app, so I couldn't check if he'd arrived at work that way. To calm my nerves, I pulled the local traffic app to check the traffic for any accidents or other delays on his route. The whole way was green: regular speeds on the freeway, and there were no accidents in Maple Fork or Harvest Valley.

Could I have really outsmarted him? Had *he* tricked *me*, lying about having a meeting? This was the guy who'd guessed every gift I ever bought him, for any occasion, just by staring at me—except for the tattoo.

How could he *not* know what I had planned today?

If he knew, he wouldn't have kissed me like that. He would have blown up and put an end to everything already.

Ivy and I still have hearts beating in our chests. He doesn't know.

Somehow, I'd hidden an Everest-sized secret from Rick. Maybe I'd succeed.

I went to the pantry, where I reached behind bags of flour and sugar, felt around a bit, then pulled out Rick's smartwatch. I'd hid it there this morning, fully charged.

Another secret I'd kept from him. I'd take any small victory at that point. I attached the watch to my wrist so it would track my steps and movements through the house. If Rick slipped in and out of the back door of the firm, no one would know he'd been there, and his watch would show that he'd been at home, walking around during the time he claimed he'd had a meeting. I hoped that would be enough to deflate any attempt at an alibi.

My phone blared with an obnoxious siren, making me lose my grip. It dropped to the carpet at my feet. Ivy startled and began to cry. I'd forgotten the grating sound I'd picked for the alarm so I wouldn't dismiss it. The adrenaline zipping through my veins was a testament to the siren doing the trick.

"It's okay, sweetie," I said, kissing Ivy's temple and smoothing back her hair. "It's just my phone, see?" I pointed to the carpet.

Ivy stuck her fingers into her mouth, then twisted to look behind her, where I was pointing.

"Want to help me pick it up so we can turn it off?"

Her fingers came out of her mouth, and she reached both arms toward the phone. I held her, Superman-style, and lowered her so she could reach the phone. As soon as she had it clutched in her chubby little fingers, she let out a triumphant laugh.

"Good job," I said and lifted her back to me. She'd already shoved the corner in her mouth. "Can you turn off that alarm? Touch that button right there."

Ivy pulled the phone out of her mouth and studied the screen. I pointed at the button with the word *stop*. "Tap right there."

She successfully turned off the alarm, grinned as if she'd discovered gravity, then tapped and swiped the screen as she'd seen me do. Everything she did was simple and content as if today weren't entirely abnormal. She had no idea that her life was about to be entirely upended.

The reminder made my body start to shake. I closed my eyes, pressed my face to the top of Ivy's, and kissed her downy hair. I hummed a lullaby, but she popped up, wanting to play with my phone rather than rest against me. I had to get moving soon, but I let myself have a couple of minutes to relish these last moments when my time with her was almost up.

She was so young that, provided I managed to save her, she'd have no memories of me at all—not even hazy ones. I hoped she'd know that I loved her more than anything, that the reason I wasn't there to see her grow up—graduate from high school, go off the college, marry and have children of her own—wasn't because I didn't love her, but *because* I loved her more than I loved myself.

I sat Ivy on the kitchen floor next to a basket of toys and watched her play. This was the time I was supposed to be loading up the boat with food and other supplies so we could leave almost as soon as he got home. Loading up the damn boat was *not* on today's to-do list. I'd grudgingly bring a few grocery bags out, but only for the sake of appearance. Same reason I left the list of chores Rick had written for me to do before he got back. I wanted to crumple it and throw it away, but that wasn't part of the plan.

My vision swam, and for a moment, I didn't know if I could go through with it. Ivy's playful babbles reached me.

For Ivy, I reminded myself. *And for Natalie and Chloe.*

I imagined Rick's other wives as my guardian angels, watching over me and standing witness to what I would do to bring them justice.

Bringing to mind their pictures—the photos of them living, not of their bodies—gave me the nudge I needed. I went to my purse, which hung on a hook near the door. I fished out my keys and the knit gloves I'd purposely started carrying in my purse. I stared at the gloves in one hand and the keys in the other. This was it. I was doing this.

Would it work?

It had to work. It *had* to.

CHAPTER THIRTY-SEVEN

BECCA

Five minutes into the drive to the mortuary, Ivy wakes up and starts whimpering in the way I recognize to mean that she's hungry. I have a few minutes before it turns into a full-on wail. I pull over and debate whether to hope she'll make it to the mortuary until I can make a bottle there. But picturing myself receiving Jenn's ashes while dealing with a fussy baby . . .

No. I need to be able to give the moment—give Jenn—my attention. She and I both deserve that much. From the shoulder of the road, I call Nancy to see if she can tend Ivy.

"Bring her on over," she says when I explain the situation.

"I owe you chocolate or diamonds or something," I say.

A few minutes later, when I drop off Ivy, she's fussy but not completely unhinged, thank heavens.

"She just woke up from her morning nap, and she's hungry," I tell Nancy, holding out the diaper bag. "Bottles and formula are in there, and—"

"Go," Nancy assures me. "Take all the time you need. Ivy and I will be fine. Really," she says, as Ivy begins crying in earnest.

Tears threaten to choke my voice, so I nod until I can speak—a single word. "Thanks." I wave at them and hurry back to the car.

When I pull into the parking lot at Gates Mortuary, Ben's already there, leaning against the back of a white sedan, looking at his phone. He's wearing Dockers and a blue button-up shirt—professional but casual. I'm glad I put on a little makeup and didn't show up wearing leggings and a hoodie. Glad I still have a decent wardrobe, even if it hasn't been used much lately.

He glances up when I pull in and straightens, slipping the phone into his pocket and waiting for me as I park. I cross the lot to him, feeling weirdly relieved. I've met him only once before, but he seems like someone I can trust. I didn't realize how much I needed an adult to talk to until he showed up yesterday.

I stop a few feet from him. "Thanks for coming. I really appreciate it."

"Happy to," Ben says. He nods toward the mortuary. "Is this"—he twirls his hand in the air—"on the record?"

I note his phone, which he's holding out, showing his thumb hovering over a red button that would begin an audio recording. Of course. He's a journalist, not a friend. He's doing his job, likely hoping for a scoop on the Banks case. Disappointing, but in the scope of everything, not earth-shattering.

"Sure," I say.

"Great. Can I record this?"

I nod. "Yeah."

He hits the red button, then slips the phone, microphone side up, into his shirt pocket. I look at the gray granite building with its manicured walkway. It looks solemn.

"If I ask for something to be off the record later, is that okay?" I ask.

"Absolutely." He smiles at that, and I'm not sure whether it's to reassure me or because he finds the question funny.

"Thanks," I say again. I have half a mind to add that I'm a virgin in journalism matters. Instead, I smile back. I have no idea what I might want off the record, but I'm glad I have the option. It's a small sense of control in a situation where I've felt entirely *out* of control for weeks.

"Then I guess . . . let's go in." I head down the walk lined with tulips that are newly opened with the spring. No doubt they were planned to give a sense of life and hope to those coming here after a loss. To me, the bright reds and yellows seem blasphemously cheerful.

Inside, we're met by Betty, who wears a nondescript navy-blue dress that could have come from any of the last four decades. I appreciate that it's not depressing, but also not something cheerful like the tulips. Her hair's coiffed in the way that tells me she's a Boomer; it probably has so much Aqua Net on it that not a hair would shift in a windstorm—helmet head, Jenn and I called it. She'd get such a kick out of Betty's—big and perfect, like Margaret Thatcher's in the eighties.

"Nice to meet you," Betty says, shaking my hand and then Ben's after I introduce him. "Come with me."

Ben gestures for me to go ahead, and we walk down a short hall with a flat red carpet that reminds me of a casino but I'm sure is supposed to look classy while being easy to maintain. Moments later, we're sitting across from Betty, who slides a black plastic box across her desk with one hand. It looks much heavier than I would have expected for its size, slightly bigger than an ice cream carton. With her other hand, she sets a small stack of papers in front of me.

"What's that?" I ask, staring at the box.

"Just some basic paperwork," Betty says. "Need to record who picks up the loved one and such. You *do* have ID on you, yes?"

"I do," I say, taking the papers. "But I meant *that*." I nod toward the box. "Your loved one."

Oh. The ashes. What's left of Jenn is right there, on the desk, inside that box, in front of me.

Betty opens a desk drawer and rummages around, closing it a moment later after finding a Sharpie. She goes over the papers, explaining each line, where to fill out information and sign. From her view, the papers are upside down, yet she knows each line by heart as if she's done it a thousand times. She probably has.

"Here is the cost breakdown for services rendered, due upon receipt of your loved one," Betty says, pointing with the orange cap of her Sharpie.

"It's not already paid for?" I confirm. I knew Rick probably wasn't going to pay for it, but I'd kind of hoped he would in the end. I gave them Arrington's contact information.

"No," Betty says. "Mr. Banks's lawyer said you'd be the one to do that. Is that incorrect?"

A glance at the charges makes my stomach drop. They include a cardboard casket that she was cremated in. Not a fancy one. No funeral service or fancy urn either, yet the total at the bottom is still over a thousand dollars.

"I'll pay for it," I say.

Betty returns to the papers and begins itemizing the list, again, tapping each line with the orange Sharpie cap. "Here's the transfer fee from the medical examiner's office. This is the fee for the car that made the transfer . . ."

"Wait," Ben interrupts. Betty looks up expectantly. He goes on. "There are separate fees for transferring the body *and* for the vehicle that did the transfer?"

"That right," Betty says in a matter-of-fact tone.

"What's next, fees for the driver and the gas?" Ben asks, his voice having an edge now.

I throw him a grateful look. Sitting here makes me feel like a deer in the headlights, unable to form clear thoughts or questions. I'm already glad I asked him to come along to have someone nearby on my side who *can* think clearly.

"I assure you, this is all very standard," Betty says. "May I go on?"

Ben looks at me, and I nod. She continues, and the heaviness in my middle continues to grow. The second page has one of those *sign here* sticky flags. She goes through a few other pages of legalese, but they don't seem to be asking for money. Then she flips the last page and reveals a brochure on the bottom. Shiny images of urns stare back at me, in all colors—blue, red, green, gold. Boxes made of different woods, some painted, some stained.

Ben takes the brochure. I smile my gratitude to him—I didn't want to look at that thing another second—then return to the page where I have to fill out my personal information. I write my address and phone number. Today, I have the mental capacity for filling out personal information, not for picking out a box to store Jenn's ashes in. Not today.

"Are you okay?" Ben asks quietly.

I'm not. I'm inches from Jenn's ashes. I'm facing a bill of at least a thousand dollars, likely several hundred more if I'm a decent enough friend to buy a box for her ashes that's not cheap. How on earth am I supposed to know what kind of box or urn Jenn would want? I'm not sure she wanted to be cremated in the first place. We talked about all kinds of things over the years, but *what to do with my body when I die* never came up.

Will Rick try to get me to send the ashes to him in jail? What about in prison after he's convicted? Can inmates *have* ashes? Doesn't matter, because he's not getting them.

I start to get tunnel vision, which tells me I'm holding my breath. I force myself to inhale deeply and then let it out. Repeat. "I'll *be* okay," I finally tell Ben. "It's a bit overwhelming."

"Understandably," he says with empathy in his eyes. I haven't had anyone acknowledge my emotions through this. I've had to be strong for everyone—first for Rick and Ivy, then the twins, then for everyone at work. That first day when the detectives questioned me for hours, they weren't unkind, but they weren't exactly friendly either. Seeing Ben's compassion, I suddenly realize just how starved I am for something so simple as someone acknowledging that this whole thing is hard.

"Thanks," I say, knowing the single word doesn't encapsulate the half of it.

With interlocked hands resting on the desk, Betty tilts her head with a practiced angle of sympathy. Too little, too late. "It's all so trying. I understand. Take your time." She reaches to the side and places another copy of the glossy urn brochure on the desk for us all to see. "These ones"—she uncaps her Sharpie and circles them—"are the priciest, but they're no better in quality or appearance than some of the others. These, however"—she draws a line along the side of one column—"are rather cheap and poor quality. The paint chips off. I've heard stories of them cracking and spilling. I do *not* recommend them." She finishes her spiel with more circles and explanations. Betty slides the brochure closer to my end of the table and then stands. "I'll let you two to look them over. Holler if you have any questions. I'll be just down the hall." She sweeps herself out of the room.

"I can't pick right now," I say. "I don't know what she'd want . . . Sorry. I'm a mess." I lick my lips, glance at Ben, and feel my cheeks get hot.

"Nothing to apologize for," he says. "This is a lot."

"I can't get over the fact that Rick won't pay for it."

"Let's tell them to send a bill to his lawyer."

Let's, as in both of us. As in, for the first time since Jenn died, I don't feel alone.

A smile of relief tugs at my mouth. "Great idea." I look at his shirt pocket where his phone still sits, still recording. "Could you turn that off now?"

"Of course." He pulls out his phone and stops the recording. He sets the phone on the desk, easily in my view, a gesture much appreciated because I know he hasn't started another recording without telling me.

"Thanks."

"I'm sure you can pick out a container later, maybe from somewhere else," Ben says. "Or come back. There's no rush, right? I mean, Betty might not be here much longer, but the mortuary will."

I nearly choke on a burst of laughter at that, and he laughs too. I'm so glad he broke the tension; it was getting unbearable.

"This isn't a car dealership," he says. "No deal expires when we walk out, right?"

"Right." After a moment, as I sign one of the spots Betty pointed out, Ben gestures to the box. "Do you think she might want her ashes scattered somewhere?"

"I don't know. Maybe." I set the pen down and slide the papers back to Betty's side of the desk. I've signed the important stuff to claim the ashes, but not the financial paperwork. Let them send an invoice to Arrington. I'm taking Jenn's ashes today no matter what Betty says.

"Let's go get some lunch," Ben says. "We can look over the brochure—or not. You can at least make a decision on a day when you're not under pressure."

"And when I don't have low blood sugar," I add, realizing I haven't eaten in hours. "I'd like that. Thanks." Even if he's just being nice because I'm a potential source, I'm glad he's here, and I'm glad he invited me to lunch.

"I'll get Betty," he says and leaves the room, returning only a few seconds later with the mortuary rep, who had to have been waiting outside the door.

"For now," I tell her as she sits in her chair again, "we'll just take her in this box."

"But—" Betty begins.

"Mr. Arrington will be paying for your services on behalf of her husband. I believe you already have his information, but I'm happy to provide it again if needed." I pick up the plastic container of ashes. "If I decide to purchase an urn through you later, I'll be sure to let you know."

"Oh." Betty looks genuinely surprised. "Would you like us to post an obituary for her?"

Why is there always something else I'm not expecting lurking in the shadows, popping out when I'm not expecting it?

Ben stands and holds out a hand to shake Betty's. "We'll be in touch on that as well."

I stand beside him and nod. "Right. I—we'll—be in touch."

We each shake hands with Betty. I pick up the temporary box—it has more of a heft than I expected, weighing several pounds, for sure. Together, Ben and I walk to the parking lot. Only when we're past the tulip-lined walkway do I sigh with relief.

"You were a lifesaver in there," I say.

"No biggie. I imagine this is a business that thrives on people who are having a difficult time."

"Definitely." I hug myself, which also means sort of hugging the box of ashes, partly because of the chilly spring breeze. Also because I need to feel held. "Imagine families who have to make these decisions just a few days after a death." I can't imagine coming here and making any decisions about what to do for Jenn right after she died. It's been a month and a half, and I'm as eloquent as a frog.

I adjust my hold on the box and can't help but think that the ashes weigh about half of what Ivy does.

"I was serious about lunch," Ben says. "I'm happy to take you out somewhere. My treat."

"Can anything we talk about be off the record?"

He cracks a smile that's sweet enough I almost wonder if he's inviting me to lunch as a *guy* rather than as a reporter. "Sure."

"Meet you at Heaps?" I suggest—a family-owned spot that has a great salad bar and the best deep-dish pizza around.

"You got it."

We head to our respective cars, and after I get in mine, I set the ashes on the floor of the passenger side. After I buckle myself, I can't help but look in the rearview mirror at Ben's car and wonder about him. He's nice. He's cute. And his ring finger is empty.

Careful, I tell myself as I put my car in gear.

I have no intention of dating anyone. I just want a normal conversation with someone who isn't upset over a missed work deadline, charged with murdering Jenn, or accusing me of not being a good enough mom and threatening to take custody of my kids.

A meal of comfort food with a good-looking guy is just what I need.

CHAPTER THIRTY-EIGHT

JENN

G loves on, I went into the garage and walked to the back of my car. I stood there for a minute, staring in the hatchback window at the blanket. Knowing what lay under it.

For Ivy, Chloe, and Natalie.

After a deep breath, I reached out and opened the hatch. As it slowly rose, up, up, I stared at the blanket. Rather, I stared at the bump in the blanket that was the plastic jug under it.

This is it. I had to reach out and grab the edge of the car to steady myself and take a few more calming breaths.

For Ivy, Chloe, and Natalie.

Finally, I reached in with gloved hands and drew the blanket to the side. Still holding the blanket, I wiped the plastic container to get rid of any lingering fingerprints. Would this be very painful? Flashes of movie scenes of people dying horrific deaths went through my head.

Stop it. No thinking more than a step or two ahead.

The jug was wiped. Next step: take it inside. But that felt like several steps: grab the handle, lift the jug out of the car, move the blanket back so it looked untouched, close the back of the car, go inside, put the jug on the kitchen counter.

For Ivy.

For Ivy. Ivy. Do it.

One swift movement later, I had the jug in my gloved hand. I commanded myself to get through each of the next steps. I closed the hatch. I walked back inside. I set the jug on the kitchen counter. Check, check, check.

I stared at the container. It didn't belong here. The color wasn't something anyone should ingest, even if it did look a lot like liquid candy. Green, like something a superhero's nemesis might drink to turn that color.

Next step: wipe the jug down better, this time with soap and water.

For Ivy.

And for Chloe. And Natalie.

With a soapy paper towel, I wiped down the jug again, still wearing gloves. I threw away the paper towel, then faced the counter and the jug again. Next step: fill up the glass.

I looked to the one I planned to use: the glass I'd set in the sink after Rick had drunk his green smoothie for breakfast, his latest obsession for maintaining his weight. His appearance has always mattered to him, something he'd always attributed to his profession and the need to look polished for both clients and the courtroom.

Stop stalling, I ordered myself. *Pick up the glass.*

I turned to the sink. The glass still had a green coating of blended vegetables, something that would serve my purposes well. I picked up the glass and set it beside the jug of antifreeze.

Next step: fill the glass.

For Ivy. For Ivy. For Ivy.

The childproof lid on the jug gave me fits, partly from the clumsy gloves but also because of my trembling fingers. I finally removed the lid and peeled off the inner foil seal.

Maybe I should take Ivy over to Becca's first, I thought. But then I checked the clock and remembered what I'd read about ethylene glycol's effects on the body. It needed to be in my system as long as possible for evidence of it to show up in my system.

Keep going. I lifted the jug and tilted it, and the antifreeze poured out fast. Nearly sloshed across the counter. I hadn't expected it to be thin, like water.

I hadn't known what to expect, really. If pressed, I would have imagined it to be a little slimy. Not as thick as one of Rick's green smoothies, but a bit viscous. When the glass was about half full, I stopped. Kale and spinach flecks were a stark contrast against the neon green.

As I stared at the glass, my fingers flexed and stretched inside the gloves. *Not yet. Not quite yet.*

I backed away from the counter and walked to Ivy, who had pulled herself to standing on a kitchen chair. She'd never done that before. She leaned against it, mostly with her face, which was tilted to the side as she gummed a ring of baby keys. When she saw me, she bounced up and down, showing off her new trick, but the movement made her lose her balance and plop back to the tile on her diaper.

I'll never see her walk. That wasn't news. But that specific thought hadn't occurred to me among the dozens of other things I'd miss. A stab shot through my chest, and I held back a whimper, not wanting Ivy to sense my worry or sadness. I needed her to *not* sense that anything was wrong. If she cried . . .

"Look at you!" I said with an overly cheerful tone. I clapped, though the sound was muted by the gloves, so I grinned to be sure she recognized my approval. She waved her arms and showed me the keys, then leaned forward and pulled herself back to standing with the chair. "Such a big girl!" I cooed.

She grinned—toothless and gummy—and lost her balance again.

The glass of green liquid beckoned me. No more ignoring it. The clock was ticking. No matter that I felt increasingly uneasy. No matter that I didn't want to do this and almost convinced myself to try to escape Rick instead.

The last thing I wanted to do was drink from the glass. Well, almost.

The actual last thing I wanted was for me and Ivy to both die at Rick's hand, with no one ever knowing how it happened, then to have Rick go off to another state, begin a new life with a new identity and another forged transcript—maybe medical school to keep things interesting. I couldn't let him get away again. I couldn't allow Rick to have another forgotten victim.

I couldn't allow my daughter to be a victim at all.

253

At least I hoped I was saving her. If all went as planned, Rick would come home and find me while Ivy was at Becca's, and he'd be arrested right away. Ivy would stay with Becca, safe.

If I didn't do this, Ivy would be dead soon. She mattered more than I did, and if my death could save her *and* bring justice to those who died before me, then I had to do this.

If I *didn't* do this, no one would get justice, and Rick would kill again.

No one but me knew about the other lives he'd stolen away.

He'd be punished for the murders he already committed, and for mine before he did it.

A few beads of condensation had formed on the outside of the glass. I nearly wiped them off out of habit, but resisted. Rick's fingerprints needed to be there.

It tastes sweet, I reminded myself. But my intellect knew full well that I was staring at poison, not lime-flavored punch.

How did anyone know it was sweet? Did someone survive antifreeze poisoning and live to tell the tale? Did a scientist put a drop on their tongue?

No more stalling. *One swallow at a time.*

I reached for the glass with both hands to be sure it wouldn't slip through the slick knit gloves. *Ivy. Chloe. Natalie.*

A baby giggle floating to me from the other room pushed me over the edge. If I wimped out now, Ivy wouldn't experience life. She wouldn't grow up and become the amazing woman I knew she had every right to be.

I lifted the glass. *It's time. Do it.*

I pressed the edge of the glass to my lips. The trembling in my hands made the glass tap against my teeth. I tilted my head back. Some dripped into my mouth. It *was* sweet. I could pretend it was bright-green Gatorade. Even better, Kool-Aid. No, that wasn't better. An image of Jonestown flashed into my mind of dead children lying next to their parents who'd poisoned them as part of mass suicide.

Not Kool-Aid. Gatorade.

I swallowed, expecting the liquid to burn on the way down. It didn't. I waited for a solid minute to see how I'd feel. Would I throw it up? Would my stomach cramp? When nothing happened—I might as well have drunk Kool-Aid, for how different I felt—I took another swallow.

One steady swallow after another, I drank. I tilted my head back until I tasted spinach. I'd drunk it all. Stunned, I lowered the glass and set it on the counter. I did it.

Well, I'd done the first big part. But I wasn't *done*. Not even close.

If I stopped here, I might pass out, and I might go into kidney failure, but Rick would come home in time to find me and call 911. He wouldn't let me die unless he was the one pulling the strings. He'd still be able to end things his way, on his timetable.

"No," I said aloud and pounded the counter with my gloved fist. I needed to hear myself say it—to make it real. I'd never again be at the whims of Rick Banks, Ryan Brockbank, or whoever he was in his heart. The devil.

A few green drops clung to the sides and bottom of the glass, lit by rays of morning sunlight streaming through the window. Should I drink more? I hadn't been able to find definitive information on how much antifreeze would do what I needed in the time I had.

I knew how much *ethylene glycol* was needed, but antifreeze was a solution, and high school math was far too long ago for me to be able to figure out how much of the toxin was in a twelve-ounce kitchen glass.

The taste wasn't horrible, and I wasn't in agony, at least not yet. I prayed I'd be unconscious before any gastrointestinal symptoms showed up. I was counting on it. To be on the safe side, I poured another glass. The second went down much easier. By the end of that one, I felt off, almost like the beginning of a beer buzz, mixed with something more.

My head felt foggy, and my limbs thick. If I didn't finish up the rest of the plan right away, I'd be unable to do it at all. I slipped off the knit gloves and tucked them next to the toolbox in the garage where they belonged. I grabbed my phone, moving a bit too fast. My vision swam. The floor seemed to crest and dip under my feet.

I leaned against the counter until the dizziness ebbed a bit, then called Becca. Normally, I'd text, but I didn't know if my fingers could do that; they felt like sausages.

"I'm on my way with Ivy," I said when Becca answered.

"Awesome. See you in a couple!"

"Yep." I meant to say more, but my mind was already getting muddled, and I didn't trust my voice. If I sounded weird and Becca became suspicious, all bets were off. I rested my forehead in my hand, my arm being held up by the counter. "See you soon."

I ended the call, hoping that those last words sounded normal. Mustering every bit of fortitude I had left in me, I loaded Ivy into her carrier and tucked the diaper bag into the car beside her. Last night, I made sure it had an almost full can of formula and two clean bottles. I'd very nearly added a couple of changes of clothing but stopped myself. I couldn't do anything that might telegraph my plans.

As I adjusted the car seat, my wrist hit the counter with an unfamiliar clink—Rick's watch. I'd nearly brought it with me. I quickly took it off, hurrying up the stairs to return it to his nightstand so it wouldn't get left out the foggier my thinking got.

Good thing too. On the way to Becca's, my head grew increasingly fuzzy. I drove slowly, sure that my reaction time was crap, scared I'd get into a fender bender or hit a dog, but we made it to Becca's. She opened her front door before I was out of the car and helped take Ivy out, still buckled in her carrier. I took the car seat's base out, glad that this was a normal part of our interactions. She wouldn't question why I was making sure she had the base. I always gave it to her when she tended to Ivy, just in case she needed to drive somewhere. This time, it wasn't *if* but *when*.

I walked to the front door and set the base inside. "Thanks for watching her. I have so much to do before Rick gets home." Entirely true, though she'd assume I meant loading up the boat.

"Of course," Becca said. She'd already gotten Ivy out of the car seat. Now she reached in for a hug with her free arm, and I hugged her back, taking strength from her touch.

When she pulled away, she looked at me closer. "Hey, are you feeling all right?"

Panic zipped through me. I put on a smile. "I'm fine!"

She tilted her head, brows raised, in the *Yeah right* way she had. She knew me too well.

"Be back soon," I added, then headed to the car quickly, knowing I was about to blow the whole thing.

"You're heading out at noon, right?" Becca asked. "So see you around eleven?"

"Yep." I didn't dare say more than single-syllable words. Before getting inside the car, I waved. "Bye!"

Ivy reached out an arm and waved back. She'd waved at other people, but this was the first time she'd waved at me—saying a final goodbye. My eyes were quickly tearing up. It was time to go, both because the chemicals were clouding my mind and because saying more would ruin everything. I swiped at a tear and got into the car.

As I backed out of the driveway, I could hardly think. I glanced at Becca's door, where she stood with Ivy. She gave me a questioning look again, but I put the car into gear and drove away.

Only I knew that I wouldn't be coming back at all. That it was really farewell.

CHAPTER THIRTY-NINE

BECCA

We arrive at the pizza joint seconds apart; on the way, I made sure that Ben made the same lights behind me. When we walk in together, a hostess—a young thing, no doubt a student at the local university, like most of the staff—greets us.

"Two?" she asks cheerfully. Her name tag reads *Kandee*. Definitely a local. Parents in this area love using "creative" spellings, though hers isn't nearly as weird as some I've seen.

"Yes," Ben and I say at the same time.

She consults the floor plan of tables on the podium before her and grabs a dry-erase marker, but before she can assign us a table, Ben chimes in.

"Could we sit somewhere private? Say, this booth?" He points at the floor plan; he's done this before. I'm guessing he's talked to a lot of sources here. But I'm not a source. I'll confirm that lunch is off the record just as soon as we're settled.

"Sure thing," Kandee says. She circles a different table, pushes a button, and grabs two menus. "This way."

She leads us to a corner booth, where Ben and I sort of end up sitting beside each other, sort of across. Our server appears quickly. Her tag says *EmmaLeigh*, but she introduces herself without a pause, so it sounds like *Emily*. Ben's taking a drink of water right then and nearly does a spit take.

"EmmaLeigh," I repeat, feigning interest. "Interesting spelling. Where are you from?"

"Oh, I grew up just a few minutes north of here. Born and raised in Red Grove."

I catch Ben hiding a smile behind his hand; the fact that we have the same sense of humor about this local quirk is like water on parched ground. I relax into the booth's padding and order a small personal pizza with a side salad.

When we're alone again, Ben shifts so he's facing me a bit more, and I do the same. "Tell me about Jenn."

My face must give away my concern about my being a source and this being an interview because he quickly jumps in. "Only if you want to. Shoot. It's hard to take off the reporter hat. I swear this isn't a trick. I'm not Ben Winsley the journalist right now. This conversation isn't official. It's off the record. All of that. Promise."

I needed that assurance—how much, I didn't know until I got it. "It's all good," I say and stroke my thumb along the fog of my water glass. "About Jenn . . ." I shrug and finally settle with something that probably sounds cliché but is one hundred percent true. "Jenn was the best friend you could ever have. We were more than close. We were practically sisters. Neither of us has family, so we became each other's family."

"Wow. Losing her is an even bigger loss to you, then," Ben says. He shakes his head as if he put his foot into his mouth. "Sorry. That probably sounded like a hollow platitude—"

"I know you mean it," I assure him, putting a hand on his arm resting on the table. "So thanks. Really. There's not exactly a good Hallmark card for something like this. There *are* no right words."

Neither of us says anything for a moment, and I appreciate that he's giving me space to think and feel. EmmaLeigh returns with our food, asks if we need anything else, then leaves, throwing a smile and waving in our direction. We're back to companionable silence as we take our first bites.

"I'm still trying to grasp that she's really gone, you know?" I say. "Even though I have her ashes in my car. Even though I'm taking care of her baby—even though I *found* her body. I *know* she's gone. But . . . this isn't how it's supposed to be." I stare at a crouton in my salad for a few seconds and wonder just how much Ben knows about the circumstances surrounding Jenn's death.

As far as I can tell, no one but the police and I know about Rick's history. Now I can't help but worry. If the press—someone like Ben—were to reveal Rick's past as part of their coverage, would it *help* keep Rick behind bars? I have no idea, but I *think* it could help. Ben could do more research. He'd know how to find the kinds of thing Jenn did, and probably a lot more.

If that information gets to the press, I have to remain secret as the source. Detective Andrus would need to think it could have been someone on his team who talked to the press, or maybe that Ben's a great reporter who dug into Rick's past and figured things out.

I reach for my purse and withdraw my phone. After unlocking it, I glance at Ben. "I, uh, learned some things about Jenn and Rick—mostly about Rick—after."

Ben raises his eyebrows, looking both curious and cautious. "What kinds of things?"

Here goes nothing.

"If I share some of them with you, promise me you'll keep them off the record unless I give the go-ahead to use them."

"You got it," Ben said. "I promise."

"And *if* I give you permission to use them—big if—you can't name me as the source."

He immediately straightens. The idea of a confidential informant has piqued his interest. "Have you shared"—he gestures toward my phone—"it with the police?"

"The majority is stuff Jenn found herself. Public information."

He visibly relaxes a bit and leans in, intrigued. "Go on."

"I've given most of it to the authorities. Everything but a couple of private recordings." I look up from my phone, which holds the recording from the pen. I made a copy before handing everything over to Andrus. "Is it legal to record someone without them knowing it?"

"This is a one-party state," Ben says with a nod. When I gave him a look that shows my confusion, he clarifies. "Only one of the two parties on a recording needs to be aware of it, not both. Some states are two-party states, meaning—"

"That both parties need to know they're being recorded," I say with a nod. "Got it."

"Did *you* record someone?" Ben points at my phone.

"No. Jenn did." I pull up the conversation she recorded at the restaurant. "A lot of what she found points the finger very much at Rick."

"Hold that thought." He reaches into a pocket and pulls out a pair of wireless earbuds. "To avoid eavesdroppers," he says.

"Smart," I say and quickly pair my phone with his earbuds. When we each have one in, I hit play.

I've heard the recording several times, but every time is a gut punch, starting with hearing Jenn's voice again. The progression of emotions on Ben's face must be like mine the first time—confusion shifting to disbelief that makes way for shock and horror.

Just as it ends, EmmaLeigh appears suddenly and asks how things taste and if we need anything.

"Everything's great," Ben says, and I smile my agreement, nodding. We wait until she's out of earshot before speaking, and then we lower our volume.

Ben takes out his earbud. "Wow."

"Yeah," I say, taking out mine as well. "She did a ton of research about him and his past before and after this recording. His parents' deaths, his previous wife's death—" Ben's mouth opens in question, so I clarify.

"*Wives*, plural," I say. "She found another one. They all died by drowning..."

"That's . . . stunning."

"And disturbing," I say. "The police have all of it, but I made copies. If you're interested."

"I absolutely am," he says, then adds "Wow" again, shaking his head.

Showing some of the documents I've taken pictures of, I give a *Reader's Digest* version of what Jenn found, along with my conclusion that Rick is responsible for all of the suspicious drownings in his life.

"He's definitely a serial killer," Ben says, still under his breath. He leans back on the padded vinyl. "I've never covered a story so potentially huge. Do you want this story out? Or do you want everything to remain quiet?"

"I do want it out the right way at the right time," I say. "Maybe after the trial—assuming he's convicted. Someone from one of the other cases might see it and realize there's evidence that can be used to charge Rick with the other deaths. Everyone who has lost a loved one because of him deserves to know what happened and who is responsible."

"His victims deserve justice too," Ben adds. "If the story comes out sooner, and charges are filed in the other cases, that might help get a guilty verdict in Jenn's case. Well, assuming the judge allows any of that to be mentioned during the trial. That's a gamble."

"I'll email you everything I have."

"That would be fantastic."

We take a break from the conversation to eat a little. As I pick at my salad, I ask, "Why do you think he did it when he did? I mean, aside from being tied down by a wife *and* a kid. You haven't read all of the information, but still—any ideas?"

"Why that specific day, at home, rather than a week later in a lake or something?"

"Especially when they were already planning a boat trip that afternoon."

"They were?" Ben asks, his voice hitting a new level of tension, something that makes me aware of how weird that piece of information looks. And that it's not part of public knowledge.

Also that it doesn't fit the picture. The more I think through it, the more I'm unsure what to make of it. My thoughts spin like a dog chasing its tail, not quite able to grab it.

"Okay, let's back up," I say, as much for my sake as for Ben's. "Jenn didn't want to go on the boating trip. She felt uneasy about having a baby on a boat, and it was still so cold."

"A month and a half later, it's *still* pretty cold for a boating trip," Ben says. He takes a sip of his drink. "Do you think that's when he was going to do it?"

"That would make sense," I say. "Jenn probably thought he'd do her in on the trip, and that's why she didn't want to go. Could he have changed his mind at the last minute to do it at home? Why not go through with it the way he'd planned?"

Ben tilts his head in thought. "Maybe Jenn refused to go on the trip after all, but Rick was determined to get it done that day no matter what, so he did it at home."

"Still by drowning, but do it at home," I say. "Like his first wife. Then he goes to work, giving him an alibi—though no one at the firm can corroborate that he was there, and the fact that someone else found the body is significant. Andrus told me that killers try to get someone else to find their victims to throw off suspicion."

EmmaLeigh shows up to top off our soft drinks, and we thank her with smiles before Ben continues, his voice lowered even more, though now that our server has left, no one is nearby.

"If he was already planning to kill her on the boat, why change the plan the day of? He spent tens of thousands of dollars on that boat. Why not *force* her on the trip—he could have bound her with zip ties or something. Or even killed her at the house but dumped her body in a lake. It doesn't make sense."

"You're right," I say.

The pepperoni feels heavy in my stomach. My mind feels as if tumblers inside it are rotating, first in one direction and then the other. One falls into place, followed by another until the answers slowly unlock to me. The truth is showing itself. I can almost make out the picture.

Rick's past says he's a serial killer who has done away with multiple wives, all by drowning. He likely killed his parents by drowning as well—or at the very least, when they died, he realized that drowning was a great way to get rid of people. My guess about them is that they'd been drinking, and when they fell asleep, he heaved them overboard. However it happened, their deaths seem to have sparked in Rick a desire to kill—or to *keep* killing.

When Jenn died of drowning, the police had plenty of probable cause to arrest Rick based only on the evidence they've already made public: Rick's fingerprints and DNA on the glass that held the antifreeze found in Jenn's system. Her DNA was on the glass, but not her fingerprints. All of that fits with the theory that he force-fed her antifreeze.

Then there's his alibi. He has no clear one for the hour before she was found—he claims he had a secret meeting, but no one saw him in the building, and even he admits that it was over about the time I found her. Plus, his smartwatch has GPS movements and steps around the house at the time of her death, meaning he might not have been at the firm that morning at all. I'm sure there are more things Detective Andrus hasn't told me or released to the public, but even the little I know is damning.

And yet. As Ben says, the way she died doesn't make sense with the boat trip planned for later that day. As far as I can tell, there's nothing that definitively puts Rick at the scene the moment Jenn died.

What if he didn't kill her, and it wasn't a home invasion gone wrong?

What if, thanks to everything she'd figured out, Jenn knew he planned to kill her and Ivy at the reservoir? In that case, she'd do whatever it took to stop Rick. She'd become a mother bear: do anything to protect her baby.

The final tumbler falls into place. I understand it all now, and I wonder how I didn't see it before. I think back on the tear-filled night Rick came over looking for comfort. I thought he was telling the truth then. I later figured he'd been lying, but maybe his frantic claims of innocence were real. When I visited the jail, he was practically manic in his insistence that he was innocent. That he didn't kill Jenn.

What if he *didn't* kill Jenn? Not because he didn't plan to but because she beat him to the punch and made sure he'd be blamed?

I realize I've been silent for a while, so I try to come up with something to say—some explanation for Rick's change in plans. "Sociopaths don't make a lot of sense."

"True," Ben says, and he looks ready to say something else, but I hurry on, reminding myself to keep my voice low.

"He's gotten away with killing before—several times." I'm not ready to tell him what I've figured out, so I go with a different tack. "He probably got cocky, but when he saw that he was losing control over Jenn, his anger got the better of him. I bet that when she said she'd never go on the boat, he snapped."

"Maybe," Ben says slowly.

We sit there, nodding without looking at each other for a moment. Then our eyes catch and hold. Does he believe me? Has he figured it out too? Does he know what I know? If so, what will he do? He blinks, which breaks our gaze. He looks away and returns to his chicken parm.

He takes a bite, swallows, and without looking at me again, says, "I'm always out to find the truth. That's my job. If Rick is a murderer . . ." Ben's voice trails off. I can tell he's choosing his words carefully, wanting to be both honest with me and true to his profession.

"If Rick is a murderer . . ." I prompt.

He looks up. "Then that's the story I'll tell. The story that will keep him locked up." His words have an unmistakable electric undercurrent, something unsaid.

He knows.

And we're on the same team. I'll have to be careful with what I say, but for this moment, having an ally, even if it's just someone who recognizes my pain, feels good.

CHAPTER FORTY

JENN

I had to get home quickly. The street was warping and moving in my vision, and the effects of the antifreeze would only get worse. Based on my reading, I'd expected to have more time.

Despite the urgency to finish the plan, I drove even more slowly on the way back. No point in upending it all with a car crash on the way home. After what felt like an eternity, I successfully pulled into the garage. For a tiny blip of a moment, I considered finishing myself off that way: fumes from the car would be painless, and I wouldn't have to get out and try to walk when I felt so off.

It has to be murder, not suicide, I reminded my foggy brain.

The point wasn't simply to die. The point was to make sure Rick couldn't ever kill anyone else and to make sure that Ivy was with Becca. If I were found dead in my car, none of that would happen.

When I pushed the button to turn off my Prius, there was no cutting of the engine. The electric motor was running, as was typical when moving at slow speeds or when stopped. With a *duh*, I realized that my car wouldn't run the gas engine until I passed out anyway. Suicide by hybrid probably wouldn't work. My legs were getting less steady by the minute. I needed to get moving.

Mechanically, I got out of the car and went into the house. I left my purse on the counter, not looking at the glass I'd left by the sink, and headed for the stairs. As I climbed them, I felt woozy, unstable. I counted each step, the only way to keep myself moving and *not* thinking ahead. One step at a time meant I wouldn't chicken out. When I reached fourteen steps, I was at the top. Now to the bathroom.

The corner tub was deep and wide. We'd used the tub together maybe once, but today its size would serve a more important purpose.

I plugged the drain and turned on the water. Without thinking—I couldn't do much thinking anyway—I tested the water and adjusted it to be nice and hot but not uncomfortably so.

Wait. This can't look like an ordinary bath.

I turned down the hot water and increased the cold. Better let anyone coming into the room think that the water had been warmer and had cooled off some. That would make the timeline muddier, the possible window for all of this bigger.

I reached into the rising water—it felt a bit warmer than body temperature. Good enough. I straightened and went to the bedroom, where I headed for Rick's dresser. Only when I reached for the top drawer's pull did I have a thought break through the haze in my mind.

Fingerprints.

My prints on my husband's dresser wouldn't be suspicious, but my prints on his prescription bottles might be.

I pulled a pair of socks out of my dresser drawer and slipped them onto my hands. They didn't have the little plastic dots on the soles that would have made gripping plastic bottles easier, but they'd do. If I moved fast enough. Just thinking grew harder to think with every minute. I had to blink several times to clear my vision. Pain in my middle began to burn and ache.

Hurry.

I easily found the oxycontin prescription Rick had held onto since spraining his ankle—and had managed to get filled several times. He always had a "good stuff" painkiller on hand if he ever needed it "in a pinch," as he put it. The bottle opened easily in my hands, and I shook out four tablets. I checked the label, though I already knew the dosage: ten milligrams per tablet. Four of those should do a lot, especially to someone as sensitive to medications as I was.

A string of other numbers and abbreviations were there after the ten milligrams—how much Tylenol was mixed in with the oxy and who knew what else. I knew that too much Tylenol could cause liver damage. Would the four tablets in my hand cause any? For good measure, I took a fifth tablet before replacing the bottle inside the drawer.

I tilted my palm over the bedspread and let the tablets fall onto it, then reached for another bottle in Rick's drawer: his Ambien. I opted for four of those. By the time I dropped the blue pills next to the white oblong ones on the bedspread, my eye-hand coordination was getting worse. Replacing the lid on the second bottle took more time. I wasn't done. Finding Rick's old anxiety medication took a little effort. I added some of those to the collection.

Lastly, I added the pills I'd bought the other day: first, I shook several Benadryl onto the bedspread. Even one of those pink tablets could make me drowsy. A few of the cold-medicine caplets finished off the pile.

The pain in my stomach grew worse, making me double over, arms over my middle. I waited for it to pass, *hoped* it would, like a labor contraction. The sharp knife ebbed a tiny bit but then increased again. I'd have to just get this done by pushing through the pain.

I rested against the side of the bed and looked at the mound of pills. Would they be enough? I couldn't know for sure. They probably wouldn't be enough to take a life on their own, but if they knocked me unconscious enough to slip under the water, then they would do their job. I hoped they'd all show up in my blood. How long did that take?

Of all the medications in the pile before me, the Benadryl was the only one I knew I'd ever taken before and could guess at my reaction to.

I pushed the dresser drawer closed, removed the socks from my hands, and put them back in my drawer. They weren't folded as prettily as I liked, but my hands wouldn't cooperate anymore.

Leaning against the bed again, I scooped up the pills in one hand. They were quite a collection. I used the water bottle on my nightstand to swallow the capsules. Next step: grind the tablets into powder. I took the bronze mortar and pestle I'd bought at an antique shop years ago—displayed on a shelf in our room—and dumped the pills into it. Resting the heavy container on my nightstand, I felt like an old-fashioned apothecary. A few strokes of the pestle later, the tablets were turned to powder.

My protein shake waited in its plastic bottle on my nightstand. I took off the lid, poured in the powdered pills, and replaced the lid so I could shake it up. Then I downed the whole thing as fast as I could.

I hoped that grinding up the meds would do two things. First, it would be more believable that Rick drugged me; getting someone to swallow a literal handful of intact pills would be hard. Second, I hoped that ground-up pills would get into my system faster than usual.

Before I could forget thanks to brain fog, I replaced the mortar and pestle on the shelf, not cleaning it out first. I was pretty sure that Rick had handled it before, so both of our prints should be on it.

My hand knocked against the dresser, and only then did I remember I still wore Rick's smartwatch. It had tracked a few steps in the house, at least. Good enough. I took it off and let it fall to the carpet between our dressers, where it would be found later.

The water falling into the tub had deepened in pitch, telling me that the tub was nearly full. My balance was becoming compromised, so I hurried to the bathroom. Or I tried to. I had to focus on the doorway first, make my way one careful step at a time, my hand bracing my weight on the wall. I'd been feeling uneasy and shaky before drinking anything, so now I was unsure how much of these sensations were from nerves and how much was from the antifreeze. This had to be too fast even for powdered tablets to be affecting me already.

As I reached the bathroom, the room tipped, and I crashed against the door frame, wincing at the impact. I rested, waiting for the world to come back into focus and stop moving, but it didn't seem to be settling at all. I'd have to do this while feeling as if I were on a ship arcing and plunging through the waves of a hurricane.

I crawled to the counter and used it to help myself stand, then held myself upright by leaning against the counter and taking steps sideways, like a baby moving along a couch. Like Ivy had pulled herself to standing on the chair this morning.

My heart tightened, and I pressed my eyes closed tight at the ache of knowing I'd never see her again. Since leaving Becca's house, I'd kept my hazy thoughts on the task at hand, but now my legs nearly dropped out from under me. I caught myself before falling again.

Be strong. For Ivy. Gritting my teeth, I inched my way to the tub and turned off the faucet. The room sounded so quiet now, loud in its own way. The silence seemed to engulf me. With it came fear, creeping into me, moving up from my toes, up through my veins and throughout my body.

I felt ready to both vomit and pass out, but I couldn't allow either. I wasn't done. This had to look like Rick had followed his own method, and that meant I had to be found in the water. Not in the reservoir, according to his plans, but on my terms, in my tub.

Natalie. Chloe.

The tunneling of my vision worsened by the minute. I nearly fell into the tub, which scared me with a jolt of adrenaline. That could have done the job, but again, I had to do this on *my* terms. I lowered myself to the carpet and took deep breaths to regain a little balance. Then, holding to the metal faucet, I pulled myself to kneeling.

Part of me seemed to be watching the whole thing from the outside and thinking that everything I'd done so far, everything I was still doing, was odd. Surreal. Impossible.

The side of the tub, cultured marble, felt good against my skin. I rested my face against it, a relief when I felt so weak. So tired. I nearly drifted off. My eyelids felt leaden, and for a moment, all I could think about was how nice it would feel to rest my head against the edge of the tub.

No. No, no, no. I forced my eyes open. I couldn't let myself fall asleep here. My eyes had to stay open until I was ready, or the game was over. I had to keep fighting. The weakness and lightheadedness got worse by the second. I didn't know how much longer I could stay awake.

Ivy. Natalie. Chloe.

I pushed myself back up on my forearms and stared into the water. Fully clothed, I gripped the edge of the tub.

For Ivy.

Natalie.

Chloe.

Ivy, Ivy, Ivy.

Tortoise slow, I pushed myself to half standing, then lifted one jean leg into the tub, followed by the other. The water seemed cold. On my knees in the tub, I braced myself on my arms, teetering to one side and then the other.

I wanted to text Becca, send her one final message, but I was in too much of a daze to dictate. Assuming my phone wasn't in my pocket in the tub. Texting her a goodbye would be stupid, though. Even through the fog, I knew that much.

I thought my goodbye instead. *Love you, Becks. Thank you for raising my baby.*

My jeans and sweatshirt soaked up a lot of water and made even little movements difficult, as if I suddenly weighed three times as much as before. I shifted to the side and leaned back, lying in the tub, looking at the ceiling. The water was pulling me down.

I wasn't afraid, and the pain in my stomach wasn't as intense.

The rippling water felt good on my neck. The soft lapping sounds of the water against the tub made me feel as if I were on a miniature beach. The gentle caress of the water along my chin and jawline soothed me like a lullaby.

Now I could relax, let go. Close my eyes. Slowly, the tide rolled in, or perhaps I sank into it. I had no sense of time, no sense of anything. I could have been in the water only seconds or for an hour. All I knew was that the water was rising. Or maybe that I was sinking.

I was vaguely aware that this wasn't a beach and that I should be afraid, but I didn't feel fear, only a warm fuzz. I embraced the haze, felt it wash over me. Slowly, oh so slowly, I slipped deeper into the water.

It reached my chin.

Went past my lips.
Covered my nose.
My hair floated above me.
The world looked strange through the water.
I surrendered to the darkness.

CHAPTER FORTY-ONE

BECCA

The trial lasted two months, and the verdict came in after just seven hours of deliberation: guilty.

Last week, the state of California charged Rick with Chloe's death. Detective Andrus tells me that agencies in other states are working to find evidence to charge him with Natalie's murder too. All of this is a huge comfort to me. Now, even if Rick wins an appeal for his conviction in Jenn's death—doubtful, though possible, considering how she actually died—he'll likely be tried and convicted for at least some of his other crimes and remain in prison for the rest of his life.

Ben asked if I thought he deserved the death penalty. Rick might be the kind of felon who deserves it, but I'd rather he rots in a cell and suffer every minute of every day for a long, long time to pay for what he did to so many.

I've come to the state prison to see Rick one last time. Weirdly, I feel that he needs to hear this news from me. I go through the same security checks as before, though they feel stricter at the prison. The setup I'm brought to is more like what I expected when I visited him at the county jail: thick glass stands between us, phone receivers for talking to the person on the other side.

My hands begin to tremble as if seeing the glass barrier is such a relief I'm near collapse. He won't be able to lunge at me this time. Rick probably wouldn't have been able to hurt me if we met in the same room as before—though the releases I signed are pretty clear that they make no guarantees for visitor safety. But here? He can't touch me.

A security guard leads me to a cubicle. "Wait here," he says, pointing to a folding metal chair.

"Thanks," I say and sit. I strain to see what's on the other side, expecting to see Rick brought in any moment. I'm both eager and anxious to get this over with. Despite how many times I've pictured this moment, I don't know how it'll play out.

I scoot the chair forward slightly. The metal legs scrape the concrete floor and throw a high-pitched screech onto the cinder-block walls. My heart's fluttering nervously, but my middle has calmed, like a lake without the slightest breeze—perfectly still. How my body is reacting is a paradox, but somehow, I understand it. I've got nervous energy, but I'm not scared. I can do this.

A heavy door clangs open, and soon I see two figures, a prison guard holding the arm of an inmate in an orange jumpsuit. Judging by the shuffling gait, his ankles are shackled.

At first, I don't recognize the man as Rick. His hair is longer with streaks of gray, and he's grown a beard. Is that because they don't trust him with a razor? Or is this look his choice? The differences go beyond hair and beard, though. The set of his mouth—lips pressed together—and his cold, dark eyes are chilling. This *isn't* the Rick I knew as Jenn's husband.

The guard pulls out the chair, and Rick sits down, his eyes drilling into mine the whole time. He scoots forward, which shows me that his wrists are shackled too. The guard says something I can't hear through the glass. Rick nods in understanding without looking at him. I don't think he's so much as blinked since locking his stare on me.

The guard walks off, and for a moment, I panic, wanting to call him back, as if I won't be safe unless someone stands at Rick's side. As if the glass barrier won't be enough to protect me after all.

I'm safe, I remind myself. *He can't get to me.*

I focus on my calm middle. On the guards on my side of the glass. This conversation is the end of the road for me and Rick. After this, I'll never have to see or speak to him ever again.

He reaches for the telephone receiver on his side, holds it to his ear, and waits. My mouth has gone dry. I think of Jenn and Ivy, of all I've been through, all *they* went through, and why I'm here.

I pick up my receiver and put it to my ear. I keep looking right at him, straight back into his eyes. He hasn't won even this small moment. He stares back as if waiting for me to break.

I refused to be cowed. I won't break the stare either. I try not to blink. This feels like a game of chicken—who will flinch? Not me. I won't give him the satisfaction of even a small victory, which is the only kind he can have now.

His face is hard. His eyes hold enough hate to fill the world. But he's also calm, which surprises me. Is it resignation? A mask? I don't know and don't care, although I suspect the latter because I've seen his mask drop a couple of times: when he was arrested and when the verdict was read.

After a good long silence, my eyes still trained on him, I speak first. "She's mine now. It's official." No need to say who. Assuming Arrington's still doing his job, Rick has known for some time that Ivy's adoption was close to being finalized.

His fingers tighten ever so slightly around the receiver. "You had no right."

"The judge disagreed." I mentally pump myself up to keep this strong, controlled tone. Hearing the judge terminate Rick's parental rights and declare her my legal daughter was one of the most beautiful moments of my life. "This is what Jenn wanted."

Rick blinks at that. One eye twitches as if hearing Jenn's name sends a zip of electricity through him. He recovers, then stares at me for several seconds. He blinks, once, twice. I wait. I smile.

He swallows, and I swear his Adam's apple bobs in slow motion. "You are the reason I'm in here," he says with venom and disgust in his voice.

He could go off on theories about why I'm supposedly to blame, but I can't take the credit for getting him locked up; all of that goes to Jenn. I just helped after the fact to make sure her plan succeeded.

"You're here because of your own sick actions."

"That's a lie." His voice is laced with ice, entirely different from the man who spoke with adoration about his wife. His hard lips curl in disdain. "I. *Didn't*. Kill. *Jenn*," he says slowly, emphatically. Only a sharp observer would notice the hint of extra emphasis he puts on *Jenn*.

"You're a murderer, Rick," I say—one hundred percent true, regardless of what he did or didn't do to Jenn. But I won't say that here, where our conversation is being recorded. "You belong here. We both know that."

He's killed multiple times. Justice demands that he stay in prison for life, even if he's technically here for the one murder he *didn't* succeed in committing.

Rick leans closer to the glass, and I have to force myself to not pull back. *He can't reach me.*

"*You* belong in prison, not me," he says.

How much has he figured out that I know?

Did he kill Jenn? Technically, no.

But he *is* responsible for her death. But for Rick, Jenn would still be here. Ivy would still have her mother. The blame for her absence lies entirely at Rick's feet, no matter what her last moments looked like.

It's all technicalities.

"While you rot where you belong, I'll be raising Jenn's daughter as my own."

"*My* daughter."

"Mine," I stay harshly, slapping my palm on the counter. I feel the fierce strength of a mama bear running through my veins. *I'm* Ivy's mother now. "The adoption is final, and there's nothing you can do about it." I smile triumphantly, knowing those words will stick in his craw. He's lost all control in a world where he used to tell it how fast to spin.

Still holding the receiver to my ear, I stand. "Goodbye, *Ryan*."

His nostrils flare at the sound of his birth name. A string of profanity comes through the receiver. I slowly pull it from my ear and grin. I have the control now. Even with the receiver several inches from my ear, I can hear him screaming.

"I *didn't* kill *Jenn!*" His face turns a darker shade of red, and his knuckles go white as he tightens his grip on his receiver. He gets to his feet and bangs the glass. His eyes are wild, his voice loud enough to draw the attention of security. Rick glances over his shoulder at the guard who's now standing right behind him. Rick sits down in the chair again and breaths heavily, making a show of calming down. "I didn't. Kill. Jenn." This time, he says the words at a normal volume. The dark tone still slithers through the wires.

"You are a murderer," I say evenly. "And you got caught."

"I didn't—"

A smile still hovering about my lips, I move to hang up. His voice gets louder, protesting, telling me not to hang up, to listen to him. Every other word is vile, something he lobs in hopes of hurting me. I flick my shoulder with a finger, showing Rick that his insults are nothing but dust to me.

I make a show of returning the receiver to its spot. His yells cut off abruptly. Now he's just a silent tantrum on the other side of some glass.

Satisfaction warms me.

He stands and bangs the glass again, but now the guard restrains him, and a second appears to help. Within seconds, Rick's under their control, looking like a rabid dog. I grin even wider, which makes him all the more furious. I wave goodbye with the tips of my fingers and wait for him to be escorted away.

A few seconds later, a vibration reaches me—the heavy door closing on the other side. Life has given me this moment to close one chapter in my life as I begin a new one with my children.

All three of them.

∽

Acknowledgments

B ook publishing truly takes the proverbial village, and *Just One More* is a testament to that. Big thanks to my amazing agent, Jill Marsal, who believed in me, and to the Women's Fiction Writers Association for its part in connecting us. Thanks to everyone at Scarlet Books and Penzler Publishing who worked to make this book a reality: the editorial team comprised of Luisa Smith, Will Luckmann, and Nadara Merrill; publisher Charles Perry; and designer Charles Brock, who created the deliciously creepy cover. And of course, I must express my enormous gratitude to the legendary Otto Penzler himself.

The writing process can feel solitary, but it's never truly completed alone. For helping this book along its way, I'm eternally grateful to Luisa Perkins and Sarah M. Eden, the other two members of our writing group affectionately called The Naked Mole Rats.

My critique partner, Julie Coulter Bellon, consistently points out holes in my work and shows me how it can be better. As my accountability partner, Luisa Perkins keeps me motivated and moving, and for this book, she provided much-appreciated revision notes.

A decent portion of this book was written in pre-pandemic days at Kneaders, fueled by their oatmeal (breakfast), sandwiches (lunch), and Diet Coke (always). Thanks to the Riverwoods location and team, who let me work for hours in the booth in the corner with the only outlet in the place. I relied on it when my laptop battery was on its last leg.

The best big brother ever, Mike Luthy, was an incredibly helpful resource on police procedure. Any lingering errors are, of course, mine.

I'm grateful to my parents for supporting me in a publishing journey that has spanned decades. Not every kid has their dreams taken seriously, but the Buddy L typewriter they got me for my fifth birthday shows that they have believed in me all along. They continue to prove their love and support with every new project I take on.

Thanks to my husband, children, and sons-in-law. In addition to being consistent cheerleaders and the reason I do so much of what I do, they know my weird writer quirks and love me anyway. I believe writing made me a better wife and mother. As my family has never known anything else, I certainly hope I'm right.

Finally, I can't forget to thank Samantha Lyon Prinster, my eldest daughter, for inspiring a certain plot point. Many years ago, after hearing that I'd fictionally offed many characters and pets, she made me promise to kill a goldfish in a book. So, here you go, cutie. I have finally fulfilled that promise. I even had him murdered for you.